The Russian Woman

The Russian Woman

Tom Hyman

St. Martin's/Marek
New York

Library of Congress Cataloging in Publication Data

Hyman, Vernon Tom.
  The Russian woman.

  I. Title.
PS3558.Y49R8   1983   813'.54   83-2923
ISBN 0-312-69614-0

Design by Manuela Paul

To Suzanne

ACKNOWLEDGMENTS

My thanks to Ira Scott Du Bey, Deputy Director and Chief Forensic Serologist of New York's Suffolk County Crime Laboratory, and to William R. Haldane, formerly of RCA's David Sarnoff Laboratories, for their valuable technical contributions; and to Alexander Dolgin, whose excellent book, *Alexander Dolgin's Story,* educated me in many of the details of life in the Russian labor camps. And my special thanks to my agent, Clyde Taylor, and my editor, Richard Marek, for their consistently first-rate editorial advice and guidance.

AUTHOR'S NOTE

Most of the details in this novel concerning the White House are factually correct. The locations of rooms, hallways, staircases, elevators, windows, bathrooms, doorways, tunnels, and firedoors are described exactly as shown on the architectural blueprints used for the mansion's interior reconstruction during the Truman administration. Similarly, the locations of specific pieces of furniture and paintings are as accurate and up-to-date as possible, given the redecorating that parts of the mansion, especially the family quarters, frequently undergo. Descriptions of the various kinds of safety and monitoring equipment, however, and the procedures used for the president's personal protection inside the mansion, are necessarily a blend of fact and fancy. When certain sensitive information was either not available to me, or obviously not in the best interests of White House Security to have revealed, I have substituted my own inventions.

PROLOGUE

The unloading commission arrived at Dzhezkazgan camp in Kingir province on March 2, 1956, and began its work.

It snowed all day. Wind whipped ice-hard crystals against the boards and windows of the prisoners' compounds, and snow piled in deep drifts against the concrete administration building and guards' barracks, and along the high barbed-wire fences. The network of rutted paths that scarred the frozen ground were softened, then finally erased, by the accumulating blanket of white.

Each day, for days past counting, thousands of hungry, ill-clad prisoners had marched out along these paths, prodded through the Arctic cold by dogs and machine guns, to labor in the forests and mines that surrounded this desolate Siberian outpost.

But on this day there were no work convoys. The prisoners remained in their barracks. They paced nervously among the tiers of bunks and whispered together in small groups to allay the agony of their suspense. A mood of uncertain euphoria gripped them all. They knew what the arrival of the commission from Moscow meant. Similar commissions were at work all through the vast system of labor camps, freeing political prisoners by the hundreds of thousands. The Khrushchev amnesty was sweeping through the Gulag Archipelago like an invisible army of liberation, undoing the injustices of the past, bringing an end to the long night of Stalinist terror.

On that first day the commission worked steadily from eight o'clock in the morning through the late afternoon, taking few breaks. Prisoners' names were called alphabetically, and one by one they edged nervously into a small, overheated room in the administration building, and stood before the four members of the commission panel to hear their cases reviewed. After the briefest of formalities, they were asked to sign a document admitting guilt to the offenses for which they had been imprisoned, and then they were pardoned. Nearly every three minutes a new prisoner emerged from the room clutching the stamped certificate of his release, giddy and overwhelmed by the sudden gift of freedom.

At five o'clock, KGB Colonel Dmitri Semenenko, the head of the commission, opened the collar of his tunic and slumped back in his chair. His long, smooth-skinned face sagged in fatigue, and his normal olive complexion seemed faded to an unhealthy yellow. The shallow sockets around his brown eyes, which betrayed his Asian blood, were creased in wrinkles. He yawned, exposing large, perfect teeth, and glanced at the other three members. There was Zyuzin, the representative of the Central Committee; Kublanov, from the chief prosecutor's office; and old General Gorelov, who represented the political prisoners. They looked as exhausted as he felt.

"How many so far, Comrade?" he asked Zyuzin.

The Central Committee member tipped his bloated head downward and gazed at the tally sheet in front of him. "One hundred and ninety-nine."

Semenenko nodded wearily. It annoyed him that Zyuzin dropped the "comrade" from his reply. It was symptomatic of the times. The Khrushchev thaw was putting the heat on the Committee for State Security. Those who once quaked at the presence of a KGB officer, now dared to be rude. And morale within the elite service had plummeted alarmingly. KGB interrogators were even committing suicide, unable to face the thought of the thousands of politicals they had sent off to serve five, ten, and twenty years in the camps, now suddenly walking the streets again, their battered souls aching for revenge.

It was a time, Semenenko knew, to lie low and consolidate, to wait out the storm. Eventually the situation would improve. While his KGB colleagues bemoaned the reversal of their fortunes, Semenenko worked to profit from the lessons of the times. He had volunteered for the unloading commissions, for example. It was unpleasant, arduous work. There were thousands upon thousands of prisoners to be freed; and the red tape that had to be overcome, the living and traveling conditions that had to be endured, and the depressing weight of looking into the faces of an endless flood of victims, whose only luck in life was to have survived their ordeal long enough to gain back what was left of their freedom, was altogether an experience Semenenko would have chosen to avoid.

But politically, the toil would advance him in the power structure. He had escaped direct blame for the excesses committed against the politicals, but that was not enough. By working on the unloading commissions, he would improve his stock with Moscow and with the KGB hierarchy.

At the age of forty, Dmitri Semenenko was one of Moscow's most accomplished secret agents. His record, as a deep cover operative at home and in a score of foreign countries, was impressive. His administrative skills were unmatched. His loyalty was unquestioned. And most important, he had managed, by instinct and good luck, to avoid identifying himself too closely with the now dead and disgraced former head of the KGB, Levrenti Beria.

Soon, when the purges were over, he would rise to head one of the KGB's major directorates; he was confident of it. Meanwhile, he need only be patient and do his penance on the unloading commission.

Semenenko repeated Zyuzin's number. "One ninety-nine. Well, Comrades, let's do one more and make it an even two hundred. Then we'll call it a day."

The others nodded their assent. Kublanov motioned for the guard by the door to bring in the next prisoner.

The four members of the panel looked across the room in amazement as a small girl walked in and stepped quickly to the front of the table. She was quite thin, and her hair hung around her face in dirty brown strands. Semenenko guessed her to be only about nine years of age. Under a nondescript wool dress she was wearing padded cotton leggings that had been patched in many places. Her coat was short, frayed at the hems and cuffs, and missing at least two buttons. Incongruously, its collar was trimmed with a luxurious piece of sable fur.

She glanced at each member of the panel, and let her eyes settle on Semenenko, sensing that he was the one in charge. Most of the prisoners, he reflected, cast their gaze at the floor, for which he was always grateful. This girl's stare, and the unspoken challenge behind it, made him uncomfortable. He flashed a wolfish smile at her, baring his large white teeth, and then snapped his fingers at Gorelov, who handed him the girl's dossier. He opened it, glanced at it, then looked up at the girl again.

"You are Zoya Voloshin?"

"Yes." Her voice was low, sullen.

"How old are you, child?"

"Eleven."

Semenenko shook his head and looked again at the dossier. The girl had been sentenced when she was ten years old. Destruction of state property: five years. Conspiracy against the state: another five years. It was grotesque, what some of these courts had done. He looked accusingly at Kublanov, from the chief prosecutor's office.

"She one of yours?" he asked.

Kublanov shook his head, a smirk on his thin lips. "She's special procedure. Read the file."

Semenenko consulted the file again, his cheeks reddening. Kublanov was right. She had been sentenced without a trial, by the KGB. No wonder. They wouldn't have dared bring a ten year old before a judge, and ask for ten years, at that. It was stupifying, the excesses he encountered. At another camp in Kingir they had freed a boy who had been sentenced when he was only eight years old!

He read through the details of the girl's history. Her mother, Valeska Sashanova Voloshin, was a 1058 also. She had been sentenced to twenty-five years. The girl's father, to Semenenko's surprise, was an American—John Framingham, a lieutenant in the United States Army. They met in China, and Framingham died there in 1946. Mother and daughter emigrated back to Russia in 1948. Her mother was promptly arrested as a spy and sent to Krivoschevo. Later she was transferred to Kolyma. Her daughter Zoya was sent to a state orphanage at the age of four.

Semenenko skimmed through a long, tedious account of the girl's "crimes," which basically consisted, beyond the guilt by association of her birth, of defacing a painting of Stalin at the orphanage, and being insolent with the authorities.

Semenenko studied her. Despite her raffish appearance, there was something captivating about the child. Her large and penetrating eyes, perhaps; or her cheekbones, a mixture of Slav and Anglo-Saxon that was complimentary to both. Her manner, too, was arresting. She was remarkably self-possessed.

Kublanov handed the girl the confession form and indicated where she was to sign it. She shook her head, refusing to pick up the pen.

"Don't be obstinate, child," Semenenko said. "This is just a formality. Sign it and you'll go free."

The girl regarded the KGB colonel suspiciously, then picked up the pen proferred by Kublanov and scratched her signature hastily across the bottom of the form.

Semenenko turned to Zyuzin. "Where is she to go?"

Zyuzin shrugged. "To her family. Or back to an orphanage."

Semenenko supposed the unloading commissions would soon free her mother, if they had not already done so.

"Do you know where your mother is?" he asked her.

"She's dead."

Semenenko nodded. He might have guessed. Not many survived Kolyma. "Do you have any other relatives?"

She shook her head. "They're all dead," she replied. Semenenko detected no emotion in her voice.

"Where will you go, then? Do you want to go back to an orphanage?"

"No."

"What do you suggest?" he asked, his voice heavy with condescension.

Zoya narrowed her eyes into a hostile stare. "I can take care of myself," she murmured.

Semenenko shook his head. "The state is responsible for you until you reach your eighteenth birthday."

The girl cocked her head to one side, as if she hadn't heard him correctly. Then a broad, challenging grin spread across her features. Her big eyes sparkled defiantly.

"You find that amusing?"

"Yes."

"Why?"

"Because in the hands of the state, I'll be lucky to live to eighteen."

The girl's impudence amazed him. Instead of crushing her spirit, the brutalities and hardships of her young life seemed to have forged an extraordinarily resilient and independent character. He was intrigued and wished to question her further, but he sensed the other commission members growing restive. They had been through a long day, and they didn't at all appreciate Semenenko drawing them into this child's problems. All prisoners had problems. It was not their franchise to concern themselves with them, nor their desire.

"You'll be sent to an orphanage, whether you like it or not,"

Zyuzin told her. "It'll take a few days to arrange it. Meanwhile, you'll remain here at the camp."

The girl regarded him for a moment, then shrugged.

It was irrational, but Semenenko felt a powerful attraction to the young prisoner. She was like a rare gem in its natural state, demanding to be plucked from the filth of her environment, demanding to be shaped, to have her worth realized and exploited. In some undefined way, she represented possibilities of power to him, a promise of triumph.

He thought of his huge apartment on Kutuzovski Prospekt, and his aging mother, rattling around in all those rooms. He thought of the *dacha* in Uspenskoye, empty most of the time. By any standard he was a rich and privileged figure in Russian society. Yet his private life was one without family or friends, more impoverished in many ways than the poorest worker's. He needed something to complete it, to make it whole.

At forty years of age, Semenenko understood himself well. He knew that he would never marry. He was not a homosexual, but neither did he find sexual comfort in the company of women. His few past attempts had resulted only in impotence and humiliation.

For him, sex could be partly sublimated in a drive for power. But that did not entirely erase the yearning, the need for gratification. And that need, he had gradually come to discover, could only be satisfied by the innocent, uncritical freshness of youth.

In this child he felt that desire—and more. He saw the opportunity to become at once a father and a lover on a continuous, safe basis. He could put an end to the dangerous liaisons that laid him open to blackmail and ruin. The possibilities this child presented excited him enormously. What he did next, he would look back on years later as an act of great inspiration.

He closed the file and handed it to General Gorelov. "I want to set an example for you, comrades," he said, relishing the shock he was about to deliver to them. "I will adopt this child, and see to her needs personally. General, check into the necessary arrangements, if you will."

The amazement on their faces amused the KGB colonel. He looked at the girl, still standing before him, her dirty hands nervously caressing the sable collar on her ragged coat.

"That is, of course, assuming this arrangement meets with your approval, Zoya," he added, grinning at her.

For the first time the girl seemed to lose her poise. It had been so long since anyone had done anything generous or kind for her, that she couldn't think how to react.

She nodded, finally, then wiped a tear from the corner of her eye and ran out of the room.

The Russian Woman

1

A WHITE AMBULANCE BEAR-
ing the legend PARKLAND EMERGENCY SERVICE in large red letters across its doors, appeared at the corner of Swann and Silver
Hill Road near the Washington suburb of Parkland Terrace and
braked to a stop. Curtains were drawn across the back windows
of the vehicle, a converted Chevrolet van, obscuring the interior.
The driver glanced at his wristwatch, then flicked a switch on the
dashboard panel. The red emergency beacon on the roof flashed
on and began rotating.

It was ten minutes after eleven o'clock in the morning, on February 19, 1982, a Thursday. The weather was chilly, in the low
thirties, and the sky was overcast by a gloomy, lead-gray shield of
snow clouds.

The ambulance turned left onto Silver Hill Road and moved
slowly through a wooded area toward the concrete and stone
bridge that spanned the Suitland Parkway, the old, narrow-laned
artery that connected Andrews Air Force Base with the nation's
capital.

As it approached the overpass, it slowed to a stop. A barrier of
long plank sawhorses blocked its path. Further ahead, halfway
across the overpass itself, a lemon yellow Maryland State Police
cruiser sat parked in the middle of the road. Two state troopers
leaned on the hood, slapping their hands together to keep warm.

For a long moment the driver of the ambulance contemplated
the barrier, as if debating what to do. Finally, he slipped the van
into low gear, steered it up onto the shoulder of the road and
squeezed around the edge of the wooden horses. Once past, he
proceeded along the overpass toward the cruiser.

Both troopers pushed away from the hood of the car and sauntered forward, signaling the ambulance to stop. The driver braked
and after a moment's hesitation, switched off the engine and rolled
down his window.

"You saw the barrier back there!" one trooper yelled. "Road's closed!"

The driver, a young male with black, close-cropped hair, dark eyes, and a tough, angular face, nodded uncertainly. He glanced at the troopers' holsters. The leather flaps were securely buttoned over the pistol butts. They weren't expecting trouble.

"I've got an old man in the back," he said, in a thickly accented voice. "Stroke victim. We're on the way to the hospital."

"What hospital?" one trooper demanded.

"Over in Morningside."

The troopers exchanged suspicious glances, then looked down at the stretch of parkway beneath them. In anticipation of the motorcade, the highway's two eastbound lanes had been entirely cleared of traffic.

"We've got a minute," one said. "Let's check."

"Open up the back," the other directed.

The driver shrugged, jumped out, and walked around to the rear of the ambulance, a step ahead of the troopers. He tugged at the rear door handle several times, but was unable to open it. His movements were slow and clumsy. Finally one of the cops, his patience worn thin, pushed the driver out of the way. He grabbed the handle himself and gave it a powerful yank. The doors flew open with a screech.

He stared inside, transfixed by what he saw. Two men sat facing him, grinning savagely. They wore Maryland State police uniforms identical to his, and they were pointing pistols at his head.

The truth, President Daniels realized, staring out the window of the speeding limousine, was that he just didn't like Premier Kamenev. He was pedantic and overbearing. He was also an incurable bore. Even now, in the euphoria of their mutual triumph, the man was lecturing him across the back seat.

The effort to play the gracious host, on top of a week of exhausting and often acrimonious negotiations, had fatigued the president. He reminded himself that in only a few minutes the motorcade would roll into Andrews Air Force Base, and after final handshakes, hugs, and smiling remarks, Kamenev, his wife, and his entourage, would at last board their jet for Moscow and be out of Daniels' hair.

Back on the president's Oval Office desk sat a two-page memorandum of understanding, initialed jointly by Daniels and Kamenev, that would form the basis for the first meaningful strategic arms reduction agreement ever reached by the two superpowers. The memorandum, the result of thousands of pages and man-hours of work, provided, in essence, for an across-the-board one-third reduction in nuclear weapons. Many details remained to be negotiated, and months would pass before a formal treaty could be drawn up, but the memorandum removed the last major obstacles to the first comprehensive disarmament agreement in history.

Despite outrage from the right wing and the military, and the reservations of some of America's allies, the talks represented to Daniels the crowning achievement of his three years in office. The accord was built on a foundation of mutual interest, and the momentum toward a final treaty was too great to be halted by minor snags. The path to this momentous agreement had been rough and controversial. Both the president and the premier had collected a lot of enemies along the way. Only their political courage—and their political strength—had made the risk possible.

Senate ratification would require an enormous amount of arm-twisting, but Daniels controlled a solid majority, and he expected to prevail. Public opinion polls, published that morning, showed an alarming dip in Daniels' popularity, but he knew that was only temporary. The public's moods shifted like beach sand. Time, and heavy doses of education, would reverse the trend against him.

Kamenev, who held both major positions of power in his government—premier of the Soviet Union and general secretary of the Communist party—seemed to have stifled the opposition to the talks among his military and the Politburo hard-liners, although deciphering Kremlin politics was a little like reading Tarot cards. One relied heavily on superstition, faith, and guesswork.

Despite the great breakthrough, Daniels felt depressed. It was simple fatigue, he supposed, and the letdown that inevitably follows any major achievement. His nerves were worn raw. Even the motorcade exacerbated his anxiety. He hated motorcades anyway. They wasted the taxpayers' money and their president's time. Daniels also considered them vulgar. A rude display of power. The long line of bulletproof limousines, the motorcycle escorts, the police cruisers, the platoons of cops and Secret Service agents, the helicopters, hovering like buzzards overhead. A posturing juggernaut of engines and armed men, barreling down a deserted highway at eighty miles an hour—just to get a few people to the airport. Ridiculous.

The traveling circus aspect of the presidency always embarrassed Daniels. Not that he didn't think that he deserved it. Nobody in Washington laid claim to a larger ego. It was just that it offended his taste. It was excessive. Ostentatious. *Vulgar.*

The president had suggested earlier that they go by helicopter. The White House lawn to the boarding gate at Andrews—ten minutes flat. No fuss, no security problems. But Kamenev, it turned out, wouldn't go near a helicopter. "They have no wings," he had muttered, in his thick English. The president, puzzled by such an ignorant remark, had reminded the premier, in a chiding manner, that the helicopter had, after all, been invented by one of his countrymen, Igor Sikorsky. Kamenev had glared back at him, inexplicably offended. An hour later Daniels found out why. Sikorsky, his chief of staff Wilbert whispered to him, had emigrated to the United States during the Russian Revolution.

Daniels smiled, remembering his unintended insult. He suspected that Kamenev just got a kick out of motorcades. His enjoyment of this one seemed transparent enough. When he wasn't lecturing Daniels, he watched the capitalist countryside roll by, his lumpy features set in an expression of pompous satisfaction.

The president saw Kamenev's finger wagging again. He was droning on about what he called "the mercantile mentality," one of his favorite subjects, and in his view, the chief evil of the American system. His terrible accent made listening to him a double ordeal. Daniels tried to tune him out, wondering why fate needed to spoil this great moment in history by inflicting on him such a tiresome partner to share it with.

Daniels slid his arm forward and made an exaggerated display of consulting his watch. It was petty, he supposed, but the motorcade would cost him nearly an hour of his tightly scheduled day, and he wanted Kamenev to be aware of his impatience. One-upmanship. He had suffered the Russian's boorish manners to get this historic agreement, now he wanted to hint that he had better things to do.

He looked past the Russian's bobbing head and flapping lips at the scenery zipping past them on the Suitland Parkway. Traces of last night's snow flurries still clung to the brown grass on the sides of the roadway. He caught sight of two Maryland State troopers standing stiffly at attention on an overpass as the motorcade swept by underneath. The excessive security was yet another presidential annoyance.

In recent weeks Secret Service Director Mack Clark had been smothering him in a blanket of protection. Much to Daniels' dismay, Clark possessed unassailable arguments for his actions. The FBI had recently gathered evidence that a team of hit men had slipped into the country, and Daniels was believed to be their target. Nothing was yet known of their whereabouts, their identities, or who might be behind them. And the list of possibilities was unfortunately very long.

A corollary to the arms reduction agreement was an understanding that both Russia and the United States would refrain from introducing more arms into the Mideast and Latin America, and would collaborate to prevent others from doing so. This understanding, widely publicized and debated, had infuriated every country in both areas. And most of them were perfectly capable of mounting an assassination attempt.

So until the hit squad was uncovered, or proven not to exist, Clark had increased the PPD (presidential protection detail), and restricted the president's travels to Camp David and his vacation retreat in Maine, both of which could be easily guarded. Daniels' public appearances had also been severely curtailed. Wags in the media were already calling him "the prisoner of the White House."

Daniels lamented the high price he paid for so much protection. It was as if he alone were forced to live in the claustrophobic confines of a police state, while his fellow citizens went about their lives unhunted, unguarded, and free.

The three men worked with rehearsed precision. Within less than a minute, the two Maryland State troopers were stripped of their weapons, handcuffed, gagged, and roughly prodded into the back of the ambulance. Quickly, the three then turned to a large pile of equipment stacked inside and began unloading it.

They removed two steel bars, each an inch and a half in diameter and eight feet in length. One end of each bar was filed to a spear-sharp point, and two feet back from these sharpened tips a stack of four twenty-pound barbell weights had been welded onto the shafts. Two feet further up the shafts was attached one end of a thirty-foot-long heavy-duty truck chain.

Struggling under the load, the three lugged the awkward assembly of bars, weights, and chain to the side of the overpass facing west above the empty eastbound lanes. They rolled the chain out along the top of the low concrete parapet until it was stretched to its full length, then positioned the steel bars welded to each end across the parapet, sharpened tips pointed outward.

From beneath a plastic tarpaulin behind the front seat, they removed an Armalite machine gun, and a U.S. Army one-man RPG-7 antitank rocket, with an accompanying rack of high-explosive, armor-piercing missiles.

The two in troopers' uniforms took up positions alongside the steel bars, checked the weapons, and then propped them carefully against the parapet in front of them.

Their plan was simple. As the president's limousine approached the overpass, the two "troopers" would shove the weighted steel bars off the parapet into the path of the oncoming limousine below. The bars would fall, points forward, like giant darts, and puncture the paved shoulders on each side of the roadway right up to the hilts formed by the barbell rings. The thirty feet of chain strung between the bars would create an instant barrier, two feet high, across the road.

The maneuver worked. They had tested it several times. The most difficult element was timing the release of the chained contraption so that it would strike the road surface at precisely the right moment. At eighty miles an hour, the motorcade normally spread out, leaving six or eight car-lengths between limousines. In their rehearsals, they had timed it carefully. The president's vehicle would be the fourth car. A spotter back at the White House east gate had radioed its position to them. They knew they must shove the bars off the parapet at the exact moment the nose of the car immediately ahead of it disappeared beneath the overpass.

The presidential limousine would either manage to stop before it hit the chain, or the chain itself would stop it. Either way, in the confusion that was certain to ensue, the "trooper" wielding the antitank weapon would have time to fire at least two rounds of armor-piercing shells at the limousine. The "trooper" with the machine gun would protect them from return fire and cover their retreat.

The hit squad would escape in the ambulance. The driver had practiced the route until he knew it by heart, and the emergency vehicle made a nearly foolproof getaway car. They could race away from their ambush boldly, clearing their path with lights flashing and siren blaring.

The driver moved the ambulance across to the far side of the overpass and backed it into a thick stand of evergreen shrubbery to hide it from the highway below. He prodded the two hand-cuffed troopers out of the back and herded them, at the point of a .22-caliber high-standard automatic, a short distance into the woods that bordered the overpass.

"Sit down," he said.

The policemen sat under an oak tree and leaned against the trunk. They looked up at the black-haired assassin, their faces strained with fear. He threaded a long, pipelike silencer onto the end of the barrel, and grinned down at them.

"Don't worry," he said. "You'll be dead before you feel anything."

He shot them quickly, a bullet each in the forehead. The second cop had managed to struggle to his feet before he was struck, and he toppled sideways onto his partner. The assassin stood over the tangled bodies for a few seconds, nudging them in the sides with the toe of his shoe, to make sure they were dead.

He returned to the ambulance and started the engine. Arms resting on the steering wheel, he waited, tapping the gas pedal impatiently. Fifty feet away he could see his companions, standing by the parapet. Far up the parkway, the first blinking red and blue lights of the president's motorcade flashed into view.

The president's eyes wandered to the premier's wife, Katya Ivanova, sitting in the jump seat directly opposite him. Her hands rested in her lap, and her expression was composed, perhaps a trifle bored. Still in her late thirties, she was a remarkably beautiful woman. Silky blond hair, flawless white skin, wide Slavic cheekbones, and the most extraordinary eyes—large, agate blue, dramatic.

She spoke better English than her husband, but was careful not to upstage him. She played her role as Russia's first lady with consummate skill, Daniels thought. At the dinners and receptions in their honor, she had moved and talked and laughed with charm and vivaciousness. She appeared completely at ease and she conducted herself with an aristocratic grace and self-possession, a sureness of manner, that set her apart. But there was more than poise in her manner. She possessed something rare—a presence that drew people to her instinctively. She was a star. And social Washington was completely in awe of her.

The president realized that he was staring at her again. He had done that often during the past week, and was trying to avoid doing so now, in the close confines of the limousine. But it was difficult. She fielded his furtive glances with bold eyes and a smile that made his groin tingle.

He had searched for flaws in her appearance that might dilute his fascination, and he had found only one. There were several scars on her face—barely visible little lines by her eyes, the bridge of her nose, and along her jawline. He had first noticed them when sitting beside her at a particularly brightly lit banquet table. Now, in the dim interior of the limousine, he couldn't see them at all.

What, he wondered, was such a sensual creature doing married to the pompous potato sitting beside him? Was it simply the power the man represented? And the good life that went with that power? Those could be strong aphrodisiacs for many women, Daniels supposed. She would have great privileges—exclusive resorts, glittering parties, fancy restaurants, foreign luxuries, servants, *dachas* in the country, chauffeured limousines, access to important and interesting people, the opportunities to travel abroad. The best of life that was possible in the Soviet Union. Perhaps she even had young lovers as well.

Daniels dropped his gaze from her lips to her knees. He watched her long, firmly muscled legs, sleek in their stockings, as she crossed them, providing him a fleeting glimpse of her thighs. He caught his breath, stirred by the sight and the fantasy it conjured. The president looked from the premier's wife to the empty jump seat next to her. A sharp knife of guilt stabbed his heart.

His wife's place.

Poor Estelle. No more motorcades for her, he thought. Nor state dinners, nor trips abroad. In his moment of triumph, she could not be there to share it with him.

Poor Estelle. She was only memories and pain.

The night he discovered the truth about her condition still burned in his mind with a horrible clarity, though it had happened nearly three years ago.

The French ambassador was making a toast to Estelle, and the applause of the hundred seated guests echoed across the huge state dining room. Then, to Daniels' surprise, Estelle was standing, making a toast of her own. At first he felt a surge of pride. It was their first big social event in the White House. A formal state dinner. Estelle had worked for weeks to make it perfect. And now she seemed to be carrying it off brilliantly.

But something was wrong. Estelle was talking incoherently, stopping in the middle of sentences, shifting the subject abruptly, forgetting her words altogether. Her eyes flashed angrily around the enormous horseshoe table. Her voice was strained, shrill. She spilled wine from her glass onto the tablecloth.

My God, Daniels remembered thinking, she's drunk. A waiter reached out from behind her to remove the goblet from her hand. From across the long table Daniels watched, horrified, as Estelle resisted the waiter's help, then hit him with the goblet. The glass shattered against the man's cheek, spraying him with wine and drawing a trickle of blood down his face.

A palpable wave of shock froze the guests into silence.

Events blurred. With the help of Sam Gordon, the Chief Usher, Daniels half led, half carried Estelle upstairs to their bedroom and summoned the White House physician, Harry Sheldon.

Estelle was alternately laughing and crying, teetering on the edge of hysteria. Daniels could not calm her down. Sheldon assured him she was just reacting to the strain she had been under preparing for the dinner. He injected her with a sedative and she went to sleep.

Daniels returned downstairs to apologize to the guests. He suffered through the remainder of the evening, shaking hands, dancing, talking, his insides churning with anxiety.

The incident was kept out of the papers, but it was to be Estelle's last social affair. A team of psychiatrists and M.D.'s examined her and reached a diagnosis: she had suffered a "psychotic episode," and needed a long rest, under medical supervision, away from the strains of the White House.

Daniels ignored their advice. Instead, he cut back heavily on their social activities, shielded her from the public, and tried to help her adjust to a reduced role as the country's first lady. But none of it worked. More "episodes" followed. Helpless, Daniels watched his wife slide headlong into madness.

The doctors insisted, finally, that she be removed to a hospital, where she could be properly treated. Daniels refused to allow it. He wanted to keep her with him, where he could look after her. He ordered a suite of rooms on the top floor converted into a kind of miniature psychiatric ward, and Estelle gradually came to spend all her time there, locked up and watched around the clock by nurses.

Three years had passed, Daniels reflected, and she had yet to show any signs of returning to normal. The doctors remained pessimistic. Only Daniels himself believed that she might still recover. He had to believe it. He had gained the presidency at the price of her sanity.

His determination to stick with her through her illness, difficult as it sometimes became, had had one ironic side benefit: the public loved him for it. No single issue in his three years in office had generated even a fraction of the support the country gave him for remaining faithful to Estelle.

The benefit was also a noose.

He was only fifty-two years old, and possessed the vigor of a far younger man. Three years of celibacy had been a strain, and increasingly, dark images of Estelle's death crept unbidden into his consciousness. He hated himself for such terrible imaginings, but he could not suppress them.

Many times he had been tempted to try a discreet affair. God knows the opportunities were there. But the frustrations of abstinence always won out over the risks of involvement. Wilbert, his chief of staff, told him he suffered his celibacy to assuage his guilt for causing Estelle's madness. Perhaps.

He looked at Katya Ivanova. She smiled again, almost as if she had been reading his thoughts. It was a strange, confiding smile, earthy and flirtatious. It seemed almost physical, so powerful was its effect on him. He smiled back, suddenly chagrined that she was leaving. He would likely never see the woman again. And he barely knew her.

Daniels bent his head toward Kamenev, who had mercifully

shut up and taken to staring out the window. Daniels followed his gaze and saw another overpass looming, with its pair of troopers standing guard. They seemed encumbered by their weapons. What a tedious job they have, he thought.

The troopers moved suddenly.

Daniels saw his driver, on the other side of the bulletproof partition, abruptly throw up a hand.

Brakes squealed.

He felt his body pitch forward, and he flung his arms in front of him. Both palms struck the glass partition behind the driver and sent a wave of pain shooting through his elbows. His chest smashed into Katya's face, and she gasped and fell sideways across the jump seats. Kamenev toppled forward and slammed headfirst into the partition with a thud, then crumpled to the floor, moaning and grasping his neck.

The limousine rocked violently and began to skid, tires screaming against the tarmac like an animal in distress. Daniels fell off Katya and onto the floor, beside the premier. His mind raced to assess the situation. It appeared as if they had just swerved to miss something on the highway.

An ear-shattering explosion lifted the limousine from the ground and bounced it sideways with a crunch of glass and metal. The taste of death rose like bile in Daniels throat.

He wrenched himself free of the tangle of limbs on the floor, conscious of a painful ringing in his ears. His upper lip felt wet. He touched it. His nose was bleeding. He looked out the right side window and saw that they were stopped broadside to the highway, ten feet in front of the overpass. Next to the car, incredibly, a length of heavy chain stretched across the entire width of the road, like a barrier closing off someone's private driveway.

Half a mile ahead, on the other side of this mysterious chain, the lead motorcycle escort and police cruisers were just braking to a stop. Behind the president, the car carrying the vice-president, the secretary of state, and the Soviet minister of defense, had come to a sideways stop halfway across the narrow grass center island. The follow-up cars, caught in the chain reaction, were scattered in a helter-skelter jumble across the entire parkway.

Agents scrambled out the doors and crouched behind the crippled vehicles, scanning the terrain for signs of the enemy. Several, toting Uzi submachine guns, raced toward the overpass. In the front seat, the agent riding with the driver lay slumped against the door, his eyes and mouth open. The driver hunched over the wheel, trying to restart the engine. Daniels could hear the plaintive whine of the starter.

He looked at his companions. Kamenev was on his knees now, his hand groping for a hold on the edge of the jump seat. A large gash across his head oozed blood. He was shouting something in Russian. His wife lay across the carpeting, hiding her face in her hands.

The driver fired the ignition and popped the shift lever into low gear. The limousine lurched over the narrow center strip, pitching and rolling like a ship in a heavy sea.

Another explosion.

The limousine shuddered violently and the shatterproof windows turned abruptly opaque. Daniels struggled to his knees, stunned and dizzy. His heart pounded. He felt deaf and his eyes stung. A bitter acrid odor assaulted his nostrils. The vehicle had stopped again, listing sharply to one side. A large hole had appeared in the front windshield; black smoke billowed through it. The driver lay still, his face pressed against the steering wheel.

Kamenev, on his knees, pounded on the side door and pulled on its handle. Daniels reached across to restrain him, but the door had already swung open and he was crawling out.

"Stay in the car!" Daniels screamed. His yell came out as a barely audible croak.

Popping noises rent the air. Through the limited view of the open doorway, Daniels saw a Secret Service agent fall on top of Kamenev to protect him, but the Russian, thinking he was being attacked, fought him off with desperate strength and staggered to his feet again. The gunfire intensified.

He watched Kamenev scamper across the grass verge, his fur-collared greatcoat flopping around his pudgy body.

Suddenly the premier's feet buckled beneath him and he pitched forward and plowed face-first into the wet grass. Daniels thought he had just lost his footing, but he continued to lie there, arms flung out from his sides, motionless.

Secret Service agents fanned out around the area before the bridge, taking cover behind the scattered vehicles and directing a fusillade of pistol and machine-gun fire at the overpass.

Agent Dan McCormick cradled his Uzi in the crook of his elbow and dashed in a crouching zigzag toward the steep grass banking that sloped up to the right to meet the roadway coming off the end of the overpass. He scrambled up the banking and hid behind a bush, level with the attackers and almost on their flank. From that position he commanded a view of the entire top surface of the overpass, and a large slice of the Suitland Parkway below.

Over the racket of the gunfire he heard a screech of tires. He snapped his head around just in time to see the taillights of a vehicle disappearing off the far end of the overpass.

Directly in front of him, two of the attackers still crouched behind the parapet. As he raised his machine gun, fire from below raked the overpass and caught one of the assassins in the chest. He stumbled backward several steps, still clutching his weapon, then slumped to the roadway.

The remaining assassin dropped his submachine gun and fled for the bushes, directly toward McCormick's hiding place.

The agent jumped on him as he dashed past, tackling him around the middle like a linebacker sacking a quarterback. On the ground McCormick wrapped an arm around the man's neck and jammed the man's elbow behind his back in a half nelson.

"I've got him!" he screamed. "I've got him!"

In seconds, other agents were on the overpass and swarming around him. They pinned the captive to the ground under the weight of their bodies. McCormick struggled to his feet, found his radio, and called frantically for a helicopter.

An agent slammed the door shut from the outside, and Daniels lost his view. The gunfire abated, but the pandemonium of the battlefield, invisible now beyond the opaque twilight of the limousine's interior, swelled anew with the mournful wailing of sirens and the clatter of helicopters.

President Daniels collapsed on the carpeted floor, coughing from the smoke. He felt Kamenev's wife, Katya Ivanova, clinging to him, trembling against him like a terror-stricken child.

CIA DIRECTOR PAUL FRIED-
rich depressed the intercom switch, watching his hand tremble as
he did so. He was exhausted. His legs were rubbery, his eyes gritty,
and his intestines felt like a smoldering dump fire. He could almost
see the acid eating away at his ulcer. No sleep last night, and only
two hours the night before. He was sixty-four. This kind of stress
was dangerous.

A dispassionate male voice answered: "Yes, Mr. Friedrich?"

"Where is Turner?"

"On his way, sir."

"It's five after eight. What's holding him up?"

"Nothing, sir," the voice replied. "He left the farm forty-five
minutes ago—by helicopter."

"Send him in the second he arrives," Friedrich ordered. "Meanwhile, tell the kitchen to send up some breakfast. Coffee, juice, and
rolls for five."

Friedrich flipped off the intercom switch, slicing his assistant's
maddeningly calm "yes sir" in half, and swiveled his chair around
to confront the others.

They sat at the conference table at the other end of the director's spacious seventh-floor office: Luther Hodges, director of the
FBI; Mack Clark, head of the Secret Service; and William Wilbert,
President Daniels' chief of staff. Each was occupied sifting through
the reports stacked on the table.

A messenger from decrypt entered and dropped another
batch of reports on Friedrich's desk. Messengers had been running in and out all night, and Friedrich's office, serving as a temporary crisis-management center, was beginning to disappear
under the blizzard of photostats, Xeroxes, loose-leaf binders,
folders, photographs, telexes, and notepads that covered every
available surface, including large areas of the floor. Along one
wall a large seascape in oils had been taken down and a detailed
plan drawing of the ambush site and its immediate environs
tacked up in its place.

The Suitland Parkway ambush was now forty-four hours old. A
progress report on the investigation was scheduled for ten o'clock
in the president's office, and the mood of the four men was grim.

Progress looked like the one ingredient their report would not contain.

Friedrich cleared his throat. "Gentlemen, you've had a chance to look over the material that's come in overnight. While we wait for Turner, it might be a good time to rehearse what we can tell the president."

The director held up a copy of that day's *Washington Post*, delivered to his desk earlier, and let the others read the banner headline: CRISIS GROWS. He turned the paper around and read the lead paragraph out loud: " 'World anxiety over the assassination of the Russian premier continues to mount. More nations join in condemning the United States. In Moscow, meanwhile, official reaction to the killing of its leader on American soil remains surprisingly muted. . . .' "

Friedrich folded the newspaper and placed it on his desk. "Let's start there," he said, "with the Russian reaction. Publicly, they haven't yet made a move. Tass, *Pravda, Izvestia,* Radio Moscow, state television, all silent so far. No denunciations of the US, no threats, nothing. The Russian people, unbelievably, have not even been informed that their leader is dead. . . . The Soviet ambassador, Voroshilov, has not so far been recalled for consultation, as we expected he might be. The Kremlin has not yet requested a meeting of the UN Security Council, something else we expected them to do. They have not, in fact, even recovered their premier's body. He's still in the morgue at Bethesda."

Friedrich paused and glanced around the table, to see if anyone had questions. No one did, so he continued: "Privately, however, the Russians have been active as hell. From our usual sources—spy satellites, AWACS, informants—we've pieced together the following: Red Army reserves have been called up and all leaves canceled. Russian divisions in East Germany, Poland, Czechoslovakia, and Hungary have been put on alert. Monitored radio transmissions indicate stepped-up warship and submarine activity. Troop and tank convoys have been spotted all along Russia's western borders. The borders themselves have been sealed. Diplomatic travel within the country has been suspended, and all foreign journalists have been confined to their hotels and apartments. Our sources in Moscow have counted twenty-three Zil limousines parked behind the barrier between the Kremlin's Arsenal and the

Minister's Building since yesterday. Chauffeurs and guards are relieving each other on six-hour shifts. This means the Politburo is meeting in special emergency session. As we analyze the situation. . . ."

Presidential Chief of Staff William Wilbert interrupted: "Who's we?"

Friedrich turned his eyes toward Wilbert, fidgeting impatiently at the far end of the conference table. It was for his benefit, as much as anything, that Friedrich was offering this little review. The director disliked Wilbert, a sentiment shared by many in the administration. He was a small, ugly man, with a sarcastic, even arrogant disposition, and a brusque manner. His thick black eyebrows always seemed creased in a scowl, and his thin lips drawn in a perpetual sneer. He was Daniels' minion—confidante, errand boy, alter-ego, hatchet man. No one felt safe around him, knowing that he had the president's ear. To rub Wilbert the wrong way—a very easy thing to do—was to risk the president's displeasure.

" 'We,' " Friedrich answered carefully, "is the alphabet soup of the intelligence community. I briefed you on this earlier. On the floor below we've assembled a USIB-coordinated group of analysts from every agency—DIA, NSA, NRO, the works. There's twenty of them down there, sifting through this stuff."

Wilbert nodded, satisfied. "Okay. Go ahead. As they analyze the situation . . ."

"As they analyze the situation," Friedrich continued, his face reddening from Wilbert's challenge, "the activity we're observing indicates that the Russian leadership is in a crisis, possibly even a deadlock of some kind. They have two problems: first, how to react to the assassination, in the absence of any information on who was responsible; and second, how to agree on a successor to Kamenev. We think they have to solve the second problem before they can tackle the first. The leadership struggle is between Kamenev's moderate and liberal factions, and Bulgakov's hardliners. With Kamenev's death, Bulgakov's side has an edge. If they prevail, President Daniels' arms reduction treaty will be dead. Bulgakov has opposed it from the start. . . ."

"The president," Wilbert interrupted, "had several hotline exchanges with President Valenkov yesterday, so he may know more about the Politburo crisis than we do."

Friedrich shrugged. "Let's review the ambush itself, then."
The director glanced expectantly in the direction of FBI Director Luther Hodges, who shifted uneasily in his chair. Friedrich didn't know the man very well. He was a former cop—police commissioner for the city of Philadelphia—and a recent Daniels appointee. He seemed unimaginative, even slow-witted, the kind of man who always did things by the book. He was well liked, however, and got high marks for his administrative skills. He had played defensive tackle for the University of Pennsylvania, and he looked it.

Hodges clapped his paws together and nodded at Friedrich, his white eyebrows twitching nervously. He was also, Friedrich was learning, a man of few words.

"We're still running tests on the weapons recovered from the site," Hodges began, in his rumbling baritone. "The antitank gun and the machine gun were both stolen from a private arms warehouse in Virginia, three months ago. Both are new."

"What about the other stuff?" Friedrich prodded. "The weights, the chain? . . ."

Hodges shook his head. "Nothing yet."

"What about the escape vehicle?"

"No traces yet. We're analyzing tire marks on the overpass, and looking for eyewitnesses."

"Any conclusions about the number of assassins?" Wilbert interjected.

"Three," Hodges replied.

"Three conclusions?" Wilbert asked, arching an eyebrow, "or three assassins?"

"Three assassins," Hodges replied, oblivious to Wilbert's sarcasm.

Mack Clark, who had yet to say a word, nodded in agreement. Friedrich felt sorry for Clark. He had lost four agents during the ambush, and he was taking incredible heat from Congress and the press for the death of Kamenev. He took all the losses personally. The fact that Daniels, along with the premier's wife, had escaped harm, did little to assuage him. He knew that it was a fluke of fate, not his agents, that had saved the president's life.

"Probably three," Friedrich concurred. "There could have been more, but there were at least three."

"My men counted two on the overpass," Clark said, his voice

harsh. "A third one must have been driving an escape vehicle. I say there must have been three because that's all there needed to be. And no group of trained killers is going to take along extras on something as dangerous as this."

Wilbert nodded. "Okay, we agree there were probably three assassins. Let's take a look at them one at a time. First, the dead one. What have you developed?"

Wilbert eyed Hodges like a prosecutor at a trial, waiting for him to answer. Friedrich noticed how quickly the president's chief of staff had snatched control of the discussion away from him. It was just as well. His tired brain was aching from the two days' marathon it had been through.

"Not much," Hodges replied. "We've sent mug shots, fingerprints, and physical descriptions everywhere—fifty state police headquarters, Interpol, Britain's SAS, West Germany's GSG9, the French GIGN, and every police and antiterrorist organization we know about. Nobody's turned up anything so far. He's not on anybody's list."

"What *do* we know about him?" Friedrich got in.

"Again, not much. His uniform we've traced. It was stolen from a Maryland State Police barracks outside Annapolis, and his underwear he bought in a nearby discount store. That's it. He had nothing in his pockets at all—not a scrap of paper."

"So we have no clues to his identity," Wilbert summarized.

Hodges shook his head. "Not a one."

"Okay," Wilbert sighed. "Now how about the missing assassin? The one nobody saw. The one we assume was driving the getaway car—if there was a getaway car. What about him?"

Hodges shrugged, unperturbed by the insulting way Wilbert had framed the question. "Nothing," he replied. "He's disappeared. We have no leads."

Wilbert expelled his breath and tipped back in his chair. "So it all really comes down to the third man, doesn't it?"

The others in the room nodded. Wilbert turned his inquisitional gaze on Friedrich. The third assassin was his baby. After his dramatic capture on the overpass, they had whisked him off to a holding cell at Andrews Air Force Base. For several hours the FBI and Secret Service had quarreled over his custody. Wilbert, acting on the president's orders, had stepped in to arbitrate. He had ordered the assassin placed in CIA custody, and formed a joint committee, consisting of himself, Hodges, Clark, and Friedrich, to oversee his interrogation.

They were holding the assassin at the farm, the CIA's nickname for Camp Peary, a 480-acre site outside Williamsburg, Virginia, 120 miles south of Washington. Disguised as an Army research and testing facility, it was actually a secret CIA camp, used for training recruits, rehearsing covert action missions, testing weapons, and debriefing defectors.

A team of CIA counterintelligence officers was questioning the prisoner nonstop. His existence was still a secret. Other than those directly involved, only the Kremlin knew about him. Daniels had informed President Valenkov of his capture on a hotline exchange immediately after the ambush.

"Obviously," Wilbert said, "this man's the key. He can tell us who he is, who the dead one is, who the missing one is, and who's *behind* them. It's really that simple, isn't it? He can tell us the whole story and we can wind up this investigation. Am I right?"

"If he knows the whole story," Hodges murmured.

Friedrich's eyebrows lifted. Hodges wasn't as dumb as he looked.

"Why shouldn't he know it?" Wilbert demanded.

"You're assuming some kind of political conspiracy," Clark said, coming to Hodges's aid. "We don't know that."

"Are you kidding?" Wilbert shot back, his thin lips curling into a snarl. "Of course it's a conspiracy! It was too well planned to be anything else! We were even warned about this hit squad in advance!"

Clark's face reddened at the implied criticism. "What's their motive?" he challenged. "Maybe you know that, too?"

Wilbert seemed taken aback by Clark's sharp answer. "I don't know their motive," he muttered. "But I can damned well make a good guess! They want to stop the disarmament treaty!"

"That doesn't narrow it down much," Clark said. "There are at least a dozen countries in Latin America and another five or six in the Mideast who don't want that treaty to go through. And all of them are capable of using assassins." He turned to Friedrich. "What do you think, Paul?"

"I think Willy's right. Everything points to conspiracy."

"Let's not overlook the Russians themselves," Hodges said. "Bulgakov's people could have planned this."

Clark's eyes widened in shock. "Try to kill our president? And their own premier? That's pretty farfetched."

"Bulgakov benefits most by Kamenev's death," Hodges persisted. "He gains power and he gets rid of a treaty he was against."

"You have a point, Director," Wilbert admitted. "But we have to look beyond *qui bono*. Bulgakov wouldn't stage anything so risky. And why would he want to kill President Daniels?"

Hodges shrugged. He hadn't thought it through. "I don't know."

"Well, forget it," Friedrich said, clearing his throat. "The Russians are innocent. In fact, the Kremlin is convinced the ambush is the work of a right-wing Cuban group, operating out of Miami."

The others looked at him sharply, stunned by such an unexpected revelation.

"Jesus Christ!" Wilbert swore. "That would be wonderfully convenient for them, wouldn't it? Do they have any hard information, or is this just wishful thinking?"

"Apparently they have information," Friedrich replied.

"Aren't they sharing it with us?" Clark asked.

"No."

The others waited, but Friedrich didn't elaborate.

"What's your source?" Wilbert demanded.

The CIA director looked out the window to escape Wilbert's penetrating stare.

"Company secret?" Wilbert asked.

Friedrich nodded, grinning uncomfortably. Wilbert muttered something under his breath, but didn't pursue the issue. He knew he was not entitled to pry into details about CIA sources.

And this wasn't just any source, Friedrich reflected. It was forbidden knowledge. Even the source's code name was a secret.

Saraband's true identity was known only to the CIA director himself, and to Byron Shanklin, the agent who had developed the source. Just thinking about it made Friedrich nervous, as if somehow someone might succeed in penetrating his thoughts and steal the most sensitive secret it had ever been his responsibility to keep.

Before he could worry about it further, Fred Turner, the deputy director of the CIA, strode into the office. Friedrich trembled with relief. Turner nodded briefly to the others, and settled into a small armchair near the director's desk.

Friedrich noted, with an older man's envy, how fresh Turner appeared, considering that he also had not slept all night. His dark blue suit was neatly pressed, his hair precisely combed, his round, baby face as pink and healthy looking as ever. Friedrich admired Turner's diligence, honesty, and brain power, but he didn't like him very much. A former Naval intelligence officer with a spotless record, he was a bit of a prig, the director thought, and too obviously covetous of his job. Friedrich knew he shouldn't hold the man's ambitions against him, especially since his own retirement was only a year away. But Turner made him uncomfortable. Friedrich retaliated by working Turner like a slave.

Friedrich's eyes traveled from the deputy director's boyish face to his slender fingers, gripping the armrests of the chair. It had just occurred to him that Turner had walked into the room empty-handed. Not a good sign.

Turner gazed shyly about the office. Friedrich waited for him to say something, but apparently he was waiting to be asked.

"What have you got for us, Fred?" Friedrich coaxed, his voice on edge.

"Nothing."

Friedrich's mouth dropped open. He felt suddenly light-headed. "Nothing?"

Turner nodded. "Shanklin's got a good team on him. You know that, of course. Carter, Robinson, and Moore. They've been sweating him around the clock, nonstop. I've listened to several hours of tapes. They're working him hard, but the bastard won't say word one."

Friedrich looked across at Wilbert. The man's face was contorted with anger. He looked back at Turner. "What does Shanklin say?" he asked.

Turner gazed at the ceiling, as if trying to recall Shanklin's exact words.

"He admits the guy is tougher than he expected," Turner said. "But he says everybody breaks eventually. He says they're working on him as hard as they can. It just takes time."

"How much time does he think he needs?"

"Four, five days—minimum."

"What do you recommend?"

Turner squeezed his hands together and glanced over at the conference table and the three grim faces staring at him. For the first time since he had known him, Friedrich realized that his deputy director was nervous.

"Well," Turner replied, "I saw the prisoner. He looked shaky to me. Two nights without sleep. I don't see anything else we can do except let them keep working on him. Give them more time."

"Do you think they're sweating him hard enough?" Hodges asked.

Turner shrugged. "I'm not a good judge of these things, Mr. Hodges. Shanklin is tough, I know that. If he says they're bearing down, I believe him. They're depriving him of food and sleep, keeping him in a cold cell with the lights on, threatening him, applying a lot of stress, that kind of thing. . . ."

"What about drugs?" Wilbert demanded. "Can't they break him with drugs?"

"We have to be careful," Clark warned. "We're already depriving him of his rights. . . ."

"He doesn't have any rights!" Wilbert burst out, unable to contain his frustration. "The son-of-a-bitch tried to kill our president! He's a terrorist, a hired assassin, the scum of mankind. Don't give me any crap about his rights!"

"Okay," Friedrich said. "He's been a bad boy. The fact remains that we need more time to break him."

"We don't have more time!" Wilbert shot back. "We're in a serious bind! The president is kicking the walls. And news will leak out about this prisoner before much longer. If not from somebody around here, then from the Russians. They're screaming at the president to break this case!"

"The president—and the Russians—will just have to show a little more patience."

Wilbert shook his head. "Not if you're not getting anywhere. He told me last night what he wants to do."

The sudden changed tone of Wilbert's voice riveted Friedrich's attention. "What's that?" he demanded.

"He wants to bring in the Russians."

Friedrich rubbed the stubble of beard on his chin. He was puzzled. "I don't follow you," he said.

"The Russians! The KGB!"

"Why?"

"Get them involved. Let them share in the interrogation."

"Interrogate our prisoner? At the farm?"

Wilbert nodded impatiently. "You're not getting anywhere with him. And the Kremlin's pressing the president hard. It was their leader who died, after all. The president sees this as an acceptable way to appease them. Show them that we're not hiding anything. And at this point, what alternative can we propose? You're two days into this investigation and getting nowhere."

It was Friedrich's turn to become agitated. The idea outraged him. "We can't let them in!" he replied. "It's crazy! And it's probably illegal. This isn't some agricultural exchange program we're talking about!"

"Okay," Wilbert answered, his voice suddenly tired. "Let's ship the assassin to Moscow. Let them break him. I'm sure they won't worry about his civil rights over there."

"*We* can break him, dammit!" Friedrich replied. "Shanklin just needs more time!"

"The fact remains, Paul," Wilbert replied, almost whispering. "You're not making any progress."

"The Russians will send Semenenko," Turner interjected. "I'll bet on it. He's their number two, after Bulgakov."

"That would be a disaster," Friedrich muttered. "Semenenko would humiliate us. He's completely unscrupulous. And too clever by half. I'll resign before I let him in here."

Wilbert glared at Friedrich. "The president may just call your bluff."

"I'm not bluffing! I'm not going to end my career in the CIA as the man who had to ask for help from the KGB!"

Wilbert let out a long breath and slumped further into his chair. "Look," he said. "In about an hour we're going to meet with the president. I can tell you right now that when he hears what you have to say, he'll chew you to pieces! Remember, the whole damned world is pressuring him for answers! And on top of all that, there's still at least one assassin running around loose, looking to take another shot at him!"

"That won't happen!" Mack Clark insisted, his voice hard and cold as marble.

Wilbert shrugged and went on: "It won't be enough to tell him that you'll try harder. He won't buy it. He'll go for the KGB idea, and you won't be able to stall him, because you aren't getting anywhere!"

"It sounds to me, Willy," Friedrich replied, "as if you *want* the Russians in here."

Wilbert shook his head. "Don't be idiotic. I don't want the

damned Russians in here any more than you do. But Shanklin and his team have got to produce! Two days and they haven't gotten a word out of him! That's not an interrogation, that's a joke!"

"I resent that," Friedrich snapped.

"Resent it all you want. But unless you can give the president a workable plan at ten o'clock I'm predicting that Shanklin's boys will have to play host to the KGB—and like it."

"You've been criticizing everything for half an hour, Willy," Friedrich said, his exasperation complete. "Do you have anything positive to offer?"

Wilbert scowled. "As a matter of fact I do."

"I'm listening."

"Bring in Warfield."

Friedrich looked at Wilbert's diminutive form crouched in the chair as if he had suddenly metamorphosed into a frog. "Warfield?" he echoed. *"Charles* Warfield?"

"Yes."

Friedrich laughed. "That's ridiculous!"

"It's not ridiculous at all. He's the best interrogator your agency ever had."

"I think I'd rather let in the KGB than Warfield."

"He broke Nosenko for you," Wilbert reminded him. "And Kubilev. And Sharansky."

Friedrich sighed. "Willy, it took him six months to break Nosenko. The others even longer. And that was several years ago. He's washed up. A bum. He was fired at least two years ago. I don't even know where he is."

"What do we have to lose, Paul?" It was Hodges, suddenly coming to life. "If the president likes the idea of bringing him in, it might buy us those extra days Shanklin needs."

"That's a point," Clark added. "I don't know anything about this guy, but if Wilbert can persuade the president to bring him in, why the hell not do it. He can't hurt us—can he?"

Friedrich shook his head in disagreement. "Yes, he can. Warfield's more trouble than he's worth. And he wouldn't agree to help us anyway."

"You have any better ideas?" Wilbert asked.

Friedrich twisted his chair around and looked out the window. He didn't have any better ideas. And he could see at least negative merit in Wilbert's suggestion. Warfield was expendable. If things went wrong Warfield would make an admirable scapegoat. And Wilbert could take the blame for suggesting him.

The director felt slightly ashamed of himself for his line of reasoning. But only slightly. He gazed across the acres of wooded Virginia countryside that protected the agency and its secrets from the eyes of the outside world. It was cloudy and sleeting intermittently—a raw, unpleasant day. He realized he had not been out of the building since the whole flap began, forty-five hours ago. Tonight, he would have to go home and sleep. He wished he were there now, drinking sherry and playing a quiet game of Scrabble with Marguerite. He peered at his watch. Nine-thirty. The president would be waiting. He cranked the chair back around and faced his deputy director, Fred Turner, sitting with his fingers laced tightly together in his lap.

"Find Warfield," Friedrich said to him.

Hiding his chauffeur's cap under his arm, the man stood at the counter of a Georgetown boutique and called for service.

A saleswoman approached him. "Can I help you?" she asked, her voice dripping with disdain.

"I want a hairbrush," he said. "It's for my wife."

The saleswoman appraised him critically for a moment, then pointed to a row of cheap plastic-handled brushes on top of the counter. "We have several here she might like. . . ."

The chauffeur shook his head. "No. I want your best. Wood handles. The best you have."

The woman raised her eyebrows in surprise. "Ah. Well, you've come to the right place."

She pulled open a drawer and began setting out a series of brushes on the glass top of the counter.

"These are all boar bristle," she said. "And they are all available in oval, half round, and full round."

The chauffeur gazed at them silently.

"This handle is Ovankol," she explained, touching one of the brushes. "A special wood made in Africa. It's like teak but not so expensive. And this one is satinwood. A lovely, very well-made brush. And this is our best. It's entirely handmade in Switzerland. The finest boar bristle set in aged macassar wood. This half-round model is seventy dollars. The full round is eighty."

The chauffeur glared at the brushes as if he found them offensive. His eyes came to rest on the satinwood model, a fat-handled brush. He picked it up and inspected it minutely. It was heavy— the most substantial brush of all those she had laid out.

"How much?" he demanded, shaking it at her.

"That one is forty-five dollars," she replied.

"I'll take it."

"An excellent choice. I'm sure madame will be very pleased."

The chauffeur nodded absently, ignoring the sarcasm in the saleswoman's voice.

"Cash or charge, sir?"

He pulled a wad of bills from his pocket, peeled off three twenties and handed them to her. She wrapped the brush in its box for him, gave him his change, and watched him as he hurried from the shop. She crossed her arms and shook her head at the other clerk.

"Some people," she said, "have no breeding."

The chauffeur carried the box with the expensive satinwood brush down the street to a post office. He purchased a padded shipping envelope there, shoved the brush inside, sealed it, and addressed it to a box number in northeast Washington.

He had the package weighed, paid eighty cents for the stamps, and left the post office, glad to be done with his errand.

What the hell did these people, whoever they were, want with a wood-handled hairbrush? he wondered. And why didn't they just go out and buy it themselves? Well, he shouldn't complain. They were paying him two hundred dollars. Not bad for fifteen minutes' work.

3

WARFIELD CONSULTED HIS stopwatch. A minute remained. He glanced down at the small folding chair beside him, vibrating from the ten pairs of pounding adolescent sneakers out on the court. The junior varsity team manager was trying to stabilize the table with one hand while writing in a fresh set of figures on his clipboard with the other.

"What's the score, Cubby?"

"Green's ahead of Red by a point, sir!"

Warfield nodded and turned his attention to the bench. He noticed "Carrot" Williams sitting at the far end, separated slightly from the other boys. His face wore a tense, mournful expression. Carrot was the only one who had not yet played in the game. Warfield wondered which ordeal the boy found more painful— endlessly warming the bench, a public reminder that he was the worst basketball player on the team; or actually playing, where his fearfulness and lack of coordination made him a humiliation.

Carrot's physical shortcomings were magnified by a wide-eyed, naive manner that encouraged the cruelty of his classmates. They teased and bullied him with a perverse relentlessness that disturbed Warfield, no stranger to cruelty himself.

Kramer, playing guard on the Red team, started to limp. Warfield blew the whistle for a time-out and called Kramer to the bench.

"Carrot, in for Kramer!" he directed.

Carrot reacted to the command as if jabbed with a cattle prod. Warfield suppressed a grimace. Kramer came running off the court, red-faced with fury.

"Don't take me out now, Mr. Warfield!"

"Sit down, Timmy. You need to rest that leg."

"Aw, come on! The game's almost over! You can't sub that wimp for me!"

Warfield fixed Kramer with his hard gray eyes and Kramer cut short his protest. Warfield glanced at the stopwatch again—fifteen seconds remained. He turned his attention back to the game.

Anderson of the Green team was dribbling the ball slowly down the far side of the court, obviously planning to keep control of the ball until the end. Carrot Williams planted himself directly in his path and waved his arms awkwardly in the air. Anderson glared at him contemptuously, then launched the ball over his head toward a teammate.

Somehow the basketball hit one of Carrot's outstretched arms instead, and for a few miraculous seconds he gained possession of it. He clutched it as if it were a live explosive, and searched about frantically for someone to pass it to. Anderson, outraged at losing the ball to him, stepped into him and shoved him hard with both hands. The ball went bouncing into a row of folding chairs along the sideline, and Carrot Williams pitched over on his back.

Warfield threw up his hands in disgust, and sent Anderson off to the showers with a reprimand. Carrot climbed unsteadily to his feet and stood, bent with hands on knees, his chest heaving.

"You all right, Carrot?" Warfield called. Carrot nodded. "Okay, we have a foul!"

Warfield retrieved the ball and walked Carrot over to the free-throw line at the other end of the court. The players began lining up under the basket. Time had expired, with Carrot's team one point behind.

"You've got two shots," Warfield said, tossing him the ball. "Take your time."

Carrot caught the ball, bounced it once, and held it tentatively up in front of him with both hands. He looked pathetic, Warfield thought, standing out there all alone, his frail body shivering with tension.

The first shot fell through the hoop.

Carrot's teammates gasped in surprise. He had just tied the score.

Warfield recovered the ball and tossed it to him for his second try. Carrot bounced it deliberately several times, relishing his sudden position of power. The fate of the game was in his hands. Warfield tried to remember if he had ever—even in practice— seen Carrot Williams sink a basket.

The boy took careful aim, his arms visibly steadier now, and released the ball. Everyone in the gym held his breath.

The ball struck the backboard, bounced against the rim of the hoop, hesitated, and then dropped through.

Pandemonium.

The Red team players jumped up and down, whooping and slapping Carrot on the back. Warfield shook his head in disbelief. Carrot's face was aglow, his eyes shining with a euphoria Warfield supposed the boy had never experienced before. Warfield himself was unaccountably moved. He felt a strong jolt of adrenalin expand from his chest to his head. There was still hope in the world, he thought. He knew the boy would carry this moment with him for the rest of his life. It was legend in miniature, the kind of small miracle that can turn someone's life around.

As his classmates dashed off to the showers, Carrot lingered behind, savoring his triumph.

"I bet you didn't think I could do it," he said, his voice trembling with excitement.

"Sure I did," Warfield replied. "That's why I put you in the game!"

"I've been practicing," Carrot explained. "After study hall, when no one's here. It paid off, just like you said it would!"

Warfield nodded and smiled. He didn't remember telling him any such thing, but he wasn't going to argue. He rested a hand on Carrot's thin shoulder and squeezed it firmly.

"If it wasn't for you," Carrot said, suddenly overcome, "I don't know how I'd ever make it through this place!" His voice broke and he burst into tears. "I don't know how I would," he repeated, and ran off toward the locker room.

Warfield felt his face redden. Adolescent hero-worship made him feel guilty. Poor self-image, the school psychologist had told him. He let Cubby stash the equipment away and ducked out of the gym by the side entrance.

Outside he paused and drew in a deep breath. The air was cold and clear. The late February afternoon sun cast shadows across the snow-buried fields beyond the cluster of brick school buildings. For the first time in a long while he felt almost serene. Harnessed to the daily discipline of school routine, he was beginning to escape his morbid preoccupation with the past. He was even beginning to understand that teaching here could be more than occupational therapy; that it could even be rewarding. He was adapting, becoming part of this small corner of western Massachusetts, with its quiet rural satisfactions and manageable discontents.

From the school gate, Warfield turned right and walked down the hill toward town. It was three in the afternoon, and the rest of the day lay clear before him: he would pick up his battered Ford from the repair shop, do some grocery shopping, change his clothes, pick up the school psychologist and take her out to dinner —and maybe, with luck, to bed.

An hour later, his arms full of groceries, Warfield pushed open the front door of the big Victorian house on High Street where he rented his rooms. In the downstairs hallway, he hesitated. Something seemed wrong, but he couldn't determine what it was. He listened for unfamiliar sounds, but heard only the hall radiator hissing steam.

It was a smell that bothered him. He removed his cap and gloves slowly and glanced into the front parlor, a musty, seldom-used mausoleum of faded prints and furniture from another era. Over the familiar odors of cat and mildew, he detected a subtle trace of lime-scented after-shave lotion. The room was unoccupied.

He started up the stairs toward his apartment, stepping softly on the worn carpet runner, realizing that every creaking tread betrayed his attempt at stealth. No matter. Just another attack of paranoia, he told himself. Old habits died hard.

But halfway up, near the landing, he saw that the door to his apartment stood ajar.

"Freeze or you're dead!"

The words came from behind him, by the railing that wrapped around the second-floor stairwell. Before the voice had closed on the last consonant of the word "dead," Warfield was in motion.

He pushed against the bannister with one hand, kicked his feet back off the edge of the stairs tread, and propelled himself feet first backward down the stairs.

Near the bottom, he twisted on his side to avoid cracking his knees. A shoe-top caught the small plant stand near the bottom step and sent it spinning across the polished maplewood floor. Warfield sprang to his feet and flattened himself against the wall. The side of his head hurt and one arm felt numb.

The voice upstairs was roaring with laughter.

Warfield stepped around to the foot of the stairs and looked up. A giant, sandy-haired figure with a ruddy complexion and deep, pitted scars on his cheeks slouched against the top stairpost. He was slipping a snub-nosed .32-caliber revolver into a side pocket of a gray plaid overcoat, buttoned across his thick chest.

"Jesus Christ, Charlie, that was magnificent! Absolutely fucking magnificent!" He slapped the stairpost with a huge hand and roared again.

Warfield ascended the stairs slowly, massaging his arm. The big man watched him as he climbed. "Still got the good reflexes, hey ol' buddy?"

Warfield glared at him, the muscles in his jaw twitching. When he reached the top step, the other man turned away from him rudely and preceded him toward the open door of his apartment.

Warfield reached him just as he stepped over the threshold. He grasped the man's coat collar from behind with both hands and snatched it forcefully down over his arms to his elbows, trapping him in his own coat.

With one hand on the coat and the other gripping his shirt collar, Warfield hauled him backward from the doorway, swung him around like a heavy garbage can, and pitched his 250 pounds toward the stairwell. The man spun around, hit the wall near the top step, shuffled his feet in a desperate search for balance, and then toppled over the edge, bellowing loudly. Halfway down he crashed through the bannister railing and plunged off the side of the stairs, hitting the floor so hard that the old house shook.

Warfield walked unhurriedly down the stairs after him. The man was on his back, still trapped in his overcoat. His florid face had been bled white. Warfield jerked him up to his feet by his hair and necktie, and pressed him against the wall.

"Next time make an appointment, Shanklin."

"You could have killed me!" Shanklin gasped.

"Yeah. I never seem to have any luck."

A cut over Shanklin's ear trickled blood down his neck and onto his shirt. He felt it with his fingers, then pushed Warfield's hand away and staggered into the front parlor, collapsing into one of the landlady's high-backed chairs. Warfield paused in the doorway, his jaw still twitching with rage.

Shanklin pressed a handkerchief to his head wound. "You're a fucking maniac, Charlie. You've changed."

Warfield said nothing. His mind was churning. He had to get Shanklin out of the house before the landlady returned. He'd invent some story to explain the damages later.

"Crazy bastard," Shanklin muttered, almost dispassionately now, stuffing his blood-stained handkerchief into his coat pocket.

"What do you want, Shanklin?"

The big man coughed and let his head fall against the chair's upholstered back. "Let me catch my breath, ol' buddy."

Warfield snatched his cap and gloves from the hallway floor and put them on. "Catch it outside. I'll be out on the street."

Shanklin caught up with Warfield ten minutes later, on the sidewalk by the public library. Warfield noticed that Shanklin was limping. He increased his pace.

"I'll make this fast," Shanklin said.

Warfield said nothing.

"Friedrich wants you back. He's got a job for you."

"Fuck him," Warfield replied.

"I know how you feel," Shanklin said. "But don't blame him. It wasn't his idea. Wasn't mine, either."

"Whose was it?"

"Believe it or not, it was the president's chief ass-licker, Willy Wilbert. Seems you got at least one friend left in a high place."

"Fuck Wilbert too."

"Well, Friedrich's been authorized to pay you a fat fee. Restore your GS rating, put you back on the pension. The whole rehabilitation. And you look like you could use a little rehab, ol' buddy."

Prickles of fear touched Warfield's spine. Shanklin, steadily regaining his composure after his plunge down the stairwell, walked alongside, letting his message sink in. Warfield turned onto a street that slanted into a steep uphill grade.

"You're not even curious?" Shanklin asked, keeping pace at Warfield's side.

"No."

"It's connected with the news."

"I don't watch the news."

"You read the papers."

"The sports."

Shanklin pulled his coat collar up over his ears. The sun was going down and the temperature was dropping with it.

"You like it up here? Playing nursemaid to a bunch of snot-nosed kids?"

Warfield didn't answer.

"How the fuck do you keep off the sauce?"

"I drink a lot of coffee and stay home at night."

"I know you're crazy, Charlie. But I didn't think you were dumb enough to want to live the rest of your life as a vegetable. Don't you ever miss the fun times? What do you do for excitement up here? Play with yourself? Maybe you're putting it to that landlady of yours. How old is she? Eighty?"

Warfield held a precarious grip on his temper. Shanklin was baiting him, and if he attacked him again, it would be dangerous.

32 . . .

Shanklin was on his guard now, and Warfield knew he was capable of breaking his neck as casually as shaking his hand.

"You should stick to whores, anyway, like I do. You get just what you want. No complications, no demands. There's a hell of a place just opened in Washington, right near the Capitol. You oughta come down, let me show you around. Remember that whorehouse I had in Egypt? Wasn't that something else? Jesus, I wish I still had that gig."

Warfield remembered. It was Shanklin's cover in Alexandria. His whores were a pathetic crew. He beat them so regularly they were often unfit to work. One night, in a drunken rage, he killed one of them. His excesses were no secret to the CIA brass. They protected him for years, and when they were finally forced to take him out of circulation, instead of busting him, they gave him a safe job—training recruits at the farm. Good covert action agents were worth indulging. Shanklin had been a good one, and despite his barbarities—or maybe even because of them—he remained something of a company hero.

"Friedrich told me you'd refuse," Shanklin said.

Warfield stopped and looked back down the hill they had just climbed. Lights were blinking on in the village. They combined with the snow, the church spire, and the wood smoke curling from the chimneys to make a New England postcard. A postcard that held a special private meaning for Warfield.

"He was right. I'm staying here."

"So he authorized me to twist your arm a little," Shanklin said, ignoring Warfield's reply.

"My arm doesn't twist anymore."

The big man laughed. "He said that if you seemed shy about coming back, we might have to call on your headmaster here and provide him with a little peek at Charlie Warfield's long and distinguished career. The uncensored version."

"Tell Friedrich I think he's pathetic."

"He probably knows that already. And I warned him you might not buckle that easily."

Warfield felt Shanklin's cat green eyes measuring him like prey.

"Spell it out, for Christ's sakes!"

"I told him we could always open up the Al Montaza incident. Finger you for the Egyptians."

Warfield felt suddenly faint. He balled his fists and jammed them hard against the bottoms of his coat pockets.

"You gotta admit, Charlie, the Egyptians would sure like to get that one off their books. Wife of an army officer and all."

"Tanya was my agent!" Warfield answered, his voice hoarse with emotion. "I didn't kill her! Friedrich knows that damned well!"

"The *Mukhabarat* thinks you did. They think you discovered she was doubling on you and so you iced her. You did clear out of town right after. Looks suspicious as hell from their point of view."

"It's monstrous," Warfield whispered. "You know it isn't true!"

Shanklin shrugged. "Yeah, maybe I do. The point is Friedrich's determined to twist your arm."

Warfield couldn't help himself. He felt tears springing to his eyes. "Don't you see? I'm no good for that stuff anymore! My nerves are gone. I couldn't stand it again, even for a day! It would destroy me!"

It was Shanklin's turn to keep silent.

Warfield pressed back his emotions and tried to concentrate. He saw immediately that there was no real choice for him; he had been naive to imagine that there was.

"What kind of job?" he asked, finally, when he had regained enough composure to speak.

Shanklin grinned, displaying his yellow teeth as he savored Warfield's torment. "Just a little Q and A work."

"Starting when?"

Shanklin laughed. "Right this minute. I've got a plane waiting for us in Pittsfield."

Warfield started back down the hill toward town, feeling weak in his legs. A sense of doom enveloped him.

"Why did he send you?"

The big man rested a hand on the back of Warfield's neck and pressed his fingers into the flesh. "Because he knew what buddies we used to be, ol' buddy."

4

THE PRESIDENT STRODE
through the doorway from the west wing into the White House
ground-floor corridor, Secret Service agent Dan McCormick at his
side. The marble walls and the ceiling's vaulted arches echoed
their conversation back at them as they walked.
Daniels did not like the ground floor, and he always hurried
through it. The paintings disturbed him. The corridor served as
the gallery for portraits of former first ladies. Even though his
route from the Oval Office required him to traverse barely a third
of the corridor's length—just far enough to get him to the west
elevator bank opposite the map room—he still had to pass by three
first ladies: Eleanor Roosevelt, Betty Ford, and Rosalynn Carter.

His unease grew from the simple fact that one day the White
House curator would ask to commission a portrait of Estelle to
hang in the corridor with the others. Under the circumstances,
how could he respond to such a request? All a president's burdens,
he reflected sadly, were not affairs of state.

"I talked to your boss today," Daniels said, looking at McCormick.

McCormick grinned. "So I heard. Lay down the law, did he?"

Daniels laughed. "If Mack Clark had his way, he'd keep me
locked up in my bedroom—like Estelle."

"Keeping you in one piece is getting to be a bitch of a job, Mr.
President."

Agent McCormick was in charge of the presidential protection
detail, and he had been assigned to Daniels as his personal bodyguard since the election campaign of 1980. Mack Clark had picked
him for Daniels' detail, so the story went, because he was the only
agent as tall as the president—six feet five inches.

McCormick was likable and easygoing—an amiable sponge. The
president, a man of fierce competitive spirit around rival politi-
cians and diplomats, felt he could relax with him, let down his
guard. It was a simple relationship, unencumbered by rivalry,
competition, or differences of opinion. McCormick was Daniels'
sidekick—literally and figuratively.

"I think Mack's overdoing it," Daniels said, as they reached the
small vestibule by the west elevator bank. McCormick pressed the
button and the car descended from the second floor. "As far as

security goes," he continued, "we've reached the point of diminishing returns, and I told Mack so. So we struck a compromise. I've agreed to no more trips or public appearances until the missing assassin is located. No more Deer Isle for the time being. Weekends at Camp David. That's it. And the uniformed guard around the White House grounds will be doubled. Mack also insists on an FBI SWAT team on the roof. Seems excessive to me, but I'll humor him."

The elevator arrived; the door hissed open. McCormick, stepping in behind the president, pressed the button for the third floor.

"You said you compromised," McCormick replied. "What did you get from him?"

Daniels shrugged. "He wanted to suspend the public tours of the White House. I vetoed that. And at night, you fellows will have your stations moved. At eight o'clock, everybody clears off the second floor until six in the morning."

McCormick scratched his ear, where he wore his two-way radio earplug. "You mean Junior won't have to spend the night out in the hallway?"

"From now on," Daniels replied, "he can sleep on the west stair hall landing."

"What about the football?" McCormick asked.

The "football" was White House slang for the thick black leather attaché case carried by a field-grade military officer who remained only seconds from the president's side wherever he went, day or night. The briefcase carried the "sealed authenticators," envelopes containing the codes necessary for the president to initiate a nuclear attack. The officer carrying it at the moment was silently trudging up the west stairs, to meet the president on the third floor.

"The football spends the night in the third floor hall," Daniels replied.

McCormick nodded. "Sounds okay. But what's the big deal about clearing the second floor?"

Daniels sighed. "The big deal is that I need a little breathing space, a place where I can talk to myself if I feel like it. Now that I'm a prisoner of this damned mansion, I need some escape."

"I can see that," McCormick agreed. "It won't hurt security, that's for sure. There's a big fence around this place, after all, and guards at all the gates and doorways. But how are we supposed to handle this down in the cellar?"

McCormick was referring to the Secret Service control room in the White House subbasement, where an agent manned an electronic panel that plotted the president's movements, tracking him, via agents' radioed messages, from building to building, floor to floor, room to room.

"That's your problem," the president replied. "I guess you'll just have to leave the second floor a big blank from eight until six."

The elevator reached the third floor and the doors slid open.

"I guess we can live with that," McCormick said.

"You'll have to." Daniels stepped off the elevator. "Anyway, I won't exactly be hard to find. I promise not to hide in the closets."

"Goodnight, Mr. President."

"Goodnight, Dan."

President Daniels walked down the third-floor hallway toward the suite of rooms on the southeast corner. The third floor—actually the fourth level of the White House, not counting the two basement levels—was a part of the mansion few outsiders ever saw. It was added onto the roof in 1927, and set back, penthouse fashion, from the main walls, hidden behind the parapets that enclosed the roof's perimeter.

Compared to the chambers on the floors below, the third floor was a rabbit's warren. The west side contained a small kitchen and sitting room, and a cluster of tiny bedrooms for some of the domestic staff, and the east side was taken up with guest rooms and a playroom with a small stage. The floor's center hall was bisected by a narrower north-south passageway, the north leg leading to a maze of storage rooms over the north portico, the south leading up a shallow ramp to an enclosed octagonal solarium over the south portico.

On the southeast corner, the former Washington Sitting Room and its adjacent bedroom and bath had been converted into Estelle's domain.

Daniels knocked softly on the reinforced paneled door and waited. After a short pause, a key twisted in the lock and the door opened to reveal a short, stout woman in a white nurse's uniform. She ushered him into the vestibule of the suite.

"Good evening, Mr. President," she whispered.

"Hello, Irene."

Irene pressed the president's large hand between her own small ones and looked up at him with a mournful expression. "I've been thinking all day, Mr. President, how lucky we are to still have you with us. Thank heaven you weren't hurt!"

Daniels put an arm around her shoulder and squeezed her gently. He liked the nurse, but she tended to dwell on the morbid. The night following the Parkway ambush, she had been on the verge of hysteria.

"I'm too stubborn to die just yet, Irene."

"God watches over you, Mr. President," she replied somberly.

"How's Estelle?" he asked.

"Very good today, Mr. President. She watched television and ate dinner by herself. She's still awake."

"I'll go in then," he said.

The nurse opened the door from the vestibule into Estelle's bedroom. "Dr. Bergmann was in," she whispered. "He wants to talk to you. When it's convenient, of course."

Daniels frowned. He knew what Dr. Bergmann wanted. It was always the same thing. He wanted to move Estelle to an institution. During the last installment of this running argument, Bergmann had tried a new tack. He had suggested that it was he, Daniels, who concerned him, more than his sick wife. He had hinted that Daniels' doting on his wife was unhealthy, that he was letting his guilt about her illness prevent him from leading a "full life."

The nurse shut the door behind the president and he looked across the bedroom, softly lit by two ceiling fixtures, their bulbs turned low by a dimmer switch in the vestibule. The colors of the walls and curtains were bright, cheerful whites and lemon yellows, the carpets beige, the furniture decorated in pretty floral patterns.

Everything in the room was designed to appear as normal as possible. But a closer look revealed that it was in fact an elaborately disguised padded cell. There were no floor or table lamps, no unupholstered furniture, no sharp objects. The exterior of the vanity table was padded, and it contained no jewelry box or jewelry, no combs, no hairbrushes, no bottles of cologne or perfume. In the adjoining bathroom, the medicine chest was empty. The bedroom walls were upholstered in an expensive, stain-resistant cloth with a thick, padded backing, and all the wall outlets had been covered.

The closets held many of Estelle's clothes. She seldom wore them, but she liked to spend time with them, fussing over them. Four pillows she had embroidered years before when they lived in the small brick colonial in Georgetown, were arranged on a chaise, and a few old rag dolls from her daughter Alice's childhood were tucked in a window seat.

Daniels sank into his familiar armchair by the foot of the bed. Estelle was sitting up, her knees drawn against her chest, her arms wrapped around them.

"Hello Stelly," he whispered.

His wife lifted her head slightly, reacting to the sound of his voice. Her eyes found him, alighted briefly on his face, and then retreated, back to their customary inward focus. Irene had combed her hair, and it shone a lustrous reddish brown. It was astonishing, he reflected, how beautiful she had become since she had surrendered to her illness. She had gained weight, and that strained, haggard look had vanished from her face, taking with it the lines around her eyes and mouth, and leaving behind a serene, otherworldly composure. As she retreated from him mentally, finding refuge in some imaginary fortress shaped from the incoherent fragments of her past, so also she seemed to retreat from him physically. By some perverse medical alchemy, her madness was transporting her backward in time, pulling her each day further away from him.

He began reciting some of the events of the past day to her in a low monotone. Daniels spent half an hour with her every evening, reviewing the day in this fashion. At first, when he had hoped the effort would be therapeutic, it had been difficult, continuing on against her blank, uncomprehending stare. But gradually he had come to ignore her reactions—or her lack of them. Now he talked simply to unburden himself. What the words did for her— whether she understood them, whether she derived any benefit from them—he could not tell.

Sometimes he imagined he saw a flicker of comprehension in her eyes. Sometimes her face would take on an old, remembered expression. And on the rare occasions when she spoke, usually in a rush of incoherent phrases, he imagined her words might be a message in code, transmitted in secret across the hostile void that separated their worlds.

It was during these tantalizing moments that it struck him how desolating her illness really was. If she had been afflicted with some physical malady, no matter how terrible, they could still have shared the bonds of communication, understanding, mutual love. But this invisible beast of madness was far more difficult to endure.

The night of the ambush he had spent nearly three hours with her, recounting the attack on the motorcade and the turbulent aftermath. He transformed the motorcade attack into an attack on her madness, in a determined effort to break through the walls, to press reality onto her. He had failed. It was from such reality, after all, that her madness was designed to shield her. Daniels had left her that night feeling curiously bereft and angry.

He talked now about the speculation in the press concerning the ambush; about the missing assassin, whom the Secret Service and the FBI feared would make another attempt on his life; about the captured assassin, and the CIA's difficulties in getting information from him. He admitted to a terrible disappointment about the disarmament agreement, now doomed by the ascent of the hardliners in the Kremlin.

Daniels felt his wife's eyes on him, and he paused in his monologue to watch her. Her hands traveled abruptly to her face, as if reacting to a slap, and she pushed her legs out straight beneath the covers. He had seen her do this before. She would sit perfectly still, hunched up on the bed, and then suddenly an inner something would disturb her, and she would react as if shaken from a trance. Each time he saw it happen, he held his breath, praying for a breakthrough that never came. It was as if she approached the edge of his world, then hesitated, afraid to advance further, and instead slipped back into her private oblivion.

This time she appeared especially agitated.

She stared intently at the far wall. "Where's Alice?" she cried.

Her words came out small and almost sweet sounding, as if from a child.

Daniels swallowed hard. "Alice is in New Haven, Stelly. Teaching. You remember."

Estelle locked her large brown eyes onto his. A moment of recognition passed. She nodded, faintly, then pulled her legs back up to her chest and wrapped her arms over her knees. Daniels bit his lip in disappointment.

When Alice was born, almost thirty years ago, Estelle had nearly died of the complications. Daniels, away on a fund-raising trip, had not been able to get back to see her until the next morning. He remembered the four days of delirium, and he remembered her crying out for Alice then. It had scared him, and he knew she had never completely forgiven him for not being there with her.

Did she remember that now? he wondered.

"She'll be here at Easter," he said, hoping to encourage more words from her. He looked at his watch, and was surprised to see that the hour had advanced past eleven.

"Eliot?"

The hairs on his neck tingled.

"Yes. It's me, Stelly!" he whispered.

She smiled briefly, gazing at his face and at the front of his shirt, as if trying to recall something about him. Daniels feared to move, lest he jar this precarious connection.

"Let's go home, Eliot."

He nodded, feeling a hard lump rise in his throat. He rested a hand gently on the blanket by her ankles. Then she was gone. He watched the inward expression cloud her eyes again, as the devil that possessed her soul snatched her back from him.

Daniels pushed himself up out of the chair, stood looking down at his wife for a brief moment, then bent over and kissed her on the forehead. "Goodnight, Stelly," he said.

Instead of returning to the elevator, he walked to the narrow stairs by the playroom and descended to the second floor. He paused in the east hall, at the bottom of the landing, and looked around him. The hall, flanked by the two major guest suites in the White House, the Lincoln Bedroom on the south, and the Queen's Bedroom on the north, served as an informal sitting area for that end of the mansion. He gazed absently at the unfamiliar armchairs and sofa, and the clutter of antiques—a mahogany tambour desk, a Hepplewhite chest of drawers, two Chinese vases converted to lamps. He hardly ever set foot in this part of the house, he realized. A huge Palladian window, an exact twin of the one in the west sitting hall at the other end of the house, dominated the space, its fanlike arrangement of panes draped in luxurious gold silk damask. A few lights from the Treasury building next door glowed through its white undercurtains.

Estelle had once talked ambitiously about her redecorating plans for the White House. Every first lady liked to leave her personal imprint, and Estelle was no different. But she never even got started. The mansion looked exactly as it had when they inherited it from their predecessors, three years ago.

Daniels' glance swept over the paintings on the walls. Over the chest of drawers by the door to the Queen's Bedroom, hung a view of the Hudson River. He stepped in closer to read the plaque at the bottom of the frame: *Robert Havell, Jr. 1850.*

Daniels knew the real reason for his lingering here. He was debating with himself whether or not to knock on the door of the Queen's Bedroom, and risk disturbing its occupant, the premier's widow, Katya Ivanova. He waited, hoping he might hear some sounds of activity to encourage him.

Only silence.

Since the ambush and the chaotic helicopter ride back to the White House, he had hardly seen the woman. He understood that the Russian ambassador was putting heavy pressure on her to move to the Soviet Embassy, a few blocks away on Sixteenth Street, but she was resisting it. Sam Gordon, the White House Chief Usher, had mentioned to him that the situation was still tense. The first night following the ambush, the Russians had insisted on posting their own three-man bodyguard at her door, and parking another four staff personnel on the third floor as well. After hours of negotiations with the Secret Service and the Russian Embassy, Gordon had managed to reduce the Russian presence to three, and move them all to the third floor. The Russians finally gave in, Gordon had said, only because Mrs. Kamenev had made a terrible fuss about it.

It had probably been a mistake inviting her here, Daniels realized. It had only exacerbated the crisis. Thinking about it made him feel sad. He had not even had a chance to talk with her. And in a day or two, she would be gone.

Reluctantly, Daniels headed down the long center hall toward his own bedroom. How deserted the place feels, he thought, with the Secret Service detail off the floor. His mind made an imaginary circuit of all the rooms around him. He counted sixteen. And except for the Queen's Bedroom and his bedroom, they were all empty. So much space, and no one to live in it.

He stopped in the tiny vestibule by his study, mixed himself a scotch and soda at the bar, and carried it into his bedroom.

He sat on the edge of the bed, sipping the drink, thinking over the events of the past three days. The ambush had created the worst international crisis in recent memory. He needed to devote all his time and energy to cope with it, but his mind kept coming back to the premier's widow. He recalled that when he had told the story of the ambush to Estelle two nights ago, he had left Katya almost entirely out of the narrative. Why had he done that? he wondered. Did he think that if Estelle knew that the premier's widow was staying in the White House that she would be jealous? Absurd.

And tonight, instead of being elated at Estelle's brief moment of lucidity, he felt anxiety. It was almost as if the possibility of her recovering might be a threat to him. Damned strange.

The president rested his drink on the night table, threw his clothes onto a chair for the valet in the morning, and crawled into bed, suddenly tired.

Before sleep, the same vision returned that had visited him the previous two nights. It was the image of Katya Ivanova squeezed against him on the floor of the limousine. He experienced again the firm softness of her thigh, pressed between his legs, and the feeling of excited fear that trembled through her. In that moment, when they both lay so near death, they had shared a peculiar, perverse sort of ecstasy.

5

WARFIELD SAT NEXT TO SHAN-klin on the helicopter ride from Langley to the farm. He gazed out a porthole window at the brown fields and woods of Virginia's Tidewater, picking out the rivers that threaded through the barren winter terrain—the Potomac, the Rappahannock, the York—still familiar to him from aerial reconnaissance photos he had been required to memorize as a trainee at the farm years ago.

He played the meeting with CIA Director Friedrich earlier that morning back over in his head. It had been a damned short briefing. About five minutes. Warfield had begun it by trying to spell out to the director the problems involved in getting subjects to talk against their will, but Friedrich was in no mood for spelling lessons. "All I have to say to you, Warfield, is this: make him talk —any way you can. There's no time limit, but keep in mind that every hour it takes you, is another hour in which the president's life is in jeopardy. I've instructed Shanklin to provide you with whatever you need."

That was it. Dismissed.

Warfield looked over at Shanklin. He was thumbing through a copy of *Hustler* magazine. He held it open to a full-page color photograph of a female nude with blotchy skin, reclining on her back. Fingers from both hands were stuffed into her vagina.

"Does Friedrich think I'm going to torture him?" Warfield asked. Over the roar of the Huey's engines and rotors, he had to shout to be heard.

Shanklin shrugged without looking up. "I dunno, ol' buddy. Sounds like he gave you free rein. Results are what count."

"If I were in your shoes, I'd be mad as hell," Warfield said, to test his attitude.

Shanklin looked up. "Why's that?"

"You're being axed. You failed to crack the assassin, so now they're pushing you aside in favor of me."

Shanklin laughed. "I don't see it that way. I'm just riding herd on this business. And nobody's failed yet. Like you told the boss, these things take time. My team will still be working on the case with you. If you break the assassin, I'll get my share of the credit."

"What if I fail?"

Shanklin picked up the magazine again and turned a page. "In that case, it'll be Wilbert's ass, since it was his idea to bring you in."

Warfield nodded. Still, Shanklin's nonchalance puzzled him. He tried to probe deeper. "I'm surprised Friedrich didn't ask you personally to squeeze the prisoner. You'd be good at it."

Shanklin glanced up from the magazine, an uncertain, preoccupied look in his eyes. "I've got a career to protect," he replied, his tone serious. "Don't want any stains on it now, at this late date."

Warfield slapped a hand down on the armrest. "What about me?"

Shanklin turned another page. "You're expendable."

Warfield turned to the porthole window. He saw the silvery expanse of Chesapeake Bay, off to the southwest, glittering coldly in the February sun. Below them, the streets of Williamsburg, Virginia, crisscrossed the brown terrain like dozens of unplayed tic-tac-toe squares.

The craft veered west and passed over a couple of small villages and then a stretch of deep woods, unmarked by houses or roads. Warfield saw a field, many acres in size, loom suddenly out of the surrounding wilderness. Dozens of one-story buildings popped into view, clustered around the field's perimeter.

Camp Peary. The farm.

Warfield recognized the officer's club, the main classroom building, the barracks, the mess hall. The helicopter swept past a solitary concrete building Warfield remembered was an explosives storehouse, over a weapons range and a jump tower, and along a mysterious swath of cleared woods, dotted with watchtowers, bunkers, and high barbed-wire fences that zigzagged through the clearing like a ski trail. Warfield shook his head at the memory of it. It was a simulated border of some imaginary hostile country. One of the favorite exercises at the farm was sending the career trainees out to penetrate it, usually in the middle of the night. According to the scorekeeper, he had died many times trying to find a way across.

"There's no way I'll use torture," he said. "No way."

Shanklin closed the magazine and threw it onto the empty seat across from them. He examined Warfield with an amused grin.

"If the president is so worried about somebody shooting his ass off," Warfield continued, "then let him come down here and squeeze a confession out of the prisoner himself."

Shanklin shrugged. "Suit yourself, ol' buddy."

The Huey hovered in midair for a few seconds, then spiraled down toward a fenced-in clearing Warfield had not noticed from above. They settled onto a paved parking lot, next to a row of government sedans and jeeps, and near a long, low cement block building, painted dark brown and artfully hidden among a thick stand of Southern pines. A Marine guard was posted at the single entrance.

Warfield and Shanklin jumped from the helicopter and trotted a short distance across the tarmac to escape the blast of the rotor blades.

"That's new," Shanklin said, pointing to the low building in the trees. "For special debriefing. Off limits to the rest of the base.

That's where your team is working. You'll stay there. It's self-contained. Even has its own kitchen, but you can eat in the mess hall."

A sedan drove up beside them and a driver jumped out and opened the back door. Shanklin climbed in and slammed the door behind him. He rolled down the window a few inches and looked out at Warfield, left standing on the tarmac.

"They're expecting you inside," he said. "I'm off to the weapons range. Got a class there at nine. You're on your own, ol' buddy."

Warfield stared at Shanklin's bad teeth, grinning at him from the back seat. Shanklin laughed, then rolled up the window and the sedan drove off. Warfield watched it until it disappeared around a corner. Then he turned and walked slowly across the parking lot toward the lone guarded door of the building at the edge of the woods. Carrying a canvas overnight bag, he felt foolish and vulnerable, like a green recruit arriving late for training camp. And the same butterflies fluttered in his gut. He forced a small laugh. The absurdity of his predicament could have been considered comic. At least by someone else.

The guard examined Warfield's freshly issued pass politely, and opened the door for him. Inside, he followed a long, narrow corridor until it terminated in a small, cluttered lounge. The room was stale with cigarette smoke and sweat, and uncomfortably hot. Three men looked up at him from battered vinyl armchairs. Warfield dropped his bag in an empty chair, peeled off his overcoat, and stood, quietly absorbing the scene around him.

A large table shoved against the far wall bespoke the occupants' long ordeal. Disorderly piles of transcripts, tapes, and folders spilled off its edges. Ashtrays overflowed with cigarette butts. Empty coffee containers, dirty plastic spoons, and torn gum wrappers littered the linoleum tile floor.

"I'm Warfield," he said.

The other three continued to stare at him, sizing him up coldly. He felt like a stranger who had just walked into a bad bar. Finally the senior of them roused himself from his seat and extended his hand.

"I'm Frank Carson."

Warfield took his hand. Carson applied an unnecessary amount of pressure to his grip. He sported crew-cut steel gray hair and rimless glasses. About fifty, Warfield judged, and muscular, probably once an athlete. He looked tough as a rock ledge.

"And that's Harold Robinson and Howard Moore," Carson said, waving toward their chairs. Warfield stepped over the debris on the floor and shook their hands. Robinson was tall, thirty-ish, fair-haired, and morose. Moore, the youngest, was thin, black, and possessed the air of an intellectual—large, intelligent eyes peering shyly from behind thick glasses. All three showed obvious signs of defeat—lethargy, yawning, disheveled clothes, red-rimmed eyes.

Worse yet, Warfield thought, they were all just sitting around, at nine o'clock in the morning, not *doing* anything. He wondered what use they would be to him in their present depressed condition. Their initial hostility was not promising. Of course they resented his being brought in over them. They would interpret it as a judgment against their competence. Trying to win them over would probably be both time-consuming and self-defeating.

"I don't know what you know about me," he began, "but I guess you know why I'm here."

Carson nodded, grinning sardonically. Moore and Robinson gazed out the window, as if to hide the reactions on their faces.

"I can appreciate you've had a tough time of it so far," Warfield continued. "Unfortunately, it's not going to get any easier with me here."

A pregnant silence.

Warfield stepped to the casement window and pushed it open, letting fresh air pour into the room. He turned to Carson. "Let's get somebody in here to shovel this place out."

Carson shook his head. "There's only one cleaning man on the base with top-security clearance," he replied. "It usually takes a few days notice to get him."

"When's he scheduled here next?"

"I don't know. Some time next week, I guess."

Warfield met Carson's squinted-eyed stare head-on. "Get on the phone and tell the commandant's office I personally asked to have him here right away."

Carson's eyebrows shot up. "Right away?"

"Right away."

"I don't think they'll buy that."

"Try them."

Robinson and Moore watched him expectantly, as he relayed Warfield's demand. A minute later he cradled the phone, his expression hardened into a surly frown. "They'll send him," he said. "Right away."

Warfield affected indifference. "Tell me about the interrogation," he said.

"The whole story's in those transcripts," Robinson replied, flicking a hand lazily in the direction of the table.

"I guessed as much," Warfield said. "I'll look at them later. Meanwhile just give me a fast fill-in. What's been the routine?"

"We've been working him in twelve-hour shifts," Carson replied. "Harold here plays the good cop, I play the bad cop."

"What do you do?" Warfield asked Moore.

The young black glanced at the others. Carson answered for him.

"Howard here is sort of the producer of the show. He takes care of the equipment, gets the transcripts done, runs interference for us with Langley and the commandant's office."

"I work out lines of questioning, too," Moore added, "for the interrogation."

"What kind of pressure are you putting on the prisoner?"

Carson grimaced impatiently. "Bright lights, a lot of yelling in his face, pulling his hair. Threats. Keeping him awake. The usual drill."

"If we could just learn his name," Moore said, "or something about him, then we could develop a better attack. As it is, all we can do is go over the details of the ambush with him. And nothing we've tried has worked. He's a hard case."

"Have you developed anything from his clothes?"

Robinson tapped out a cigarette and lit it with a shaky hand. "The FBI report is on the table. Nothing that'll help us."

"What about a doctor? Has he been checked over?"

"Yeah," Carson replied. "Two docs here at the farm took him apart. That report's on the table, too. Nothing in it. The guy's never had any operations, no knife wounds or anything interesting. Nothing unique. They haven't been able to trace his dental record. Oh yeah, he's not circumcised."

Robinson laughed.

"What's funny?" Warfield asked.

"Just our little joke," Robinson said. "We figure at least he's not an Israeli terrorist."

Warfield sighed. "Where is he now?"

"In the basement," Moore said. "Next to the interrogation room."

"Who's with him?"

Moore glanced over at his colleagues, then back at Warfield. "The guard's there, outside his cell."

"That's all?"

"Well, he's probably asleep."

Warfield sat up as if he'd been slapped. "Asleep? . . ."

Moore looked embarrassed and frightened. "When we were told you were coming . . . they told us to knock off. Wait until you got here. . . . We . . ."

"Jesus Christ!" Warfield yelled, rising up out of his chair, genuine anger spilling out of him. "But you don't let the son-of-a-bitch go to sleep! At nine o'clock in the morning! You're losing the entire advantage of two days' work!"

Moore swallowed. "I thought that, but Shanklin said. . . ."

Warfield saw Carson flash Moore a warning look. "What did Shanklin say?" he demanded.

After a tense moment, Carson broke the silence. "He told us you'd been kicked out of the agency. He didn't understand why they wanted to bring you in, but he told us you probably wouldn't last. He told us to follow orders, but we don't have to volunteer anything."

Robinson, for the first time since Warfield had entered the room, actually smiled. Moore was biting a fingernail. Warfield stroked his chin slowly, trying to calm himself.

"The talk around camp," Moore said, trying to soften the confrontation, "is that you were a great interrogator. . . ."

Warfield ignored Moore and turned to Carson. "I appreciate your honesty."

Carson shrugged. "Yeah, well . . ."

"Obviously you all need a good night's sleep."

"That's the truth!" Robinson said, sounding almost cheerful.

"In the morning I'll put in reassignment requests for all of you."

Carson eyed Warfield suspiciously. "What's that mean?"

"It means, Carson, you dim-witted baboon, that I'm finished with you! Now get the fuck out of here!"

Nobody moved. Carson bunched his fists.

"Get out, goddammit!" Warfield bellowed. "Get out!"

They left.

For a long while Warfield just stood, contemplating the paper on the table. He knew he should at least go down and wake the prisoner. But then what? He had no plan and no one to help him carry one out if he did have one. He swept the stack of documents and transcripts off onto the floor and kicked them around until they covered the entire surface of the ugly green linoleum. Then he collapsed into one of the vinyl easy chairs and buried his face in his palms. He sat, slumped over, still as a meditating yogi, for a long time.

A banging noise brought him back to reality. He was shivering. He opened his eyes and saw an old black man in coveralls shutting the casement window. The temperature in the room had plummeted. The man turned to him and waved his arms at the floor. "You sure you want me to clean this up? Might be better we just nail the door shut and start all over again down the hall. . . ."

Warfield ate lunch by himself at the camp mess hall and returned to the lounge in the low building in the restricted area, his mind preoccupied. The cleaning man had stacked all the documents in neat piles on the big table. Warfield picked up a folder from the top of a pile and opened it.

> Transcript, 2.21.83. 0100 hrs., Camp Peary debrief. TOP
> SECRET NODIS. Frank Carson interrogating.
> C: I'm just going to sit here and read this magazine. . . .
> When I finish this magazine, I'll go get another one. . . .
> We'll go on like this all night, if we have to. . . . You'll
> just sit there in that chair until you decide to start
> talking . . . and you'll stay awake as long as we have to
> keep you awake until you start talking. . . . I've just had
> a good eight hours of sleep myself, so I'm real well
> rested. . . .
> (Interval)
> C: You don't sleep until you talk, you fucker. . . .
> (Interval)
> C: Sit up! . . . I said sit up! . . . (sound of slapping)
> (Interval)
> C: You're a stubborn son-of-a-bitch, aren't you? . . . But

we'll wear you down. You'll talk sooner or later. They all do. . . . the longer you wait the harder it's going to be. . . .
    (Interval)
C: Sit up, you bastard, and keep your eyes open! . . .

Warfield closed the folder and heaved it in the direction of the metal wastebasket in the corner. It hit the rim and knocked the basket over.

He looked at the telephone, sitting on a stack of documents. An idea was beginning to germinate. Vague, unformed, uncertain, but at least an idea. He picked up the receiver and dialed a long-distance number.

He listened to the hollow burr on the other end—five, six, seven, eight rings. He was about to hang up when the receiver clicked and a raspy voice answered: "Who is it?"

"Herb? That you?"

"Who's this?"

"Charlie Warfield. And don't ask for any explanations. Just listen. I'm at the farm, outside Williamsburg. I've got a problem you can help me with. Can you drive down here right now?"

"Of course not! I'm between classes. Are you drinking again?"

"I'm very sober, Herb. I need your advice. Serious business."

"What the hell are you up to? What are you doing at the farm?"

"I'll tell you when you get here."

"Damn it all, Charlie," the other voice protested, "it's a three-hour drive down there from Washington!"

"It's important."

"Well, Jesus . . ."

"How soon?"

There was a long pause at the other end. A faint metallic echo alerted Warfield to a tap somewhere on the line.

"You still there, Herb?"

"I'm here. Eight o'clock tomorrow is the earliest."

"That's great! Don't tell anybody where you're going. Not even Louise."

"This better be good!"

"It is. Bring your black bag and a change of clothes. You'll need them both. And don't forget your security pass. They'll call me from the gate when you get here."

Warfield cradled the phone and exhaled. He felt marginally less miserable.

A sudden knock at the door startled him.

"It's open!"

The young black interrogater, Howard Moore, walked in, his lips taut with anger.

"You can't do this to me," he said.

"Can't do what?"

"You lumped me in with Carson and Robinson. You didn't give me a chance."

Warfield frowned. "You're better off out of this, Moore. It's a mess and it's only likely to get worse."

"That's just being condescending," Moore said. "I want to stay with this. I believe I can help. This is my field. Debriefing. Interrogation."

Warfield considered it. He supposed Moore was right. He was being unfair to him. And Moore had at least tried to be cooperative when Warfield first came in.

"Do you know what you're getting into?"

"Hell, I'm in it already! You owe me the chance, damn it!"

The expression on the young man's face seemed caught somewhere between plaintive and unyielding.

"You're making a mistake," Warfield said. "But it's your life. Have a seat."

Moore perched unsteadily on the armrest of the easy chair by the window. He was thin and bony, Warfield noticed, all knees and elbows and Adam's apple. His movements were jerky and ungraceful, and his clothes were an afterthought. He was intelligent, but timid, high-strung. He reminded Warfield of Carrot Williams, his maladroit basketball player back at the school. But he saw possible strength in Moore: mental toughness, determination.

"Tell me," Warfield said. "Is there something peculiar going on here that I should know about?"

Moore looked startled. "What do you mean?"

"I don't know exactly what I mean. Maybe it's just my paranoia, but I swear there's something fishy about this interrogation."

Moore shook his head, still puzzled.

"Look," Warfield said, bending toward Moore to emphasize his point. "The country's in a serious crisis, right?"

"Yeah? . . ."

"They should be doing everything humanly possible to break this assassin. The joint should be crawling with world-famous experts and specialists in a dozen different fields. Instead, we find Carson and Robinson down here, playing Good Cop, Bad Cop, and tucking the prisoner into bed at night. An interrogation like this would embarrass a backwoods country sheriff. Who picked them for this job?"

"I don't know."

"Who picked you?"

"I was assigned through the commandant's office. I don't know who actually picked me."

"Damned strange," Warfield muttered.

Moore shrugged defensively. "So we didn't get anywhere. We only had three days."

"And you wasted them."

"So that's why you're here, to get things rolling, right? I don't see anything odd."

"I do," Warfield said. "It almost looks as if somebody doesn't *want* the assassin to talk."

"Nobody's trying to sabotage anything," Moore insisted. "Despite what you think, we worked like hell the past three days. And we had a lot of help and advice. You should know better than anyone that it's not easy to break a determined man. And this son-of-a-bitch is determined, I can promise you that."

"Any man can be made to talk," Warfield answered.

"But there aren't many ways to do it," Moore countered.

"That's true."

"In fact," Moore said, "there are only two. You can wear him down—with persuasion or drugs—or you can torture him."

"That's about right," Warfield admitted.

"The problem with wearing a victim down," Moore said, "is that it takes time. So that leaves squeezing him."

Warfield nodded.

"I figure they must have sent you down here to squeeze him."

"Maybe," Warfield said. "But I'm not going to do it. It doesn't work that fast anyway. If our assassin is as tough as you say, he could easily last for weeks. And we don't have weeks."

"What's that leave us, then?"

Warfield slipped his hands into his pockets and studied the green linoleum, its scarred tiles freshly waxed by the cleaning man.

"We have to find a third way."

Howard Moore scratched an elbow again. "Well, there's always black magic."

Warfield looked up from the floor and smiled thoughtfully. "I was thinking along the same lines," he said.

6

AFTER DINNER THE GUESTS followed the waiter from the small upstairs dining room through the west sitting hall and the center hall into the Yellow Oval Room. It was arguably the most attractive salon in the entire mansion, its pleasing, spacious proportions furnished with Louis XVI pieces. From its windows on the south portico balcony it offered a spectacular view of the Jefferson and Lincoln Memorials and the Washington Monument. Daniels liked the room, and did most of his entertaining, official and private, here, leaving the cold, museum-like expanses of the floors below to the tourists and the occasionally inescapable big state dinner or diplomatic reception.

The guests gravitated toward the warmth of the fireplace—Secretary of State Stewart Wellman, his wife, Caroline; William Wilbert, the president's chief of staff, his wife Susan; and the widow of the Russian premier, Katya Ivanova Kamenev.

The dinner, planned weeks earlier, had almost been cancelled because of the crisis. But Daniels had decided to go ahead with it. The guests were close friends and he needed the chance to unwind a little. And keeping his social schedule would convey a good impression—that the administration was not in a panic, that this president had the crisis firmly under control. His inviting Madam Kamenev had raised a lot of eyebrows among the staff, but he had defended it easily—it was a show of solidarity with the slain Russian leader, and a gesture of sympathy to his widow.

Daniels had wanted the evening to be informal. But at the White House, with its enormous staff, a dinner for six tended to be run a little like a rowboat with a twelve-man crew. Sam Gordon, who was in charge of these affairs, inevitably erred on the side of ostentation. Daniels watched in exasperation as six waiters filed in through the double doors to take drink orders. The White House, Daniels had long ago discovered, possessed a will of its own. Its staff, aware it would still be here long after he was gone, carried on the traditions of the nation's first residence in almost stubborn defiance of its present occupant. He had found it more difficult to direct their efforts than that of the federal bureaucracy. Of course this all should have been Estelle's responsibility.

The president caught Wilbert's eye and motioned him over. "Walk with me down the hall for a minute," he said. Wilbert followed Daniels out into the west sitting hall. "I don't want the others to see us talking shop," Daniels explained.

Wilbert cocked his head sideways, studying the president with his customary skeptical grimace. "You just don't want to make Wellman jealous. He thinks you never tell him anything."

Daniels grinned. "He thinks *you* have too much influence over me."

Wilbert bristled. "Did he tell you that?"

Daniels changed the subject. "Tell me what's happening on the Hill."

Daniels and Wilbert conferred thirty or forty times each day, on every matter affecting the president. Wilbert had been with him since his first congressional race in Ohio in 1953, and shared an intimacy with him that Daniels allowed no other person. Wilbert's loyalty bordered on the familial, if not the fanatic, and in exchange for it, Daniels trusted Wilbert to play many roles—manager, adviser, confessor, Devil's advocate. His "yes, but" man, Daniels called him.

"It's all bad news," Wilbert replied. "Cathcart is accusing you of withholding information from the American people. Naylor is saying we're trying to cover up a bungled investigation."

Daniels snorted indignantly. "The usual partisan rhetoric."

"Yeah, but it's true. And I'm getting it from our side of the aisle as well. The worst news is that Jenson wants to form a select subcommittee to investigate the ambush. He's announcing it at a news conference tomorrow."

"Can we head him off?"

Wilbert loosened the knot of his tie. "You know how stubborn he is."

Daniels stared into his drink. "We'd better go public with this right away, then, confession or no confession. We already have a four-day delay to explain away."

"I agree," Wilbert replied. "If it leaks before we get it out, the press will tear you to shreds—and so will the Republicans. That loose assassin will have to get in line just to get a piece of you."

"We'll have to work out carefully exactly how much to reveal," Daniels said. "Get Hodges, Friedrich, and Clark into my office first thing. I'll make an announcement in the press room auditorium at midday."

"They'll pick you apart," Wilbert warned.

Daniels looked offended. "I can handle the press. They'll accept the need for some secrecy. What the hell, somebody's trying to kill me. Don't I get any sympathy?"

"Not from the press," Wilbert replied. "Anyway, the announcement won't change much—just give everybody some fresh bones to gnaw on."

Daniels tasted his drink. "It won't change much, because we still don't know much ourselves. How's that man of yours working out? Warfield?"

Wilbert shrugged. "So far nothing. Friedrich says he's dismissed the old interrogation team. That sounds like a step in the right direction."

Daniels rubbed a hand over his curling gray hair. "I'll give him about two more days. Then I'm asking the Russians in."

Wilbert bared his teeth, as if in sudden pain. "Friedrich'll have a heart attack. He might even resign."

The president shook his head. "He's a loyal team player. And he's too close to retirement to make any grand gestures."

"You can't blame him for hating the idea."

"He doesn't see the big picture. We owe the Russians. It was their leader who got killed after all, not me."

"So I've told him, but I side with the director on this one. We should tell the Russians to mind their own business. Let them rant and rave all they want. What can they do to hurt us? Start World War Three? Letting them in will just be an admission of weakness. And it'll cost you politically."

"Maybe not, if the initiative comes from me. It all depends on how things are framed, as usual. And you're wrong, they can do a lot of damage. Bulgakov and his gang are tightening their grip on the Central Committee. That's bad enough. And if I give them any excuse, they'll sabotage the treaty I worked out with Kamenev."

Wilbert loosened his tie a little further. "The treaty's already dead, Eliot. It just hasn't been buried yet."

"That's what I like about you," Daniels sighed, leading his chief of staff back down the hall. "You're such an incurable optimist."

Inside the doorway of the Yellow Oval Room a waiter met them with a tray of fresh drinks.

"Sometimes," Daniels said, taking one, "I think everybody would have been happier if *I* had been killed, instead of Kamenev."

"That's not funny."

"I mean it. The Russian ambassador would be getting plenty of sleep, I'd get a great funeral, the country'd have a good cry, and Premier Kamenev would be talking in public about a great new spirit of U.S.-Soviet cooperation to be forged in my memory." Daniels paused in his monologue and took a sip from his glass. "And Catlin," he added, "would be sitting in the Oval Office, wetting his pants waiting for you and the Democratic leadership to tell him what to do."

Wilbert stared across at the other guests, still clustered by the fireplace. His eyes twitched nervously, as they always did when he was about to zing his boss. "And Kamenev's wife," he said, "would she be happier too?"

The president narrowed his eyes. "What's that mean?"

Wilbert shrugged elaborately. "I've just been noticing how adaptable she seems. She fits in too well. Doesn't she have an escort?"

Daniels' face reddened. "She's a house guest. She doesn't need an escort."

"What happened to all those Russian bodyguards?"

"She has some staff on the top floor. The rest are at Blair House."

"She shouldn't be staying here, Eliot," Wilbert muttered.

Daniels, irritated by Wilbert's badgering, raised his voice. "Why the hell not? It's an act of simple courtesy. We were in that limousine together. I'm trying to show her—and the Russians—that we're sorry for what happened."

"I understand that. But why couldn't you have left her at Blair House?"

Daniels looked across the room. He didn't *know* why, exactly. He felt his chief of staff's dark eyes peering accusingly at him from under that thicket of brow, and he felt suddenly angry.

"I've known you for twenty-eight years," Wilbert went on. "Hell, I've *studied* you for twenty-eight years, like the subject of an endless Ph.D. thesis. You're vulnerable to that woman."

"That's ridiculous!"

"With Estelle sick, you're a lonely man," Wilbert continued, softening his tone. "Just be careful. For one thing, you're courting a public-relations disaster."

"I'm tempted to tell you to mind your own business," the president said.

"You are my business," Wilbert replied. "Sorry."

Daniels saw Wilbert's wife, Susan, guiding Katya Ivanova across the room toward them, and he broke off his argument. Susan, short and dark haired with pretty features, and a lively, intelligent manner, seemed quite overshadowed by the Russian woman. In a floor-length black evening gown, unadorned by a single accessory, Katya Ivanova looked solemnly magnificent. Her white blond hair, normally pulled back in a bun, was swept up in a French curl, revealing a long, graceful expanse of neck. Her wide mouth and full lips bore only the subtlest trace of lipstick, and her eyes wore no makeup at all. And it was her eyes that first commanded one's attention. They were an odd, transparent blue. By some unique prismatic quality of their lenses, they seemed to reflect back more light than normal, and the hue and density of their color altered dramatically in response to even slight changes in her expression or the position of her face.

"No Communist should be that attractive," Wilbert muttered, just before the women arrived within hearing distance.

At eleven o'clock the Wellmans and the Wilberts said goodnight and were escorted down the grand staircase to waiting limousines.

President Daniels found himself alone with Katya Ivanova. She stood next to him by the Yellow Oval Room fireplace, cradling an empty wine glass between thumb and forefinger and watching the flames. An awkward silence began to grow, and Daniels, the least shy of men, found himself ransacking his brain for the right conversational gambit to end it.

"I love all the fireplaces in this house," she said, breaking the silence herself. "I have so many bad memories of the cold."

The president seized on her remark gratefully. "If the Secret Service had its way, it would plug them all up."

"For heaven's sake! Why?"

"There's always been something of a phobia about fire around the White House," he replied. "I suppose it goes back to 1814, when the British burned the original one down."

"The British did that?" she exclaimed.

Daniels laughed at her surprise. "They did indeed. We weren't always allies. And there was another, more recent fire, during the Hoover administration. Christmas eve, I think, 1929. It was in the west wing, and I don't know how it got started. The old building was a terrible firetrap, I guess. During Roosevelt's years they actually put buckets of sand around the corridors. It was during the war and everyone was worried about sabotage. FDR used this room as an office then, and he liked to work on the sofa in front of the fire. His legs were paralyzed, of course, and he couldn't get up from the sofa without help. The staff was under strict orders never to leave him alone in the room without first putting out the fire. Sam Gordon told me that some days they lit and extinguished the fire a dozen times."

He felt Katya's eyes on him, attending his words with apparent interest. He was aware of a powerful tension between them. He wondered if she felt it, too.

"Everything changed during the Truman administration," he continued. "The entire inside of the house—except for the top floor—was gutted and rebuilt. And fireproofed. Beneath this old herringbone parquet there's about half a foot of concrete, and the stairwells have firedoors. There's even a fire escape on the roof." He pointed toward the high ceiling. "You can't see them, but tucked behind the fancy molding up there are smoke detectors and heat sensors. Every room has them. They're wired up to a master panel down in the subbasement, and somebody sits there and watches it all the time. One night last year I was in a meeting with a bunch of political advisers in the Treaty Room, next door. About midnight, the doors burst open and six uniformed White

House guards rushed in, brandishing fire extinguishers at us! Cigar smoke had triggered the damned alarm!"

Daniels shook the ice cubes in his glass thoughtfully. "A lot of things can go wrong at the White House, but fire isn't one of them. It would take a direct hit by the Russians to get this old fortress burning."

He saw Katya's lips part in shock, and suddenly he realized what he had just said. They stared at each other and burst out laughing.

"You could hold me hostage here, as insurance against that," she said.

"That's a damned good idea," he replied, surprising himself. "At least you can sit and talk to me for a little while."

Katya hesitated. "It's late . . ."

"But you only live down the hall. Have a nightcap with me."

Before she could refuse, he picked up a clean wine glass from the tray left by the waiter and filled it for her.

"Unless you want something stronger? . . ."

"No, please. Wine is perfect."

Daniels handed her the glass and saw, standing in the doorway, a brawny woman in an ill-fitting gray skirt suit. He was certain he had never seen her before. She had thick lips and dark bangs, and was staring at him reproachfully. He was still recovering from the surprise when he noticed the flush of embarrassment on Katya's face.

"I'm sorry," she said. "It's Irina, my secretary. Excuse me."

Katya took the woman firmly by the arm and steered her around the corner and out of sight. Daniels heard a sharp exchange in Russian, and a moment later Katya reappeared.

"Irina is staying upstairs," she explained.

"She looks fearsome," Daniels said, settling onto the sofa alongside Katya.

"She *is* fearsome," Katya replied.

"Is she your secretary—or your chaperone?"

Katya shook her head, a defiant smile curling the corner of her mouth. "No. We have a different word. In Russian she is called a *stukach.*"

"Sounds bad. What does it mean?"

"I don't know the English word for it. She reports on me."

Daniels looked puzzled. "Reports? To whom?"

Katya sighed. "Everyone of prominence in the government has

at least one *stukach*. She has been mine for years. She is an informer for the KGB. She was assigned to me as my secretary, but her true job is to spy on me."

"That's awful! Does she know you know she's spying on you?"

"Yes, of course. No one admits it. It is just accepted, something you learn to live with."

Daniels grinned conspiratorially. "We'll throw her out in the morning."

Katya's hands flew up in alarm. "You mustn't! Please just don't think about it. I've sent her off to bed. She does what I tell her. I can report on her, too, after all."

Daniels, surprised by the intensity of Katya's reaction, changed the subject. He brought her up to date on the investigation. She listened politely, but he sensed that she did not really want to hear more. The conversation shifted to other, less consequential matters. The president's eyes followed the strands of stray blond hair that curled around her ear, and admired the extraordinary smoothness of her skin. The inroads of age showed in only a few hairline wrinkles across her neck. He noticed again the barely perceptible scars on the bridge of her nose and the corners of her eyes.

"How did you acquire these little marks?" he asked, impulsively touching his finger to her temple.

"Are they ugly?" she demanded.

"No, not at all! I think they're attractive!"

She gazed into the fire. The logs had crumbled to a bed of embers. "A childhood accident," she said in a low voice.

"Where did you spend your childhood," Daniels asked, eager to shift the conversation to more neutral territory.

"I spent most of it in a state orphanage until I was ten."

Daniels was surpised. His staff had told him she was from a prominent family. "Then what happened? You were adopted?"

Katya didn't answer. He thought she hadn't heard his question, but after a pause she glanced at him, as if gauging how much she should confide in him.

"No," she said. "I was sent to Dzhezkazgan."

Daniels grinned self-deprecatingly. "To the despair of many of my staff, my geography is almost as bad as my skill with languages. Where is that?"

"In Kingir province."

"If it's that hard to pronounce, it must be a small town."

Katya smiled weakly. "No. It's a very large labor camp."

"Labor camp?"

"Yes."

The president set his glass of scotch down on the side table and stared at the Russian woman in astonishment. "You were sent to a labor camp at the age of ten?"

She nodded.

"My God! What had you done?"

"I was rebellious at the orphanage," she replied, her voice taking on a steel-hard quality Daniels had not heard before. "Specifically, I was sentenced to the camps for defacing a painting of Stalin."

"How long was your sentence?"

"Ten years."

Daniels swallowed. He felt as if he had steered their conversation right over a cliff. He feared to hear more, but felt at the same time a fierce compulsion to know.

Katya obviously sensed the reaction her words had stirred. "But I was lucky, in a way," she added. "I only served a year. They let me out in 1956, during the Khrushchev thaw."

"Where did you go?" Daniels asked. "How could you have become such an educated, accomplished woman?"

Katya reached her hand across the sofa and pressed it gently on top of his. The sensation of her touch pulsed through him like a small electric current.

"It's past midnight. Too late for the story of my life," she said. "I already feel guilty, taking up so much of your time."

Daniels rested his other hand on top of hers. "Don't say you feel guilty. I enjoy your company. I wish we had more time."

They walked slowly beneath the dimmed chandeliers of the deserted center hall, past the top of the grand staircase, and into the east hall. She turned to face him in front of her door.

"When are you returning to Moscow?" he asked.

"Tomorrow night. The funeral is in two days. Will you be there?"

Daniels shook his head. "No. The security risks are too great. Both our governments agree on that."

"I'm sorry."

"I'm sorry too," he replied. "Sorry about the circumstances. I feel responsible for your husband's death. Our system of justice is sometimes slow and clumsy, but I promise you we'll find those responsible."

Katya looked at him. She was a tall woman, much taller than his wife, and she had barely to tilt her head to meet his eyes directly. "You must not apologize," she said. "It happened. It cannot be undone. The important thing is that *we* are still alive."

Daniels nodded, his eyes captured in hers. "I'll see you before you leave?"

"Of course."

She held out her hand.

He took it, wondered briefly whether to shake it, or kiss it. Instead he bent forward to kiss her on the cheek, as he might the wife of a friend. She turned toward him, and their lips met. She slipped her hands around his neck and pressed herself against him for a lingering moment, then pushed away.

"I will tell you a secret," she whispered.

The president, his heart racing, watched with regret as her hand found the doorknob and twisted it open.

"What?" he asked.

"I hated my husband."

She closed the door and was gone.

7

IN THE CHILLY HOUR BEFORE dawn a Chevy van parked in front of a dilapidated brick warehouse in a run-down section of northeast Washington. The building was boarded up and padlocked.

The driver of the van sat hunched behind the wheel, watching the street to make certain that no one had followed him. The van had undergone a remarkable transformation in the past three days. It was now green, instead of white, and the red letters that had spelled out PARKLAND EMERGENCY SERVICE on its doors were gone, along with the flashing roof beacon and the siren on the hood. The license plates had changed from Maryland to Virginia, and the side windows, once curtained, now bore crude hand-paintings of desert scenery.

After a ten-minute wait, the driver moved the van a block further down the street, parked it, locked it, and walked back to the brick warehouse.

He was of average height, with a narrow waist and wide shoulders, and he walked with a barely perceptible limp, the result of an accident years before that had cost him all the toes on his right foot. He was extremely strong physically. Even his olive tan Mediterranean face seemed muscular. The wide cheekbones and cleft chin bulged like tight knots under the skin. His eyes were black and set deep under a thick brow that grew in one continuous line straight across his forehead. His ears were small and cup shaped, and his nose descended from his brow in an almost perpendicular drop, giving his face a caved-in appearance.

Papers in the wallet in the back pocket of his jeans identified him as Nikos Andropoulous, Greek immigrant and restaurant employee. He was, in fact, a Turk. He was known by international police agencies and intelligence services only by a single name: Kemal. No photographs of him existed. His history and origins were obscure. He was thought to be about thirty-five years of age, but no information about him was considered reliable.

He was known by his reputation alone. Among the world's league of professional assassins, he ranked near the top. He was skillful and resourceful; without fear, sympathies, or compassion. In a lifetime of killing, he had terminated the lives of several hundred strangers on five continents.

Kemal unlocked a small side door in the warehouse and let himself in. A reek of oil, dust, mildew, and urine assaulted his nostrils. He pulled a penlight from the pocket of his Navy pea jacket, and followed its narrow beam of light to a stairwell and up three steep flights. At the top landing he stopped and trained the beam down a long, empty corridor, listening for any unfamiliar sounds.

Silence.

He walked the length of the corridor. The floorboards creaked and groaned under his weight. At the far end, he paused before a wooden door with flaking paint and an upper panel of frosted glass, painted black from the inside.

He twisted the knob and pushed the door open.

His flashlight beam explored the corners of a large room, about thirty feet square, with high ceilings. A single, hard-backed chair sat in the center of the floor, facing the far wall. It was the only object in the room.

Kemal closed the door, stepped to the chair, sat down on it, and turned off his flashlight. He thrust his hands into the pea jacket pockets and tucked his chin under the fold of his turtleneck sweater.

He waited.

Gradually his eyes adjusted to the darkness, but nothing was visible save the thread-thin slices of daylight that squeezed past the edges of two boarded-up windows along one wall. He felt suspended in a void. He focused on the luminous dial of his wristwatch. Six-thirty in the morning. He yawned, and his mind wandered. Briefly he dozed, then woke again, shivering from the cold.

At 6:45 footsteps sounded in the corridor outside; he became instantly alert. The door opened and a powerful flashlight beam spilled across the floor and stopped at his chair. The door closed and the flashlight went off.

"I hate this," Kemal said.

"You're breaking my heart," the voice replied.

"Why don't you just put a bag over your head," Kemal said. "And meet me in the daylight."

The voice, known to the assassin only as the Instructor, laughed mirthlessly. "I like this arrangement. In any case, the bag would go over your head, not mine."

Kemal didn't pursue it. What did he care, anyway? He was only in this for the payday.

Still, the bastard in the dark behind him had unusual advantages. If he failed to deliver on his part of the arrangement— leaving the cash payments by the door—then Kemal could not find him and kill him.

"You want to know about the rest of the money," the Instructor said.

"Yes."

"You haven't earned it yet."

"I did my part! The other two fucked it up!"

"You have a point, but the job's not done."

"I told you! I could have done it alone! It was *your* plan to bring in the others!"

"And you trained them. So they became your responsibility."

"I want the money. Nobody refuses to pay *me.*"

The Instructor laughed.

Kemal remembered the Instructor's pistol. The bastard had showed it to him, the first time they had met here. He had shone the flashlight on it for him—a silenced Mauser parabellum. A ridiculous cannon to carry around, Kemal thought, but he respected it. He made an easy target, he realized. The Instructor could just train his light on him and blow him apart with those nine-millimeter rounds. He'd rot in this old warehouse for months. The rats would eat him before anybody found him.

"I didn't guarantee results," Kemal said. "I want the money."

"You'll get it when the job's done. We're going to improvise another plan."

The assassin waited in the dark for the Instructor to continue. He heard the floorboards squeak behind him as the man changed position. Despite himself, the hairs on the nape of his neck tingled.

"We're still working out the details," the Instructor added. "The new plan will be ready tomorrow. Meanwhile I want you to go to see the Korean. Pick up a package from him."

"What kind of package?"

"Just pick it up and bring it here tonight. Midnight. Pay him ten thousand dollars. The money's in an envelope I'll leave by the door. When you bring the package, I'll pay you the remaining two hundred and fifty."

"I want more money, now."

"You ought to do this for free."

"No. I've done my contract. I'll pick up the package for my standard rate. Fifty thousand dollars."

"Ridiculous."

Kemal said nothing.

"You're a greedy bastard," the voice said.

"I'm in a high-risk profession."

"This is just an errand."

"Then hire an errand boy."

The Instructor laughed. He had a large, rusty laugh that reverberated through the empty room. Kemal supposed that he must be a big man.

"All right, fifty thousand," the Instructor said.

Kemal allowed a tight grin of triumph to crease his lips.

"One other thing," the Instructor said. "Kill the Korean."

Ever since the ambush on the parkway, Harold Wicks had been thinking that he was just born unlucky.

A retired GS-12 from the Government Accounting Office, Wicks had spent all that morning in the parkway woods, shivering in the cold behind his camera, waiting to snap a photograph of a ring-necked pheasant. Finally, attracted by the corn Wicks had scattered around, the bird arrived. It was just before eleven o'clock. Wicks shot two rolls of film, packed up his camera, tripod, and telephoto lens, and started back to his house in Parkland Terrace. Ten minutes later, at eleven-fifteen, the president's motorcade was attacked.

Ten minutes, he thought. If the damned bird had only showed up ten minutes later. With the telephoto lens and the clear view he had had of the overpass from his hillside location, he could have caught the whole thing on film.

The whole thing! He would have the only photographs of the event in the world! Every magazine, newspaper, and TV network on earth would be bidding for the rights.

If only the damned bird had showed up ten minutes later!

Wicks stacked the color slides back into their plastic holder and tossed them onto the light box. On an impulse, he picked up the envelope that had contained the slides and peeked inside. A strip of unmounted film had fallen to the bottom. He knocked it out onto the glass surface of the light box and looked at it over the illumination. The strip contained three spoiled frames that the developer had not bothered to mount. He knew they were from the front of the roll. To secure the film properly on the uptake sprocket required advancing it the distance of three frames and clicking the shutter three times. Occasionally, if the camera happened to be pointing at anything, and the lens cap was off, that early part of the film would yield an image or two.

Wicks picked up his magnifier and centered it over the strip of film. The first frame was half-black, and half a dark gray blur. The second frame showed a treetop, out of focus, and a patch of sky. The third showed a stretch of road, a bush, and the front half of a vehicle.

Wicks studied it for a moment, and decided that the vehicle was the ambulance he had seen approaching the overpass while he was reloading. He remembered worrying that it might scare the bird away.

The face of the driver was visible, and in surprisingly sharp focus. Part of the lettering on the side of the vehicle was legible: PARKLAND EMERGEN . . .

He remembered thinking that the ambulance was connected in some way with the police roadblock on the overpass, because it had driven right around the wooden horses set across the highway. If only he had been more interested in that motorcade, instead of his damned bird!

"Parkland Emergency Service," must be what the lettering spelled out, he decided. He looked in the yellow pages of his telephone directory under ambulance service. No listing. Nothing. Curious, he thought.

Wicks went to the telephone in the kitchen and called information for three area codes: 202 for Washington, D.C.; 301 for Maryland; and 703 for northern Virginia. None had a listing for anything with Parkland Emergency in its title. He called Walter Reed, Bethesda Naval, and several other hospitals in the area. None knew of any ambulance service called Parkland.

His heart began to beat a little faster.

Was it possible that the hit squad had used this ambulance to get to the overpass? He puzzled over the matter for a long time. Everything they needed—the chain, the weights, the bars, the weapons—could have been hidden in the back of the vehicle, he reasoned, including the hit squad itself. And it provided an excellent camouflage both for approaching the troopers guarding the overpass and for getting away after the attack.

And as far as he knew, no escape vehicle had yet been located. Which meant that the driver—the man Wicks could see sitting behind the wheel of the ambulance in his photograph—had gotten away.

A wild hope began to flicker in Wick's chest. By God, maybe he wasn't so unlucky after all! Maybe this tiny piece of film was an incredible piece of luck—a vital clue in identifying one of the killers at the Suitland Parkway ambush. A killer who was still at large!

If his reasoning was correct, this inch and a half of celluloid could be worth a lot of money.

He sat and contemplated his next move.

8

DR. HERBERT ROSENSTOCK AR-
rived at the farm at eight o'clock in the morning. He walked in on Warfield lugging a beat-up black leather satchel and wearing a murderous expression.

"This better be good, Charlie," he exclaimed, slamming the black bag onto a chair. "This better be the best thing since cinnamon toast!"

Warfield pushed himself up from the table and held out a hand. "It's good to see you."

Rosenstock was ugly. His short, frail body was balanced on an outsized pair of feet and topped by an enormous head with a long beak of a nose and small dark eyes hidden under thick glasses. Assuming it was no use, he neglected his appearance shamelessly. His long, lank white hair was washed but uncombed, his clothes clean but unpressed and ill fitting. His size-thirteen shoes were badly scuffed, the leather tops cracked from repeated exposure to rain. His pathology students called him "Frodo."

Rosenstock's physical shortcomings had spawned psychological ones. He was rude, profane, and socially maladroit. His basic strategy in life was to stay on the offensive—attack before being attacked, reject before being rejected.

What he lacked in the externals he made up for in brainpower. Magnificently complex, his mind was capable of vast comprehension, sustained concentration, precise, intricate reasoning, and nearly total recall. In the forensic sciences he was an acknowledged giant, widely published and much sought after as a consultant, lecturer, and expert trial witness. In a dozen related fields, both medical and criminal, he was equally brilliant. He possessed an M.D. degree, but had long ago abandoned practice when he discovered that he had no patience with his patients. He didn't get along with his professional colleagues, either.

Warfield liked him. He had met him years before, when the CIA had called him in to supervise an autopsy on one of its agents. Rosenstock had traced the cause of the agent's death to a form of poison unknown in the West at the time. It had been developed in a KGB laboratory in Hungary and administered to the victim, Rosenstock determined, via a pinprick in the leg from an umbrella.

Rosenstock accepted Warfield's handshake hastily, then plopped down on the couch by the wall. "You're healthy looking for a change," he said, conversationally. "The last time I saw you I wouldn't have given you six days to live. Your eyes were as yellow as a canary's ass and your liver was as big as my ego."

Warfield grinned at him bleakly. "Nothing's that big. And I'm off the sauce."

Rosenstock reached for his black bag. "I was afraid of that," he said. "So I brought my own." He zipped open the bag and pulled out a bottle of Jim Beam sour mash whiskey.

Warfield's mouth fell open. "What the hell are you doing?"

"What do you think I'm doing? It's eight o'clock in the morning. I need an eye-opener!"

Rosenstock picked up a styrofoam coffee container from the table, peered into it, decided that it was reasonably clean, and splashed it half-full of whiskey. Warfield watched him as he knocked it down, and felt a trace of annoyance. Rosenstock exhaled loudly, shivered violently, then lit up a nonfilter cigarette and sat back, an expression something like contentment settling across his comic face. Warfield drew a deep breath. He had forgotten how much energy it could take to cope with Rosenstock.

"Okay," Rosenstock rasped, suddenly businesslike again. "What's this all about?"

Warfield looked at him intently. "I want you to examine a body for me."

"Is that all you shanghaied me down here for?"

Warfield raised a hand. "Hold on. This isn't just any body."

The corners of Rosenstock's lips curled skeptically. "You're scaring me half to death."

"The body I want you to look at is a live one. He's downstairs in a cell. He's one of the assassins from the Suitland Parkway ambush."

Rosenstock's eyes bulged in surprise. "They caught one?"

Warfield explained. Rosenstock listened attentively, then pored over the reports and transcripts on the table. Finally, he downed another shot of whiskey and slumped back against the sofa.

"It's a son-of-a-bitch," he admitted, much subdued from his earlier mood. "Do you think you can get a confession out of him?"

"If I had a lot of time, yes. But they want it in a couple of days. For that, I'll need a miracle. I've already lost time just worrying about it."

"Any ideas on what to do?" Rosenstock asked.

"Just one. I've been toying with it all night. It's the only approach I can think of that might actually work."

"What do you want me to do?"

"Two things. First, give our prisoner a thorough physical examination. I want to be sure he's healthy before I try anything."

"Leaning toward the rubber hose and pliers?"

Warfield shook his head emphatically.

"What's the second thing?"

"See if your forensic genius can't find us a few clues—things about the assassin that might tell us something. I can't tell you what to look for, exactly. I'm just groping myself."

Rosenstock grimaced. "I'll need a few things. Mainly a telephone. I'll have to start alerting some special labs. The tricks of the profession these days boil down to lab tests and computer analysis."

"Whatever you need. Speed is the main thing."

Warfield picked up an envelope from the table and took a wristwatch from it. He handed it to Rosenstock by the string of the attached tag.

"Take a look at this, too. The assassin's pockets were empty. All he had on him was this watch. And he fought like hell to keep it."

Rosenstock turned the watch over in his hand. "A gold Cartier? No wonder. These things run several thousand bucks. Is it genuine?"

"According to the FBI lab."

"Times must be good in the assassination game."

"I'm hoping he stole it. The Bureau is still trying to trace it."

Rosenstock handed the watch back. "Let me see the lab reports. They might show me something."

Warfield returned the Cartier to its envelope and stood up, stretching. "Let's get a quick breakfast. We can start back here at nine. One of the interrogators, Howard Moore, will join us."

The two men walked across the compound toward the mess hall. Rosenstock turned the collar on his beat-up greatcoat against the chill. Warfield noticed that he had the buttons lined up in the wrong holes.

"Why did they drag you into this?" Rosenstock asked.

Warfield studied the pebbles on the path in front of his feet. "I guess it's because they don't know what else to do. And they're desperate for results. It was Wilbert who pushed the idea. I met him some years ago, after the Berlin tunnel stunt, when I was riding high."

"Why the hell did you agree?"

"They didn't give me a choice."

Rosenstock blew out a thin cloud of vapor in the frosty air. "They figure you're expendable, then."

"Expendable and deniable. They hope, if they put enough pressure on me, I'll cut corners—squeeze the prisoner and make him talk. If I succeed and no one finds out how, they'll take the credit. If word does get out, they'll disown me—or even prosecute me—and still have what they want. If I fail to get anywhere at all, they'll just throw me aside like a disposable syringe."

"Then why are you trying so hard?"

Warfield pulled a tissue from his pocket and wiped his nose. The sudden change from a warm room to the cold air always triggered his sinuses. "I don't know. They're paying me for this. And they've promised to reinstate me if I succeed. I'll get pension money."

Rosenstock snorted. "That's not the reason! I know you better than that. You want to succeed, for your own sake. You're like me, a big ego."

"I'm used to failure, Herb."

"No you're not! No one ever gets used to that. You want to show them up. Shove it down their throats. I don't blame you."

Warfield shrugged.

"You have any hunches," Rosenstock asked, "who's behind this hit team?"

"It's impossible to read. Whoever planned it was very careful.

We don't know their motive. We don't even know for sure who their target was—Daniels, Kamenev, or both. And we don't know if they're going to try again."

They arrived at the door of the mess hall. Rosenstock paused. "So what's your plan? What are you going to do to your prisoner?"

Warfield grabbed the handle and opened the door. The smell of hot food and the sudden din of voices and clattering china rushed out at them. He looked at Rosenstock, a tight grin on his face.

"I'm going to scare the living bejesus out of him," he said.

9

PRESIDENT DANIELS PUSHED open the French doors from the Oval Office and charged out into the Rose Garden, Paul Friedrich at his heels.

Daniels loved to walk, even in winter. It was his chief form of exercise. He liked to conduct affairs of state on foot. Members of his staff and cabinet, lobbyists and congressional leaders knew that an appointment with the president often meant a brisk constitutional around the south lawn. At Camp David, he often walked for hours, meeting his appointments on the wooded trails. Aside from its physical and psychological benefits, walking for Daniels was a tactical weapon. There was nothing like getting someone out of breath to encourage him to be brief, and to see things the president's way.

Friedrich was accustomed to the routine. He hated it, as he hated all forms of exercise, but he was resigned to it. He once estimated that he had logged over fifty miles on foot with the chief executive. He had also noted that the faster Daniels walked, the more serious the matter he wanted to discuss. And this morning Daniels was moving at a furious pace, forcing the director to take little jogging half steps to keep abreast.

Daniels led him directly down the lawn toward an area called the Mounds, at the far end of the circular drive. Friedrich watched the Secret Service agents fan out around them, just out of earshot, their dark glasses glinting in the pale February sun. In the past, the bodyguards had been satisfied simply to stake out stationary positions along the perimeter of the fence. This new procedure, Friedrich knew, was part of the response to the ambush.

He waited for Daniels to open the conversation, but the president remained silent. Along the fence on the east side, Friedrich could see the long line of tourists forming for the ten o'clock White House tour. A few in the line waved. On most days, he experienced a certain satisfaction, being on the inside of the fence, looking out. Today, he wished he was out there in the line, with nothing more serious on his mind than where to have lunch after the tour.

"This man Warfield," Daniels began. "Is he making any progress?"

"Not so far, Mr. President," Friedrich answered.

"Does he have a plan of attack?"

Friedrich nodded. "He says he does. But he won't share it with anyone. He's difficult. You have to give him a long leash."

"He has a few stains on his record, I understand."

Friedrich wondered who had told the president that. Probably Wilbert, to cover himself in case Warfield blew it.

"True," he replied. "He was dismissed from the agency four years ago by my predecessor. He had been a brilliant agent, but an operation went wrong in Egypt, and he cracked. We kept him on, in counterintelligence, and he did well there for a time, but he developed a serious drinking problem. Since he's been on his own, he's conquered it, I'm told."

"Aren't we putting a lot of our eggs in his basket, Paul?"

Friedrich wondered how blunt he should be. He knew the president understood damned well what was going on. They had brought Warfield in—on Wilbert's insistence, at that—because the man was expendable. Warfield could be pressured to squeeze a fast confession from the assassin and take the blame for any questions about methods that might surface later on. It was dangerous politics, because both Warfield and the situation were unpredictable, but there was more to be gained than lost by throwing Warfield into the breach.

"He used to be good," Friedrich replied. "And he's hungry now. Anxious to redeem himself."

"Do you have someone watching him?"

"Of course."

Daniels changed the subject. "What's happening in the Kremlin?"

"Apparently Bulgakov now has Sokolov's backing."

"I thought Sokolov was a liberal?"

"He's hard to label. But his joining Bulgakov's camp surprises me. Either he's being opportunistic, or Bulgakov has something on him."

"Does Bulgakov have the votes, then?"

"He may have."

Daniels regarded his CIA director with a cold eye. "That's pretty vague."

Friedrich said nothing, but he was quaking inwardly. With *Saraband* inoperative, his Kremlin intelligence was dramatically less authoritative. He had hoped, in vain, that Daniels wouldn't notice the difference.

The president slowed his pace, forcing Friedrich to do the same to stay alongside. The director averted his gaze toward the sky. It was a gentle day. A soft breeze danced in the bare branches of the enormous elm at the east end of the Mounds. John Quincy Adams had planted it, Daniels once told him. The president seemed to know the history of every tree on the property. He wondered how the man found time to learn such trivia. He liked and respected Daniels, but he didn't feel close to him. He was less gregarious than most heads of state he had met. Aloof.

Daniels looked squarely into Friedrich's eyes. "There's been a new development," he said.

Friedrich felt his stomach tighten.

"Mrs. Kamenev came to see me this morning," Daniels began.

"Yes?"

"She plans to defect."

The words seemed to vibrate in the air. Friedrich caught his breath. The president's voice betrayed strong emotion.

"No reaction?" Daniels asked.

Friedrich cleared his throat. "Did she give a reason?"

The president held his gaze on the director. "Of course," he said. "She told me she's been working for us for over three years. Spying for us."

Damn that woman! Friedrich thought. What an idiotic thing to do! He forced himself to meet the president's eyes. "Yes," he admitted. "Operation *Saraband*."

"She thought I knew all about it, of course," Daniels continued, his voice harsh. "She was under the impression that the president of the United States would know about the most important intelligence source his government had ever developed."

Friedrich had long dreaded this sort of confrontation. But he had his arguments ready: "There are some things, Mr. President, tht it's better for you not to know. This, surely, was one of them. It would have done you no good to have known that she was working for us. There would have always been the danger that you might have unintentionally given her away. Such things have happened. I think it was just too big a secret to risk sharing. Even with you."

The president stopped and turned to face Friedrich. He stepped in close and pressed his forefinger against the director's chest. The rude, almost bullying gesture startled Friedrich. He stepped back and caught his breath. He found himself trembling.

"There are some things you have to be in a position to deny!" he blurted out.

"I might have bought that argument before the ambush!" Daniels thundered, "but Goddamn-it-to-hell, Paul, it was your duty to tell me immediately after that attack! It's inexcusable that you didn't! I've got that woman in the White House with me! I could have compromised her unknowingly, for Christ's sake!"

The director felt the blood drain from his face. He had a terrible vision of his career ending in disgrace, right here on the south lawn. "I just thought it better . . ." he stammered.

"I'm the president, goddammit," Daniels said. "And you're making me look like a horse's ass!"

In that instant, Friedrich perceived the real source of the president's fury. He must have gone through the floor when Mrs. Kamenev revealed her role as *Saraband*. Not knowing about it had embarrassed him in front of her.

"I'm sorry," Friedrich said. "I'll offer my resignation, of course."

Daniels turned without a word and started back across the lawn to the White House. The director followed, suffering the president's ominous silence now more acutely than his reprimand.

"I don't want your resignation, Paul," he said abruptly. "I've got enough trouble on my hands without going through the trauma of trying to find a new DCI. This administration is going to hold together through this crisis, by God, and come out the other end in one piece!"

Daniels' anger seemed to evaporate. Friedrich risked a return to the subject of Mrs. Kamenev. "How determined is she to defect?" he asked.

"What do you mean?"

"It will complicate things with the Russians. And, of course, we lose our most highly placed agent inside the Soviet Union."

Daniels dismissed Friedrich's words with a wave of the hand. "I have no intention of trying to persuade her to return against her will. She'd be risking her life to go back. And anyway, since the premier is dead, we have to assume she's lost her access. I think it's time we rewarded her for what she's done."

Friedrich nodded. Losing *Saraband* was going to hurt. It was hurting already.

"Is there any chance Kamenev knew what she was doing?" Daniels asked. "Or anyone else in the Kremlin?"

"There's no evidence she was ever compromised. Her information was excellent even as late as three days ago. It was through her we learned that the KGB thinks the hit team may be the work of right-wing Cubans."

They reached the borders of the Rose Garden. Friedrich glanced along the rows of pruned, bare rose stalks, bristling with thorns. It struck him as a sinister sight; as if someone had stuck rows of dead sticks in the ground, to mark a burial.

The president kicked gently at the layer of wood chips mulched around one of the bushes. "I've already discussed her defection with the Soviet ambassador," he said. "He's foaming at the mouth about it; they plan to protest. I had to give them something to placate them."

Friedrich's heart sank. "What was that?"

"As you know, they want to monitor our interrogation. I told them they could. I'm going to announce this afternoon that we have a prisoner in custody, and that we're inviting the Russians in to participate in the investigation. I'm telling Wilbert and the press office to put as good a face on it as they can—unusual example of U.S.-Russian cooperation, first time the two governments have worked together on this level, bodes well for future relations, and so on."

Friedrich swallowed hard. Daniels regarded him sympathetically.

"I don't like it, either, Paul. But there's no other way. We'll just have to live with it. They're sending a Dmitri Semenenko from the Ministry of Foreign Affairs on tomorrow's Aeroflot flight. I'll bump him over to you, probably with the vice-president and Wilbert in tow, as part of a little red carpet treatment."

"He's KGB," Friedrich said.

"I guessed as much. Keep an eye on him."

"Don't worry."

Daniels laughed. "Maybe it's all for the best. Maybe they really will help us break this thing."

"I admire your optimism, Mr. President. My fear is they'll get in our way."

Daniels didn't seem to be listening. He started walking slowly back toward the colonnade. "Why do you think she agreed to spy for us?" he asked.

Friedrich shrugged. "She came from a distinguished family, I believe. Intellectuals, professors, writers, dissidents. Stalin wiped them out completely after the war. She had ample reason to hate the government."

"And yet she married a government official, the man who became premier, at that. Seems strange. How was she recruited?"

"One of our agents—Byron Shanklin—recruited her. He's remained as her case officer, even though he's stationed at Camp Peary. He was in West Germany three years ago, when Kamenev and his wife came on a state visit. He contacted her through a servant—a chauffeur, I believe—and persuaded her to work for us."

"A hell of a coup."

"Shanklin's one of the best."

"Is he?" Daniels challenged. "Wasn't he in charge of the interrogation—before you brought in Warfield?"

The director felt his cheeks burning. "Yes, but only indirectly. I mean he wasn't doing any of the actual interrogating."

"Who else knows about *Saraband?*"

"Just Shanklin and myself. She's been carefully protected."

"Let's keep it that way. From now on, she's my responsibility. I'm assigning a Secret Service detail to her, and she's staying at the

White House." Friedrich nodded. "Meanwhile, prepare your man Warfield for the Russians."

"He won't like it."

"I suppose not. But he doesn't have any say in the matter."

Friedrich looked up at the south facade of the White House, his eyes following the row of windows on the second floor. Which room had the president put Mrs. Kamenev in? The Lincoln Bedroom? The Queen's Bedroom? Or up on the top floor, where they kept Daniels' crazy wife? Or was she in the president's own bedroom?

Good God, it was possible! The woman was attractive, and Daniels was a lonely man. And it explained his sudden possessive behavior perfectly.

The director felt acid rising in his stomach again. The Russian woman in bed with the president! An appalling thought. Would Daniels do something that dangerous?

10

BACK IN THE LOUNGE AFTER breakfast, Warfield described his plan to Rosenstock and Moore.

"Risky as hell," Rosenstock said, when Warfield had finished. "You'll have to be lucky to pull it off."

Warfield shrugged.

"It's goddamn brilliant," Moore exclaimed. "We'll make it work!" He grabbed a pad and pencil from the table and started to compile a list of necessary items.

For an hour they thrashed out the details. Moore finally held up the pad and read off the long list he had amassed. "Anything else?" he asked.

"Only one I can think of," Warfield answered. "We need a woman to play nurse."

Moore rubbed his temple with a bony forefinger. "Damn, that's right," he replied. "I think I know just the one. Nan Robertson.

She works with the special decrypt instruction unit here. She's young, a real All-American type. Perfect nurse."

"Does she have clearance?"

"If she's in decrypt she's cleared pretty high."

With two phone calls, Moore arranged it. "She's coming over after lunch," he said.

"Good. If she's okay and willing, I'll brief her on the project. We won't need her until tomorrow."

Moore went out to begin collecting the many items they would need. Warfield and Rosenstock reviewed the plan again, looking for flaws. When Moore returned, an hour later, Warfield decided it was time to begin. He pulled on one of the white jackets Moore had obtained. He patted the sides. The cloth was stiff with starch and pinched him in the shoulders. "Where the hell did you find these, Howard?"

"The busboys at the mess hall wear them. Your real gowns won't get here until tomorrow. Don't worry, you both look terrific!"

Warfield glanced across at Rosenstock, who was stuffing a stethoscope into the side pocket of his. "At least he *looks* like a doctor," he said.

"I *am* a doctor," Rosenstock grumbled, picking up his bag. "Let's get going. It's eleven o'clock. I have to get the tests off to the labs this afternoon."

Warfield held up his empty hands. "Shouldn't I have a stethoscope, too?"

Moore grabbed a clipboard from the table, shoved a pad of legal paper into it, and slipped it under Warfield's arm. "That's all the prop you need. Looks perfect. I'll be over at the infirmary, getting things started. Good luck!"

Warfield and Rosenstock walked down the narrow stairs to the basement, then along a stark, low-ceilinged corridor. Three guards waited for them at the far end. It struck Warfield that he had been at the farm a whole day and had not yet even seen his prisoner, the man upon whom so much would depend in the hours to come.

Now he was eager to face him.

The oldest of the guards, a beefy, tired-looking man with a large wart on the back of his neck, held out his hand to Warfield.

"I'm Emerson," he said, in a deep baritone. "This is Trippet and Frady."

The two younger guards nodded in greeting.

"This is Doctor Herbert Rosenstock," Warfield said. "He and I are going to give the prisoner a physical examination. I want all three of you fellows outside the cell. We may need you."

Emerson nodded solemnly.

"Let's go," Warfield murmured.

Emerson led them to a green steel door with a small peephole at eye-level. He slid the cover of the peephole back, looked inside, then unlocked the door. Warfield stepped in first, his pulse quickening.

The cell was narrow and bare, the air inside stale and uncomfortably hot. The assassin was sitting on his bunk, his legs drawn up, his back against the cement block wall. He was dressed in the shirt and pants of his stolen trooper's uniform, minus his belt and shoes. Warfield was surprised at how small and young he appeared, even with a five-day growth of beard.

Despite his youth, he emanated an unmistakably dangerous aura. His face was a swarthy brown, his ears slightly cauliflowered, and his neck very thick in proportion to his head and shoulders. A deep scar marred his lip at one corner, and another scar cut a white swath through one eyebrow. A street brawler, Warfield thought.

"I'm Doctor Warfield," he lied, speaking in as relaxed and conversational a tone as he could muster. "And this is Doctor Rosenstock. We'd like to examine you, please."

Taking his cue from Warfield, Rosenstock stepped briskly to the foot of the assassin's cot and cracked open his bag.

"Remove your clothes," he commanded.

The assassin turned his head just far enough to bring his stare, like the barrels of a shotgun, to bear on Rosenstock's face. Otherwise, he made not the slightest movement. Rosenstock looked up at Warfield. "Now what?"

Warfield called in the guards and instructed them to remove the prisoner's clothes. Frady and Trippet grabbed his ankles and wrists and held him while Emerson yanked off his shirt and pants, socks and underclothes. The assassin offered no resistance. Rosenstock pulled a hospital gown from his bag and handed it to Emerson. With considerable awkwardness, they managed to stuff the assassin's arms through it and tie its pairs of drawstrings across his back.

With the guards holding him, Rosenstock began his examination. He took his pulse, blood pressure, and temperature; listened to his chest, back, and heart; palpated his stomach and back; peered into his eyes, ears, nose, and throat; examined his teeth, his testicles, his hands and feet, the surface of his skin; and tested his reflexes. Warfield admired Rosenstock's efficiency as he watched him slap a needle into the assassin's arm and rapidly fill six small test tubes with his blood.

Warfield scribbled a few meaningless notes on his clipboard to keep up his end of the charade. They had agreed beforehand not to ask the prisoner any questions at all. Warfield was counting on the sudden change of routine and personnel to unsettle him.

Rosenstock progressed smoothly from the standard examining procedures to a special set of his own. He looked over the man's teeth again, and the entire surface of his skin, but this time he used a magnifying glass. Then he laid out, with a fussy meticulousness that seemed uncharacteristic of him, several rows of specimen jars on the floor.

He removed a handful of swabs from his bag and began collecting samples of the assassin's bodily fluids. He inserted the swabs in every orifice—nose, mouth, eyes, ears, navel, urinary tract, and anus—and sealed the specimens carefully in the jars. Then he went on to gather other samples. He snipped off strands of the assassin's thick black hair, and cut slivers from his fingernails and toenails. Finally, he took up a thin scalpel and scraped the backs of the assassin's arms, hands, and neck, depositing the scrapings on glass slides as he worked. Unable to prevent these indignities, the prisoner affected a bored unconcern.

Satisfied that he had collected everything he needed, Rosenstock labeled all the specimens and packed them, along with his instruments, back into the black bag.

"You wanna let him go now?" Emerson asked, his big hands still clutching the assassin's right arm and leg.

"Not yet," Warfield said.

Rosenstock fumbled around in the capacious bag again and produced a long pair of barber's shears. He glanced over at Warfield. Warfield nodded.

Rosenstock applied the shears to the assassin's disheveled hair, and began snipping it off close to the skull, like a gardener trimming a hedge. The assassin twisted his head violently to one side and bellowed. His scream was high pitched and piercing. At least his mouth works, Warfield thought.

"Hold him still!" Rosenstock yelled.

Emerson threw an arm around his neck from behind and squeezed him in a hammerlock. Trippet grabbed him hard by both ears.

The prisoner stopped thrashing. Tears of rage welled from the corners of his eyes. Rosenstock calmly continued his clipping. When he had chopped his hair to within a half inch of his skull, the doctor put away the scissors and rummaged in the bag for an electric razor.

"Let's stop here," Warfield decided. "We can shave his head easier when he's out."

Rosenstock picked up his bag. "That's it, then," he muttered.

"Let him go," Warfield said.

The guards released their grip on his arms and ears. The assassin collapsed back against the cot, his hands pressed to his skull. The guards filed out of the cell, Rosenstock and Warfield behind them.

"Didn't like losing his hair, did he?" Rosenstock said, as soon as they were out of hearing. "He must think he's Sampson."

Warfield nodded. "It hit him right in the *machismo*."

"I'm on my way, then," Rosenstock said.

"Okay. Moore should have the helicopter ready for you. Get back here as fast as you can."

"We'll be working all day and night on this. Some of the labs are way the hell off on Long Island. I'll be back late tonight, with whatever we've got."

Warfield shook his hand. "Thanks, Herb. Good luck."

Rosenstock displayed his crooked teeth. "I'll try to surprise you."

Warfield turned to Emerson, standing in the corridor with his hands on his hips, an expression of utter bafflement spread across his features. He was aching for an explanation.

"No more food for the prisoner," Warfield said. "Just water. Don't let him out of the cell for any reason. And don't talk to him. Keep the peephole open and watch him constantly. If he says anything, or does anything you think out of the ordinary, call me immediately."

"Yes sir."

"Keep two men here at the door at all times. Don't let anybody else near the door without my specific permission."

"Yes sir."

"I'll be back down here at midnight to give him a shot—a sedative."

Emerson nodded, his eyes growing steadily in circumference. He looked about to burst. "What's going on, sir?"

"You know better than to ask that."

"Yes sir." The guard's face seemed to deflate like a punctured balloon.

Warfield turned to go. Several steps down the corridor, he stopped and looked back at Emerson and the other two guards, standing behind him. "And I assume you all know better than to talk about this. At all. To anyone."

Emerson straightened up, his pride offended. "Of course!"

"Good. I'm counting on it. Tomorrow morning I'll need you to help move the prisoner out of here."

"Move him out of here?" Emerson repeated. "Where are you taking him?"

"To the infirmary."

"Is he sick?"

Warfield laughed. "No. Not yet, anyway."

11

THE KOREAN CLEARED A SPACE on the workbench in his basement, spread out a square of felt cloth, and carefully centered the object on it.

He cackled to himself and rolled his wheelchair a few feet back from the bench, to admire his creation. It had taken him twenty-five hours to design and assemble the device. Truly impressive, he thought, by any standard. He laughed again, a short explosion of noise that sounded almost like a bark.

He felt the pain coming back, disturbing the tranquil appreciation of his achievement. With his teeth he pulled the fireproof woven glass glove from his hand, zipped open his sleeve, and unlatched a compartment on the side of his wheelchair. He reached in and withdrew a small ampule of morphine, placed the ampule between his teeth, then brought his arm up and pressed the needle into the flesh just above the inside of his elbow.

He zipped the sleeve closed again and sat patiently, waiting for the painkiller to work its way through his body—what was left of it.

The Korean had survived to the age of fifty-three against great odds and at great cost. He had given up large parts of himself along the way. Both legs he had lost long ago in a land-mine explosion during the Korean War. His tongue, his genitals, and one eye had been removed from him in a North Korean POW camp. His right arm he had left behind in Lebanon, building a bomb for a group of Palestinian terrorists. His left ear, melted into scar tissue against his head, he had lost making hand grenades for the Monteneros in Argentina. One-eyed, speechless, and nearly deaf, he suffered constant pain from the accumulated assortment of violations his body had endured. His existence was made bearable only by painkillers and opium.

The Korean got around well in his electric chair, and the prosthetic device he used in place of his missing right arm was a technological marvel built to his own design. It featured interchangeable hands for performing specialized kinds of work. It had made his bomb-building at least marginally safer. To protect what was left of his flesh and bones, he wore an armored mesh cloak over his trunk and one remaining arm, and a motorcycle helmet with a specially made bullet-proof visor.

When the morphine began to block the pain, the Korean reached over with his real hand, lifted the device from the cloth, and examined it lovingly beneath the workbench light.

It was a hairbrush—an expensive one, made with stiff Himalayan boar bristles, and a thick, round, satinwood handle. In the day and a half the brush had been in his possession, he had subjected it to an invisible, but profound transformation.

He had sawed the wooden shaft in half, between the handle and the shank holding the bristles, and carefully hollowed out the interior of both halves down to a thickness of a sixteenth of an inch. Each half he had then equipped to perform entirely separate functions. Into the handle end he had fitted a miniature microphone attached to an equally small transmitter. It contained its own power cell and its own transmitting antenna, a tiny ferrite rod wrapped with hair-thin silver-plated copper wire. It broadcast its signal in the VHF range, and could be picked up by a sensitive receiver from a distance of approximately half a mile. It was self-activating, turning itself on automatically when sound waves of a certain volume struck its vibration-sensitive switch.

The Korean had faced a problem with the positioning of the microphone. The miniature pickup would not work if it were entirely enclosed within the handle. After some thought, he hit upon a solution. On the back of the handle, following the pattern of letters in the manufacturer's name, he had drilled a series of tiny, evenly spaced holes through to the hollowed-out interior and glued the microphone against them from the inside.

To pick up the bug's signal, the Korean had modified an off-the-shelf very low noise figure receiver of Japanese manufacture that was about the size of a large book.

Preparing the bristle half of the hairbrush had been the greatest challenge of all. The customer's requirements were demanding. The device must kill everything within a range of twenty-five feet "with the maximum possible degree of certainty." Normally he would simply have packed the hollowed-out core with C3 or C4 composition plastic or Dupont EL-506 sheet explosive, stuck in a lead azide detonator, and been done with it.

But a simple explosion, even a powerful one, might not kill. Without the fragmentation effect of the preserrated metal casing of a grenade flying like shrapnel in all directions, one could survive a concussion from fairly close up, especially if the path of the blast wave was partially blocked by something—a car door, a piece of furniture. Bombs frequently failed to kill for just that reason.

For "the maximum possible degree of certainty" he needed something better.

The Korean had carefully considered the alternatives, and finally opted for a combination blast and incendiary device. Because the amount of charge was limited by the space inside the shank, he created the most potent mixture he could concoct. For the incendiary effect, he mixed thermite (powdered aluminum and iron oxide) with magnesium. They required a high temperature to ignite, but once burning they were fierce as a volcano and almost impossible to extinguish. To spread the incendiary in the widest possible circle, he added a brownish yellow material known as composition "B." It consisted of two high explosives—TNT and RDX, the most powerful nonnuclear explosive known—stabilized in a wax base. To detonate the charge, he pressed an engineer's special cap into the waxy substance. The detonator, in turn, he wired to a miniature reed decoder switch, which could be activated by a tone signal broadcast on an unused frequency of 96.5 hz, in the subaudible band, from a 100-watt portable transmitter he had modified for the purpose. To power the electronic switch, he tapped into the cell already built into the other end of the brush to power the microphone transmitter. Once the switch was activated, after all, the microphone would no longer need its power source. The brush, in fact, would no longer exist.

For its size, the bomb was the most potent and sophisticated device he had ever created. A triumph of his special genius. He imagined the spectacular effect it would create. At a velocity of 9,300 meters per second, the detonation would create a shock wave of shattering intensity—twice that of the standard army hand grenade. And the metal incendiary, particularly the magnesium, would burn with a blinding white flame, its 2,000-degree Centigrade heat igniting everything it touched.

The device possessed, without question, "the maximum possible degree of certainty." No one within fifty feet of it would survive.

The Korean wiped the surfaces of the brush and placed it back in its handsome gift box. He repacked the tissue paper around it, closed the lid, and placed the box in a larger box on the floor, which contained the control units—the receiver for picking up the bug, and the transmitter and amplifier for triggering the detonator—already packed in protective styrofoam. The box, in turn, he stuffed inside a canvas overnight bag and zipped it closed.

He wondered briefly about the destiny of his creation. Of course he knew it would be used to kill somebody, and he didn't care to know who that might be. His only interest was in knowing that his creation would perform properly. His reputation was at stake, after all, on everything that went out of his shop. This one, particularly, he felt proud of.

He left the canvas case on the floor by the workbench and wheeled himself over to the small elevator that ran to the top of his two-story house. At the second floor he wheeled himself into the front bedroom and over to the window overlooking the deserted winter beach across the street.

All that remained now was to wait.

He opened a compartment in the side of the chair and drew out a long pipe with a small bowl, a box of matches, and a ball of brown opium. He kneaded the ball in his hand and then tamped it into the bowl. When he had fired it up, he closed his eyes, sat back in the chair, and puffed earnestly, sucking the coils of the dragon in to entwine around his brain, and take him to the happy place.

Warfield filled the last cardboard box with the last stack of material from the table in the lounge, folded the four flaps together on the top, and set the box on a pile of other boxes. He was tempted to throw the stuff away, but he knew better than that. In a bureaucracy nothing was ever thrown away. Things got lost, or shredded, or forgotten, but nobody was ever given the authority to discard anything. The amount of worthless paper that had accumulated in the five days since the parkway ambush was staggering. But it would all have to be stored somewhere, and allowed to rot away.

A young woman appeared at the open doorway and knocked on the side of the frame. He looked up.

"Charles Warfield?" she asked.

"Right. Come in! You must be Nan Robertson."

She stepped slowly into the center of the room and looked around. A Vuiton pocketbook was slung over her shoulder. Her face was partially hidden under a wide-brimmed felt fedora, but what he could see of it looked tanned, healthy, and attractive. She wore black slacks, a purple sweater, a silk designer scarf, low-heeled Italian shoes, and silver bracelets. Her open coat was suede leather trimmed with fur. Warfield blinked. This was Moore's idea of the All-American girl?

"Moving day?" she asked, her voice pleasantly soft.

"Sort of," he said. "We're transferring our act over to the infirmary. Sit down. Is it Miss Robertson, or Mrs?"

"It's Miss," she said. "But I'm also known as Mrs. Latham. At least to my husband's friends and our tax accountant."

"How about 'Ms.', then?"

"I hate that. Just call me Robertson," she said. "Like one of the guys." She pulled off her hat, peeled off her coat, and tossed them on the sofa. She was tall and slender. Fashionable was the word that would instantly leap to anybody's mind, Warfield thought. And probably rich.

"No matter how hard you try, 'Robertson,' you'll never be one of the guys."

She sat down, crossed her legs, and smiled, looking him directly in the eyes. She was wearing a very wet kind of lipstick.

"Thank you," she said. "Howard told me you needed someone for a special assignment."

"Yes, it's not an especially *big* assignment. But it's important as hell. I need someone to play the part of a nurse for a couple of days."

"Oh?" She sounded disappointed.

"You don't have to be a great actress, but you might have to be good at improvising. You'll be in a situation with no room for mistakes."

"Is that all you can tell me?"

"For the moment. Are you still interested?"

"Of course."

"Tell me about yourself."

"What do you want to know?"

Warfield shrugged. "How a pretty girl like you ends up working for an ugly boss like the CIA."

Nan Robertson's eyes narrowed. "Don't 'pretty girl' me, Mr. Warfield. I'm thirty-two and I have a Ph.D. in linguistics. And a brown belt in karate."

Warfield hastened to apologize. "No offense. My little ironies are always getting me into trouble. How come only a brown belt?"

Nan Robertson laughed. "More irony? If I had said a black belt you wouldn't have believed me."

"You have a black belt?"

"I have only the little leather belt you see on my slacks. I lied to impress you."

Warfield grinned. "That's okay. Lying is more important in tradecraft than karate."

"I'm glad you agree."

"What else did you lie about?"

Nan Robertson thought for a moment. "My age," she said. "I'm thirty-three."

"Anything else?"

"Not so far."

"Okay, back to my question. What are you doing in the CIA?"

"It's sort of the family trade," she answered, suddenly self-conscious.

Warfield started to say something, then stopped. He repeated her last name to himself, and felt a jolt of realization. He stared at her in awe.

"Your father was Harlan Robertson?"

She nodded.

"Jesus! Why didn't you say so?"

"I don't like to trade on my father's reputation."

Warfield studied her, still trying to adjust to the idea. Harlan Robertson was one of the few great men ever produced by the gray machinery of the American intelligence establishment. He was in a class with Donovan and Dulles. No, in a class by himself. Unique. He had died in a freak boating accident off Bermuda in 1979, five years after his retirement. There were persistent rumors that it wasn't an accident. The KGB was known to have set a price on his head.

"I met him once," Warfield said. "In Berlin. He was an extraordinary man. I'm sorry about his death."

Nan smiled a faint thank you.

"How long have you been in the company?"

"Since 1980."

"What did you do before?"

"After college I worked in an ad agency, did some fashion modeling, some photography, some reporting for a radio station, and some house-wifing, in that order. Then some dubbing for foreign films. You no doubt remember me as the voice of Lucy Harker in Werner Herzog's *Nosferatu.*"

Warfield laughed. "I thought you sounded familiar. How did that glamorous background get you here?"

Nan shrugged elaborately. "It wasn't glamorous. It was trivial. Rich girl thrashing around aimlessly to justify her existence."

"Are you telling me you've found happiness in the CIA?"

Nan didn't answer him. She looked past him out the window, her jaw set, her lips compressed. Warfield felt the sudden weight of a depressing suspicion.

"Revenge?" he asked.

She nodded.

"That's a bad reason to do anything."

"Maybe. But I like it. I've got a goal. I'm motivated. It's made me work hard at something for the first time in my life. Even if I never get back personally at the bastards who killed my father, I'll be satisfied just to know that I'm replacing him in some way. And that I'll do my share of damage in return."

"If your father was killed, as you think, you should consider it a tribute to him—that his opponents thought him so important."

"He was retired!" she said, her face tight with anger. "He wasn't a threat to anyone anymore. The KGB knew that! They killed him anyway."

Warfield sighed. He knew all the arguments about the ethics of espionage. But he also knew he was hardly the one to lecture her on the subject. He understood her feelings only too well.

"Obviously you're hired," he said. "Moore will give you your costume and fill you in on the details tonight. We start things rolling at six tomorrow morning. In the infirmary. Be there on time."

The assassin pressed the door buzzer and waited for the Korean to answer. The house was one of a row of dilapidated family homes, jammed together along a strip of Maryland shore front. The public beach across the street looked forlorn, its untidy jumble of concession stands and bathhouses boarded up for the winter.

Kemal looked down the street in both directions. No cars or pedestrians in sight.

The door opened to reveal a tiny man in a wheelchair, draped in what looked like chain mail and wearing a motorcycle helmet with the visor pulled down. He stared up at the assassin. One of his hands rested on a control panel on the wheelchair, the other —an artificial prosthesis of some kind—was pointed at the assassin.

Kemal's eyes fastened on it. Instead of fingers, two short pistol barrels, one stacked on the other, like a miniature over-and-under shotgun, grew from the steel fist. Kemal had heard about the Korean, but had not anticipated his paranoia. The Korean wheeled the chair back several feet and Kemal stepped inside, shutting the door behind him.

"Please . . . hand . . . me . . . your . . . weapons . . . ," a voice said. Kemal stared open-mouthed at the figure in the wheelchair, momentarily confused. The voice repeated the request. It sounded flat, mechanical, like the voice of a computer. The assassin spotted the source of the sound—a small metal box strapped to the Korean's throat, with a speaker grille on its front. He wondered how it worked.

"Please . . . hand . . . me . . . your . . . weapons . . . ," it said again.

The assassin shrugged, opened his shirt and pulled the .22-caliber High Standard Trophy automatic from its custom shoulder holster and dropped it into the Korean's lap. It was his favorite killing gun. He had planned to use it on the Korean.

"Is . . . that . . . all . . . or . . . do . . . you . . . have . . . more? . . ."

Kemal directed a malicious glare at the visored figure, and reached into an inside coat pocket and removed his backup, a small .22-caliber Astra Constable automatic. He added it to the one already in the Korean's lap. He felt the small face studying him impassively from behind the visor. Through the tinted glass he saw that one side was fused into an ugly mass of scar tissue, melding ear, cheek, and eye together, like a melted wax image.

The Korean's one good eye appeared glazed, the pupil dilated. Heroin, Kemal guessed, or opium.

"Now . . . please . . . may . . . I . . . have . . . the . . . money? . . ."

Kemal jerked the packet of bills from his side coat pocket and tossed it on top of the pistols.

The Korean opened the packet with his flesh-and-blood hand and riffled through the bills. Kemal watched him, his eyes caressing the hundred-dollar notes. What a shame it would be to have to leave those behind, he thought.

The Korean opened the compartment in the side of the wheelchair and dropped the packet of bills inside. The twin barrels of his mechanical fist never wavered from the assassin's chest.

"You . . . may . . . go . . . down . . . to . . . the . . . basement . . . now. . . . The . . . package . . . you . . . want . . . is . . . by . . . the . . . workbench. . . ."

The Korean pointed toward the basement door at the back end of the hallway. Kemal hurried down the steps, found the canvas case, and zipped it open. He saw the box inside, but didn't check its contents. He hadn't been told what it was supposed to contain, and he knew from experience that it was better not to know what you didn't have to know. His responsibility was simply to deliver it to the Instructor.

He gazed quickly around the basement workshop, his experienced eyes recognizing the tools and materials of the bombmaker's trade. A series of shelves, set low against the back wall, were lined with dozens of large olive-green military ammunition boxes, each neatly labeled. He scanned the labels, astonished at the variety and number of explosives they contained: black powder, smokeless powder, single- and double-base propellants, mercury fulminate, nitroglycerin, lead azide, lead styphnate, PETN, tetryl, RDX, TNT, military dynamite, E.C. blank powder, amatol, ammonium nitrate, Composition "B," C-3, C-4, EL-506, ammonium picrate, HBX-1, nitro-starch, picric acid, guncotton, even a box of photoflash powder.

The man was crazy to keep such an arsenal in his basement, Kemal thought. Not only were most of the explosives illegal to possess, but many were very unstable, needing only the right amount of heat, shock, or friction to set them off. They should all be stored in a bunker, not a house in a crowded neighborhood.

On a higher shelf he saw boxes of detonating caps, timing devices, reels of primacord, and assorted fuses.

Suddenly the idea he had been searching for came to him.

He pulled out the ammo box containing the C-4 plastic, an explosive he was familiar with, removed a one-pound block, and set it on the workbench. Hastily, he scanned the shelves, and found the other items he required—a box of blasting caps and a coil of safety fuse. He rolled out eight feet from the fifty-foot coil of fuse, and cut it off. He found cap crimper pliers lying at the back of the workbench, and quickly crimped the end of the length of fuse into the blasting cap, then inserted the cap into the puttylike block of C-4. He stuck the block back into its ammo box, and returned it to the shelf, alongside the other boxes.

All that remained was to ignite the coil of fuse. He knew it would burn at the rate of forty-five seconds a foot. So eight feet meant six minutes until detonation. He picked up the lighter from the bench, struck it, and held it to the end of the orange coil of fuse until the powder train ignited and began to spit a jet of flame.

Excitement seized him as he headed up the stairs, the canvas case containing his package slung over his shoulder. In six minutes, the neighborhood was going to hear one hell of a bang.

At the top of the stairs, he encountered the Korean, his wheelchair rolled squarely in front of the door, blocking his exit. The double-barreled fist was trained on him again, and in his other, real hand, he was pointing Kemal's own High Standard at him.

"Please . . . return . . . to . . . basement . . . and . . . cut . . . fuse . . . or . . . you . . . will . . . die . . . here . . . with . . . me. . . ."

The firepower trained on him gave the assassin pause. The son-of-a-bitch must have a TV monitor set up down there. And he didn't see it.

The assassin edged back through the basement door and down the steps. At the bottom his mind raced. He could cut the fuse cord, of course, but now he had tipped his hand to the Korean. The bastard might shoot him anyway, after he cut the cord.

He noticed an elevator door next to the stairwell. He reached over and pressed the button. He heard a click and an electric hum as the car began its descent. It reached the basement, stopped, and its doors slid open. The assassin stepped inside, and punched the button marked "2." The doors closed, and the lift began its ascent to the top floor of the house.

The instant the elevator's doors opened on the top floor, the assassin flipped the switch on the panel to put the elevator out of service and ran out into the corridor. He glanced at his wristwatch, then realized it was pointless. He hadn't checked it when he first lit the fuse. A guess told him he had about a minute to get clear. He tried not to think of the hundreds of pounds of high explosives that would detonate beneath him when the flame on the powder train reached the blasting cap.

With the elevator out, the Korean was now effectively trapped on the ground floor below him, unable to get to the basement to try to defuse the bomb, and unable to come after him on the top floor. His only choice was to get out of the house.

Kemal had to beat him to it. He dashed into a bedroom and checked its windows. One opened on the side of the house. The drop was about fifteen feet to a cement driveway. The other opened onto the roof over the front porch. Kemal unlatched it and slipped out onto the slanting surface.

Gripping the clumsy load of the canvas case in one hand, he reached up under his pants leg and pulled out a tiny Derringer pistol from a leg holster. Too puny a weapon, he realized, against a man in an armored suit. He jammed it back in its holster.

Fighting down a ballooning sense of panic, he crawled to the edge of the roof, flattened himself out on his stomach and craned his neck around to look underneath. The front door was open, the wheelchair parked just inside. The Korean didn't know how little time remained.

He could not jump from the porch roof without being shot, the assassin realized.

He scrambled back up the roof and into the bedroom again.

The side window was the only other way out. An impossible jump.

He stood in the room, momentarily paralyzed with fright. His eyes froze on his reflection, caught in a mirror over a chest of drawers. He could see his own terror etched on his face.

He was trapped on top of what amounted to a munitions dump. And he would be blown to pieces before the sweep hand on his watch made another circuit of the dial.

The pores of his skin opened in a spontaneous reaction to the panic that gripped him, soaking his body in a bath of sweat. He had narrowly escaped death before. But this was idiotic, crazy! He had trapped himself with his own carelessness. He couldn't die like this. He had to do something!

He ran to the side window again, raised the sash, and looked out. He would have to try to jump clear of the cement drive. If he could fling himself out far enough, he might hit the hedge that divided the yard from the one next door. It would take a superhuman push. More likely he would break a leg or ankle on the cement, and be unable to get clear of the house in time.

It was jump or stay in the room.

First the canvas case. He held his breath and flung it out toward the hedge, praying it would cushion the package enough to prevent that exploding as well. It landed directly on top of the hedge, then bounced and rolled several feet, without detonating.

Kemal jumped right after it, climbing out on the sill, standing on it, and pushing off with all his strength. He hit the hedge with his legs and fell backward onto the cement, knocking the wind out of his lungs, and bruising the back of his head.

Gasping painfully, he staggered to his feet and grabbed the canvas case. With panic alarms clanging in his head, he beat his way through the hedge and ran across the neighboring lawn, bent so close to the ground that his elbows nearly scraped the grass.

He reached the van, parked across the street, opened the door and threw the canvas case on the passenger seat. His lungs still rasping, he forced his arms and hands to move with astonishing rapidity, finding his keys, inserting them in the ignition, depressing the accelerator, cranking the starter motor, shifting the gears, engaging the clutch.

Bullets, fired from the Korean's wheelchair on the edge of the porch, ripped through the side panels of the van.

A sudden tremor distracted him. He glanced toward the house. The foundation was shooting out sideways in all directions, followed by a billowing apron of debris and smoke, like a rocket during the first seconds of lift-off. The Korean's wheelchair was rolling from the porch like a tumbleweed in a windstorm. For a fraction of a second, the house seemed to hang suspended on the cloud of debris, then crunched back to earth.

Kemal jammed down on the accelerator and the van spun its tires along the street.

The house blew apart in a series of concussions that beat like ocean waves against the van.

He rode the vehicle down the street like a bronco buster, debris falling in a shower around him, the day growing rapidly darker.

Three blocks away, he slowed the van to a halt, and looked back. A cloud of smoke mushroomed skyward.

He drove back to Washington slowly, the canvas bag with its mysterious package safe on the seat beside him. A shame, he thought, that he wasn't able to recover that ten grand.

12

HERB ROSENSTOCK SLOUCHED through the doorway of the infirmary's west wing, and stopped to gawk at the activity in front of him. The entire wing had been closed off from the main building and was undergoing hectic renovation. A ward on one side was swarming with carpenters, painters, and electricians. In one wall a big hole had been punched into the adjacent room. Rosenstock peered through the scar and saw two men kneeling on the floor, surrounded by a tangle of tools, color-coded wires, electronic devices, and testing equipment.

In a third room further down the hall he found Warfield, writing on a pad of legal paper. The hospital beds had been removed and replaced by a pair of beat-up metal desks, an assortment of chairs, a typewriter, and two telephones.

Warfield looked up from the clutter and grinned. "Herb! Thank God you got back in time! How do you like our new headquarters?"

Rosenstock dropped his cigarette stub on the floor. "Looks like you're building a missile control center. Will it all come together in time?"

Warfield held up both hands, fingers crossed. "We're bringing the prisoner in later tonight. We start at dawn tomorrow, ready or not."

Rosenstock plopped onto a chair and dropped his satchel on the floor beside him. "Christ, I'm exhausted! I've never worked so hard in one day in my life. At least not since medical school."

Warfield rubbed his eyes and yawned. "You're not the only one."

"Does this joint produce anything resembling coffee?" he asked.

"We have a rough imitation," Warfield replied, rising from his chair. "I'll get us some."

He collected two plastic containers of coffee from the machine in the corridor and brought them back to his desk. Rosenstock tasted his. "Jesus! A man could die from shit like that!" He pulled out the bottle of sour mash whiskey from his bag and dumped a generous amount on top of the coffee, stirring it in with his finger.

"What did you find out?" Warfield asked.

Rosenstock smiled enigmatically and took a long, slow sip of his bourbon and coffee mixture. "That tastes miles better," he said.

"I'm not enjoying the suspense, Herb."

"I don't have all the test results yet," Rosenstock said. "I'll be collecting more by telefax later tonight and tomorrow. Analyzing all this stuff is no giggle, I'll tell you."

"Did you *find* anything?"

"Yes, as a matter of fact. The guy's left-handed. You can tell that from the development of his wrist and forearm muscles. . . ."

Warfield slumped down in his chair and closed his eyes. "For Christ's sakes, Herb. . . ."

Rosenstock held up his hand. "Now hold on, I'm just warming up. Don't be so impatient! The calluses on his fingers and palms indicate he's worked at manual labor, probably most of his life. I picked up some traces of barium, lead, and antimony from his eyebrows and the back of both hands, too. That tells me that he was the one who fired the submachine gun. . . ."

Warfield picked up his pad and started taking notes.

"I've got it all written down for you," Rosenstock said. "I'm just giving you a brief summary of the main points."

"I'm listening."

Rosenstock blew a thin plume of smoke across the room. "He's about thirty years old, and he's Hispanic. Cuban."

Warfield sat up. "How do you know?"

"By a kind of triangulation. Computer analysis is part of it. It's possible now to isolate blood factors unique to certain racial strains. He comes up Hispanic. Determining the Cuban part is a bit more difficult, but it goes something like this: there are antibodies in his blood for several varieties of tropical diseases found in the Caribbean, and he has parasites in his intestines that are specific to several islands—Hispaniola, Puerto Rico, Jamaica, and Cuba."

"But then he could be any number of nationalities," Warfield argued. "Puerto Rican, Dominican . . ."

"No, I don't think so," Rosenstock said. "Not when all the pieces of the puzzle are laid out. His dental work is almost certainly Cuban. Cuban dentists before Castro were all trained either in the States or in Spain. This one was trained in Spain. The Spanish fondness for certain amalgams is distinctive."

"Castro came to power in 1959! If he had his dental work done in Cuba, the dentist was probably Russian trained!"

Rosenstock grinned, the edges of his crooked teeth peeking out under his lips. "Good point! The answer is that both he *and* his dentist are most likely Cuban refugees—probably part of the exodus of the sixties. I think the assassin was born in Cuba and then came to Florida with his family when he was a teenager. That scenario would fit his blood profiles and the other evidence perfectly."

"Couldn't any Hispanic have gone to a Cuban dentist in Florida?"

"Yeah, but this guy's been going since he was fifteen."

Warfield pondered the information. "Okay, let's say he's Cuban. What does that mean? Omega Seven? Alpha Sixty-Six?"

Rosenstock shrugged. "That's what the Russians think, isn't it? According to that briefing paper from Friedrich's office."

"Yeah," Warfield replied. "Or that's what they want *us* to think."

"Isn't the information from a high-level source?"

"That's exactly why I distrust it. It's too pat. The Russians love to slip us disinformation. They know how extraordinarily gullible we are."

Rosenstock laughed. "That's probably to our credit."

"Probably, but the Russians may just be seizing an opportunity to exploit us. Omega Seven or Alpha Sixty-Six is who they would *like* to be guilty of the ambush. It works to their benefit. Right-wing anti-Socialist fanatics, running amok in capitalist America, etcetera, etcetera."

"There's paranoia in that kind of reasoning," Rosenstock said.

Warfield smiled. "Healthy skepticism. And remember, the FBI has put those groups through a sieve, according to their reports. They're convinced that none of them are involved."

Rosenstock shook his head. "They don't know every member of every group. A lot are illegal aliens. No prints, no records. And most FBI work I've seen has been shoddy as hell. They miss as much as they turn up, and what they turn up they misinterpret. These assassins of ours could be some right-wing splinter group nobody's ever heard of."

"And they could just as easily be working for Castro," Warfield said. "He has a lot to lose from the Daniels-Kamenev accord. No more weapons from Russia, no more exporting revolution to the Americas. For Cuba, the treaty would be the diplomatic equivalent of a kick in the teeth."

"Plausible," Rosenstock agreed.

Warfield scratched his neck slowly with the eraser end of the pencil. "Maybe. Anyway, our assassin knows the answers. All we have to do is ask him in the right way and he'll tell us."

"That's all you have to do," Rosenstock agreed.

"Did you turn up anything else?"

"Yes I did. Microscopic pollen samples from his clothing, his earwax, his nasal passages, and under his fingernails show a surprising amount of cotton and jute fibers."

"What's unusual about that? Couldn't they just come from the clothes he's wearing?"

"No. The cotton is raw fiber. There are even traces of the chemical defoliant used to make the leaves fall off before it's picked. It's raw cotton, Charlie. He seems to have cotton dust all over him. The same with the jute."

"What would jute be used for?"

"It's a cheap fiber. Most of it comes from India. It's used for rope, twine, carpet backing, burlap, that kind of thing."

Warfield tapped the pencil against his teeth. "Okay, so he's been using rope or burlap bags, or something. What does that tell us?"

"I don't know. I'm more interested in the cotton boles."

"You have any theories?"

Rosenstock drained off his coffee and bourbon, threw the empty container toward a wastebasket in the far corner and missed. "Maybe he goes south and picks cotton between hits."

"Not in February."

"New Zealand? Australia?"

Warfield laughed. "They grow wool, not cotton. Anyway, it's probably not important."

Rosenstock shook a finger at him. "Don't ever say that! Every thing's important when you don't know anything!"

"Okay. Now tell me how accurate is all this fiber analysis and trace evidence and blood profiling?"

"Damned accurate. I'm not saying it would all stand up in court, at least not without follow-up tests and more complete analysis, but I'd stake my rep on everything I've told you so far."

Warfield stood up. "No miracles there, but you found more than I expected. Put it in writing, and send the bill to Langley. And go home immediately and get a good night's sleep."

A pained expression creased Rosenstock's forehead. "That's it?"

"I guess so. You've been a big help to me. You've given me some leverage with the assassin, and that's what I needed most."

Rosenstock fumbled to extract the last cigarette from his pack. "There's still more test results in the pipeline, coming along from some of the labs. . . ."

"Call me immediately if there's anything new."

Rosenstock snared the cigarette and saw that he had broken it. He crumpled the pack angrily in his fist. "I want to stick around, damn it!"

Warfield smiled. "Why?"

The doctor tossed the crumpled pack at the wastebasket and missed it again. "Because I want to see how this comes out!"

"You were complaining yesterday how busy you were."

Rosenstock nodded, his tone defiant. "Yeah, but there's busy and there's busy. This case has me hooked. And I think you're gonna need me."

Warfield shook his head. "I can always call you. Go home and get some sleep."

Rosenstock raised a palm. "You said it yourself, yesterday, on the way to the mess hall. They see you as disposable. If you fail, they'll feed your ass through one of their shredders back at Langley. You need more troops. I can help lower the odds against you."

Warfield frowned. "Why stick your neck out for me, Herb?"

"I told you why! Because I'm interested! I'm an old bastard who doesn't get many thrills out of life anymore."

"I don't want to be responsible for you."

"Bullshit, Charlie. I'm responsible for myself!"

Warfield capitulated. He was grateful, actually. "I guess you could still play doctor for me," he admitted. "Our assassin's going to need close medical supervision."

Rosenstock found another package of cigarettes in his bag. He tore off the top and banged one out against the side of his palm. "Hey," he said, exhaling his first drag noisily. "I almost forgot."

"What?"

"Our assassin's name is Raoul."

Warfield regarded Rosenstock as if he had just grown another head. "What did you say?"

"His name is Raoul," Rosenstock repeated. "He had a tattoo removed from his right forearm, but I could just make out the original scar with a magnifier. It shows a heart with the words *Raoul Ama Carmen* inside it. 'Raoul loves Carmen.' A noble sentiment for a killer, don't you think?"

Warfield collapsed against the back of the chair. "You son-of-a-bitch! And you knew this before you left here this morning."

Rosenstock grinned sheepishly. "Well, I was thinking I'd save it in case I couldn't persuade you to keep me on. No harm done. Just a little chip to bargain with. I mean, I'd have told you, Charlie, no matter what."

Warfield nodded wearily. It was two o'clock in the morning. He needed sleep. Tomorrow was going to be the most important day of his life. "I thought of one more thing," he said. "What about the dead assassin? Shouldn't you run your tests on him, too?"

Rosenstock squinted at Warfield. "You didn't hear?"

Warfield felt his chest muscles tighten. "Hear what?"

"Well, naturally I thought of that. I had the helicopter drop me at Walter Reed after I left here this morning. The body's gone."

"What?"

Rosenstock shrugged. "They lost it, believe it or not, some time between last night and this morning. They think somebody switched toe tags in the storage locker next to the autopsy room. They cremated him by mistake, thinking it was a different corpse. They were sorry as hell about it, but didn't think it was all that big a deal, since they had already done an autopsy."

Warfield pressed a fist to his mouth. "Incredible!"

"A coincidence, a stupid blunder," Rosenstock said. "That's all. Routine in our great medical institutions. It probably doesn't matter."

Probably not, Warfield thought. But still it frightened him. Like all men whose work put their lives at risk, he was superstitious. And this struck him as the worst possible omen.

The Instructor opened the door on the top floor, aimed his flashlight down at the floor just inside the door, where Kemal had placed the package, then raised the beam across the room to the assassin's back, pressed against the chair.

"Did you get the Korean?" he asked.

"Yes."

"How?"

"I blew him up."

"Did you see him die?"

"Nobody could have survived that explosion."

"What happened to the ten grand?"

"It went with him."

"You sure?"

"I'd have kept it if I could."

A silence grew. Kemal heard the Instructor bend down and pick up the package. The beam of light stayed on his back. He watched his silhouette dance across the cracked plaster of the far wall and felt the hairs of his neck tingle with apprehension. Would they try to kill him now?

"Am I going to sit this one out?" he asked.

"No."

"How come I'm not the one using the package?"

"It's too complicated. You've got another assignment."

"What is it?"

"You're taking a job as a dishwasher."

"What do you mean?"

"Instructions are in the envelope I'm leaving for you. Also a hundred grand. Fifty for picking up the package and fifty for this new job."

"Where am I going?"

"A little farm in Virginia," the Instructor said.

They evacuated the entire neighborhood—over five thousand people. Fifteen houses near the beach were burning out of control, another ten were set ablaze. Smoke blackened the sky for miles. Three hundred men and thirty fire engines and emergency vehicles answered the six alarms that went out during the course of the late afternoon and evening.

Explosions continued for several hours at the site of the original blast. Firemen refused to approach it until late in the evening, long after the surrounding fires had been brought under control.

One fireman turned over a wheelchair on the scorched lawn and discovered a body underneath, clad in a strange steel mesh cloak and a motorcycle helmet. He pushed the helmet's visor back and saw the face, one side badly scarred. He dragged the body a few feet across the lawn, then noticed that most of its limbs were missing. He dropped it back on the ground.

Half an hour later a stretcher team arrived. The medic took one look at the truncated form and shook his head. They zipped the Korean in a body bag and tossed him into the back of an ambulance.

An hour later the body reached the morgue. Two attendants carried the bag inside and settled it on an autopsy table. One zipped the bag open and peered inside.

"Jesus!" he whispered. "This guy's alive!"

13

AT SIX O'CLOCK IN THE MORN-
ing they filed silently down the infirmary corridor and into the
room next to the special ward. When they were all inside, Warfield
closed the door.

The small room's single hospital bed had been shoved against
one wall, and the shade drawn tightly against the window. The
wall across from the bed drew their attention immediately. It had
been torn apart and put back together again, with heavy sound-
proofing and a double-paned glass window about two feet high
and three feet wide cut into it. The window—hidden at the moment behind a black cloth drape—opened onto the larger ward
next to it. It was one-way glass. The small room could see into the
ward, but the ward saw only a mirror. A low bench and control
panel were built into the wall beneath the glass. On the panel a
series of switches operated two cameras and three microphones
hidden in several locations in the ward on the other side. Two
monitor screens, two sets of earphones, and a video- and sound-
taping system occupied another portion of the bench.

Warfield sat at a swivel chair by the control panel. The others
crowded behind him.

"Ready?" he asked.

A murmur of assents.

"Here goes, then."

He drew a deep breath and flipped a switch on the control panel
that doused the overhead light, plunging the room into sudden
darkness. He flipped another switch and a dim red light illuminated the panel. In quick succession he tripped more
switches, activating the microphones, the cameras, and the taping
systems.

"Okay, Howard," he said.

Moore stepped up to the drape covering the one-way glass and
slowly pulled it aside.

Through the glass they saw a hospital room, its freshly painted
walls gleaming faintly in the early morning light. High up on the
wall on one side two windows were visible, covered by heavy
mesh grilles. On the wall directly across from them were bunched
the room's few furnishings—two metal chairs, a dresser, a bedside
table, and a narrow hospital bed.

The assassin was in the bed, sleeping. He lay on his back, his head resting on two big pillows. One arm extended outside the covers to accommodate a thin plastic tube taped to his wrist and leading to a bottle of glucose solution suspended from an I.V. pole by the bed. Another plastic tube, a nasal catheter, ran from the oxygen outlet valve in the wall over the bed down one nostril of the assassin's nose and into his pharynx.

His head was heavily swathed in bandages.

Rosenstock bent over Warfield's shoulder to get a better look. "He's been asleep for about ten hours," he said. "I've given him a shot of ketamine hydrochloride. When he comes to he'll feel unpleasantly confused. I gave him a big enough dose so there should be some emergence reaction—irrational behavior, maybe hallucinations." Rosenstock grinned. "Other than that, he should be ready to greet the day with a smile."

Warfield turned up the volume controls on the microphones—one by the head of the bed, one planted in the ceiling, and a third hidden in the wall near the door. A hum crackled over the speakers on the control panel. Each of the two monitor screens were lit, showing the bed from the cameras' positions at opposite corners of the ward.

"How do we wake him up?" Moore asked.

"Like this," Warfield replied. He touched a button near his left hand. A harsh buzzer sounded in the other room, and blared back in over the speakers. He lowered the volume and watched the bed.

The assassin moved his head. Slowly his eyelids separated. For a long moment he remained still. His eyes closed again. Then he blinked them rapidly, and tossed his head from side to side. He stopped, opened his eyes, and stared at the ceiling.

Suddenly he bolted upright, his hand groping for the tube that ran into his nose. He fingered it nervously, as if it might hurt him if he disturbed it. Then his eyes fell on the other tube leading to the glucose bottle, and on the needle taped into his wrist.

From his wrist he looked up slowly and saw himself in the one-way glass across the room.

The four in the control room watched him, transfixed. Over the speakers they could hear his sharp intake of breath.

He reached up with both hands and felt the bandage that encased his head. Astonishment contorted his features.

"Jesus," Moore murmured. "He's really spooked."

The assassin tore at the tape on his wrist and yanked out the needle. The plastic tubing bounced onto the floor, trickling a tiny stream of blood and glucose onto the black tile. He grabbed the tube in his nose, yanked it a couple of inches, then grimaced in pain.

"That thing goes all the way down his throat," Rosenstock said. "He'll throw up if he tries to yank it out like that."

The assassin seemed to recognize that possibility. Instead he pulled the tube free of the oxygen valve in the wall and jumped out of bed, the tube trailing from his nose.

"He's moving awfully fast for a guy full of ketamine," Warfield said.

"Yeah," Rosenstock agreed. "Amazing."

The assassin grabbed a chair and dragged it over to one of the windows and climbed up on it. For the first time the effects of the drugs were apparent. He staggered trying to mount the chair and nearly fell over backward. On the second try he steadied himself on the seat and pulled himself up to the window. His hospital gown, open in back, exposed his naked backside.

A minute passed while he took in the view. The windows on that side of the infirmary looked out onto a part of the mock border— a strip of cleared woods with a high fence, guard posts, search-lights, rolled barbed wire. Warfield had picked the room because of that view. It would further confuse and disorient the prisoner.

He climbed down from the chair and walked over to the one-way mirror. Warfield and the others shrank back instinctively as his face loomed near the glass.

"Are you positive he can't see through that?" Moore whispered nervously.

"I'm positive. As long as the light's off in here. But make sure nobody lights a cigarette."

They watched the assassin as he stood, not two feet from them, seeming to stare directly into their faces. He felt the bandages on his head, tentatively at first, as if debating with himself whether or not to risk removing them.

He decided on the risk. He tore into the headdress with his fingers, unraveling it frantically, pulling it off in a long ribbon of increasingly blood-soaked cloth. At the crown of his head a patch of sticking plaster about four inches in diameter adhered to his shaven skull. With barely a second's hesitation, he ripped it off, grunting from the pain as he did so. Beneath the plaster, across an area of pink, swollen flesh, lay a neat three-inch-long surgical incision, stitched together with plastic thread. Each end of the incision terminated in a dime-sized scab.

Warfield heard Nan Robertson, behind him, whisper "My God!" in a shocked voice.

"Don't lose your breakfast," Rosenstock said. "The incision is only skin deep. I doubt that it'll even leave a scar. The hair'll grow back over it in any case."

"It's realistic as hell," Warfield said.

"*He* sure thinks so," Moore added.

The assassin, his head bent forward, was eyeing the scar with an expression of frank terror. Warfield felt his own skin crawl, watching his victim cope with the shock of his discovery. In ripping off the plaster he had opened the stitches slightly, and a trickle of blood was oozing down the side of his scalp.

The assassin's face disappeared from the one-way mirror. Warfield glanced at the monitor screens. The left one showed him at the door of the ward, tugging on the knob with both hands. The microphone over the door picked up with harsh clarity the rattle of the hardware and the assassin's rapid breathing.

"He's hyperventilating," Rosenstock said. "Really worked up."

The assassin pounded on the door for several minutes, then abandoned the effort and made rapid, erratic circuits of the room, trying to fathom his situation. Finally, he dropped down on the side of the bed and sagged forward with exhaustion.

"The ketamine's doing its job," Rosenstock said. "He feels like he's been sacked twenty times by the Dallas front line. Bells are ringing, the room is swaying, and his skin seems to be three sizes too tight for his body."

Warfield looked around for Nan Robertson. She was standing beside Rosenstock, dressed in nurse's whites, complete down to the cap and RN button. She was biting her lip nervously.

"It's time to visit our patient," he said. "Are you ready, nurse?"

"Ready," she answered, brushing the front of her dress. "I'll have to get my tray from the kitchen."

"Go ahead then. And don't worry. There are two guards by the door. They'll jump in immediately if he gets out of line."

"I can handle it," she said, and headed toward the door.

Warfield, Rosenstock and Moore hunched in front of the glass, waiting for Nan's appearance on the other side.

"I hope she *can* handle it," Warfield whispered.

After a long, nervous minute, they saw the door open in the ward and one of the guards, Frady, usher Nan into the assassin's presence.

She strode forward, balancing a breakfast tray in front of her. Warfield felt a twinge of guilt sending her in first, when the prisoner's reactions were still untested.

The assassin cringed as she deposited the tray on the dresser and surveyed the mess he had made of his bandages and the tubes. She stood over him.

"What on earth have you been doing! You *must* get right back into bed! You are a sick man! A *very* sick man! Do you hear me?"

Nan bent down, picked up the pile of bandages and the IV tube and needle and flung them on a chair with disgust. The assassin, barely moving, followed her with agate-hard eyes. She approached the bed, yanked back the covers, grabbed him firmly by the arm, and pushed him back against the pillows. He resisted feebly, then fell back.

"I'm calling Doctor Rosenstock right away!" she scolded. "He'll be furious with you."

Rosenstock grinned at Warfield. "She's okay!" he exclaimed. Warfield shrugged.

Nan produced a thermometer from the pocket of her uniform and jabbed it under his tongue. He didn't resist. She picked up his wrist to measure his pulse.

Moore tensed. "Christ, we forgot to get her a wristwatch!"

Warfield saw that Nan had just realized the same thing. She gazed at her bare wrist, then glanced worriedly toward the one-way glass. Warfield held his breath.

"Oh, damn!" she exclaimed. "I left my watch in the kitchen. I'll take your pulse later."

Warfield exhaled.

"Cool," Rosenstock murmured.

The assassin seemed to be relaxing a little. His eyes roved over Nan's face.

"Why the hell doesn't he *ask* her something?" Warfield muttered. "Who am I? Where am I? Who are you? What day is it? Why am I here?"

"Don't expect too much," Rosenstock cautioned. "He's groggy and confused. And there's still plenty of resistance in him."

"Confused? Hell, he's scared silly." Moore whispered. "I never saw anybody soften up so fast."

Warfield wondered. When the initial shock wore off, he might regain his equilibrium. Or worse, see through their deception. They'd have to keep the pressure on. Crack him before the day was out. Or risk losing him for good.

Nan pulled the thermometer from his mouth, read it, inserted it back into its holder, and wrote something on a small pad she fished from her pocket.

The assassin watched her closely. Warfield noticed that she was afraid to meet his stare. No great harm there, he supposed. Any nurse would naturally be intimidated in such a situation. But he could sense the balance of control subtly shifting. She picked up a large glass of orange juice and a paper cup with some pills in it and held them out to him.

"This may be a mistake," Rosenstock said.

"Take these pills, please," Nan ordered. "They'll make you feel better."

The assassin looked from her face to the pills and juice in her hands and back at her face again.

"Maybe he's *unable* to talk," Warfield sighed. "Did you check to see if he had a tongue when you examined him?"

Nan hesitated, not sure what to do. "If you don't take your medicine," she said, her voice losing its conviction, "you'll never get well."

"What's in those pills?" Warfield asked.

"Nothing," Rosenstock replied. "Placebos. It's a test to see if he'll cooperate. We have to compromise him in stages."

"I don't think he's going to take them," Moore said.

Nan was losing her poise. She thrust the orange juice glass and the cup against the assassin's chest.

He batted the glass and the cup of pills violently with the back of his hand and sent them flying. The glass shattered on the tile floor.

Nan froze, speechless. Warfield bunched his fists.

"Very well," she said, her voice quavering. "Very well!"

The assassin lurched from the bed. He swung at her awkwardly, striking her on the breasts, then grabbed her uniform at the neck and yanked on it. The top half of the dress tore open. Nan shrieked, then grabbed his arms and tried to push him away. He held on, ripping the fabric from one shoulder, exposing the strap of her bra. Then he lost his balance on the puddle of orange juice and toppled over backward, pulling her down with him.

Warfield punched the alarm button and Frady and Trippet rushed into the ward and swarmed on the prisoner, pinning his arms and legs to the floor. Nan scrambled to her feet and dashed from the room.

The assassin started to scream.

He bellowed with such volume and intensity that the speakers on the control panel vibrated from the overload. He wailed on and on, as the guards handcuffed him and carried him back to the bed. It was a cry torn from the center of his being.

Warfield shuddered and clapped his hands over his ears.

Kemal boarded the olive tan military bus that shuttled twice daily between Williamsburg and Camp Peary, transporting base workers, staff, dependents, and supplies. He sat in the back, by the window, avoiding the eyes and conversation of the other passengers.

An hour later he was inside the base itself, walking unchallenged past the two-story frame building that served as the base headquarters. Security was as laughably porous at the farm as it was anywhere else, he realized. As long as you looked like you knew where you were going, people rarely challenged you. Americans were incredibly trusting and stupid. Contemptible.

He found the mess hall kitchen and sauntered into the dirty office at the back, knocking with his fist on the edge of the open doorway. A skinny man in a gravy-stained chef's apron looked up from a disordered stack of invoices on the desk in front of him.

"Who the hell are you?"

Kemal affected a timid manner and lowered his eyes. "Dishwasher."

The chef nodded impatiently. "Oh yeah? Let's see your card."

Kemal produced the forged ID from his back pocket and handed it across. The chef glanced at it and pronounced the name on it with deliberate difficulty: "Ni-kos . . . An-dro-pou-lous? That your name?"

Kemal nodded.

"You Greek?"

He nodded again and grinned shyly.

The chef handed the card back. "How old are you?"

"Twenty-nine."

"You're the first white dishwasher I've ever seen here. What's your problem?"

Kemal looked at him in confusion. "I dunno."

The chef shook his head, exasperated. "Why are you a dishwasher? That the best you can do?"

"I guess so."

"Live in town?"

"I'm looking for a room."

"Where'd you work before?"

"At the Steak House . . . in Williamsburg."

"Got a reference?"

Kemal produced a persuasively wrinkled and folded letter of recommendation and placed it on the desk. The chef didn't bother to open it.

"Police record?"

"No."

"How much school you have?"

Kemal studied the floor, the picture of humility. "Sixth grade. In Athens."

The chef curled a lip. "That's six more than you need to wash dishes."

"Yeah," Kemal agreed.

The chef returned to his stack of bills. "Okay, Nikos. You're hired. Get a uniform from the supply office in the building next door. They'll give you your tickets too, and base pass. Report back here for work at thirteen hundred."

Kemal looked at him, his brow creased in puzzlement.

"That's one o'clock."

Kemal nodded and smiled and walked out, whistling softly to himself.

14

ROSENSTOCK ADJUSTED THE
new white surgeon's gown Moore had acquired for him. Warfield
bent over the control panel, reloading the videotape spools. Nan
Robertson was on the bed, head propped against the wall. She had
pinned together the front of her torn dress and kicked off her
sneakers.

"I should never have pushed those pills on him like that," she
muttered. "I could see he was about to explode. I'm sorry."

"Don't apologize," Warfield said. "You did a first-rate job."

"What did I do with my stethoscope?" Rosenstock muttered.

Moore pointed to it, hanging from the back of a chair. Rosenstock stuffed it into the pocket of his gown, grabbed his black bag,
and paused for one last look through the one-way glass. The assassin was sitting on the bed, his hands cuffed together in front of him,
his head slumped forward.

"We've got him on the ropes," Rosenstock said. "Time for round
two."

"Good luck," Warfield murmured.

They watched Rosenstock burst into the assassin's ward, surgeon's robe flapping, expression stormy. The assassin looked up,
startled by the intrusion, then lowered his head again. His mood
was hard to read, Warfield thought. Since his screaming fit, he
seemed to have fallen into a lethargy.

Working with concentrated fury, Rosenstock removed the catheter from the assassin's nose, reinserted the IV needle in his wrist,
then slapped the diaphragm of the stethoscope smartly against his
chest and held it there, listening impatiently. The assassin submit-
ted to the rough handling without complaint. Rosenstock's
brusqueness, playing on the ingrained fear that doctors command,
seemed to cow him totally.

Rosenstock shook his head, indicating some disappointment
with the information he was getting through the stethoscope. He
listened briefly at several other locations on the patient's back,
then stuffed the stethoscope back in his pocket. He examined the
stitches in the assassin's head wound, then cleaned the wound with
alcohol and slapped a strip of cotton gauze over it.

"That should hold you," he muttered. He completed the examination, peering quickly into the assassin's eyes, nose, and ears.

Warfield tensed when he pulled the assassin's mouth open and inserted a tongue depressor. He studied his throat for a few seconds, then tossed the depressor at a wastebasket by the side of the bed, and—typically—missed it.

"The cotton gauze reminds me," Warfield said to Moore. "Do you have any ideas about the cotton dust Rosenstock found in the guy's earwax? Cotton and jute, I think."

Moore grinned maliciously. "You think my race might give me some special insight into cotton? From all those years my granddaddy picked it?"

"Don't be so sensitive, Howard."

"All I can tell you is the obvious," Moore said.

"What's the obvious?"

"We're talking about raw cotton. Our prisoner's been hanging around bales of the stuff somewhere."

"How do you figure that?"

"Because raw cotton is baled in burlap. Burlap is made from jute fiber."

"That wasn't obvious to me. Where does that take us?"

"I don't know," Moore replied. "I can't get any further than that."

Rosenstock completed his examination and pulled up a chair beside the bed. He studied his patient for a while, focusing on him impersonally, as if he were a mouse in a lab experiment.

"How do you feel?" he demanded.

No answer.

"Headache?"

No answer.

"Weak?"

Still no response.

"How's your memory?"

The assassin's eyes locked on Rosenstock. The mystery of his situation is getting to him, Warfield thought. He wants to talk.

"Do you remember the interrogation?" Rosenstock asked. "Last week?" He was starting to establish a critical part of the deception —that a week had passed that the assassin could not recall.

Still no response.

"Do you remember the shock therapy?"

No response.

"Do you remember the operation?"

The assassin bared his teeth. The question clearly disturbed him.

Pretending unconcern at the lack of response, Rosenstock dipped into his bag again and brought out a hypodermic syringe. He held it up to the light and squeezed the plunger forward until a drop of liquid oozed from the end of the needle.

"I'm going to have to schedule you for more electro-shock therapy," he muttered, almost as if talking to himself.

The assassin's Adam's apple bobbed in his throat as Rosenstock approached his arm with the hypodermic. "No!" he cried.

Warfield bent toward the speakers.

"Yeah, you heard it," Moore whispered. "His first word—'no.'"

Rosenstock grabbed the chain of the handcuffs to hold the prisoner's arms steady and pressed the needle against his forearm. The assassin twisted free of Rosenstock's grasp and swung his handcuffed fists around like a baseball bat. He struck the doctor on the side of the head. The syringe bounced to the floor and Rosenstock followed, toppling over in the chair and landing with an echoing bang on the hard tile.

Warfield hit the panic button again. In seconds the guards were through the door and grappling with the prisoner. They wrestled him flat on his back and sat on him. Rosenstock, his glasses hanging precariously from one ear, shook his head and hoisted himself slowly to his feet.

While the guards held the assassin down, Rosenstock attached a new needle to his hypodermic and jabbed it roughly into the man's right forearm. He removed the IV tube from his wrist and the guards then wrapped him in a straightjacket. It took the three of them to do the job.

Rosenstock stumbled into the control room and sat on the bed, next to Nan. He rubbed his neck slowly.

"You all right?" Warfield asked.

"Hell yes!" he replied, angrily. "Next time I really will operate on the son-of-a-bitch. With a rusty hatchet!"

Nan wet a washcloth and held it to Rosenstock's cheek.

"He's stronger than I thought," Warfield said, suddenly depressed.

"The ketamine's unpredictable stuff," Rosenstock admitted. "It's hard to calculate the effect—especially without a medical history of the damned patient."

"You think it's the drug that's making him violent?"

"Seems likely. I've given him a tranquilizer to bring him down."
Warfield slapped the arm of his chair in exasperation. "We were counting on the stuff to soften him up, not piss him off!"

"I'll increase the dosage," Rosenstock replied.

"How do you know that won't make him even more violent?"

Rosenstock adjusted his eyeglasses thoughtfully. "I don't," he admitted.

"It's unfair!" Harold Wicks complained. "Damned unfair!"

His wife nodded sympathetically, and sipped her cup of herb tea.

"I've been to every damned TV station, newspaper, everywhere! They all had the same question—how can I prove my photograph isn't a fake? It's maddening!"

"They probably get a lot of phony tips and evidence on things like this, dear," she said. "Why don't you just take it to the police?"

Harold Wicks stared at her, incredulous. After thirty-five years of marriage, her naiveté still amazed him.

"Because they'd just confiscate it," he muttered.

"But if it's important, they'd know, wouldn't they?"

"They wouldn't know a damned thing. But that's not the point. The police wouldn't *pay* me anything. They'd just take the photograph and that would be the end of it."

Helen rested the cup carefully in the saucer. "But dear," she persisted. "You just told me no one wants to buy it. Why not give it to the police? They might need it as evidence."

Harold Wicks pounded the table in anger. "No, by God! I'll burn it before I'll give it away! It's damned unfair!"

15

AT SIX THAT EVENING WARfield decided that the time had come.

He looked through the one-way glass. The assassin lay flat on his back in the bed, eyes closed, hands still bound around his waist by the straightjacket. They had abandoned the IV tube and let him eat a small dinner earlier.

"Remove his straightjacket," he told Emerson, standing by the control room doorway. "And no handcuffs, either."

Emerson went off toward the assassin's ward, Frady and Trippet trailing behind him.

"You ought to keep him tied up," Rosenstock said. "He's scared, but he's violent."

"I thought you sedated him."

Rosenstock shrugged. "I wouldn't count on it to keep him still."

"I'll risk a feeble punch or two," Warfield replied. "The main thing now is to alter the atmosphere. We've driven him to the edge, now we have to entice him back."

"You're the matador," Rosenstock said.

Warfield smiled grimly at the doctor's metaphor. He watched through the glass as the guards removed the straightjacket from the assassin. He seemed limp, disinterested.

Warfield picked up a loose-leaf notebook he had prepared, and stood up, trying to beat down the sudden twinges of stage fright. The others had done their jobs. They had terrorized the terrorist, exactly as planned. Now he would offer him salvation.

Moore and Rosenstock wished him good luck. Nan helped him into his white doctor's jacket and surprised him with a light kiss on the cheek.

In the assassin's ward, the fading winter daylight filtered through the steel mesh covering the windows, and cast a watery gray pattern across the floor, heightening the room's sterility. The assassin was sitting up, staring vacantly into space. His eyes were glassy, his demeanor listless. The hospital gown hung loosely from his shoulders.

Warfield approached the side of the bed. He had agonized at length on how to begin the session. The terrible time pressure finally convinced him that he must gamble boldly from the start.

"Good afternoon, Raoul."

The assassin turned his face toward him slowly. His drowsy lids blinked in slow motion as he brought his eyes to focus on him. Warfield saw him nod, and felt a flood of relief. Raoul was his name! thank God!

"I'm Doctor Warfield," he continued, "How are you feeling?"

The assassin regarded him blankly. He appeared almost in a

116 . . .

trance, but the trickles of sweat on his shaven head, and the bunching of the muscles around his neck bespoke tremendous stress.

Warfield sat by the bed and balanced the notebook on his knees. The notebook served both a practical function and a psychological one. The front pages contained Rosenstock's forensic report. These were followed by pages of Warfield's own notes—mostly subject groupings of possible lines of questioning he might pursue, depending on how the session developed. The rest of the notebook was bulked out with a couple hundred pages of irrelevant type-script Moore had obtained for him from the base records library.

He turned its pages, pretending to refresh his memory. He let time pass—a minute, two minutes, three. He wanted his presence to contrast sharply with everything that had preceded it. When he had stretched out the silence as long as he dared, he closed the notebook and looked up at his patient.

"You probably don't feel very good, is that right?"

The assassin stared at him, holding himself rigid, as if movement might cause pain.

"That's perfectly normal," Warfield continued, "after this sort of operation. Anesthesia, weakness, dizziness, disorientation—all those are natural reactions and no cause for alarm. After a few days those unpleasant sensations will subside and you'll feel much better."

Warfield concentrated on the assassin's eyes. Did he understand what he was telling him? He fought back the dreadful suspicion that the man might not understand English.

"It's all perfectly normal," he continued, "for you to have a serious memory lapse after this kind of procedure. Sometimes the lapse is only temporary, sometimes it remains permanent. Fortunately, the worst loss of memory usually involves only the events of the previous five or six days. So as you can see, that's nothing to be alarmed about. Events further back in the past may also be blurred or unclear, but they will almost certainly improve with time. . . ."

Warfield thought the assassin had nodded yes. Perhaps not. It was difficult to tell, because his head kept drooping to his chest.

"Let me explain the operation we performed," Warfield said. "It's a new technique, and still in the experimental stage. Two small holes were drilled in your skull and thin electrodes inserted in each hole. One electrode was pushed into an area of your brain called the septum, located in the limbic system. The other electrode was installed within the amygdala. Simply put, electrical stimulation of the septum causes pleasurable sensations, stimulation of the amygdala causes unpleasant ones."

The assassin blinked rapidly.

"The reason for the procedure, of course," he went on, "was your refusal to cooperate with our interrogators. You had committed the most serious crime, and it was imperative that we find out who was behind it immediately."

Warfield let the words sink in, then expanded on them: "For a week you were kept in a special hospital cell, with the electrodes implanted in your skull, and interrogated around the clock. When you refused to answer questions, we stimulated the amygdala. When you cooperated, we rewarded you by stimulating the septum."

As far as Warfield could judge, the assassin seemed to believe him. And why shouldn't he? The procedure worked exactly as he described it.

"It took a few days," he continued, "but gradually you began to talk, to tell us what we needed to know."

The assassin sucked in his breath.

"Finally, of course, you confessed to everything."

The assassin glanced around the ward, as if some unseen menace might be lurking there.

"There is nothing to be ashamed of," Warfield said. "It's impossible to resist this sort of treatment."

Warfield stopped and opened his notebook. He mustn't rush, he told himself. Let the assassin digest it all. Let it fester in his mind. And give him plenty of chance to speak.

"There is sometimes minor brain damage," Warfield went on. "Usually to the memory, but sometimes to other areas, like motor functions or speech. Sometimes it's necessary to use drugs or electro-shock therapy to help restore proper brain function."

The assassin stared at him. There was something unnerving in his gaze. An accusation and a threat.

"So far the question of further treatment remains unsettled. Doctor Rosenstock favors electro-shock. I'd like to see a milder program of drug rehabilitation first. What we decide really depends on you. . . ."

118 . . .

Warfield looked at the man's hands. They were clasped together in his lap, the knuckles white with tension.

"What I want you to do today, Raoul," he continued, "is help us determine the extent of your memory loss. That way we can measure progress in the days ahead. . . ."

Warfield paused. The moment would come, not long from now, when he had no more to say. He tapped the loose-leaf binder in his lap, to call it to the assassin's attention.

"Now that we have your confession, right here, you have nothing more to fear. The electrodes won't be used on you again. The holes in your skull will heal with only the smallest scars remaining. I promise you that you'll be treated with dignity and respect from now on. . . . It will be my job to guide you through these difficult days of recovery, to help you restore your memory—as much as possible, at least. . . ."

He let the idea of incomplete memory hang in the air, but the assassin no longer seemed interested. He had taken to staring at the far wall again.

"If you cooperate with me today, then tomorrow, or perhaps the day after, I'll bring you a television set, so you can catch up with what's been happening in the outside world. And when you feel better, you'll be allowed to go outside for exercise. We have a beautiful place here, and the staff is friendly. You'll be much better off here than in prison. . . ."

Absolutely no response. The man possessed incredible self-control. Yet Warfield sensed an enormous struggle within the prisoner's drugged brain. If he could just break away those last mental barricades still protecting him, punch a hole through those last inner defenses, then the truth would come tumbling out.

He leaned forward, put his hand on the edge of the bed, and looked the assassin directly in the eye, a conspiratorial smile on his lips.

"Between you and me, Raoul," he whispered, "you stood up to the electrodes extremely well. I was amazed. It took two entire days of almost constant stimulation of the amygdala before you began to crack. It must have been horrible. You have nothing to be ashamed of, I can tell you that. Most men would have confessed far sooner. . . ."

Warfield leaned back in his chair, letting his prisoner absorb these additional pieces of the imaginary past. He glanced surreptitiously at his wristwatch. Only fifteen minutes had passed. Christ, it seemed like an hour! Keep calm, he told himself. Plenty of time. Don't rush. Convey tranquility.

"So, Raoul," he said, working to keep the strain out of his voice, "let's start by you just telling me how you feel."

Warfield waited, but no reply was forthcoming. He had blundered, pushed a question too soon. But he was running out of monologue.

He thought of his audience on the other side of the one-way glass—Rosenstock, Moore, and Nan Robertson—waiting for some sign of a breakthrough.

Suddenly he saw the whole thing falling apart in front of him. All the effort, planning, and ingenuity going down the drain. It had all been a crazy idea to begin with, anyway; a desperate scheme that he had convinced himself would work, because it was the only thing he could think of that *might* work. Now he stared into that familiar chasm of defeat, and saw nothing to cling to that might prevent his fall.

He had been arrogant to think he could succeed with such a risky, hastily conceived and executed plan. The human being in the bed beside him might not talk for days. He had survived the psychodrama Warfield had thrown at him, and if he held out only a few hours longer, he would begin to see that he had weathered the worst they could throw at him. Beyond this lay only the plodding routine of interrogation, the weeks-long browbeating and wearing down that was the stock-in-trade of counterintelligence methods.

Beyond this was failure. Defeat.

Warfield felt the anger coming back that had seized him when Shanklin had first come to yank him back into everything he had learned to hate.

Maybe he would torture the prisoner, he thought. Why not? What did he have to lose? The CIA expected it. The assassin deserved it. He could imagine that he might even enjoy squeezing this recalcitrant bastard. The ends would justify the means, as they always did. Trade a little integrity for a little success. He needed the success more.

He looked at the open pages of the notebook, then at the assassin. His stubble of beard, his sluggish, clouded appearance, reminded Warfield of a skid row bum, strung out on dope and alcohol. Was there any point in continuing? The whole exercise suddenly struck him as a transparent sham, a desperate effort, doomed from the start. He fought down the despair rising in his throat. He must not give up, he told himself. Not yet.

He reached into the side pocket of his tunic and brought out the assassin's gold Cartier wristwatch. The man's eyes fixed on it in instant recognition. Warfield hefted it a few times, teasingly, then tossed it into his lap. The assassin jumped in surprise, then lifted the time piece gingerly in both hands and turned it over.

"It's a beautiful watch," Warfield said. "You can have it back if you tell me what time it says."

The assassin peered at him suspiciously, then looked back down at his watch.

"Can you read the time on it?"

The assassin nodded.

Warfield felt the blood rising in his face. Now was the moment. The subtle momentum of this act of compromise, like the tiniest spark in a pinch of tinder, might be fanned and strengthened.

"Read it back to me, then."

The next few seconds stretched out like years. The assassin studied the face of the watch, squinting his eyes in concentration. Warfield dug his fingernails into his palms. He heard his pulse pounding in his ears. *Talk, damn you, talk!*

"Six-forty-two."

Warfield swallowed. He felt like a drowning man, plucked at the last possible moment from the undertow. Euphoria washed over him. It was all he could do to keep from grinning triumphantly at his invisible colleagues on the other side of the mirror. He had done it! He had made him talk!

"Okay, you win back the watch," he said, keeping the elation out of his voice. His mind churned furiously. He must follow up on this, before the momentum was lost.

"Let's test your motor reflexes," he said. He tore a page from the back of his loose-leaf binder, inserted it into his clipboard, and handed it across to the assassin, along with his pencil. "Write the time down on the paper."

The assassin gazed down at the clipboard, picked up the pencil, fumbled with it; then, with painstaking care, printed out the numbers on the page.

"Okay," Warfield said. "Now copy out the date."

The assassin squinted at the small calendar area on the dial and then printed out the date below the time.

"Now sign your name."

The assassin looked at him. Warfield met his gaze, hoping his face betrayed no guile. The assassin bent to the clipboard and began an awkward scrawl, stopped, then began again. Under the scrawl, he slowly printed out a series of block letters. Warfield's pulse raced. He waited until the prisoner had finished, then gently lifted the board from his lap, trying to hide his excitement.

He placed the clipboard on his own lap and let his eyes focus on the letters that marched across the middle of the paper: RAOUL FERNANDO MARTINEZ

Warfield, restraining the impulse to jump up and cheer, nodded slowly. "That's good, Raoul. Very good."

He sensed that the assassin was pleased. Small triumphs—for both of them. "Let's test your memory a little, okay?"

Martinez nodded.

"What did you have for dinner this evening?"

"Arroz con pollo."

"Say it in English."

"Chicken and rice."

"Good."

Warfield paused a beat, then made a breathtaking *segué:* "Can you remember your mother's name?"

The answer came immediately: "Carmen."

"Your father?"

"Franco."

"What was the name of the town you were born in?"

"Santa Clara."

"In Cuba?"

"Yes."

"You remember your birthdate?"

"July ten, nineteen-fifty."

"That's good. When did you leave Santa Clara? Do you remember?"

"Nineteen sixty-two."

"Where did you go?"

"To Miami."

"Florida?"

"Yes."

"Tell me about your father."

The assassin hesitated before answering. Warfield saw his fists clench.

"He was killed by Castro."

"I'm sorry."

"He was *abogado*. A lawyer. He worked for the old government. For Batista."

Warfield nodded, his excitement soaring. The dam was breached! He must now encourage the flow, enlarge it, channel it in the right direction.

The trickle rapidly became a flood. For five hours Raoul Fernando Martinez told his life's story: his days as a child in a rich suburb of Santa Clara. The coming of Castro and the end of the good times for his family. The torture and execution of his father at El Moro prison. His mother's mental breakdown. His struggles as a boy of twelve to support himself and his three younger sisters working in an agricultural cooperative. The isolation from his friends at school. The escape to the United States, arranged through family connections in Florida.

The tapes turned on their spools in the control room and captured it all—the key dates in the assassin's life, his family names, addresses, places he had worked, his early friends in Florida. There were enough leads to keep the FBI busy for months.

Warfield was eager to steer him into more sensitive areas, but noticing that the Cartier watch, now on the assassin's wrist, read midnight, he decided to end the session for the day. He was exhausted, and he suspected Martinez was more so. He wished him a good night's sleep. They would continue in the morning.

He left Martinez—how thrilling it was just to have a name to pin on the man!—and hurried to the control room.

They cheered him when he walked in. Moore pounded him on the back in glee. Rosenstock shook his hand energetically. Nan Robertson embraced him and kissed him hard on the cheek.

"Wonderful!" she cried.

"Some show, Charlie!" Rosenstock agreed.

"I thought I'd go crazy waiting to find out what he'd written on that paper!" Moore exclaimed. "You were unbelievable! Just sitting there, holding the guy's signature in your hand!"

Warfield flopped down on the bed, a grin splitting his face. His

. . . 123

euphoria was premature, he knew, but God, how good it felt, he thought. He had forgotten how good it felt.

"Don't celebrate too soon, gang," he warned. "We don't have a confession from him yet."

"It's all downhill from here," Rosenstock said. "Once they start talking, they don't stop."

"That watch bit was brilliant," Moore said. "But I hope you remembered to advance the date on its calendar."

Warfield laughed. "That's what originally gave me the idea to give it back to him. One more ploy to persuade him a week had passed."

Moore placed a hand over his heart and sucked in his breath in an exaggerated show of relief. "Praise the Lord," he murmured.

Warfield lay back against the pillow and closed his eyes. The sounds of the others' voices began to recede. Fatigue overtook him and within seconds he was asleep. The others tiptoed from the room.

Nan lingered behind. For nearly a minute she stood, watching the rhythmic rise and fall of Warfield's chest. When she was satisfied that he was sound asleep, she withdrew a pin and a glass slide from the pocket of her uniform. Gently she grasped the forefinger of his right hand and pricked it with the pin. A drop of blood oozed up; she squeezed it onto the glass slide, and sealed it with a small round piece of plastic.

Warfield mumbled faintly and moved his hand. Nan returned the pin and slide to her pocket and slipped from the room.

Kemal pulled the last rack of clean glasses from the steaming washer and stacked it on top of the other racks in the corner. He wiped his face with a dish towel and looked around the kitchen. Midnight and the place was empty. The other dishwasher had left an hour ago. Through the glass partition across the room he could see one of the cooks still in the office, talking on the telephone.

He sat on a milk crate and lit a cigarette. He needed to put together a plan, and fast. Another day with these dishes and glasses and he would self-destruct. He saw the cook emerge from the office and head in his direction. He was short and fat and waddled as he walked.

"What's *your* name?" he demanded, with an obvious homosexual inflection.

"Andropoulous."

"Don't you have a first name?"

"Nikos."

"You're new."

"Yes."

The cook stood close to him. Kemal smelled cologne and perspiration. The cook rubbed his forehead. "Some cunt at the infirmary," he muttered.

"What?"

"She called in a dinner order for that hush-hush patient of theirs. I thought they were *torturing* him. Some torture! The bitch wanted *arroz con pollo!* Of course, sweetheart, I told her. Would he like it served in his room or at *pool*side? In his room, she says. Well, the commandant says give them whatever their little hearts desire. So she got her *arroz con pollo.* Room service!"

The cook placed a cigarette between his lips and motioned for Kemal to light it for him.

"Now the boy who takes the food to the infirmary calls in sick," the cook complained. "The lazy little bastard! I'll fuck his ass for him!"

Kemal looked up at the cook speculatively. "Who's taking the food over tomorrow."

The cook shrugged.

Kemal's lips parted in a thin smile. "I'll do it," he said.

"You will?"

"Sure."

"Aren't you a sweetheart," the cook replied.

16

THE NEXT MORNING WAR-field brought the assassin his breakfast and sat beside him while he ate it.

Many questions waited to be asked: What were the names of the other members of the hit squad? Who was the one who got away?

Where is he now? What kind of vehicle had they used in the attack? How and where had they trained? What was their goal? Did they plan another attempt on the president's life? Who was behind them?

Warfield knew that he needed to be extremely careful. He had convinced Martinez that he already had his confession, and was now only helping him regain his memory.

"What did you do on the cooperative?" Warfield asked, expanding on familiar ground between them. "You said you worked there to support yourself and your sisters."

"The Castro government sent us there. I cut sugar cane."

"Did you pick cotton?"

"Cotton? No. There is no cotton in Cuba."

"But you worked with cotton somewhere, didn't you?"

Martinez looked puzzled. "No."

Warfield shrugged. "I thought you had."

So much for Rosenstock's fiber evidence, he thought. He changed the subject, edging closer to the target area.

"What do you last remember, before the operation?"

The assassin looked at his knees, bent up in a tent under the blanket.

"Why did you operate on me!" he demanded, suddenly angry.

"You wouldn't talk," Warfield said. "We needed an immediate confession."

"I don't remember!"

"You will, eventually," Warfield lied. "That's why I'm trying to help you. What *do* you remember?"

The assassin just shook his head.

"Do you remember the torture?"

"No."

"Do you remember the confession?"

"No."

"What's the last thing you remember, then? Before waking up in here?"

Martinez concentrated on the question, staring directly at the one-way mirror across the room. His eyes watered and he looked to be in considerable pain. Was Rosenstock overdosing him? Warfield wondered. Maybe that exotic chemical cocktail of his was a bad mix.

"I remember you—and the other doctor. He examined me. Cut off my hair."

Warfield nodded. "Then what?"

"He gave me a shot. It put me out. Then I wake up here."

"That was eight days ago," Warfield lied. "They interrogated you for seven days after that."

"Who did it?"

"The same men. Carson and Robinson."

The assassin ran his fingers over his short stubble of beard, his eyes narrowing in disbelief. Warfield felt a momentary surge of panic, but recovered beautifully. "We've shaved you every third day since the operation," he said.

"I don't remember." Tears welled up in the assassin's eyes.

"It'll take time," Warfield assured him. "What about the operation? Do you remember any of that?"

"No."

"When your brain's ready to remember, it will."

Warfield sensed it was time to make his move. He steeled himself mentally, determined to make it happen.

"Let's work backward," he said, sneaking up to the transition as casually as he could. "You remember when they brought you here —in the helicopter?"

The assassin nodded.

"They brought you directly from the Suitland Parkway. . . ."

Martinez nodded again.

"Do you recall the ambush itself?"

The assassin looked at him for a few seconds before replying. Warfield met his gaze, the picture of bland innocence.

"Of course," he replied.

"Can you describe it for me?"

Martinez let out a sigh. "Enrico and I are on the bridge, waiting for the cars to come. I'm nervous about the timing. We have to push the chain off at just the right second. The cars come. We hit it just right. Then Enrico has trouble with the rocket gun. I scream at him. Hurry up! I see the men already coming out of the cars with their guns. Enrico hits the car, but the shell, it doesn't go through. It explodes outside. He loads again. But now they are shooting at us. I start shooting, too. Enrico fires another rocket. It hits right, but I see they are not all dead inside. One gets out, I shoot him. I scream at Enrico—fire again! But they shoot him. I see him go down. . . ."

Martinez paused. Warfield waited. *Don't stop now!*

"Then what did you do?"

"I turn to run. I look for the van. But it's gone already! I'm mad. The goddamn Turk, I think. He's gone! I run for the bushes, but they catch me. . . ."

"Wait a minute," Warfield said. "Try for more detail. You look around for the van? . . ."

"The ambulance! The Turk is supposed to wait. But the bastard runs out! He sees Enrico go down and he runs out."

"Can you see the Turk?"

"I see the back of the van. The Turk is driving like hell to get out of there. . . ."

"Describe him," Warfield said.

"I can't."

"Try."

To Warfield's astonishment, Martinez began to cry. Tears spilled in a flood, trickling through the stubble on his cheeks. Heavy sobs racked his chest. Warfield stared at the notebook and waited for the attack to subside. Martinez lay back on the pillows and closed his eyes. When Warfield looked up, he was rocking his head back and forth like an autistic child.

"You remember where you first met the Turk?" Warfield asked him.

Martinez stopped the rocking motion.

"Describe the place."

"Outside the dark room," Martinez whispered.

"The dark room?"

"At the warehouse. We got our orders there."

"Why was the room dark?" Warfield asked. He knew he had phrased the question in a risky fashion, slipping from supposedly guiding the assassin in the recovery of his memory into direct interrogation. But Martinez offered so little resistance, he couldn't help pushing him. The payoff lay so tantalizingly close.

The door burst open.

Warfield spun around in his chair to see one of the guards, Frady, beckoning to him urgently. Warfield gestured emphatically for the man to close the door and go away, but he persisted.

Warfield went to the door, furious at the interruption. "What the hell's the matter?" he demanded.

Then he saw Shanklin, standing at the far end of the corridor. He stepped out of the ward and let Frady lock the door behind him.

Shanklin ambled forward, an ominous grin stretched across his pebbly features. "Sorry to disturb you, ol' buddy."

Warfield clutched Shanklin's arm and pushed him back down the corridor, away from the assassin's ward. Rosenstock, Moore, and Nan Robertson clustered at the open doorway of the control room.

"What the hell is this all about? You interrupted me right in the middle . . ."

"Hold on," Shanklin growled. "The boss wants to see you. Now. A chopper's waiting for you on the pad."

"What for?"

"That's for him to explain, ol' buddy, not me."

Warfield could barely restrain the rage that boiled up in his chest. "Can't the son-of-a-bitch wait until I finish what he sent me down here for?"

Shanklin laughed, a boozy rumble that resonated from deep inside his barrel-shaped torso. "I'm just relaying the message. A jeep's outside for you. They'll take you to the pad."

Shanklin swiveled on his heels and lumbered off down the corridor. Warfield strode into the control room, smashing his fist into his palm. He was tempted simply to ignore Friedrich's order. But what was the use in that? He threw off his white doctor's tunic and pulled on his jacket.

The others remained subdued, sharing his distress.

"Don't worry," Rosenstock said. "We'll keep him on hold till you get back."

"It's time for a lunch break, anyway," Nan said.

Warfield slipped on his overcoat. "I'll get back as soon as possible. For God's sake, don't let anything happen to him. We're almost home."

"We'll watch him," Moore promised. "Don't worry."

Warfield raced out the door of the infirmary and collided with someone lugging a stack of covered lunch trays. He hit the man hard enough to knock him off balance and send the stack of trays flying to the ground.

"I'm sorry!" Warfield said, bending to help him pick up the trays. "At least nothing spilled."

For a fraction of a second their eyes locked. Then Kemal snatched the trays abruptly from Warfield's hand and took them inside.

"It's time, Mr. President."

It was Daniels' personal secretary, Frances Ware, standing by the office door. Daniels picked up a single sheet of paper from the desk, folded it once, and slipped it in his jacket pocket.

"How do I look?" he asked, stepping out from behind his desk.

Frances appraised him rapidly. "Tie and shirt okay. Makeup okay. But change your expression. You look harassed."

"Hell, Frances, I *feel* harassed!"

As he walked past the Fish Room and the Cabinet Room, flanked by an escort of aides and Secret Service agents, like a prize fighter on his way to the ring, Daniels cast his mind back over the morning. He had placed over a hundred phone calls. Most were to congressmen, telling them in advance what he was about to announce publicly, and trying to persuade them to drop their plans for the select subcommittee hearings on the parkway ambush.

The rest of his calls went to those involved in the investigation itself. Never in his political career had he been so blunt and threatening. The words he used varied from agency to agency, from individual to individual, but the gist of his message was the same. He wanted results or resignations. And he wanted them immediately.

At the door to the Pool Room, the small auditorium built over FDR's west wing swimming pool by Nixon as a briefing room for the press, he paused behind the outstretched arm of Dan McCormick. McCormick watched the far end of the room, waiting for a technician's signal that the networks were on live pickup.

"Okay," he whispered, dropping his arm to let the president past.

Daniels moved behind the podium and glanced at the faces. Every seat and all the back and side wall space was filled with reporters. Their expressions were strained and expectant, as if he were a judge about to pass sentence on them.

He focused his attention on the television camera at the back, the eye through which the country was now watching him.

"I'm going to make a few brief statements," he said. "There will be another press conference two days from now, during which I will answer any questions."

The reporters had been told in advance that Daniels wasn't taking questions today, but some groaned in protest anyway.

"First, I want to announce that we have in custody a suspect in the Suitland Parkway ambush. For reasons of national security, we have not revealed this until now. That is all the information I can provide today.

"Second, in recognition of the serious loss suffered by the Soviet people, I am inviting a representative of their government to participate in our investigation."

Daniels paused and inhaled slowly. The auditorium seemed frozen in suspended animation. One more bombshell to go, he told himself.

"And third, I want to announce that the widow of the slain Russian leader, Mrs. Katya Kamenev, has asked for and has been granted asylum in this country. She will have her own announcement to make on this matter in a short time. Thank you."

Daniels stepped briskly from the platform and out of the room, his bodyguards closing ranks swiftly behind him.

The press broke from its trance and stampeded toward the exits as if the place were on fire.

17

FRIEDRICH WAS WAITING FOR Warfield as he stepped off the elevator on the seventh floor. It was so unusual to see the DCI outside his office that for a moment Warfield thought it must be someone else. The director appeared haggard and distraught. The bags under his eyes had swollen to twice their usual bulging size, and his normally well-pressed clothes looked as if he had slept in them.

Friedrich greeted him with an anxious question: "Are you getting anywhere?"

Warfield's impulse was to complain about being pulled away at so crucial a moment, but he stifled it. "Yes, I am."

"Give me the gist."

"His name's Raoul Fernando Martinez. He's Cuban. From Florida. Anti-Castro. The dead one's name was Enrico. The one who got away is called the Turk. The getaway vehicle was an ambulance."

"That's it?"

"So far. A few more hours and I'll have the whole story."

Friedrich steered Warfield down the corridor toward his suite of offices at the far end. In the outer vestibule a large group of people were standing around idly, like a crowd at an auto accident. He noticed a smattering of Secret Service lapel pins among them.

"Listen," Friedrich said, his voice whispering sharply near his ear. "I had to call you back here because there are new developments. Complications. You won't like them any more than I do, but just go along with them. Understand?"

Warfield spread his hands, mystified. "Do I have a choice?"

Friedrich didn't answer. A secretary opened the door to his office and he pushed Warfield inside ahead of him.

From a long suede sofa at the back of the office three men stood up. Warfield had never met them before, but he recognized two of them.

"Gentlemen," Friedrich said, shifting into a forced heartiness. "This is Charles Warfield."

The first hand he shook belonged to William Wilbert, the president's chief of staff. Wilbert said nothing. His mood was grim.

The second hand was Vice-President Chester Catlin's. Catlin offered a phony smile. His palm felt cold and moist—under stress.

"The Vice-President and Mr. Wilbert are here as President Daniels' personal representatives," Friedrich explained, casting Warfield a severe look. "They'll report back to him on this meeting."

It was Wilbert who would be doing the reporting, Warfield supposed. The vice-president's role was usually ornamental. A squat, smooth-faced man in his early fifties, Catlin had been assigned by President Daniels as a sort of informal watchdog over the intelligence community. The job was meaningless, but Catlin took it very seriously.

The third man's hand was warm and dry, and it squeezed Warfield's fingers with self-confident strength.

"This is Dmitri Semenenko," Friedrich said, with a strained clearing of the throat. "From the—uh—Soviet Ministry of Foreign Affairs."

There was an awkward pause. Warfield felt the blood draining from his head. He glanced at the others. Friedrich refused to meet his eyes. Wilbert stared at him with the same grim expression. Catlin looked complacent. The information Warfield's brain had just received was snapping around inside it like a lightning bolt.

Dmitri Semenenko was not from the Ministry of Foreign Affairs. He was from the Committee for State Security. The KGB. Head of the First Chief Directorate, responsible for the six thousand or more operatives working outside the Soviet Union, he was second only to KGB Chief Mikhail Bulgakov himself. Friedrich might more plausibly have introduced Count Dracula. Had the man defected? Warfield wondered. Or was this some bizarre joke? Some supreme new idiocy in Washington's handling of its foreign affairs?

"What a pleasant surprise," Warfield murmured.

Semenenko caught his sarcasm and chuckled good-naturedly. "The pleasure is mine, Mr. Warfield!"

Warfield studied him with rude curiosity. He saw a tall, dignified figure, with wide cheekbones, shallow eye sockets, and a high forehead. More Mongol in appearance than Slav, his face was tanned, and his silver hair expensively cut and layered, just covering the tops of his large ears. He wore a dark pinstripe suit, which draped his elongated frame with a perfection achieved by only the most meticulous of tailors. He laughed easily, and spoke English with only a trace of accent.

During Warfield's years with the CIA, he had been the invisible man in the KGB hierarchy. And during Kamenev's long regime, he had dropped even further into the shadows. In its many attempts to construct a biography of him, the CIA had managed to acquire little more than a handful of vague descriptions and a page or two of conflicting information, most of it from defectors. There were rumors that he had a fondness for sex with children.

His sudden materialization in Director Friedrich's office was an extraordinary event, Warfield realized. And judging from the mood of the others in the room, he knew he wasn't going to like the reason why.

Friedrich retreated behind his desk, the others returned to the sofa. Warfield chose the neutral territory of a captain's chair located in a corner midway between Friedrich and his guests.

"Mr. Semenenko," Vice-President Catlin began, his Tennessee accent comic in its solemnity, "is here on an important mission. His stay is highly confidential."

Semenenko flashed an ingratiating smile, revealing even rows of teeth. "I think Mr. Warfield can guess why I'm here," he said.

"I can't guess anything," Warfield replied. "Enlighten me."

Friedrich gestured impatiently. "President Daniels has decided to share our information concerning the assassination of Premier Kamenev on the Suitland Parkway jointly with the Soviet government—and to ask its assistance in solving this crime. Mr. . . ."

"The president," Catlin interrupted, pompously, "is eager to demonstrate to the Soviet government that we have nothing to hide; that we are as eager as they are to get to the bottom of this dreadful incident. . . ."

Friedrich regained the initiative: "Mr. Semenenko has already been briefed here. He's fully up to date on the status of the investigation." Friedrich paused, and this time the vice-president didn't interrupt. "So it is the president's wish that Mr. Semenenko be permitted to monitor our interrogation of the captured assassin."

Warfield felt light-headed. Had everyone lost their senses? He looked at Wilbert for confirmation. "You mean you're going to let him into the farm?"

Wilbert, hunched in a private cloud of depression at the end of the sofa, nodded. "That's about the size of it, sport."

"I'm sure there's nothing at Camp Peary that Mr. Semenenko is not already quite familiar with," Catlin intoned.

Warfield hid his anger behind sarcasm. "Should I let him take notes? Bring along his Sony recorder and Polaroid?"

"You're to cooperate with him fully," Friedrich declared.

Semenenko, sensing the general embarrassment, rose from the sofa. Warfield felt the energy in the room flow toward him.

"Gentlemen," he said. "I appreciate your courtesy and cooperation. This is a difficult matter, and I understand Mr. Warfield's feelings. I intend to do no more than place myself at his disposal.

We'll work matters out between us, I'm certain. I have the highest regard for his professionalism and competence."

Warfield grinned ironically at Semenenko's praise.

"It speaks well of both our countries," Catlin interjected fatuously, "that we are able to cooperate in this unprecedentedly civilized fashion. . . ."

Friedrich waved at Catlin, as if to tell him to shut up, then rose to signal that the meeting was over.

They filed from the office, to be swallowed instantly in a confused babble of voices, as secretaries, aides, and bodyguards surrounded them. Warfield found himself walking down the seventh-floor corridor, with General Dmitri Semenenko at his side and two very burly KGB guards behind him.

In the elevator Semenenko made a surprising suggestion. "I'm excited to be in Washington, you know. I've heard so much about your capital. Before we rush off to the 'farm,' as you call it, why don't you join me for dinner?"

Warfield's mouth, falling open regularly the past hour, did so again. "Dinner?"

"Yes. Exactly," the Russian replied, showing his teeth. "There's a small restaurant near the White House they told me about at the embassy. Sans Souci. It's five o'clock now, so we can have an early meal, enjoy a profitable discussion, and be at the farm by the middle of the evening."

As their footsteps tapped over the huge CIA seal in the front lobby floor, Warfield fumbled for some plausible reason to object, but the general's authoritative manner intimidated him momentarily. Through the glass of the revolving doors he could see a Russian embassy limousine, parked and waiting for them at the curb.

"I insist," Semenenko said. "I have already made the reservation."

Warfield stared alternately into a glass of Perrier water and across at his dinner companion, his mind tormented by the thought of the assassin, Martinez, left hanging on the verge of major revelations. He watched Semenenko lift a forkfull of *Coquilles St. Jacques* to his mouth. He handled his fork like an American, holding the tines concave side up. Instinct and training, Warfield thought. He adapts to a new environment instantly.

He felt Semenenko's eyes measuring him. The Russian had been chatting steadily for nearly an hour about a string of inconsequential subjects—trivia about Washington, Americans, the price of things, places to shop, the best restaurants—like a tourist on a holiday. Warfield supposed Semenenko was testing him, purposely prolonging his discomfort.

"You do not like your food?" Semenenko asked.

Warfield glanced down at his partly consumed *Veau Normande*.

"Not much appetite, I'm afraid."

"What a shame. You are spoiled, having these wonderful restaurants. For me, this is a rare treat."

"You could defect," Warfield replied. "Like Kamenev's widow."

The KGB general raised his eyebrows.

". . . And tell them I persuaded you," Warfield added. "I could use the credit."

Semenenko allowed a slow grin to crease his face. "Of course. A small joke. You Americans have a sense of humor very much like our own."

"How's that?"

"We enjoy irony, too. Russians love to say one thing when they mean the opposite."

"In Russia that's no doubt necessary," Warfield said. "In this country we can say what we mean."

Semenenko looked at him sharply. "You have something you wish to say?"

"Yes. I want it clear to you that no matter what the director or anybody else has promised you, you're not going to participate in my interrogation."

Semenenko laughed. His teeth seemed enormous, suddenly, in the dimly lit restaurant. "My dear fellow, I have no intention of interfering with your work. I'm here to observe, that's all. Do you object to that, too?"

"I'll force myself to live with it. But this is my show. I'll share whatever information I uncover, because I have no choice, but otherwise I don't need your help."

The KGB general didn't answer, or even register the slightest trace of annoyance. Instead, he glanced about the rapidly filling room. "This is a popular restuarant with the Washington elite, I understand," he said.

Warfield shrugged.

The Russian pointed a discreet finger at one of the tables on the raised level at the back of the restaurant. "There's Senator Iselin from South Carolina. The man with him is a procurement officer for the Navy."

Warfield looked over. He saw two men in business suits, talking quietly.

"One of Iselin's companies—Datatron, in Charleston—has a lucrative contract with the Navy. Cost overruns may get Iselin in serious trouble. He's up for reelection, and he's trying to head off a scandal before his opponents hear of it."

Warfield followed Semenenko's gaze to the next table.

"There's a reporter from the *Washington Post*," Semenenko said. "Sara Findlay, and a network correspondent, Robert Hart of ABC. They've been having an affair. She's pressuring him to divorce his wife."

The KGB general continued around the restaurant, identifying other diners, revealing surprising secrets about them.

"That's a clever parlor trick," Warfield admitted.

Semenenko smiled his cannibal's smile. He motioned toward the front of the restaurant. "You see the table to the left of the door?"

Warfield nodded.

"The man there is Frank Latham. The woman I don't know."

Warfield saw someone in his late thirties, with rimless spectacles. The woman was much younger, early twenties, and attractive.

"And who is Frank Latham?" Warfield asked, tiring of Semenenko's game.

"He works for the Department of the Interior. You know his wife."

"I do?"

"Yes. Nan Robertson."

Warfield looked at the man again.

"She's separated from him," Semenenko added, enjoying Warfield's surprise.

"I see."

Semenenko studied Warfield's face carefully. "She's spying on you, you know."

Warfield tried to hide the sudden shock.

"Friedrich instructed her to watch you."

Warfield stared at his Perrier glass, stifling his anger with difficulty. Of course, it made sense that Friedrich would do that, considering what was at stake. Hell, he'd have done the same thing. But he should have anticipated it. The rust was showing. And it was galling in the extreme to be told so by Semenenko.

The Russian laughed, enjoying Warfield's discomfort. "Let's have some coffee," he said, "to round off this magnificent meal. And a brandy. Would you join me in a brandy?"

"I don't drink," Warfield snapped.

"Of course not. How rude of me to forget."

The bastard knows he's getting to me, Warfield thought. Don't underestimate him. Be careful.

"I fear I'm boring you," Semenenko said. "Perhaps we should talk about something else."

Warfield shrugged.

"What about Egypt, for example?"

"What about it?"

Semenenko flashed his teeth. "You were in Alexandria in the early seventies."

Warfield sipped his Perrier. It was warm and flat. Semenenko leaned forward and spoke in lowered tones: "I was there too, you know. In Cairo. I was the *resident.*"

Warfield focused on the Russian's snifter of brandy. He imagined the warm sensation of it down his throat. Delicious fire.

"If that's true," he replied, "I'm surprised you didn't end up getting shipped off to the Gulag."

Semenenko laughed. "You're right! We overplayed our hand badly. But I was one of the few who saw it coming. I knew Sadat planned to turn against us. I protected myself. By the time he sent us packing, I had gotten myself transferred to Kuwait, and escaped recrimination. Better that that, I was on record predicting the whole debacle."

"You fared better than I did."

"Perhaps. But results are all that count. Egypt threw us out and brought you in. We lost our most important strategic position in the Mideast. And we were humiliated besides."

Semenenko tasted his brandy, his pale eyes measuring Warfield over the rim of the snifter. "You had a clever operation going in Alexandria. We always wondered how you managed to enlist so many of the money changers to spy for you."

"Very simple. They liked money—and they hated the Russians. They knew what you were up to—trading Egyptian pounds for black market American dollars and sending them back to Moscow. Individual greed they could sympathize with. Institutional greed offended them. They were delighted to spy on you."

Semenenko nodded sadly. "Yes, we condescended to them, took advantage of them, like a colonial power. We learned a lesson in Egypt."

The KGB general signaled the waiter for the check. "You learned a lesson there, too, I understand," he said.

Warfield stiffened in his seat.

"If I may take the liberty to reprimand you," Semenenko continued, his tone almost fatherly, "it is only because I admire your professionalism. Your downfall was the result of breaking a basic rule of our trade: you fell in love with one of your agents. You were the victim of your own indulgence."

"That simple, is it?"

"At bottom, yes. In the moral universe of espionage, ruthlessness is the cardinal virtue, vulnerability the cardinal sin. You sinned, my friend, and you paid the price for your transgression."

"Is that what they teach you in the KGB? And do you have a special course on female vivisection as well?" Warfield had raised his voice. Several heads in the restaurant turned to stare.

Semenenko spread his hands. "You see. The whole affair has made you irrational. You assume it was us. In fact it was not us at all. It was the *Mukhabarat.*"

Warfield stared at him.

"Yes," Semenenko said. "The Egyptians. Tanya was spying on them, wasn't she? She was spying on her Egyptian husband for us, and spying on both of us for you. We knew about you, and took advantage of it. We used her to feed you disinformation. But somehow the Egyptians caught her. They were embarrassed to confront us, so they decided to get rid of her."

The Russian's glib explanation jabbed at him like a taunt. He fought to swallow his rage, but felt it choking him. "You offering any proof?"

"Of course not."

Warfield felt suddenly flushed and dizzy. He excused himself and rose quickly from the table. Halfway to the men's room he changed his mind and headed for the front exit. He needed to breathe fresh air, to get away from the claustrophobic spell this man cast.

Outside a blast of winter chill slapped against him.

And blinding light. He pulled up his collar and squinted, trying to orient himself on the sidewalk. He saw several limousines parked by the curb, and a dense crowd, jostling and shouting in the glare of the lights. The mob formed a tight semicircle around the restaurant entrance, like a crowd of fans at a movie premier, waiting for a glimpse of the star. Warfield turned right, then left, then stopped and shielded his eyes from the lights, trying to find an open path through the crowd. A murmur of excitement pulsed in the air around him.

"That's him!" a voice yelled.

The crowd surged forward, closing the ring around him. He ducked to his left and tried to slip away along the edge of the building wall. A gloved hand lifted a small cassette recorder into the air in front of him. Another hand thrust a microphone against his chest. A third hand pinned his arm to the wall.

A petite blond woman materialized in front of him. Her neck strained forward intently out of a heavy fur collar. She was shouting something at him. A movement in the patch of black sky above her caught his eye. A large camera lens loomed over her head and pointed at his face. Another camera hovered off to his right. Voices in the crowd shouted at him.

"Your name's Warfield, right?" . . . "Who's the man they caught?" . . . "We hear he's confessed!" . . . "Is it a right-wing plot?" . . . "Are you the interrogator?" . . . "Why haven't you turned him over to the police?" . . . "What is the president hiding?" . . . "Who are you having dinner with?"

The small blonde, crushed against Warfield's chest by the press of bodies behind her, somehow kept her balance and her microphone in position. "You were forced out of the CIA," she cried. "Why did they hire you back? Are you secretly torturing the suspect?"

A microphone on the end of a boom swung into view near Warfield's forehead. Someone jostled the arm holding it, and the mike cracked against Warfield's skull.

"What comment do you have?" the blonde demanded.

Warfield grabbed the boom with his left hand and snatched it free, yanking out the plug on the other end of the mike cord and sending the TV soundman's tape machine crashing to the pavement.

"Don't you have anything to say?" the blonde screeched.

Warfield clutched the woman's collar firmly in his fingers and began to push her backward. "Yes, I do," he muttered, his clenched teeth inches from her mouth. "Fuck you, sister!"

Warfield broke into a run, twisting like a halfback. He pushed someone's face, stepped on a foot, knocked a recorder from someone's hand, and broke through onto open pavement. He dashed south down Seventeenth Street and crossed Pennsylvania Avenue in the middle of traffic. On the far side he paused and looked back. They were charging after him like a pack of hounds, the less-encumbered reporters out in front, the cameramen straggling behind. Leading the chase was the little blonde.

Warfield turned and ran again, down Seventeenth Street past the White House and the Ellipse. At Constitution Avenue he swung to the right and continued, at a slackened pace, along Potomac Park. The lights of the Lincoln Memorial glowed in the night sky ahead of him. When he reached the corner of Twenty-third and Constitution, he ducked into the park and flung himself down on a bench.

The pack of reporters was nowhere in sight. Beyond the wild pumping of his heart, he heard only the distant growl of Washington traffic. Around him in the park an eerie stillness reigned. He sat until he had caught his breath, then returned to the sidewalk, trying to decide what he should do.

A figure loomed out of the shadows near the edge of the park. Warfield started. The figure was barely twenty feet from him. The shape of its silhouette told him who it was: the blond reporter.

She jogged up to him. Her face came into view under the streetlight. She looked very young.

"I'm with the *Post*," she said. "Elizabeth King. You sure run fast!"

"Not fast enough, I guess."

The woman grinned with satisfaction. "I was on the track team at UCLA. I hold the woman's record in the thousand meter."

"My lucky day."

"You *are* Charles Warfield, aren't you?"

"I admire your persistence—and your running form," he replied, "but you can ask questions until you drop. I'm not going to answer them."

The blonde pulled a piece of paper from the side pocket of her fur-collared coat and unfolded it.

"Okay," she said. "Just look at this for me."

She shoved the paper against Warfield's chest. In the dim light from the streetlamp, he could see only that it was a photocopy of a photograph. King produced a penlight from her pocketbook and shone it on the paper.

"All I want to know is, is this guy one of the assassins?"

Warfield saw the three-quarter profile of a dark-haired man, sitting behind the wheel of a van. The face was curiously familiar.

"Where did you get this?" he asked.

"Some guy—amateur photographer. He's been pestering the paper all week. He claims he took this at the Suitland Parkway overpass, just before the ambush. He thinks the ambulance was their getaway vehicle."

Warfield looked at the photo again. Yes, it was an ambulance!

"But nobody believes him," he said, hiding his surprise.

The blonde sighed. "Right. Should we?"

"No. It's nothing."

"You sure?"

Warfield folded the photostat and tucked it into his inside jacket pocket. "I'll do you a favor," he said. "I'll ask my people to check it out for you."

"How can I trust you?"

Warfield smiled. "I'll call you. Tomorrow."

"Give me a number. I'll call *you*."

"Not possible, I'm afraid."

Warfield stuck his hands in his pockets and started off at a fast pace down Constitution Avenue. The blonde kept up with him.

"You won't do it," she worried.

"I will. If there's anything to tell you."

"You remember my name?"

"Sure. Elizabeth King. At the *Post.*"

"The number's 546-2430. That's my direct line."

"I'll remember."

"No you won't."

She wrote her name and number on a slip of paper and stuffed it in his pocket. She followed him for several blocks, trying to pry more information from him. Finally, she gave up and hailed a cab. Some time later Semenenko's limousine found him. It slowed down alongside and stopped. One of the bodyguards opened the back door and Warfield stepped in.

Semenenko's eyes glowed with amusement. "Your free press in action, eh?"

Warfield didn't answer.

"Now," the Russian said, suddenly very businesslike, "tell me about this interrogation of yours."

18

PRESIDENT DANIELS TAPPED his finger on a plaque over the marble mantelpiece in his bedroom. "This was removed from here once," he said. "By the Nixons, I think. Estelle found it and had it put back."

Katya Ivanova bent forward to read the plaque's inscription:

> *In this room lived John Fitzgerald Kennedy*
> *with his wife, Jacqueline, during the*
> *two years, ten months, and two days he*
> *was President of the United States,*
> *January 20, 1961 to November 22, 1963.*

"Mrs. Kennedy composed it herself," he said. "Estelle was a great admirer of hers."

Daniels lifted a silver-framed photograph from the mantel and handed it to Katya. "That's us with Alice, on her graduation from Yale. Ten years ago."

The Russian woman held the frame delicately with both hands and tipped it forward to direct the reflection on the glass away from her eyes. The photograph showed his daughter, a tall, coltish girl with long straight hair, standing on a lawn in a black graduation gown, her father and mother beside her. Even in the photograph, Daniels exuded power and confidence. His wife Estelle wore a nervous smile, and her eyes looked downward, toward the grass.

"She's beautiful," Katya said, in her carefully pronounced English. "Both of them are beautiful."

Daniels accepted the photograph back and returned it to its place on the mantel. He opened a door off the bedroom and ushered Katya into a small dressing room at the southwest corner of the mansion. It smelled musty from disuse.

"This was Estelle's room," he said. "I haven't been in here in months. She was going to redecorate it—in light blues and whites —and make it into her personal library. She loved to read."

The president concluded the tour of the family quarters in the west sitting room, where the waiter had left a portable bar and a tray of clean glasses. Daniels poured a glass of white wine for Katya and a scotch and water for himself. He had canceled a working dinner with his foreign policy group to spend this time with her. He knew he was ducking responsibilities, but he desperately craved a break from the pressures he had been under the past week. What he needed now, more than anything, was to spend a few hours as a normal human being, not a head of state. He needed a large dose of sympathy, shared feelings, intimacy. He needed the company of a woman.

No. That was not quite it. He needed the company of this woman.

"It must have been about then," he said, settling onto the sofa next to her, "when Alice graduated from Yale, that Estelle started showing the strain. At least that's when I began to notice it. I was getting ready to run for the Senate, and she begged me not to. She wanted us to stay in Ohio, where I'd been governor, and go into private law practice. I promised her that if I lost the Senate race, I'd leave politics."

Daniels rubbed his chin, remembering. "But I won. Just barely. By less than a thousand votes. There were two recounts before the issue was decided. We moved from the governor's mansion in Columbus to a brownstone in Georgetown. And Estelle never really adapted to the life here. With Alice grown up and gone, she felt lonely and useless."

"What a terrible shame," Katya said. "She should have enjoyed an ideal life. So many privileges."

Daniels smiled. That's what he had thought, too.

"I suppose I neglected her," he said, feeling a need to come to her defense. "I was rarely home before ten or eleven, hustling to get my career as a senator launched. And it spilled over into the weekends. A million things always seemed to need doing, and increasingly Estelle wasn't there to share them with me. I began to resent her for it. I felt she was sabotaging my career. She never wanted to go anywhere, never wanted to entertain. We had fights sometimes, but mainly she just withdrew from me. She spent all her time alone."

Daniels sipped his scotch and looked out the big arched Palladian window at the somber face of the old Executive Office Building, its massive gray stone exterior illuminated in shades of ghostly pale by the streetlamps along West Executive Avenue. He hadn't intended to launch into such a monologue about Estelle, but now he felt compelled to continue. He wanted this woman to understand him.

"I'd come home and find her in bed, even at six o'clock, crying to herself. She saw psychiatrists, but they didn't help. The doctors would prescribe pills—tranquilizers, mood elevators, that kind of thing—to get her through the day. She began to depend on them."

"Did you ever think of separating?" Katya asked.

"No. Not once. And if she did she never mentioned it. The crunch came when I decided to run for president. At first I wasn't going to, because of Estelle. I thought if we went home, she would improve. But the pressures on me to run were heavy. I looked good in the polls, and I had a lot of support. I must have listened to a thousand arguments during those months, persuading me to run, convincing me that I could make it. I would make a great president, they said; I owed the country my leadership. Only Estelle was arguing on the other side. And of course none of the people around me even took her into account. They didn't know the depth of her problem, because we'd kept it a secret. Even her family wanted me to run!"

Daniels saw a skeptical smile curl the corner of Katya's lip. "I think you have rationalized how inevitable it was," she said. "That's how we remember things. The greatest force must have been you. You must have wanted to be president very much."

Daniels gazed up thoughtfully at the big English cut-glass chandelier that dominated the sitting hall. "I was ambitious, of course," he admitted. "Hell, I was consumed by the idea. It's hard to explain the feeling. It goes beyond the mere wish for power. Or the high-flown notion of doing something for your country. It's the challenge. If you've been a politician all your life, it's impossible to resist. Impossible. At least it was for me. I had eaten, slept, and dreamed politics since I was twelve. I didn't *know* anything else. The thought of tucking my tail between my legs and retreating to practice law out in the sticks for the rest of my life, when I had a shot at history, made me ill. It would have been cowardly not to run."

Daniels shook his empty glass and thought about a refill. He had been drinking too much in the past week, but what the hell, it had been a week for it. Katya was still nursing her glass of wine.

"My father was a day laborer," he said. "And a drunk. He died of cirrhosis of the liver. My mother took in laundry. Neither of them had got past the eighth grade, and no one in either family had ever been to college. I was ashamed of all of them. I dreamed of redeeming my family name, making it so respectable that no one could ever think of it except in terms of awe and envy."

Daniels gave in and mixed himself another drink.

"Yes, I wanted to be president," he continued, dropping a handful of ice cubes on top of the scotch. "So I rationalized Estelle's situation. I thought, well, what the hell, I'll probably lose the election, and that'll be that. And if by some miracle I *did* win, well, Estelle wouldn't really be any worse off than she had been when I was a senator. I'd get her better doctors; we'd get through it somehow. And after a term, we'd go back to Columbus and put our lives back together again. . . . But the campaign was awful for her. The media zeroed in, and the rumors started. That she was an alcoholic, that she had been in a mental institution. That I was sleeping around. It pushed Estelle over the edge. The day we moved into the White House she was so tranquilized that she fell down during the afternoon reception. I put her to bed, and went to the inaugural balls alone. I had made it. I was president. I had won. But Estelle was a casualty."

"You followed your destiny," Katya said. "As you had to. Mental illness was your wife's destiny. Had you never run for president, she would have been ill just the same."

"I refuse to take the tragic view," Daniels replied. "A medicine will eventually come along that will put those chemicals in her brain back in their proper order. I firmly believe that."

"You believe science can change fate?" Katya asked, as if he had uttered a blasphemy.

Daniels nodded. She regarded him carefully. Her gaze, hard as a diamond and even less innocent, seemed to mock him. I confessed too much, he thought. She doesn't like me.

"I should go up and see her now," he said. "Why don't you come and meet her?"

Katya swallowed. "Are you sure?"

"Of course. I'd like you to see her. After all I've told you. . . ."

The nurse, Irene, met them at the door.

"She's had her dinner," she whispered to Daniels. "And I've prepared her for bed."

"Thank you," Daniels said. He introduced Katya. The nurse eyed her with obvious suspicion. She guarded Estelle's room like a forbidden temple.

The president walked in first, letting Katya hang back in the shadows until he had greeted Estelle. He bent down and kissed her on the forehead and smoothed her hair with his palm. She gazed up at him and smiled dreamily. Irene had combed her hair, and she appeared unusually tranquil.

"I have someone I want you to meet, Stelly," he said.

The Russian woman stepped over to the foot of the bed. Estelle leaned forward and peered at her, as if she couldn't quite make out what was there.

"This is Katya Kamenev," Daniels said. "She's Premier Kamenev's widow. You remember I told you about the accident. She was there, too. Now she's going to stay here with us for a while."

Estelle fixed her eyes intently on her husband, then on Katya. Daniels felt a chill. There remained a sentient entity inside that disturbed brain that reacted logically to the outside world. He sometimes suspected that she even possessed a kind of supernatural awareness.

"I just wanted you to meet her, Stelly," he repeated. He placed his hand over his wife's, which were folded together primly on top of the coverlet. She pushed his hand away.

"Do you want to dance?" she asked Katya in a clear, bold voice. Katya blinked.

"Don't mind it," Daniels whispered. "She . . . talks about different things."

"Will you dance?" Estelle repeated. The words came out sweetly, in a singsong, little-girl voice. She pulled a pillow from behind her head, hugged it to her, and began rocking back and forth, as if swaying to the sounds of a waltz.

"Will you, won't you," Estelle murmured. "Will you, won't you . . . will you, won't you . . . join the dance?"

Daniels cleared his throat, embarrassed. "I talk to her every night," he explained, "for about an hour. Sometimes she seems to understand. She asked about Alice the other night. . . ."

As they watched, Estelle's face took on a rapturous glow. She appeared lost in some childlike fantasy. "I often think of the irony," Daniels continued. "I talked to her less before she was sick, when we could still communicate. If I had spent as much time with her then. . . ."

His wife's eyes shone, and her body tensed suggestively. Her hand strayed to her breast, and she began caressing it slowly, provocatively, her fingers cupping it through the cotton nightgown and massaging it in languorous, sensual strokes. Her body trembled and shuddered. A small cry of pleasure escaped her lips.

Daniels pretended to ignore her bizarre performance at first, uncertain how to react. He wondered what had triggered it. Katya?

Estelle kicked the blanket down. Her eyes roved alternately from Katya to her husband. They brimmed with lust. Estelle pulled up her nightgown and opened her legs. Daniels stared at her naked thighs, totally dumbfounded. She brought her hand down and stroked herself, grinning at him lasciviously. He hadn't slept with Estelle in over three years, and the sudden sexual display stirred him even while it shocked him. Katya turned away.

Daniels reached down and pulled the blanket up over Estelle's legs. "I'm sorry," he said to Katya. "This wasn't a good idea."

Estelle's movements ceased; the rapture on her face vanished. She fixed her gaze on Katya, as if seeing her for the first time. Her expression shifted mercurially from fright to anger to evil cunning, all in an instant.

"It's all right, Stelly," Daniels said, trying to mask his irritation. "It's all right."

Estelle kept her eyes locked on Katya. The Russian woman tried to smile back, but managed only a kind of false grin.

So swiftly that neither Katya nor Daniels registered the motion, Estelle grabbed the plastic pitcher of ice water from her night table and hurled it past the foot of the bed. Its edge caught Katya on the scar above her nose. The impact popped the lid free and ice water drenched Katya's face and shoulders and spilled down the front of her dress.

"You're bad!" Estelle screamed. "Bad!"

Transfixed with shock, Katya stood, letting the water drip to the floor. The nurse came running in. Daniels dashed into the bathroom and returned with an armful of towels. He handed one to her, and wrapped another one around her shoulders.

"Are you all right?"

She nodded, wordlessly, and dried her face and neck. Daniels threw another towel on the floor to absorb the water on the carpet. He looked up to see Katya retreating toward the door.

He glanced at Estelle. She was lying with her back against the pillows, staring vacantly at the ceiling. Irene stroked her forehead and crooned to her in a low, comforting singsong. Daniels burned with anger. The perversity of it! It was monstrous that she should punish him so much!

He hurried from the suite and down the stairs to the east sitting hall. Katya was just opening the door to the Queen's Bedroom. Seeing him, she stopped and turned. Her hair was soaked and clung to her neck in thick strands. Her face was wet, too. From tears. Daniels reached out and rested his hands on her arms.

"I'm sorry," he said.

She managed a faint smile. He tried not to let his gaze fall below the level of her face, but he failed. The front of her black silk dress, wet as a bathing suit, clung to her breasts like a second skin.

The president pulled her to him. He kissed her damp neck and embraced her.

"I'm sorry," he repeated, unable to think of anything else to say. He was sorry for so many things. For her. For Estelle. For the death of Kamenev. For all the trouble they were in, and all the trouble that seemed to lie ahead. He was sorry most of all for himself. Needing this woman so much frightened him.

Katya pulled back and looked up at him, her eyes filled with an inexplicable sorrow of her own. He started to say something, but she pressed her fingers against his mouth.

"We will comfort each other," she said.

19

WARFIELD SLIPPED BACK INTO his white doctor's gown and buttoned it, his eyes returning repeatedly to the assassin on the other side of the one-way glass. It was eleven o'clock at night; Martinez had gone to sleep.

"He was quiet as a corpse after you left," Moore said. "He ate dinner, went to the bathroom twice. The rest of the time he stared at the wall. Didn't say anything."

Rosenstock crushed a butt out on the floor with his shoe. "I shot him up with ketamine an hour ago," he said.

Warfield nodded. "We've got to finish this as fast as we can. Things are getting complicated. Don't plan on any sleep tonight." He glanced over at Semenenko. In deference to his status, they had found him a leather executive swivel chair. He was sitting in it now, directly across from the one-way glass, legs crossed, arms relaxed, acting the part of the undemanding guest. Warfield found his cooperativeness unnerving.

Howard Moore and Nan Robertson reacted to him by pretending he wasn't there. Semenenko noticed and seemed amused by it. Rosenstock, on the other hand, acted almost perversely pleased by the Russian's presence, as if the situation had needed a little more excitement. The doctor mugged at Semenenko frequently, winking at him whenever he could catch his eye. His efforts to discomfort the Russian weren't having the least effect.

On the way back from Washington, Warfield had explained to the KGB general how they had tricked the assassin into talking. He did not tell the Russian about Rosenstock's forensic report, however, or about the photograph of the face in the ambulance. The information they had yielded so far was ambiguous.

"Enjoy the show, General," Warfield said, picking up his clipboard and notebook. Howard Moore followed him out into the hallway.

"Before you go in," he said. "There's something interesting in the latest FBI report. I didn't want to tell you in front of him." Warfield stopped to listen.

"A Korean named Jaegwan Kim died in a hospital in Annapolis this afternoon," Moore began. "He was fatally injured when his house exploded. He was a bomb-maker, a free-lancer. The place was apparently loaded with high explosives. Blew up half the neighborhood. Before he died, he had made a bomb for somebody. They blew his house up, he said, to keep him from talking. He said he thought that the bomb was connected with an attempt to kill the president."

"Did he identify anyone?"

"Unfortunately no. He described his contact as dark, Mediterranean. Greek, he thought. That's all."

"Christ, that's not much help. Are you thinking it could be the Turk?"

"Could be. But the weirdest part of the story is the bomb itself. It's hidden in a woman's hairbrush."

Warfield laughed. "It must be another hoax. The crazies always come out of the woodwork on something like this."

"Maybe. But the Korean was no hoax. He would know how to build something like that. He said it was designed to be detonated by remote control. Has a listening device built into it as well."

"It sounds farfetched as hell, but you're right, we can't ignore it. We'll brainstorm the possibilities later—who might plant it, where, how, and so forth. If there's even a chance it might figure in another assassination try, we'd better be ready."

"Okay. I'll give you the whole report after your session. Good luck in there."

Trippet unlocked the door to the ward as Warfield approached. The pallid, bleached white of the overhead florescents cast a bleak, shadowless light throughout the assassin's room. It matched Warfield's mood.

Warfield sat by the bed, opened his notebook and shook the assassin's arm. Martinez rolled over and opened his eyes.

"We must continue," Warfield said.

The assassin stared into space for a few moments, then closed his eyes. Warfield shook him roughly. Martinez resisted, groaning softly. Finally he made an effort to come fully awake. Warfield's mental picture of Semenenko watching him through the one-way glass spurred him into sterner action.

"Sit up, please," he commanded.

The assassin propped himself up on one shaky elbow. He looked dreadful. His eyes were bloodshot, the corners filled with a pus-like discharge. His face possessed a strange waxy gray sheen. Was Rosenstock overdosing him?

"What's the matter?" Warfield demanded.

"Weak."

"Is that all?"

"Can't talk. . . . Hurt all over."

"You must try. If you sit up and answer my questions, we'll let you rest."

The assassin nodded feebly.

"Good," Warfield said. "We were talking earlier about the Turk. You used to meet the Turk at a warehouse. Outside a dark room, you said. Do you remember why the room was dark?"

"So we couldn't see him."

"See who?"

"The Instructor."

"The Instructor?"

Martinez nodded.

"He gave you your orders?"

Another nod. Warfield understood immediately. A cut-out. They took their orders from someone they couldn't identify. *Bad news.*

"What do you remember about the Instructor?"

The assassin stared at the wall.

"Look at me. What do you remember?"

Martinez turned his face toward Warfield. An expression of dread clouded his features. "Can't," he rasped.

"Why not?"

The assassin appeared confused. Warfield waited, fighting his own impulse to press him hard.

"Afraid."

"What are you afraid of?"

Martinez didn't answer. Warfield felt his exasperation threatening to overwhelm his facade of the patient psychiatrist. He should never have left him earlier. Now the momentum was lost. Warfield imagined Semenenko in the other room, smirking at this spluttering spectacle. His carefully trained pet was not in a mood to do his tricks before an audience.

"What are you afraid of?" he repeated. "Try to concentrate."

Sudden pain distorted Martinez's face. He gasped for breath.

"What's the matter?"

"Don't feel good."

Warfield wondered if the prisoner might be malingering. "You're not cooperating," he warned. "I know you've been through a tough time, but there's absolutely nothing wrong with your health. Now what are you afraid of?"

"You know!"

"I know what?"

"What it is!"

Warfield paused. There was a potential trap here. If he really did have the assassin's confession, he would know what Martinez was afraid of.

"I want to confess!" the assassin said.

Warfield started. "Go ahead, then."

"A priest!" Martinez said.

"What?"

"I need a priest!"

"Why not confess to me?"

The assassin shook his head. Sweat beaded his brow. "Need a priest . . . *por favor!*"

Warfield considered it. If it'll make him talk, why not? "I'll get you a priest tomorrow," he promised.

"Now!" Martinez cried, his voice hoarse. Then very softly: "Now, please. . . . Now. . . ."

Warfield bit his lip. The thought of another delay was anathema to him. "All right," he said. He headed back toward the control room. Moore met him in the doorway.

"You heard him," Warfield said. "Let's get him a damned priest! If we don't have one at the base, bring one in from town! And get him here fast!"

Moore disappeared toward the office at the front of the infirmary to use the telephone. Warfield called Rosenstock out of the control room and pulled him down the hallway. "Are you sure you're not shooting too much crap in his veins? He looks sick as hell to me."

Rosenstock denied it. "Ketamine isn't a great breakfast drink, but it isn't dangerous. The stuff makes him feel strange, but the doses I gave him won't hurt him, Charlie. I swear! He's just strung out, depressed. And it's making him feel sicker than he really is."

"I'll take your word for it, Herb."

"It's psychosomatic! Don't worry about it!"

Warfield hesitated. "What's the Russian doing?" he asked.

"Cleaning his fingernails with a pocketknife."

Warfield sighed. "Maybe he'll slip and stab himself in the heart."

"Too small a target," Rosenstock said.

"Yeah. I'm going back in to keep Martinez talking. When Moore gets that priest here, bring him right in."

Warfield returned to his chair by the assassin's bed and studied his notebook for a few minutes, plotting a way to get around Martinez's puzzling fear about the dark room.

"The priest is on his way," he said, finally. "Meanwhile, just relax and try to concentrate on remembering. Forget about the warehouse and the Instructor. Let's concentrate on the Turk. Tell me what you remember about him."

The assassin sat up, rigid, his face close to Warfield's. His pupils were dilated. They seemed to look right through Warfield to a place a thousand miles away. The assassin reached up with one hand and clawed the air as if cobwebs entangled him. He clutched Warfield's arm, digging into the flesh with urgent pressure. Warfield pried his fingers loose, but he groped frantically for another hold, like a man drowning.

Warfield tried to push him back against the mattress.

Martinez twisted violently, as if something invisible was attacking him. He beat the blanket with his hands and kicked his legs out convulsively. Warfield dropped his notebook on the floor and pressed his palm against the man's jugular, to read his pulse. It was faint, and too rapid to count.

The assassin jerked upright again, and tilted his head toward the ceiling. He held that position for some seconds, and then his back began to arch. Warfield saw the muscles around his neck swell into knots. He slumped to his side, twisted over, and grabbed for Warfield's shoulders, his face a mask of terror.

"Yo no mira!" he screamed. "I can't see!"

"Rosenstock!" Warfield yelled.

The doctor was already at the door, Nan crowding in behind him.

The assassin squeezed an arm around Warfield's neck and clung to him like a baby. His mouth opened and closed rapidly. *"Madre de Dios,"* he groaned, and relaxed his grip.

Rosenstock ran to the other side of the bed, pulled him back against the pillows, and slapped the stethoscope to his chest. "Goddammit!" he swore. "We need a CPR unit! Not one for miles!" He jumped onto the bed, straddled the assassin, and began pounding violently on his chest, hitting him just beneath the rib cage with the heels of his palms. Martinez's body bounced obscenely on the mattress under the doctor's frantic efforts. Warfield stood watching, hands at his side, helpless.

After ten minutes Rosenstock stopped his pounding and crawled off the bed, wheezing from his effort. He fished a cigarette from his shirt pocket and began patting the other pockets in a painstakingly deliberate search for a match.

No one else seemed able to move or speak.

Moore walked in a minute later, followed by a short, balding priest in a black cassock.

"You're too late, Father," Rosenstock muttered. "The son-of-a-bitch is dead."

20

SLEEP WAS OUT OF THE QUES-
tion.

Daniels felt like a traveler who had arrived at the edge of the map. The country that lay ahead was *terra incognita.* Exciting, unknown, dangerous.

His sexual prowess had astonished him. Their first coupling had been frantic and short lived, so urgent was their arousal. Shortly after, they had made love a second time, and had settled into a long, sensual exercise that mounted slowly to a shattering climax. Katya, encouraging him with skilled hands and erotic sighs, had metamorphosed into a wild being, clawing his back, and screaming out in a passion so abandoned that it seemed to cross into a kind of terror. Daniels' orgasm was so intense, that second time, that he nearly passed out. The experience had left him spent and shaken, but had thrust him into a state past fatigue, a kind of tingling, dreamlike high.

He had begun a journey from which he knew he would not retreat. There would be consequences, but tonight he would not think about them. Tonight he wanted as much of this woman as he could take. The cataclysmic sexual union had stimulated his curiosity to an obsessive pitch. His desire to discover her life, to fill in that unknown part of the map, consumed his thoughts.

She lay turned on her side away from him. He rolled against her, and moved his hand onto her breast.

"If I didn't think it might kill me," he whispered, "I'd make love to you again."

He felt her laugh. He was pleased she was still awake. He let his hand roam down from her breast through the valley of her waist and up the round hill of her hip. He had not yet seen her naked. They had thrown off their clothes and made love in the dark. There was so much yet to discover.

"You once told me that you hated your husband," Daniels said. The statement had haunted him ever since she had uttered it.

"Yes."

"Why?"

"He was an unpleasant man. I never loved him."

"Why did you marry him?"

He felt her tremble.

"I don't know where to begin," she replied. "It's not a simple thing to explain." She rolled onto her back and patted his thigh. "It would take all night to tell you. Who's going to run your country tomorrow if you don't get some sleep?"

Daniels laughed. "Most days the country would run better if its president never got out of bed."

"You don't really believe that."

"Tonight I do."

A silence fell. Daniels traced a finger around Katya's ear and down the soft contours of her neck. He could just make out her profile in the dim glow of light that filtered through the drapes from Lafayette Park. A very straight nose. A high forehead. Voluptuous lips, a rounded, strong chin.

"Tell me *some*thing," he said. "I know so little about you."

"You don't want to hear."

"Of course I do. After all the talking I did, I'd think you'd want to get back at me."

"No. My story is ugly."

Daniels laughed. "It can't all be ugly."

"Most of it."

Katya's resistance only provoked the president's curiosity. "I don't believe you," he said. "Tell me part of it. Let me judge for myself."

For a long time Katya was silent. Daniels could hear only her soft breathing and the distant hum of traffic around the park. After a while he thought she had decided not to tell him, after all. Well, there was a limit to how hard he should press her. He closed his eyes.

Then, in a tight, barely audible voice, Katya spoke. "My mother was the daughter of a Russian professor at the University of Peking. She met my father there. He was an American, a liaison officer with the Chinese forces during the Second World War. Before they could get married he was killed in fighting in 1945 between the Nationalists and the Communists. I was born a month later, so I never saw him. His name was John Framingham. I don't even have a photograph of him."

"He must have family here," Daniels said. "We can find out. What happened to you and your mother?"

"She wanted to return to Russia. She had grown up in Leningrad; some of her mother's family was still there. My grandfather warned her that it might be unsafe to return, but she persisted, and finally, when I was three, we left Peking for Leningrad. They arrested my mother at the border and took us off the train. I don't remember the name of the place, but it was awfully cold. We were kept for weeks in a horrible, unheated building, until some sort of trial was held. I was too young to understand what was happening, but it was later explained to me. They considered my mother a spy. Everyone, it seemed, who had been outside Russia—even our returning prisoners of war from Germany—were considered spies or traitors. And most went to the camps. My mother was sentenced to twenty-five years and sent to Krivoshchekovo. They took me away from her and put me in a state children's village."

"Did you ever see your mother again?"

"No. She sent me letters. Later, I was able to piece together her fate from other prisoners I met. She lived in a women's barracks there—five hundred women crowded in bunks. It was very hard for her, because she was young and beautiful, and accustomed to a privileged life. To be beautiful at a camp was a curse. The male prisoners and the camp personnel had the run of the women's barracks, and the attractive ones were forced into a kind of prostitution. . . . My mother attached herself to a protector—a male trustee in a good position at the camp. He looked after her in exchange for her favors. This was a common thing. The women were the slaves of their protectors.

"After several years, new orders came and the women prisoners were separated from the men and taken to new camps. That was very bad for the women, because in the women's camps they were forced to do the same heavy labor as the men.

"My mother was sent to one of the worst places—Kolyma. She was put out on the lumbering detail. No one survived that very long. She lived through six months of it, then died two weeks before the amnesty commissions reached her camp. That was in February 1956."

Katya turned on her side, facing Daniels, and drew her knees up.

"I was moved to a different orphanage when I was six. I don't remember much about those early years, except that I was always cold and hungry—and dreadfully lonely. I was told from the time I was old enough to understand that I was the child of an American and a traitor, and that I should be grateful that the state bothered to clothe, feed, and shelter me at all.

"By the time I was ten years old, I was very rebellious. I defied the staff and the authorities at the orphanage. They stole our food, beat us, tormented us. One thing we hated especially was the indoctrination. Day after day they hammered socialist dogma at us. It wasn't that we questioned it, we just hated the endless drilling. It was a torture to endure. We came to despise Lenin and Stalin as much as the people running the orphanage.

"There was a big painting of Stalin that hung in the main hall of the dormitory. One night five of us defaced it. We ripped the canvas with a knife and smeared feces all over Stalin's face. It caused a terrible scene the next day. The orphanage reported it to the police. They held their interrogation right at the dormitory. All of us were questioned, and no one confessed. They took away our food. We didn't eat for three days.

"I was the leader of the group who had done it and I felt it was up to me to end the suffering of the others. So I confessed that I had defaced the painting myself. I remember how proud I felt, telling those men that I had done this unspeakable thing.

"Of course it was all simply childish mischief, but they told me that I had committed a terrible political crime, and that I would have to be punished. I was arrested and taken away. A judge sentenced me to five years for destroying state property, five more for insulting the leader of the Soviet people, and ten for conspiring against the state. Twenty years altogether."

Daniels sat up, his heart flooded with outrage. "Barbaric," was all he could think of to say.

"Normally no one under twelve could be sentenced as an adult. They sentenced me that way because my records were incomplete and full of errors. I had been born out of the country and had no family left in Russia except my mother, and she was already in a camp. Someone had set my age down wrong somewhere, and the mistake could never be straightened out. To correct an error meant admitting that one had been made, and this no one could afford to do.

"So they believed they were sentencing a twelve year old. And I didn't care, to tell you the truth. At the time it seemed as if anything would be better than the orphanage. I was actually glad to go to the camp."

"Was it better?"

"No. I was sent to a camp of mixed adults and children. Conditions there were very harsh. The women suffered the most, and many of us died.

"The camps brought out the worst in everybody. There was no compassion or decency possible. The strong survived, the weak died. They had a saying in the camp—'nado zhits'—'you have to live'. That attitude excused any behavior that helped you survive.

"My first day there one of the kitchen staff spotted me and tried to bribe me to sleep with him for some sausage and bread. I was a virgin, of course, but I understood what he wanted plainly enough. He was a pig—the sight of him made me sick. I refused him. A week later he gave me some food anyway. Then he turned me in, claiming that I had stolen it. I was sent to a punishment cell. The guards there raped me. Six of them.

"I wasn't hurt seriously. Several days later I had put it out of my mind. There were too many other things to worry about—food, warmth, physical safety. It sounds horrible, I know, but even at the age of ten I was already hardened to the brutality. And things like chastity and virginity were meaningless at a labor camp. Less than meaningless—a joke.

"We children were probably the worst people in the camp. We had no decency at all. Where could we have learned it? We tormented the older prisoners, stole their food, their possessions, reported on them, made life even more of a hell for them than it was already. And the camp authorities didn't care. We had a certain invulnerability, being so young. By Soviet law we received the same food ration as the adults, and we worked a lot less.

"Of course I hated it. I dreamed of other worlds; I dreamed of this country. I remembered little things my mother had told me about it, things she had heard from my father, I guess. One day a woman I had become friends with showed me a postcard she had received years before from a relative in the United States. It showed a photograph of a village in New England. I couldn't read the English, but she told me it was in a place called Massachusetts. I remember how wonderfully exotic the name sounded. Massachusetts. It was an American Indian name, she said. The photograph showed a white church and some small houses and a store.

"She died soon after, and I took her postcard. I thought about that village every day, and came to have a fantasy that I lived there. I filled the town with imaginary people and made up stories about their lives. Someone took the card, finally, but I remember it so well that I could draw it from memory. Some day I want to go to Massachusetts and find the real village. If I could, I think that I would live there for the rest of my life. . . ."

Katya sat up and hugged her knees against her chest, suddenly choked with the emotions her story had brought back. "Of course," she said, when she was able to continue, "I didn't serve twenty years. I served less than two. After the Twentieth Congress there was the amnesty—in 1956. I was pardoned when I was eleven.

"I had no family left alive anywhere, and nowhere to go. The day I was freed was the worst day of my life. I wanted to die." She fell silent. Her story seemed to loom over him in the dark, a past whose dimensions he could never fully understand. It intimidated him, in some undefined way. It was an experience of life he could not compete with, and could not do anything to change. Yet nothing about her suggested such a brutal past.

"How could it be?" he said, his voice soft but insistent. "You are educated, cultured, traveled—all the things one associates with privilege. And you are, after all—or were—Russia's first lady. How did you overcome so much? Something very good must have happened to you later on."

"Yes, of course," she replied, her tone flat.

"Your life must have improved a great deal after camp."

"Yes," she said. Her voice sounded far away. He reached out to touch her, to bring her back to him, this creature who was more of a mystery now than ever. He closed his eyes, unable to fight off the demands of sleep. It must be near dawn, he thought. In an hour or two he would have to get up, face another difficult day.

". . . In some ways it got better," Katya said. "In some ways worse."

21

OTIS SPENGLER'S CHAUFFEUR noticed the difference right away.

"Looks like they're guarding Fort Knox, Mr. Spengler," he said, glancing at his boss in the rear-view mirror.

Spengler patted his forehead with his handkerchief. Police seemed to be stationed everywhere over the Naval Observatory grounds. As the limousine approached the old Admiralty mansion, the home of the vice-president, Spengler saw men crouching beside the ornate dormers on the roof. Near the house's main entrance, a police van was parked in full view, with several officers standing near it.

Spengler chuckled out loud. "The pompous bastard," he said. "I'll bet he loves it."

The chauffeur hopped out, opened the door, and reached in with both hands to pull his employer out of the back seat. At 375 pounds, Spengler was unable to extricate himself from the limousine without help.

Two Secret Service agents frisked Spengler, one patting his voluminous coat from behind, the other working the front. Spengler chortled. "A lot of territory to cover, ain't there, boys?" he said.

The vice-president met him at the door. Spengler was surprised. They shook hands.

"Hello, Chester," Spengler said, patting the envelope in his coat pocket. "I thought those fellas might mug me."

The vice-president looked preoccupied, Spengler thought. He motioned for Spengler to follow him to the back of the house. Near the kitchen he opened a door leading down to the basement.

"What's this?" Spengler demanded.

"I'll explain," Catlin muttered. "Just go down, please."

Spengler peered down the narrow staircase. Walking down those steps would be difficult. And coming back up would be agony.

"Don't you have an elevator?"

"It doesn't work. Just go on down!"

The vice-president led Spengler through a maze of furnaces, trunks, and cobwebs to a long workbench against the far wall of the basement. He snapped on an overhead light and turned to face his visitor. Spengler, still puffing noisily from the short walk, fished out his handkerchief and dabbed his forehead. He felt the crackle of the envelope in his breast pocket, so he pulled that out also and dropped it on the bench.

"Ten thousand," he said, and added, as he always did on these occasions, "a campaign contribution from the Spengler Construction Company."

The vice-president looked at the envelope but didn't touch it.

"Aren't you gonna count it?" Spengler asked. "You always count it."

Catlin shook his head. He bent down and pulled a metal case out from beneath the bench. It was a silvery aluminum, the kind used to carry camera equipment, and it was locked with a small padlock. Catlin set it on top of the bench, then turned to Spengler. "I'm not going to open it," he said, his voice cold. "You can take my word for its contents."

Spengler tucked his handkerchief back into his breast pocket and gazed at the case, thoroughly mystified. "Well?" he demanded.

"Two hundred and fifty thousand dollars, Otis. In hundreds. Everything you've given me. I want you to take it all back."

Spengler looked from Catlin to the case, then back at Catlin. "What the hell are you talking about?"

The vice-president cleared his throat. "I want you to take it all back. I want to get it all out of here. Right now! This morning! I never want to see any of it again, ever! Do you understand?"

Spengler pulled out the handkerchief again. "Understand? You're talking crazy!"

"I'm scared. I'm scared and I'm not afraid to admit it. Do you realize how close I came to becoming president last week?"

Spengler realized very well. He had experienced a brief few moments of soaring euphoria at the prospect. "Chester, I'm disappointed in you. You can't give the money back. You've already taken it. It's all clean, untraceable. It's yours."

The vice-president scowled at Spengler and pointed toward the basement ceiling. "You saw them when you came in. Secret Service. Police. They're swarming all over this place, following me every step I take. And there's a hit squad somewhere still gunning for the president. Do you realize that if Daniels is killed they'll be in here, within hours, moving our belongings over to the White House. It's just not safe! I can't keep large amounts of cash. I want it out of here! Right now! And you're taking it with you, dammit!"

Spengler mopped his brow. "I want you to think this over carefully . . ."

"I *have* thought it over! If I become president, I'll be in a fishbowl! Somebody—some reporter somewhere—will dig this business up! I'll be ruined!"

Catlin slapped the top of the case with his pudgy fingers. "It's all there. Two hundred and fifty thousand. Take it, and let's never discuss this business again. No more envelopes. Ever."

Otis Spengler let out a thick sigh of exasperation. "Listen," he said. "It's a lot more than two hundred and fifty thousand. It's more like half a million. Where's the rest?"

A stricken look transformed the vice-president's features. "It's gone," he said. "Spent. That's all that's left."

Spengler studied Catlin. He was actually wringing his hands in anguish. His cowardice was even greater than his greed.

"It won't change anything for me to take it back, Chester. You might as well keep it. You earned it. It's your commission."

"No! I'm through with all that! I've got to think about the presidency. . . . What that'll mean. . . ."

Spengler snorted in disgust. "Listen to me, you damned fool! You're already compromised. You sold yourself! You might as well enjoy the proceeds of the sale!"

"No!"

Catlin picked up the case and the envelope and thrust them both against Spengler's massive chest. "I'm ordering you to take them! Don't argue any further! And I want you to stay away. I don't want you to call me or send me any letters. Nothing. Do you understand?"

Spengler slipped the envelope back into his breast pocket and hefted the aluminum case by its handle. It was surprisingly heavy. He looked at Catlin and nodded sadly. "Maybe you'll change your mind," he said. "Think about it. I'll hold the cash for you. Put it in a Bahamas account. If you change your mind, just let me know. We'll work out something safe."

Spengler mopped his brow again and moved his ponderous bulk toward the stairwell and began his slow ascent of the steps. At the top he paused to catch his breath. "What if they stop me at the door?" he asked. "And want to open this case?"

"They won't do that," Catlin muttered. "They don't bother anything going out."

Later that morning Spengler's chauffeur dialed a telephone number somewhere in Virginia. A man answered on the eighth ring.

"Yeah?"

"This is Ortega."

"What is it?"

"We made another delivery."

"Okay. Did you catch it?"

"Taped it all. That wafer mike's a beauty. Catlin really incriminated himself. He . . ."

The voice at the other end cut him off abruptly. "Just leave the tape in the usual place. Your payment will be there."

The line went dead.

22

of the assassin's death at ten o'clock in the morning. Paul Friedrich delivered it to him in person.

"We're investigating it," Friedrich told him, from his nervous perch on the edge of an Oval Office sofa. "I've called the appropriate authorities in Virginia—district attorney, medical examiner. They've promised to keep a lid on it."

"What's your guess?"

"It looks as if Warfield killed him with an overdose of some kind of drug."

Daniels cursed under his breath. "An accident?"

"We assume so. Warfield claims he had him talking. The tapes back that up. Something went wrong last night, right in the middle of the interrogation."

"Was Semenenko there?"

"Yes. Apparently he saw the whole thing."

"What did we get from the assassin before he died?"

"Not enough. We know who he is, we know his background. And we have some leads on the one that got away. But that's about all."

"You told me he was an anti-Castro Cuban."

"Yes, but apparently he wasn't identified with any group we know about. He took his orders from a source he couldn't identify."

Daniels closed his eyes and pressed the heels of his palms against the lids. His senses were still crowded with images of Katya.

Memories of the night before blossomed and faded—glimpses of her breasts in the shadowy light, the feel of her smooth, supple flesh, the sounds of her passion.

And her story. It clung to the edges of his consciousness, creating in him an inexplicable longing for her, as if her past were some forbidding gulf that might keep her forever at a distance.

He knew it would only be a matter of days before rumors would begin circulating. There was no way to prevent that. And his political experience told him that the public was not ready to accept a romance between himself and the widow of the Russian premier. He would need time to work it out. And luck.

The president forced his mind back to Friedrich. "What should we do with Warfield?" he asked. "Can we bring him up on some kind of charge?"

Friedrich nodded carefully. "We can get Virginia to press charges for manslaughter. But we have to be cautious. He could expose details of the interrogation."

Daniels clenched and unclenched his fists. "It's exposed already. You must have seen the circus outside the Sans Souci last night. The networks ran footage of it all night."

Friedrich shrugged. "At least Warfield didn't tell them anything."

"They seemed to know everything already. What about the death itself. How many know about that?"

Friedrich estimated ten.

"Put a lid on it," Daniels ordered. "Where's Warfield now?"

"Still at the farm."

"Quarantine him. Don't let him talk to anybody. Don't let him go anywhere. Lock him up if necessary. And I want your inspector general's report as soon as possible. We're going to have a hell of a lot of explaining to do. What about an autopsy?"

"One's under way now. I'll have the results for you later today."

Daniels fought off a yawn. "For once I guess Wilbert was wrong."

Friedrich didn't understand the president's reference. "I'm sorry?"

"He pushed you to bring in Warfield. I know you were against it. I'm sorry I let him do it."

"At least Warfield's somebody we can lay a lot of the blame on," the director said.

"That's a consideration," Daniels admitted. "But not much of one. What about the Russian? Semenenko? How did he react to the death?"

Friedrich's face reddened. "Amusement would be the most accurate description."

"Where is he now?"

"In Washington. At his embassy."

"Keep him occupied or he's apt to start trouble. Sic the Inspector General on him. He was a witness, after all. Put him through a long interview." Daniels surrendered to another yawn. "I wish I'd stayed in bed," he said.

"I'm not getting much sleep, either, Mr. President. I'm counting the days to retirement. Only three hundred and forty-three left."

Daniels laughed. "I hope the hell you make it!"

Warfield lay on his narrow cot, hands clasped behind his neck. He had showered, shaved, and dressed, consuming as much of the morning as possible. Now there remained nothing to do but count the tiles in the ceiling. And think.

Rosenstock must have overdosed the assassin. It was the only plausible explanation. By this evening copies of an autopsy report would be circulating. And the inspector general would be calling sometime soon. Charles Warfield's neck was perfectly positioned for the sacrificial ax. When the whole story of his bizarre interrogation became known, the CIA would have to offer him to the blade —to protect itself and to satisfy the screams for blood that would descend on it from everywhere.

What the hell, he thought. He was guilty. It had been his idea to bring in Rosenstock. His idea to shoot the assassin full of drugs. His idea to fake a brain operation.

And yet he had come so damned close! Another hour or two. That's all he had needed!

Instead, he was left with a dead body and a collection of useless clues—a trace of jute and cotton, a story about a blacked-out room in a warehouse, and somebody called the Instructor and somebody else called the Turk. Plus a photo of a man in an ambulance and a confession from a dying Korean about a bomb in a hairbrush. The only thing they added up to was a fiasco. A fuck-up so spectacular that he knew that years from now, when all the heads had stopped rolling, it would become a classic scandal, right up there with the U-2 incident and the Philby defection.

Warfield laughed out loud. At least no one was going to ruin his reputation. He had beaten them to it years ago.

In Egypt.

Had it been bad judgment? Loss of nerve? Bad luck? The law of averages? Or was it, as Semenenko had said, his own fault?

The faces in the cramped room on Saad Zaglul swam before his eyes again. The blank dead faces, unable to explain the catastrophe that had befallen them.

It was better not to disturb the bones. But it was impossible to put them to rest. Now, with a fresh calamity on his hands, they hovered on the outskirts of his mind, a crowd of ghosts, staring in mute accusation.

And Tanya. My God, poor Tanya.

Warfield tore his thoughts from the grisly images and sent them careening away aimlessly through his past life. The little clapboard house in Wilkes-Barre, Pennsylvania, materialized before him, and the cheerless street with no trees. There was the boy next door, the one who stole his bicycle. And the fourteen-year-old girl down the block who told him about sex and let him touch her. The rose-patterned wallpaper in the bedroom where his father died of black lung, and the hushed voices and strange medicinal odors. His mother, old and wrinkled at forty. His sister, pregnant and married at sixteen. His first wife, Jane, gone after a year. A kaleidoscope of sadness. There must have been pleasure in his life, but he seemed no longer able to recall it.

He dragged his thoughts back to the present. They had brought him no breakfast. He wondered if they would bring him lunch. Not that he cared.

No one had told him anything. He wasn't under arrest. They had just locked him in his room and posted a guard outside. And what about the others—Rosenstock, Moore, and Robertson? Were they being questioned? Were they being encouraged to turn against him?

Drowsiness began to overtake him, and in its shadow the memory of Egypt crept back again. He let it come, let it sidle up and whisper in his ear its sad laments.

He is sitting on a small pier at dusk. Behind him the enormous neon sign of the Al Montaza Hotel blazes across the sky, its florescent blue and red clashing with the soft evening watercolors of the horizon. In front of him, the mouth of the Nile delta. Purple and gray, black and pink. *Inky smudges of boats—river traffic, small open dinghies spluttering through the channels with low-powered outboards; graceful, silent dhows, their triangular sails carving the air in lazy slices. Beyond, the silhouettes of the sea traffic— river steamers, oil barges, freighters; the faint twinkling of the red and green lights of the channel markers, and the muffled clanking of the bell buoys. The raucous decibels of the daylight hours soften and die, the heat cools and the pungent smells of the delta invade the senses like a heady musk.*

He sits. The night chases the evening. Silence spreads. The traffic on the river changes. The small boats find their berths, others anchor and douse their lights. At long intervals small voices drift over the water. From El Alemein to the west a desert breeze brings the astringent odor of eucalyptus. The sky blackens. The lights of the Al Montaza burn stark against it, a neon fire.

He waits, glancing every few minutes at his watch, and at the small boat under the pier, with the carefully stowed cargo of clothes, food, and forged documents. The arrangements are all made. Everything is in order. Nothing has gone wrong. He watches the cars that come and go through the entrance gate into the gardens of the hotel.

But she does not appear.

He walks the pier to shed his tension. Every detail of the plan is scorched on his brain like a brand. Every contingency has been allowed for. Nothing can go wrong.

Tanya!

Has she changed her mind? Did they catch her, somehow? He is filled with a sudden foreboding. There was no doubt that she would come, but the window of time for her escape begins to close.

She has only to leave the hotel during the dinner. A short walk through the park to the gate. Five minutes. No one would notice her gone. Oh God please don't let anything be wrong!

And then he sees her. A small figure in white, moving away from the brightly lit entrance and into the shadows of the palm trees. Then down the drive through the small park to the gate that borders the street.

Tanya!

He watches her intently, holding his breath. No one is following. No one notices. She is walking fast, coming through the gate, crossing the street and slipping along the row of cars and trucks that line the walkways to the piers. Her long gown and high heels make her pace awkward. He stands up from his hiding place behind the small shed and gestures with his hand. Another minute and they will be away, out of the delta channel and into the dark folds of the Mediterranean.

He hears an engine start and the clank of a truck gear engaging. He snaps his head toward the noise. Down the street he sees the truck pull out of the line of parked cars. Shifting rapidly, it roars and bucks down the street toward Tanya. Sensing something, she crosses back to the other side of the street, seeking the shadows of the palm trees lining the borders of the park.

Alongside her, the truck slows. He sees the glint of metal in the back, peeking between the wooden slats.

Gunfire punctures the night air.

Tanya topples in the grass under the trees. He starts to rush out, then ducks back out of sight.

The truck has stopped. Another vehicle, a Citroën sedan, materializes and pulls up behind it. Two men jump quickly out and run toward the crumpled form.

They pick her up and carry her, limp like a white sack between them, and throw her in the back of the Citroën and drive away.

The truck follows after them.

He runs to the spot, feels the wet blood on the grass under the palms, and finds an earring.

There is no more he can do.

He wanders the streets of the city until dawn. At first light, he returns to the spot and looks again at the blood on the grass, dry and dark as Egyptian coffee. He finds the footprints of the men from the Citroën in the soft soil by the edge of the park fence. One man's shoes' prints are peculiar. His right foot is several inches shorter than the left one.

There is nothing more he can do.

The neon of the Al Montaza fades out against the sky, handing the watch to the dawn. The swollen sun hunches up from behind the Sinai in a halo of smoke, the Devil rising from the underworld, and blows its scorching breath across the city.

His heart is as dry and empty as the desert.

The door into the Oval Office burst open and William Wilbert charged in, head bent forward pugnaciously. Two Secret Service agents trailed in his wake. Daniels' mouth opened to protest the intrusion, but Wilbert began talking immediately.

"Agents Cooper and Farris," he said, pushing them forward unceremoniously. "They were both with her when it happened." Cooper, the senior of the two, his face white and quivering, blurted out his story all in one breath: "Mr. President, we accompanied Mrs. Kamenev in the limousine to the Office of Immigration an hour and a half ago, for her interview for citizenship papers. After the meeting, she wanted to go shopping in Georgetown. We stopped outside a small dress shop on M Street. Agent Farris waited by the limo, I waited inside, near the front of the store. Mrs. Kamenev went into the back to try on a dress and didn't come out. I asked the woman clerk to check on her. She looked and discovered she was gone. We found a back exit, leading into an alley. We believe she was taken through there."

The President eyed Cooper harshly. "Taken?"

"Yes sir. Kidnapped."

Daniels felt his stomach lurch. "Did you see anybody actually grab her?"

"No sir. We looked around the streets nearby and couldn't find her. But Farris saw a black limousine with DPL plates cruise down M Street twenty minutes earlier. We guessed what might have happened. We broke in on the police frequency and asked them to issue an emergency bulletin. Ten minutes later a patrol car in Arlington reported it had spotted a limousine going west on Memorial Parkway. There was a blond woman inside. They remembered the plate number. DPL 46."

"DPL 46 is the Russian Embassy," Wilbert explained. "What were they doing in Arlington?"

"It's the route to Dulles airport," Friedrich said.

Wilbert nodded, a tight-lipped scowl on his face. "Aeroflot 52— Washington, Helsinki, Moscow. Departs at noon."

Daniels jumped angrily from his chair. "It's not going to happen," he said, his eyes flashing. "Not in a million goddamn years!"

Farris and Cooper edged back a step, toward the wall. Wilbert folded his arms together, bracing himself for a flood of presidential directives.

"Call Dulles airport," Daniels commanded. "Tell them to stop that flight. Direct order from me." He punched the intercom. "Frances, get the helicopter on the lawn and tell the crew to stand by. Get Dan McCormick in here with half a dozen of his men. Get Hodges and Clark on a conference line. And get the Russian ambassador on another line."

Daniels flipped off the intercom and glanced at Friedrich. "Semenenko could be behind this. Find him and tell him all cooperation on the Suitland Parkway investigation is off until they release Katya. And if he's personally involved in this, tell him we'll kick him the hell out of the country."

Friedrich pushed himself quickly off the sofa. "I'll get on it right away," he said.

Wilbert, over by the fireplace, cradled the phone he was using. "The flight's just loading," he said. "The airport can't confirm that Mrs. Kamenev is on board. But they'll hold the flight on a routine delay, check the passenger manifest, and get back to us."

The intercom buzzed: "Mr. President, Mr. Hodges and Mr. Clark on sixty-four."

Daniels lifted the receiver. "Luke? Mack? Listen to me. We believe the Soviet Union is trying to kidnap the premier's widow. We think they're putting her aboard the noon flight to Moscow at Dulles Airport. We're holding the plane. Get as many of your men out there as possible as *soon* as possible."

Frances was on the intercom again: "Ambassador Vordshilov, Mr. President. On sixty-five."

Daniels punched another button on the console: "Mr. Ambassador?"

Voroshilov knew why Daniels was calling: "Yes, Mr. President," he replied, his voice calm and placating. "Mrs. Kamenev has decided to return home. I hope you will not interfere."

"If Katya wants to go home, I'm not going to stop her."

"I'm pleased to hear that."

"But I intend to hear it from her own lips."

There was a pause on the other end. "It is the position of the Soviet government," Voroshilov said, "that this is an internal matter, involving a Soviet citizen. . . ."

"It is the position of the United States government," Daniels interrupted, "that you're not taking her anywhere!" He slammed down the receiver. "So much for international diplomacy."

Wilbert looked up from the telephone by the fireplace. "I've called the Virginia State Police. They'll cordon off the airport, block all roadways in and out. They've promised a hundred men within twenty minutes."

Daniels nodded. "Okay. That'll slow down the press, at least. Now call the National Guard. I want all the airport runways blocked and a ring of military trucks around the jet. They might ignore the tower and try to take off without permission."

Wilbert went back to the phone. A roar drowned out the voices in the office as the president's helicopter loomed over the lawn outside. Daniels yelled for Frances.

"Set up a communications link," he told her. "Situation room to the airport. The news people will see the helicopter and know something is up. Tell Jerry to stall them. Promise them we'll have an announcement for them later in the afternoon. If we're lucky we can settle this business before they find out what's going on."

Dan McCormick arrived with a contingent of six agents.

"Take the helicopter to Dulles," Daniels told him. "I want you to be my eyes and ears at the airport. And I want you to bring Mrs. Kamenev back on the chopper with you when this is over."

McCormick pulled open the French doors onto the Rose Garden and led his men toward the helicopter pad.

Daniels followed him to the door. His head was churning. He had an overwhelming urge to board the helicopter. He knew it would be foolhardy to go to the airport himself, but every nerve in him cried out at him to go.

He glanced back into the office. Wilbert had walked up behind him. "I know what you're thinking," he said. "Don't do it!"

Daniels stared at him without answering.

"Clark and Hodges and McCormick can handle it. They're the professionals. Don't get in their way. You can direct them from here."

"If I go," Daniels said, "the pressure on the Russians to release her will be tremendous."

"And what if they don't?" Wilbert persisted. "What if there's a standoff? They'll make a fool out of you. And think of the press!"

"This means a lot to me," Daniels said.

"I know what you're feeling," Wilbert replied. "But it's wrong. You'll be taking completely unnecessary risks. And you'll be putting your interests ahead of the country's. She's not Helen of Troy!"

"Her life is in danger! That's reason enough! I'm responsible for her!"

Wilbert shook his head violently. "You're not responsible for her! Come to your senses!"

Wilbert then did something that astonished him as much as the president. He grabbed Daniels by the arm and held him, physically restrained him, from going out the door. The president glared murderously at his chief of staff for several tense seconds. Wilbert held his grip. Finally, with a dejected sigh, Daniels relaxed and nodded. Wilbert released his arm and stepped back, trembling with relief.

A minute later the helicopter lifted off. The president stood nervously in the doorway and watched it as it bent its ponderous bulk westward and disappeared over the roof of the Old Executive Office Building.

Warfield slept fitfully until late in the afternoon. He awoke feeling agitated and depressed.

A jeep drove up to the building and blew its horn. He pushed himself to a sitting position and looked out the window. Someone from the mess hall was bringing a stack of covered containers to the outside door. His face looked familiar.

Warfield heard a low exchange of voices. After a pause, the guard unlocked his door and deposited the stack of covered trays on the floor. Warfield dragged himself from the cot and carried the stack over to the table by the bed.

He opened the containers, one at a time. The first held a reddish brown soup, presumably tomato. The second a slice of meatloaf, a pile of mashed potatoes, and a serving of gray green string beans. The third contained a slice of apple pie.

Maybe he would eat the pie. And ask the guard for a cup of coffee from the machine down the hall.

No, he had better eat the whole dinner, he told himself. It might make him feel better.

He set the container of soup on the table and searched for the spoon. He found it in the tray with the pie, wrapped up in a napkin with a fork. No knife. He smiled bitterly. Someone had had the foresight not to provide him with a weapon.

Warfield dipped the spoon into the soup, filled it, and brought it to his lips. He hated cold soup. Maybe if he offered the busboy

174 . . .

a tip he'd get it to him hot next time. Not that he planned on a long stay.

Warfield stopped. He looked at the spoonful of soup.

The busboy. He remembered now. It was the same busboy he had bumped into in front of the infirmary the day before yesterday, bringing food for the assassin, Martinez.

Warfield lowered the spoon back into the bowl. *But that was not all.*

He jumped up, banging the inside of his knees against the edge of the bed, and rummaged frantically underneath for his notebook, pulling out the photocopy the blond reporter had given him in Potomac Park the night before.

He unfolded it and studied the face peering out the windshield of the ambulance.

The similarities were immediately obvious. The same black hair, furtive eyes, pushed-in nose.

Warfield's hands trembled as he gazed at the photo.

That busboy was the missing assassin. The Turk!

23

PRESIDENT DANIELS AND HIS chief of staff hurried from the elevator across the carpeted corridor of the subbasement to the vaulted amphitheater thirty feet beneath the White House called the Situation Room. From this command post, protected by tons of reinforced concrete and a sophisticated alarm and surveillance system, the president had at his instant disposal all the awesome weapons of the world's most advanced technological power. From long banks of computers and video terminals, White House Communications could reach out instantly to any government or individual, could issue commands to any U.S. embassy, military base, missile station, plane, ship, or submarine anywhere on the surface of the earth. And with its dozens of spy satellites roaming the reaches of outer space, it could see anything—from the movement of tanks across Eastern

Europe, to the time on a wristwatch of a farmer in Uzbekistan.

Manned continuously by a staff of Signal Corps officers, it was nicknamed the Throne Room, because it embodied such extravagant, arbitrary omnipotence. From this subterranean chamber the president of the United States could literally call down the destruction of the world—and watch it happen on video monitors a half hour later.

The mood in the room was tense, subdued. A dozen officers sat at their stations around the walls, waiting to carry out the president's commands.

Daniels slipped into the broad leather chair in front of the central monitor bank in the middle of the room. Two officers immediately took seats facing him. One was a stenographer, to record his orders, the other a technical specialist, to operate the master control panel. Wilbert rolled up another chair and sat behind the president.

Daniels looked over the low bank of monitors at the technical specialist, a red-headed captain with a freckled face. "What time is it in Moscow, Captain?" he asked.

The officer consulted his video display. "Eight in the evening, Mr. President."

"Alert them at the Kremlin," he ordered.

"Yes sir."

The officer punched a button to activate the Hotline, the special telecommunications link between Moscow and Washington reserved for emergencies. Within ten seconds, an alarm bell would begin ringing in a similar room somewhere inside the Kremlin.

"Now put me on that helicopter," Daniels said.

The captain began punching a series of commands into the keyboard in front of him.

Daniels turned to Wilbert. "If we can hold them on the ground long enough, they'll have to let her go."

Wilbert nodded. "Maybe. But you should let them take her."

"Forget it, we're committed."

"A confrontation is dangerous," Wilbert argued. "Someone could miscalculate. This isn't worth starting a war over."

Daniels glanced impatiently in the direction of the Signal Corps captain, still busy at his keyboard. "Okay. We need a quick solution, then. Something that will save face for the Russians, but still get Katya off that plane."

"You're talking about a trade?"

"If we can, why not?"

"Like what?"

"You're my chief adviser," Daniels said, maliciously. "Think of something."

Wilbert sighed. "Thanks for giving me the easy ones."

The screen in front of Daniels flashed on, and slowly resolved into a black and white image of the flight deck of the presidential helicopter, en route to Dulles airport. The center of the screen was dominated by another Signal Corps officer, manning the ship's communications, and by the elongated figure of Dan McCormick, hovering over him. Off to one side, the back of the pilot's head and shoulders were visible.

"Dan!" the president called. "Can you read me?"

McCormick looked back up into the camera's eye. "Yes, I can, Mr. President."

"What's the situation?"

"All traffic is being cleared from the area," McCormick replied. "And all take-offs delayed. Airport security confirms that Mrs. Kamenev boarded the plane, accompanied by three Russian officials. Aeroflot 54 is now taxiing to runway four-left."

"Taxiing? They're supposed to stop it!"

"Hold on," McCormick said. Daniels saw him bend over the radioman's shoulders and press a headset against his ear. The faint crackle of radio static drifted out into the air-conditioned stillness of the Situation Room.

McCormick looked up into the camera eye again. "Dulles Control says that 54 is not answering their request," he said.

"Jesus Christ!" Daniels exploded. He gestured violently at the red-headed captain. "Patch me into Dulles Control!"

The officer nodded, hesitated briefly over his keyboard, then began punching keys. "You're on now, Mr. President," he said. "I have to warn you that this is not a secure frequency."

Daniels ignored him and bent forward to the pencil microphone protruding from the panel before him. "Dulles Control! This is President Eliot Daniels! Can you hear me?"

A thin voice crackled at the other end. "Loud and clear, Mr. President."

"Good! This is important. We must prevent the Aeroflot jet from taking off!"

"We copy, Mr. President. When Aeroflot Fifty-four reaches the holding point at runway four-left, it will wait for take-off clearance from air-traffic control. We'll again request they delay."

Daniels cleared his throat. "They won't wait for any such thing! Tell them to stop right where they are, right now! On my orders!"

"We copy. Stand by. . . ."

"Dan!" the president called, looking at his monitor. "How far are you from the airport now?"

"Eight nautical miles, Mr. President. We'll be over the field in six minutes."

Daniels drummed impatiently on the armrests, waiting for the control tower's reply. A babble of words and static poured from the speaker in front of him—cool voices conveying urgent messages, rerouting flights, holding others. His orders had thrown the day's business at one of the world's largest airports into chaos, and it was scrambling frantically to accommodate him.

The control tower voice came back: "Mr. President. Ground control has requested Aeroflot hold immediately, and is waiting for acknowledgment. I'm following Fifty-four on binoculars from the tower now. It's still moving toward runway one-right. It'll reach the holding point in about a minute."

Daniels looked across at the Signal Corps officer, sitting impassively at the control console. "Can the Aeroflot captain hear our conversation with the tower?"

"Yes, sir, he can."

Daniels glanced at Wilbert. Wilbert shrugged.

"Can we get a secure connection?" he asked the corpsman.

The man shook his head. "That would have to be on a military channel, Mr. President. The airport doesn't have that capacity."

Daniels expelled a long, exasperated breath. "Well, the hell with it. Let them hear us. Dulles Control? I've ordered police, FBI, and National Guard units to the airport. Make sure you allow them immediate access to the runways. In the meantime, I want you to block the path of that jet. It might try to take off without waiting for clearance."

"We copy, Mr. President, but that would be a dangerous maneuver. He still needs our Standard Instrument Departure and a radio number code from us first."

"No," Daniels said. "Their pilot knows you've cleared all the other traffic out of the sky. He could chance it. You have emergency vehicles—fire trucks, ambulances—near the runways. How long will it take you to get some of them out there to block its path?"

There was a prolonged silence at the other end.

"Hello!" Daniels yelled into his mike.

"Yes sir, I'm here. I'm trying to locate the airport manager, Mr. President. He can authorize that. I can't."

"Where is he?"

"We're paging him now, sir. Stand by. . . ."

The president turned to Wilbert to vent his frustration. "We need the permission of the airport manager to stop a kidnapping!"

Suddenly a heavier, older voice boomed over the speaker. "Yes sir, Mr. President. This is Collins, the airport manager. I'm authorizing a dozen emergency vehicles to move to runway one-right immediately."

"Thank you, Mr. Collins! How long will it take them to get there?"

"The holding point on one-right is several miles from here, and it'll take a couple of minutes to get men in the vehicles and headed out there. Say five minutes."

The president shook his head. "That's not soon enough! Is the control tower still on the line?"

"I'm here, Mr. President."

"What's the plane doing now?"

"He's stopped at the holding point. He's just replying to our demand for a hold. Stand by. . . ."

The Signal Corps officer interrupted: "I have Moscow on the line, Mr. President. A read-out is coming up on the monitor to your left."

Daniels glanced at the smaller video screen to his left. He saw a quick march of green phosphor words across the screen—first in Russian, then in English: "Greetings to the president of the United States from the premier of the Soviet Union. I await your message. . . ."

Daniels looked over at the military aide waiting by the steno-type machine and dictated his message: "Greetings to Premier Bulgakov. I apologize for the call. Representatives of your government have taken Mrs. Kamenev on board your Aeroflot flight 54, now ready for take-off from Dulles Airport. We have reason to believe that this was done against her will. I urgently request you direct them to delay the flight and allow representatives of our government to ask Mrs. Kamenev in person whether or not she wishes to return to the Soviet Union. Otherwise, we cannot permit your flight to depart."

The aide read back the message. Daniels nodded and hastily affixed his signature to the steno pad. The aide then typed the message directly into the hotline teletype. Daniels watched as it appeared on his monitor. Two minutes later, the Russian translation appeared below it, indicating that Moscow had received the message.

Aboard the helicopter, Dan McCormick put down the headset he had been holding and stepped up to the front of the flight deck.

"We're approaching Dulles," the pilot said.

McCormick bent forward and surveyed the panorama visible through the wide curve of the windshield. Ahead and to the right, about two miles' distance, he saw the control tower, architect Eero Saarinen's unmistakable tall, pagodalike structure, presiding over the sprawling acres of runways, hangars, access roads, and parking lots.

"The tower has us in view," the pilot said.

"Aeroflot Fifty-four isn't going to wait!" the radioman yelled.

McCormick gripped the backs of the pilots' seats and fixed his eyes on the approaching airport, his mind making rapid calculations. If the jet took off, it was possible that it could be forced down by U.S. interceptor jets before it cleared American airspace. They could scramble in minutes from nearby bases. But that was a dangerous option. If the Russian plane refused to be forced down, then the next level of escalation would be to shoot it down. That was out of the question, of course, even as a threat.

The plane had to be stopped on the ground.

"Can you see runway one-right?" McCormick asked.

Both pilot and copilot studied the maze of airport pavement ahead of them. The copilot found it first. "Over there!" he said, pointing to his right. "At two o'clock. There's the jet, too, at the holding point. He's about three miles from us."

McCormick saw it: a long, swept-wing Ilyushin 62, its four engines mounted in pairs against each side of the rear fuselage.

"He's throttling up, too," the pilot said, his voice deadpan.

McCormick glanced back toward the camera eye, mounted on the bulkhead over the lounge door. "What do you want to do, Mr. President?"

No reply. McCormick looked into the lounge, where his six agents sat, nervously checking radios and weapons, then forward out the windshield. In about one minute, he judged, the Ilyushin could be down the runway and airborne.

"Take us toward the runway," he said. The pilot nodded.

The flight deck crackled with the president's voice again. "I'm still waiting for a reply from the Kremlin, Dan. What's the situation now?"

"He's about to leave," McCormick said. "Nothing down there to stop him."

Another silence. He could feel President Daniels' tension in it, communicated almost telepathically. A dramatic idea seized him. It was dangerous, but something had to be done immediately.

"I think we can block him, Mr. President!"

The pilot craned his neck around, looking at the Secret Service agent as if he had lost his senses.

"Don't do anything risky, Dan," the president said.

"We'll lose him if I don't!"

Another silence. Daniels didn't press his argument. McCormick could read his boss' mind. He knew how much that Russian woman meant to him. The others on the helicopter would also be put at risk, but that was their job—taking risks for the president.

"Use your own judgment, then," Daniels' voice said.

McCormick smiled at the camera. That was as close as Daniels dared come to saying "okay." The agent pressed his hand down on the pilot's shoulder. "Tell the control tower we're heading directly for that runway!" he said. "Tell them to tell the Russian pilot that we're setting this chopper down right in his path. If he wants to take off, he'll have to run over us."

The pilot shook his head. Technically he was in charge of the aircraft, and could refuse any order he thought unsafe. Sensing he was wavering, McCormick went for the jugular, and challenged the man's professional pride: "You can do it, can't you?"

"I guess so, but . . ."

"Then the faster you get us there, the better!"

The pilot throttled the helicopter forward. Its nose pitched abruptly downward as the huge blades bit deeper into the air, churning like an angry insect toward runway one-right. McCormick, one hand tight around a bulkhead grip, bent forward to study the scene. The end of the vast runway, nearly three miles in length, was now directly below, and rising toward them. From the opposite end, the Russian Ilyushin faced them, vapor pluming up from its exhausts.

"How much of this strip does he need to get airborne?" McCormick shouted, over the engine's roar.

"I don't know," the pilot replied.

"Ask the control tower!" McCormick snapped. He watched the surface of the runway loom just beneath them.

"They say eight thousand feet!" the pilot said, his voice suddenly losing its laconic deadpan.

"Take us further up the runway!"

The pilot complied. McCormick watched the broken white center-line slide by thirty feet below. Ahead, the silhouette of the Ilyushin began to grow.

"They're moving!" the copilot shouted.

Heavy jet fuel vapor billowed up from behind the craft, creating a hazy penumbra around it, and even from dead-on a mile and a half away, McCormick could see the vibrations as the Ilyushin rolled forward.

"The tower says they've started take-off," the radioman yelled from behind. "He warns us to get clear!"

"Set it down right here," McCormick ordered.

The pilot, sweat popping out on his forehead, dropped the helicopter swiftly to the tarmac, bouncing it hard on its undercarriage.

"Cut the engines!" McCormick demanded. "They have to see we're committed!"

The chopper's rotor blades drooped to a stop, and the craft sat dead on the center of the runway, parked sideways to present the maximum visible target, its red beacon pulsing steadily from the tail. The large porthole windows and the windshield framed the faces of the crew and the Secret Service agents, as they watched Aeroflot 54, bear down on them.

Wilbert jumped out of his chair and waved his arms in agitation. "Christ, Eliot, order them out of there! They'll all be killed!"

Daniels sat rigid, his eyes trained on the video image of the helicopter's flight deck, and the frozen forms of the men on board. "It's too late," he whispered.

The Ilyushin was rolling fast, shrinking the distance with alarming rapidity, and for a few terrible seconds McCormick believed he had made an enormous mistake.

The jet was scarcely a quarter of a mile away now, and its size made it appear closer. Its wing surfaces suddenly blossomed, like a giant bird ruffling its feathers, as the Russian pilot raised spoilers and lowered flaps to stem the aircraft's momentum. Black smoke poured from the burning rubber of the landing gear as the brakes locked in.

The Ilyushin's nose began to wobble and shudder, and in the now-silent helicopter they heard the thunderous roar of the jet's four mammouth engines reversing thrust. Instinctively everyone dropped to the helicopter floor. Only McCormick stood, his eyes focused on the looming face of the Russian pilot, willing him to stop in time.

The screeching abated, the thunder of the jets faded. The Ilyushin came to a bucking halt barely ten feet from the helicopter's fragile flanks. The jet's gigantic bulk overshadowed the chopper entirely, blocking the view of the terminal building and the control tower.

Beneath the Ilyushin's right wing McCormick spotted a distant fire truck speeding toward them, leading a long column of other vehicles. A chorus of sirens, still faint, swelled to fill the silence. McCormick turned and faced the camera lens, his heart still pounding. He started to say "We won that round," but he was too shaken to get the words out.

24

WARFIELD FOUND AN ASPIRIN bottle in the bottom of his shaving kit. He emptied the pills onto the bed and filled the bottle with small samples from his uneaten dinner—a pinch each of meatloaf, mashed potato, string bean, and pie. Finally he soaked a piece of his paper napkin in the soup, wadded it into a ball, and stuffed it in with the other samples and snapped the plastic lid back in place.

He tucked the bottle into his shirt pocket and buttoned the flap. He checked his watch. It was six-thirty and dark outside. Most of the base personnel would be at the mess hall.

He pounded on the door for the guard. "I have to go to the head!"

The guard unlocked the door and stepped into the room, eyeing Warfield cautiously. He had come on duty at six; Warfield had not seen him before.

"Hold your arms out in front of you, please!" The young corporal removed the pair of handcuffs from his belt and slapped them around Warfield's wrists.

"This is really not necessary, Corporal Ostrowski," he said, reading the Marine's name tag.

Corporal Ostrowski didn't reply. Warfield shrugged and let himself be escorted down the corridor toward the john.

Inside, Warfield went through the pretense of taking down his pants, dropping the toilet seat, and sitting on it. He let five minutes pass, mentally rehearsing his plan of action. Ostrowski was about six-three and 230 pounds, he judged. Probably not long out of boot camp. Big and tough, but green.

Warfield flushed the toilet, pulled up his pants, and buckled his belt, a task made difficult by the handcuffs. He wasted another few minutes washing and drying his hands. He could hear the young Marine outside the door, shifting his weight impatiently on the creaky wooden floorboards.

Warfield stepped out briskly, grinning at the guard, and started back down the corridor, relieved to see it was still deserted. The guard fell into step behind him.

"I discovered something very important in there, Ostrowski," he said, looking over his shoulder. "You want to know what it is?"

The guard barked out a sharp "Sir!"

"I discovered that it's almost impossible to wipe your ass with handcuffs on."

The Marine didn't laugh.

"What you can do, though," Warfield added, "is this!"

In a blur, he whirled and dropped his chained hands over the guard's head, clamped his fingers together at the back of his neck, and brought the young corporal's face forward to meet his rising knee. The impact, carried from the point of the chin up his jawbone to his ears, knocked him unconscious instantly. He collapsed to the floor so heavily that Warfield was pulled on top of him, the chain of his handcuffs caught under the guard's throat.

Warfield untangled himself, pulled the key from the guard's belt case, and worked to unlock the cuffs, a clumsy business that consumed nearly a minute of nerve-racking effort.

He dragged the Marine's bulk down the hall and into his room, and quickly handcuffed him to the bedspring, gagging him with the pillow case. The Marine's pistol felt cumbersome in his hand, but the clip was loaded and it was no time to be fussy. He stuck it behind his belt at the small of his back.

The corridor was still empty. He buttoned his overcoat and hurried out the door.

Outside he ducked into the shadows at the side of the building and plotted his next move. He saw two ways to escape. One was through the woods to the perimeter fence. That was the easy way. The camp boundaries were patrolled at hourly intervals after dark, so getting over the chain-link fence was no problem. The problem was the risk of getting lost in the acres of woods around the camp. He hadn't time for that.

The other way out was faster. Steal a car and bluff his way through the main gate. The risk there was in the timing. Once the word got out that he was loose, they'd automatically close the gates and increase the sentry. He estimated a minimum of ten minutes before someone discovered Ostrowski and raised an alarm. Ten minutes. He would have to chance it.

Voices punctuated the evening air as people filtered from the mess hall and fanned out across the base. The moon was nearly full in a cloudless sky. It illuminated the parking lot in back of a nearby barracks so brightly that Warfield was afraid to risk entering it. He decided to move further on, in the direction of the administration building.

He would have to be brazen, he decided, or run out of time. He strode purposefully toward the long, low structure that housed the camp's main offices. Directly in front of him he saw a Cadillac Seville, parked in a visitor's space, a key chain dangling invitingly from the ignition. He stepped in, started the engine, and drove slowly toward the main gate, a half mile away.

The gate was busy. Two buses waited to get in, and a line of four vehicles waited to get out. He drove up behind the last car in the line and forced himself to sit calmly behind the wheel while the sentries processed the passes. He looked at his watch. Exactly ten minutes had passed since he had left the young Marine handcuffed to the bed. The odds were good that he'd make it through, he thought.

His own inattention nearly defeated him.

The guardhouse, he realized belatedly, rarely checked passes going out. Yet it was checking them now. Two guards were standing at the windows of the two cars ahead of him, and a third guard was approaching him. There was an obvious reason. They were looking for him.

He lowered his window. The sentry placed a gloved hand on the door and bent down to peer inside.

"What's the delay?" Warfield demanded.

"We're checking all ID's, sir."

"Going out? That's damned inconvenient. Mine's in my luggage."

"Sorry, sir. You'll have to get it. Word's just come down. We're looking for somebody."

Warfield shook his head with feigned annoyance. "I'll have to pull over to the side and dig it out."

The guard stepped back. Warfield edged the Cadillac back from the line and surveyed the scene before him. The cars waiting to go out completely blocked the narrow exit lane. The entrance lane, on the left side of the sentry box, was momentarily empty, but a big olive green Camp Peary bus was moving toward it.

Warfield's right hand settled on the shift-box lever and slipped it from "D" to "L," so the car would remain in first gear. He stepped on the gas pedal hard. The automobile spun gravel, fishtailed wildly for about ten feet, then shot through the narrow gap between the bus and the entrance lane like a whale through the locks of a canal.

For three miles he jockeyed the Cadillac down country lanes, driving on the edge of control, one foot on the gas pedal, the other on the brake. On a dark strip of dirt road just past a gas station he abandoned it, and walked back to the station and stole a VW Rabbit parked in front. Half an hour later he abandoned that in turn on a side street in Williamsburg.

From a drugstore he placed a call to Rosenstock's house in Arlington. There was no answer. He didn't have Howard Moore's number, and had no idea where he lived. That left Nan Robertson. She lived in Williamsburg, he remembered, somewhere near William and Mary College. He consulted the tattered pages of the directory hanging in the booth, and dialed her number. No answer.

He rented a car from an Avis garage several blocks from the drugstore and drove south, with no destination in mind.

He passed through Newport News and Norfolk, then took the toll bridge and tunnel that crosses Chesapeake Bay from Cape Henry to Cape Charles, and followed Route 13 up the narrow peninsula of Maryland. At a town called Salisbury, he stopped at a diner and consumed a plate of scrambled eggs, ham, and toast.

Back in the car, he drove east, to the ocean, parked and walked along a deserted stretch of winter shoreline, watching the waves shatter the lace patterns of the moonlight.

Pressure seemed to be building inside him, as if he were being pumped full of air. He ran along the hard sand by the edge of the water, slowly at first, then increasing his pace until he was racing with the abandon of a sprinter.

A mile down the beach he flopped onto the sand, gasping from the exertion. The pressure remained. He could not outrun it. He staggered to his feet and started back, throwing rocks at the water, shouting curses over the roar of the breaking surf.

In the car again, he steered south, retracing his route down the peninsula. At stretches along the empty back roads he pressed the gas pedal of the Buick to the floor and watched its speedometer flutter around the hundred mark. Outside the town of Exmoor a police cruiser gave chase. Speeding through stop signs, Warfield outran it.

He turned the radio volume up full and spun the dial impatiently past a raucous garble of rock, country music, and call-in shows.

Back at Cape Charles he recrossed the bay and stopped in Newport News. He rented a room in a motel and called Rosenstock's number again. His sister Louise answered.

"I'm sorry, Mr. Warfield. He's not here. I expect him tomorrow."

"Tell him I'm staying at the Captain's Cabin. The number is 471-3200."

Warfield paced the tiny box of his motel room for a few minutes, then went outside and walked downtown. It was ten o'clock and sharply colder. He wore no hat or gloves; the wind penetrated his thin overcoat.

The pressure still swelled, pushing against his consciousness, leaving him no room to think. He knew what was happening to him. Delayed shock, triggered by Martinez's death. He had suffered it once before, in Egypt. It was a terrifying sensation, a crushing stress akin to suffocation or drowning. Impossible to tolerate, impossible to escape, it could drive its victim to suicide.

He stopped to ponder his direction in front of a saloon. Through the partially curtained windows he saw a crowd of customers pressed up to the long, mirrored bar. The dim, rosy light brought back an intense flood of memories.

He thought about it, shivering on the sidewalk, then summoned up the willpower to walk away.

But before he reached the end of the block he turned around, walked back, and went inside.

25

VLADIMIR STEPANOVICH BElieved he enjoyed the best life in all Russia. He held the rank of colonel in the KGB, a position of great status and influence. He had a wonderful wife, Valeska, and two handsome, talented children. He had a large apartment on the edge of Moscow's Lenin Hills, and a *dacha* outside Kaluga. He owned a Mosvitch automobile that was only one year old. His salary and special privileges gave him and his family access to the special Party stores on Moscow's Granovskovo Street, and the elite Kremlin Polyclinic on Kalinin Prospekt. And best of all, his work took him all over the world, a privilege to which very few Russians could even aspire. In fifteen years he had traveled to forty-five countries.

Of course there were others in the party and government bureaucracy with equivalent, and even greater status. What made his situation so perfect was that no serious responsibility went with it. He was totally insulated. No bureaucratic infighting, no subordinates trying to do him in, no superiors taking advantage of him. And on top of all this, he loved his work.

Vladimir Stepanovich was an electronic communications specialist. And his special bailiwick within that sophisticated technological domain was a very narrow one: antennas.

The KGB employed him full time for a single technical responsibility: installing and overseeing the maintenance of the antennas placed atop Soviet embassies in the world's capital cities. These antennas played an important role in Russia's electronic espionage effort. They were used to eavesdrop on a wide range of the host country's domestic communications.

Only rarely did his work inconvenience him. The events of the past twenty-four hours had been particularly unusual. Moscow Center had actually wakened him at five o'clock in the morning, told him to pack his bags and diplomatic passport, and be on that day's flight to the United States. From Dulles airport, he had been whisked by limousine to the Russian Embassy on Sixteenth and H Street. Total time in transit: sixteen hours.

He yawned as Yuri Kropatkin, the cultural attaché—and senior KGB resident—unlocked the door on the fifth floor that led to the embassy's roof.

"Tired already, Vladimir? And you haven't even begun work!"

The antenna specialist grunted. "You would be, too. It's one in the morning here and nine o'clock in the morning in Moscow. The jet lag is terrible! And I never stay in one place long enough to adjust!"

"Don't complain to me!" Kropatkin said. "You must be the highest-paid TV repairman in the world."

Stepanovich colored at the remark. He didn't like self-important officials who belittled his work. Lack of respect from his KGB colleagues was the one drawback of the job. He dismissed it as simple jealousy, but it rankled nevertheless.

"Do you have everything you need, Vladimir?" Kropatkin asked, his tone friendly, but still mocking. "I have a screwdriver in my desk downstairs if you need it."

"*Yeb tvoyu mat,*" he retorted, in the all-purpose Russian obscenity. "Fuck your mother."

Stepanovich lugged his box of tools up the narrow stairs that led to the roof. Once there, he paused to take in the magnificent view. To the south, the panorama jumped out at him: the great dome of the Capitol, far down Pennsylvania Avenue on his left; the magnificent spire of the Washington Monument, the Lincoln and Jefferson Memorials; and in the distance to his right, the Custis-Lee Mansion in Arlington Cemetery. He had visited them all on past trips to the United States. Next to Paris, he considered Washington the most beautiful capital in the world.

Stepanovich made a circuit of the small flat area of the embassy roof, checking the status of each antenna. When the new embassy opened up on Wisconsin Avenue next year, they would all have to be removed and reinstalled. That could mean an entire week in Washington. Maybe he could persuade them to let him bring Valeska.

He examined the leads of the largest antenna, a high-frequency configuration on a sixteen-foot mast with a rotor so it could alternately monitor Pentagon or State Department radio traffic. A smaller antenna on a short mast diagonally across from it was also a high-frequency model, trained on the CIA's communications facilities. He gave them a cursory check and then moved over behind a wooden shed sitting incongruously in the middle of the roof. It contained highly sensitive computer monitoring equipment, whose functions even he was not allowed to know completely. On the back side of the shed another mast held a small, peculiarly shaped vertical quarter-wave antenna, used to intercept government limousine communications.

A fourth antenna nearby was a high-gain pickup used to receive and transmit the embassy's own coded radio traffic to and from Moscow Center and the Ministry of Foreign Affairs.

There was a fifth antenna on the roof, as well. Stepanovich plucked one of its guy-wires and smiled to himself. It was the only one he had not personally installed—a seventy-five-dollar, U.S.-made TV antenna.

Stepanovich often wondered how useful all this sophisticated interception equipment really was. The U.S. government was intimately familiar with most of it. The FBI had photographed him installing the antennas with telephoto lenses from every surrounding rooftop—the University Club to the north, the Corporation for Public Broadcasting to the south, and the National Geographic building across the street. He knew they must have a fat dossier on both him and the antennas.

That's why he was out here tonight, in the dark of the moon. Instructions—straight from General Semenenko himself—had specified that this new antenna be installed in secret.

Stepanovich unlocked the small door to the shed and crawled inside. He turned on the small bulb in the ceiling and looked for the package that had been placed there for him earlier in the day. He found it, pulled it out onto the floor, and unwrapped it.

It took over an hour to install it. Again, Semenenko had been specific—the antenna must be erected *inside* the shed, away from prying eyes. As a result, the mast could only stand five feet high. The antenna Stepanovich mounted on top of it was an expensive microwave dish, about a foot and a half in diameter. It was a super high-gain antenna, capable of picking up and amplifying signals from a very weak source, like a small electronic bug. The most difficult part of the installation, Stepanovich discovered, was setting the dish in proper alignment with its target. He was forced to do it by line of sight, and even with the bright moon, it was a tedious chore, requiring him to walk back and forth from the shed to the edge of the parapet.

Finally he was certain it was properly aligned. A few degrees off from dead center wouldn't affect its performance much, anyway. The White House was a broad target at this close distance, a half a mile down Sixteenth Street.

Finished with the work on the roof, he packed his tool kit and locked the shed door. All that remained to complete the job was to run the leads down to the fourth floor and attach them to the special transceiver in the communications room, directly beneath the shed.

Tomorrow, with any luck, he could spend all day shopping.

26

THE SUDDENLY ABORTED
take off had thrown the tourist compartment of Aeroflot 54 into
pandemonium. Hand luggage, purses, and magazines had
bounced around the cabin and one passenger who had neglected
to fasten his seat belt had been thrown against the seats and injured.

Minutes after the first shock had worn off, passengers began
clogging the aisles, speculating on what had happened, and competing for window positions to watch the unfolding drama outside.
The three flight attendants cared for the injured, calmed the hys-
terical, and tried to persuade everyone to return to his seat. As
time passed, and the plane remained stationary, the passengers
turned restless and angry, demanding an explanation for the
emergency stop and the interminable delay.

Up front, in the first-class compartment of the giant Ilyushin,
which had been sealed off from the rest of the aircraft, the atmosphere was far different. An eerie stillness prevailed, broken only
by the low voices of two KGB bodyguards, sitting in the forward
row. The remaining seats in the compartment were unoccupied,
save the one in the far right corner, where Katya Kamenev sat, her
head resting against the cushion, her coat drawn tightly around
her. A glass of vodka had spilled on the tray in front of her during
the sudden stop, and she had not moved to right it.

She turned her head to the side to look out the window.
Through the Plexiglas she could see a broad area around the Ilyushin. Hundreds of men in uniform stood out on the runway, forming a human fence around a handful of jeeps and trucks parked
close to the aircraft. Beyond, she watched a caravan of buses drive
up and park one behind the other, bumper touching bumper,
until they formed a huge outer ring, enclosing the two aircraft, the
soldiers, and the vehicles in a kind of mammoth corral.

The imprisoning wall of buses heightened her sense of desolation. Depression descended on her, pressing against body and
spirit so heavily that it was an effort to speak, to move, to think.

The image of the town on the postcard flashed into her consciousness. As a young girl in the labor camp, it had symbolized
freedom to her, an abstract vision of happiness that she had
yearned for the way a caged bird yearns to experience the sky. She

did not understand then what freedom meant. She did not know then that she had traded the labor camp fences for a bigger, invisible cage, a prison that would travel with her to the ends of the earth.

By agreeing to this kidnap ruse, without even questioning its purpose, or what new problems it would create for her, she knew she was only perpetuating her own enslavement. She should have refused. But she needed something. Something only Semenenko was in a position to give her. Only when she had that, could she hope to smash at last through those invisible walls.

The door from the tourist compartment popped open and a stewardess walked to Katya's seat, conspiratorial pleasure in her eyes. "I have a surprise for you, Madame Kamenev," she said.

Katya looked up, startled.

"Don't go away," the stewardess said. "I'll be right back."

She returned to the tourist cabin, and reemerged seconds later, with her surprise in tow, a tall girl of about nine years of age. She stepped aside, put an arm on the girl's shoulder and urged her forward. The girl was extraordinarily pretty, with long wavy brown hair framing a broad face, wide mouth, and dazzling blue eyes. She wore a light skirt and white ruffled blouse under a smart wool vest buttoned in front. A small, new-looking leather purse was clutched self-consciously in her hand, and a tinge of inexpertly applied makeup was visible around her eyes.

Katya gasped, then cried out, overwhelmed. She pulled the girl to her across the empty seat and hugged her fiercely. "Zoya, Zoya, Zoya! . . ."

Her composure evaporated utterly; tears streamed down her face. She released the girl and let her settle in the seat beside her. The intensity of Katya's emotions brought Zoya to tears as well, as much from embarrassment as joy. She fought to hold them back, but they welled up in the corners of her eyes and escaped down her cheeks. Katya produced a tissue and wiped them away, kissing her repeatedly.

"You've grown so much!" she exclaimed, her voice cracking. "And I've missed you so much!"

Zoya cleared her throat of a sob. "I missed you too, Mother."

"My darling! How did you get here? Tell me everything!"

For an hour they sat together, oblivious of the airport drama swirling around them. Katya fussed over the girl, and asked a thousand questions, trying to absorb as much of her daughter's life as she possibly could, trying to cram years of lost motherhood into a few minutes' time.

Zoya's shyness gradually melted under the affectionate on-slaught, and she began chatting animatedly, eager now to impress the strange and wonderful woman who was her mother. She told her that she dreamed of becoming a ballet star, so she could travel around the world. "Mrs. Shabov thinks I can qualify for the Regional Juniors program. But it's awfully hard work. It takes so much dedication. Uncle Kolya thinks I should stick with biology. It's safer, he says. Not so competitive. I wish I could decide. . . ."

When had she last talked to her daughter? Katya wondered. Was it two years ago? More? She remembered how she had missed her own mother. It was the harshest pain she endured all those years growing up in the orphanage and the labor camp. She must get Zoya back, she told herself. She must!

"Perhaps you don't have to decide yet, my darling."

Zoya looked doubtful. "I'm almost ten," she said.

Katya bit her lip, remembering. "Next week is your birthday!"

Zoya nodded. "Aunt Valya and Uncle Kolya are going to have a party for me. I wish you could be there. I know you'd like them. Uncle Mitya is nice, too, of course. He wants me to come live with him. . . ." The girl broke off in the middle of her sentence and looked at her mother with a sudden painful intensity. "Are you going to stay with me now?"

Katya met her daughter's troubled eyes. "I hope so. Do you want me to?"

The girl nodded eagerly, then stopped, as if uncertain of some-thing. "If you wanted to," she said.

"Of course I do!"

"Will you come back with us to Moscow, then?"

"I don't know," Katya replied. "How would you like to come and live in this country?"

Zoya frowned. "Here? America?"

Katya nodded, pressing her hand on top of her daughter's.

Zoya appeared distinctly frightened by the idea. "At school they say it's bad here. . . ."

Before Katya could reply, the door to the flight deck opened and the tall, slim form of General Dmitri Semenenko stepped into the first-class compartment.

The two KGB bodyguards moved to his side. Semenenko waved them back to their seats and stepped down the aisle. He patted Zoya on the head and smiled down at her.

"You are looking beautiful today, young woman," he said.

Zoya thanked him in a subdued voice.

"Your mother and I must have a chat in private," he told her.

As if on cue, the stewardess who had brought her in materialized in the aisle. "Come with me, Zoya," she said, holding out her hand. "I'll show you how our kitchen works."

Reluctantly, the girl went off. The door to the tourist compartment clicked shut behind them.

"A beautiful child," Semenenko said, as he slid into the seat beside Katya. "A beautiful child indeed."

A redhead in aquamarine stretch pants leaned down the bar toward Warfield and twiddled an unlit menthol-filtered cigarette next to her lips. Warfield turned toward her. All her colors clashed —hair, eye shadow, lipstick, rouge, clothes. The flesh on her arms and face was chalky white and saggy, beginning to lose its fight against gravity.

"If you was a *gentleman*," she said, in a hillbilly accent, "you'd offer me a light."

Warfield squinted at her face. "If you had any brains," he replied, "you wouldn't smoke."

Warfield directed his gaze back to his glass. It contained two ice cubes floating in a double shot of whiskey. He had consumed four just like it in the past hour. Drink by drink, he was rubbing out the past and future both, erasing memory and care.

The redhead, still determined to start a conversation, tried a fresh approach. "What do you think's gonna happen?" she asked him.

"Happen about what?"

She sighed extravagantly, jiggling her breasts. "My God, *you* know! Up there! At the airport!"

She waved her cigarette in the direction of the television set, mounted on the wall over the end of the bar. The picture kept switching from a broadcast studio somewhere with an anchorman and a commentator, to a very long telephoto lens shot of runway one-right at Dulles, and the distant, indistinct shapes of a Russian passenger jet and a helicopter, surrounded by buses and bathed in white floodlights.

"You know what *I* think," she cooed. "I think he's in love with her."

"Who?"

"The *president!* He's in love with the Russian woman. I mean, it's pretty obvious. He's got that wife of his, crazy as a june bug. Then along comes this Russian *princess!* I mean, she's a knockout! And she's staying right there with him in the White House!"

"Maybe she sleeps on the couch."

"That's why he won't let her go," she continued, ignoring his remark. "She's got him hooked, but good!"

Warfield drained his bourbon and focused on the TV screen. The station was showing a film clip from the previous week. The Russian woman was answering reporters' questions outside Blair House. She was attractive, Warfield guessed, in a certain wide-cheeked Slavic way. She seemed familiar. Maybe Slavic women all looked alike. Since recognizing the Turk at the farm, every face was starting to look like a face he'd seen before. Paranoia, the school psychiatrist would say, aggravated by alcohol.

"My name's Rosalie. What's yours?"

"I don't remember."

Rosalie regarded him suspiciously, then laughed. "You're too much! What's your story, anyway?"

"My story?"

"Everybody has a story. You tell me yours, I'll tell you mine."

Warfield shook his head.

"I'll bet your wife left you, right? Drowning your sorrows?"

Warfield gazed at her, heavy lidded.

"I left *my* husband five years ago. Smartest thing I ever did. He was good in the hay, when I could keep him there. But he liked to spread it around, if you know what I mean."

Warfield signaled the bartender for a refill.

"Well, two can play *that* game," she muttered.

She stared absently into her drink, then commenced a detailed reconstruction of her life. It had not been a good life—or a particularly interesting one—and Warfield shut the words out, letting them pour over and around him along with the smoke, the juke-box noise, and her musky perfume. He fastened his watering eyes on the neat rows of bottles behind the bar, and concentrated on drinking his way to oblivion.

"Your new lover," Semenenko said. "He must be very devoted to you."

Katya said nothing.

The KGB general motioned with his hand toward the flight deck at the front of the jet. "He enjoys this," he said. "Americans are an impatient people. They love action."

"Why did you bring Zoya here?" Katya demanded.

Semenenko affected surprise. "Why, little darling, a simple show of gratitude—for your agreeing to go along with our kidnap-ping."

"And will you now tell me the point of this insane business?"

Semenenko patted Katya's arm. "I need your help."

"You promised there would be no more!"

Semenenko sighed. "Yes, but your new romance has provided us with an opportunity I cannot pass up."

"What are you talking about?"

"We believe Daniels is hiding information about Kamenev's assassination from us. We must find out. I want you to help us eavesdrop on him, that's all. Just as you did for me with Kamenev."

"I can't do it."

The general frowned. "You underestimate yourself. Of course you can do it."

"He trusts me."

Semenenko reached over and set Katya's spilled vodka glass upright on the folding tray. "Exactly."

"I don't wish him any harm."

"He won't be harmed. But we're entitled to know who's behind your husband's assassination, aren't we?"

Katya made no reply.

"Aren't we?"

"After Kamenev, you said I could retire from this."

"Yes, yes, I remember," Semenenko said. "And I meant it. But this is an emergency. And I ask for so little."

"How do you expect me to get such secrets?"

Semenenko laughed. "All I ask is that you try. Just for a few days, that's all. Then I'll keep my promise."

For the first time since the general had sat down beside her, Katya looked him directly in the eye. "You must give me back my daughter," she said.

Semenenko reached out and stroked the palm of his hand tenderly across Katya's cheek. "Just do this one last thing."

Katya yanked his hand away with angry force. "Don't touch me!"

The general's face registered her insult like a seismograph. "I don't expect gratitude from you," he said. "Or loyalty. Or love. What I ask is a small degree of cooperation. That's all. In payment for all I've given you!"

"Yeb tvoyu mat!

Semenenko frowned. "You're still the little camp slut at heart, aren't you?"

"Yeb tvoyu mat."

"I've spoiled you. Pampered you with servants, special schools, travel. The best of everything! I created a woman of the world. You'll give me some credit?"

"Yes," she replied. "And don't forget my face! That's your creation, too!"

He ignored her taunt. "I've lavished the affection of a father on you," he said.

Katya sneered at him. "Haven't you gotten your rubles' worth?"

"I haven't asked for so much."

She laughed derisively. "You've not asked. You've taken! Everything! My whole life!"

"I've given your life meaning!"

"You've given me nothing."

"And I've loved you more than any man you've known."

Katya stared at him, genuinely shocked. "You've loved what I've brought you, that's all. You've loved me the way a man loves a weapon—for the power it brings! That's how you've used me—as an instrument of your insane lust for power! You're not capable of any kind of real love. You're deformed inside. A eunuch! And you'll remain one, no matter how much power you steal."

Semenenko's face drained white. "You're an ungrateful slut."

Katya spat on him.

He raised his hand and slowly wiped the saliva from his cheek.

He regarded her with a sort of melancholy resignation, as if she were a pet cat who had unexpectedly bitten him, and now would have to be dealt with in a new way.

"You are not going to use my daughter as you used me!" Katya warned. "I know it is on your mind!"

Semenenko didn't reply. For a long time they sat in rigid silence, like a *tableau vivant*, looking past each other to the walls of the compartment. Semenenko found his voice first.

"Very well," he said, his tone elaborately careless. "You can have her. In exchange for this one last deed. Full custody." He snapped his fingers toward the bodyguard sitting in the front row. "Boris! Bring it here, please."

Boris lumbered down the aisle and handed the general a small wooden box. Semenenko placed it in Katya's lap.

She opened the lid and looked inside. "A hairbrush?"

"Yes. Put it in your purse. It contains a microphone and transmitter. At night leave it on the table by your bed. If you sleep in the president's room, take it with you. We can pick up your conversation from the embassy."

"For how long?"

"A week. That's all I ask."

"And if I get the information sooner?"

"You'll be free sooner."

"I want to stay in this country."

"Whatever you wish."

"And I want Zoya here with me. Now."

Semenenko glanced at his watch, ignoring Katya's demand. "I must get back to the flight deck," he said. "We're involved in tough negotiations with Daniels. I'm making Daniels fight for you. I want your release to be as convincing as your capture."

"I want Zoya now!"

Semenenko grinned sardonically. "Little darling. You can see, if you think about it, that to let Zoya off the plane with you now would seem very peculiar. It would throw the sincerity of our effort to kidnap you into question."

He pushed his long frame up out of the seat. "Do your job first," he said. "And then I'll give you Zoya."

Sounds began to blur. Rosalie's voice blended with that of the TV reporter's and shreds from other conversations in the bar.

"My husband Stevie used to get in fights all the time. Seems every time we went out anywhere, there was some bum there wanting to fight him." . . . *"The situation as of this hour remains at a stalemate. The president, according to senior aide William Wilbert, is sticking to his last proposal, that the Russians allow him to talk to Mrs. Kamenev at a neutral spot outside the aircraft."* . . . "She's a commie, ain't she? He oughta let them take her back where she belongs." . . . *"Or that he be allowed inside the aircraft, to meet with her in the presence of several of his aides and FBI Director Hodges."* . . . "One time one guy nearly killed him. Said he was carrying on with his wife. He was, too, the bastard." . . . *"The Russians, represented by a Ministry of Foreign Affairs spokesman, Dmitri Semenenko, have so far refused."* . . . "They'll rape and torture her, send her to prison for the rest of her life. That's what those Russkies do." . . . *"There is now speculation that some kind of bargain is being worked out. That the president is thinking of making some concession that will allow the Russians to save face."* . . . "He gave me a black eye when I yelled at him about it. If he didn't fight in a damned bar, he fought with me later. . . . Serves her right, damned Commie!"

Later, without knowing how he got there, he was outside, leaning on Rosalie. The frigid night air revived him marginally. Rosalie gripped him by the waist and steered him along the sidewalk. Warfield concentrated on his walk, thinking out each movement ahead of time. The pavement pitched and rolled beneath him like a ship's deck in a storm, undermining his efforts to remain upright.

Rosalie helped him into her car, bought a bottle of whiskey somewhere, and drove him to his motel. A few swigs from the bottle on the way picked Warfield up. He managed to get out of the car by himself and fumbled through his pockets for the key to his room.

"I've got your keys!" Rosalie sang out in a teasing voice. She shook them over her head as if they were castanets and started down the long carpeted walkway to room 7, humming a tune in a loud off-key soprano. Warfield started after her, weaving precariously along the carpet. He caught up with her by the doorway; she was having trouble lining the key up with the keyhole.

Warfield started to giggle. His degradation was progressing nicely. He felt in the side pocket of his coat, pulled out the whiskey bottle, unscrewed the cap, and took a drink. It burned beautifully going down. The Devil's nectar. He squinted at the bottle. Half full. Cause for concern. Would stores be open? He endeavored to focus his eyes on his wristwatch, but failed. In the process he lost his balance and fell over, striking the walkway on his back. He heard the dull shattering of the whiskey bottle echo into an inexplicable volley of sharp pops, like firecrackers. Rosalie loomed above him, then lurched against the door. He saw her sliding along the plywood paneling, scratching it with the key as she fell.

He drifted up from unconsciousness groggy and confused, his inebriated brain slowing him like a reptile in the cold. The smell of whiskey teased his nostrils. The weight on him. What was it? It was so heavy he could barely push it off.

That woman. Rosalie.

Alarms were ringing in the back of his head, but he could not stir himself from the fog of stupor that enveloped him.

The woman was wet. He was wet. The whiskey? Could half a bottle make so much wetness?

He located the key on the carpeting and succeeded in unlocking the door. He dragged Rosalie inside, locked the door, and found the wall switch for the overhead light. Every move required extraordinary concentration, painstaking effort.

Blood was everywhere. Had he cut himself on the bottle? No. Too much blood. The alarms were sounding louder and louder. The woman had been shot! He staggered to the bathroom, ripped off his clothes, and tried to wash the blood off them. How did it happen? He couldn't have done it, he thought. He was no longer carrying the Marine's gun. Someone else had done it. Who? God, his brain didn't want to work. He vomited in the sink.

After a minute he felt marginally more clear headed, but he was becoming desperate for a drink. He picked up the telephone but could not steady his hand to dial anything. He threw the phone down.

Get a drink, he thought. That's what he had to do. Worlds could collide, it wouldn't matter. He must drink. And he must drink now. He went outside, picked up the broken neck of the whiskey bottle, and gazed at it sadly.

He searched for the car keys, found them in a pocket with his wallet, then remembered that they had driven out in Rosalie's car. He couldn't drive now, anyway. Crazy.

Maybe she was dead. Maybe she was dying and would soon be dead. He should find out, he told himself, mumbling some of the words out loud. He should find out. He should help.

He groped for the telephone again and tried to dial Rosenstock's sister.

He sat on the bed, looking at Rosalie, her aquamarine stretch pants turning black with blood. He struggled with every nerve he could command to steady his hand enough to dial the number. Rosenstock would help him. And he would have a drink. If only he could dial his number. Good ol' Herb, he'd do it for him. If only he could dial. . . .

Over and over again, he inserted his index finger in the hole by the first digit, twisted it to the right, let it rotate back, and tried the next number, until he missed and had to begin the sequence all over again. The farthest he ever made it without a mistake was four numbers.

Such a simple task, he thought, as he stared at the defiant dial. He should weep for his pathetic failure, but he felt nothing except the pain of his thirst. He dropped the telephone to the floor.

27

THE PRESIDENT WAS ASLEEP, sprawled out on a narrow cot that had been brought into the Situation Room during the night. His stockinged feet protruded out over the bottom edge, lending his inert form an uncharacteristic air of vulnerability. The lights had been dimmed, and the large subbasement chamber was quiet, save for the electronic hum of the equipment and the whisper of voices from the fresh crew of officers manning their stations.

Daniels had stopped the Russian plane from taking off, but he had been unable to persuade the Kremlin to release Katya. The first break in the stalemated negotiations did not come until midnight, and Daniels, exhausted, had turned over the bargaining of details to Wilbert and fallen instantly asleep.

Wilbert now shook him awake.

"They're releasing her," he said.

The president propped himself up on one arm and blinked his eyes. "What time is it?"

"Four in the morning," Wilbert replied. "I closed the deal with Semenenko directly. We agreed to let them have access to all the reports of the investigation—the autopsy, the tapes, the interrogation, the works. And we agreed to let them share all decisions concerning the future conduct of the investigation. Equal partners. They agree to release Mrs. Kamenev immediately. Her Secret Service bodyguard is out there now, ready to receive her. Hodges is still there, too, with a crowd of FBI agents."

Daniels cast the blanket aside and pushed himself to a sitting position. His gamble had worked. He felt enormous relief. "Where's McCormick and the helicopter?"

"Right where they've been since midnight. Back on the south lawn."

Daniels nodded, kicking his feet into his shoes. "Alert the crew," he said. "I'm going out there to meet her. We'll bring her back to the White House on the helicopter."

Wilbert sank down on a chair. "The hell you will!"

Daniels pulled off his wrinkled shirt. "Don't argue with me now," he warned.

"Listen, there are three network camera crews out there. When she comes out the door of that plane, they'll be all over her—and all over you, if you go out there."

"You're exaggerating. The press are all back on the observation deck, two miles away."

"That was four hours ago. They found a way onto the runway over a remote fence somewhere. They're all over the place now."

"I tough it out with the Russians, then you want me to run from the press?"

"You got her released. That's great. Don't spoil the victory by making it personal. Your popularity is sliding because of this woman. Don't make it worse."

"Fuck my popularity."

Wilbert persisted. "This is an easy one, Eliot! Let her come out by herself. We've got plenty of brass out there. Let Hodges meet her. Or I'll go out there myself. We'll put her in a limousine and drive her back."

Daniels shook his head. "I know you're looking out for my best interests. But I want to go out there! So I'm going. And you're coming with me."

Wilbert made no reply.

"Besides," Daniels added, letting a corner of his lip twist into a smile. "If anybody's watching TV at four o'clock in the morning, they deserve to see me out there. Why disappoint them? Hand me that clean shirt, will you?"

Wilbert dropped his argument and picked up the shirt from the neat pile of clothes left by the president's valet and handed it across. He had survived as long as he had by knowing when to lay off.

General Semenenko walked to the special communications console in the aft section of the flight deck. The radio operator handed him a microphone. "Embassy, Comrade General."

Semenenko accepted the instrument and depressed the button on its side. "Mr. Stepanovich. Are you there?"

"Standing by, Comrade General."

"Very good. You realize this is an open channel?"

"Of course."

"Madame Kamenev and the American president should be boarding the helicopter momentarily."

"I understand."

"The flight back to the White House takes fifteen minutes."

"I understand, Comrade General."

Vladimir Stepanovich sat in the small room off the fourth-floor decoding complex, the embassy's most restricted area. One hand was on the radio mike to Semenenko, the other was on his stomach. He swallowed to fight down the waves of nausea, and took deep, rapid breaths to subdue the violent attacks of trembling that vibrated through his body.

He had never been so terrified in his life. He prayed that the general had not detected it in his voice. He had not bargained for this. Not at all! Installing antennas was one thing. Murder was another. What a nightmare! How could he have imagined that this trip to Washington would end up in something so horrible?

He looked at the detonator box before him, its key sitting in the "armed" position. In fifteen minutes—the moment President Daniels' helicopter arrived over the White House lawn—he would move the key from "armed" to "detonate," and kill everyone on board.

He should have known that the day would come when he would have to pay for his easy life. Semenenko had told him as much when he had recruited him for this last job. "You've had a good life, haven't you?" he had said, in that condescending way of his. "Oh yes," Stepanovich had replied, so eagerly. "A wonderful life!" "Well, the time has come for you to earn it, Comrade."

He felt the trembling become stronger than ever. "God help me!" he whimpered.

Dan McCormick walked in from the communications deck and stood nervously confronting the president across the narrow helicopter lounge. "We've got a problem," he said.

Daniels reacted with a surprised frown. "What?"

"We can protect you out on the runway, since the whole area is sealed off. But we'd rather you let us take Mrs. Kamenev back in her limousine."

"For Christ's sake, why?"

"We have her bodyguard detail here. There's not room for all of them in the helicopter, and they absolutely refuse to let her out of their sight. They're anxious to redeem themselves."

"I understand that. They can meet her at the White House."

"It'll make things safer, Mr. President. . . ."

"Jesus Christ," Daniels muttered, slapping the sides of his thighs in frustration. "All right, Dan. All right. Take her in the car."

McCormick departed to pass the word to the bodyguard detail. He returned minutes later to brief the president on the procedure he was to follow for greeting Katya.

"The steps are up, and they've opened the doors on the Aeroflot. She's coming out any minute. You should go down now. The press people are cleared way back. The limousine with her bodyguard detail will pull up beside you at the bottom of the ramp. They'll take her from there. We'll lay on a police escort. We've already posted troopers along the route. It'll be fast. Probably beat your helicopter back."

From a porthole window Wilbert watched two uniformed Russians emerge in the doorway of the jet; he guessed they were the Aeroflot pilots. They looked bedraggled and weary from their long ordeal of waiting. The limousine for Mrs. Kamenev, and another one from the Russian Embassy for General Semenenko, were inching their way through the cordon of police and National Guardsmen. The buses that had encircled the aircraft were departing in a long, snakelike line down the side of the runway.

Daniels slipped on his overcoat and moved toward the helicopter exit. Wilbert watched him trot through the chill predawn across the short stretch of tarmac separating the two aircraft, and stop at the foot of the mobile staircase. The president looked up the staircase, exchanging words with a tall man in a long gray coat. Wilbert recognized him as Semenenko. The general stood aside and the Russian woman appeared from behind him, grim faced. Semenenko patted her familiarly on the shoulder. A surprising gesture, Wilbert thought.

At the bottom of the steps Daniels met her. For a moment he just looked at her, as if uncertain what to do or say. She reached a hand out toward him. He took it and then threw his arms around her and pulled her to him in a long, tight embrace. Semenenko grinned at them from the top of the mobile stairs, and then descended to his waiting limousine. The encircling bank of floodlights bathed the scene in a bleak glare, lighting the set for the TV cameras—and for history.

Wilbert gritted his teeth so hard that a piece of filling broke loose from one of his back molars. "Eliot," he whispered. "You dumb bastard."

The radio crackled, making Stepanovich jump.

"Are you there, Comrade?"

"Yes, Comrade General!"

"Madame Kamenev will not—repeat, *not*—be with President Daniels on his helicopter. There's been a last minute change. Do you understand?"

"Yes, Comrade!"

"You may stand down, then."

"Yes, Comrade!"

Stepanovich dropped the microphone and wept with relief.

Semenenko ducked into his limousine and rapped the window behind the driver's head, signaling him to start back to the embassy. The general settled against the upholstery and blew a plume of cigarette smoke in the air. A shame, he thought. A great shame. That would have been so fast. But the virtue of his plan, he reminded himself, was its flexibility.

He would have another opportunity this evening.

28

WARFIELD'S HEAD WAS SPLIT

asunder.

Bright spear-shafts of light stabbed through the open fissure, and he gasped from the pain. Something touched him, pressing against a spot near the base of his skull. It sent a jolt of agony down to his toes.

"You're a goddamned mess," a gravelly voice announced, close to his ear. "But I'm afraid it's too soon to issue a death certificate."

Warfield discovered that the light was entering through his eyes, not a hole in his brainpan. "That you, Herb?"

"Your ears are still functioning."

Slowly, Warfield forced his eyelids apart. Everything hurt. The slightest movement seemed to dislodge pieces of his brain and send them crashing around the walls of his skull like loose cannonballs. Gradually a white ceiling came into focus, then the top of a window drape, pulled shut.

"You've got a herniated lesion on the back of your head. Mild concussion, maybe. Other than that, the only thing wrong with you is a bad case of alcohol poisoning. What the hell happened?"

Warfield blinked his eyes carefully. "I fell off the wagon."

Rosenstock snorted. "You fell off the goddamn edge of the earth! You've been out for twelve hours."

"Where am I?"

Warfield was startled to hear Nan Robertson answer. "In my house," she said.

He craned his neck around cautiously and found her. She was sitting on a chaise longue, her legs folded under her, her elbows on her knees. Her hair was tousled, and she wore no makeup. She looked tired, but attractive.

Warfield focused on Rosenstock again. He was sitting at the foot of the bed, the habitual cigarette dangling from the corner of his mouth.

"How did I get here?"

"I got your message," Rosenstock replied. "Nan lived the closest, so we brought you here."

Warfield palpated the bump on the back of his head. The simple movement of his arm required effort. Pain and mental depression seemed to paralyze him. He felt a desperate thirst for alcohol.

"I'm sorry," he said.

"Just take it easy for now," Rosenstock advised. "You'll feel better in an hour or so. I've given you a shot."

Warfield clenched his jaw at the thought. "They should suspend your license," he groaned.

Rosenstock laughed. "They probably will."

Warfield looked down at his chest. Memories of the previous night began to sneak back in nightmarish glimpses.

Blood.

He sat up, ignoring the pain. "My God! The woman!" he cried. "The woman! Rosalie! She . . ."

"She's in the hospital," Rosenstock said. "She'll live."

Warfield sank back against the pillow and covered his eyes with his hands. "Jesus."

"Nan and I got to the motel at about five. We found you, nude and unconscious on the bed. The woman was on the floor. She had three bullet holes in her. Most of the blood was on the outside door and the carpet beneath it. Judging by the blood on your coat and pants, you must have dragged her into the room. What the hell were you doing?"

Warfield tried to remember. He felt Nan's eyes on him, regarding him with a mixture of curiosity and fear. She must wonder, he thought, what kind of maniac she had gone to work for. He needed a drink.

208 . . .

"I left a bar with her," he said. "I was loaded and had no idea what I was doing. She got me back to the motel. She was opening the door, I remember that. I was holding a bottle of booze. I slipped and fell and heard the bottle break. Then she fell on top of me. I passed out, came to later, and dragged her inside."

Rosenstock nodded. "Any reason anyone would shoot her?"

"Sure. They were aiming at me and missed. I fell just as they opened fire. They probably thought they had killed both of us."

"You're lucky they didn't check," Rosenstock said. "And you're lucky you picked such a lousy motel. There were no other guests. No one saw us, and I guess no one saw you. Except the gunman. Still, your fingerprints must be all over the place. And the desk clerk can probably give a fair description of you." Rosenstock paused. "You *sure* you didn't shoot her?"

Warfield sighed. "I'm not a mean drunk."

"Thank God for that. If she recovers I assume she'll vouch for you."

"You took a hell of a chance sneaking me out of there."

Rosenstock agreed. "We were going to report it, but Nan guessed that you must have escaped from Peary. And the police would have turned you over to the CIA. We called an ambulance and got you the hell out before it arrived."

Warfield managed a weak smile. "Thanks, I think," he said.

"You did bust out of Peary?" Rosenstock asked.

"I clobbered a guard, stole a car."

Rosenstock grimaced. "Then you're in worse trouble than I thought." He slid his glasses back up on his nose and studied Warfield as if he were a patient he wasn't sure was going to get well. "You didn't bust out just to get a drink, did you?"

"I don't know." He didn't feel like trying to explain, or even trying to talk at all. He focused his gaze on the neutral territory of a framed photograph on the wall near the bed. It was an old daguerreotype, showing a row of brick buildings. One was a saloon, with a warehouse next to it. He could just read the lettering on the brick face of the warehouse—J.C. Fields & Sons, Dry Goods. He looked at the saloon again. It reminded him that he needed a drink.

Rosenstock held up a small plastic bottle with bits of food inside. "I found this in your shirt pocket. What is it? Leftovers for your pet mouse?"

Warfield looked at the pill bottle, then at Rosenstock. "Give me a drink and I'll tell you."

Rosenstock laughed. "You and alcohol don't mix. It's nothing to be ashamed of. Just a matter of individual chemistry."

"Never mind the temperance lecture," Warfield said. "I need a drink to level me out. I'm not going to get drunk again."

Rosenstock shook his head. Warfield felt anger welling up inside him like a volcano. He swallowed to suppress it. "What difference is one more gonna make?"

Rosenstock blew a plume of smoke through his nose. "We've got work to do. You have to be sober for it."

Warfield closed his eyes. "We don't have anything to do! It's all over. Any idiot can see that."

Nan unfolded her legs from the chaise. "I'll get some coffee," she said, and disappeared into the kitchen.

"You'll feel better in an hour," Rosenstock said. "I promise. Just hold on until then."

Warfield stared at Rosenstock with undisguised contempt. "You're torturing me."

Rosenstock stubbed out his cigarette. "I'm beginning to think we should have called the police. You'd be less of a pain in the ass in jail." He stood up. "I've got a couple of store errands I promised to run for Nan. She'll fix you something to eat. Stop feeling sorry for yourself. Get your mind back on the case. Somebody tried to kill you last night. He'll probably try again. Think who he might be. I'll be back."

Warfield watched Rosenstock's stooped shoulders hunch out of the doorway with a sensation of relief. Nan reappeared a minute later with a cup of coffee and left it by the bed. He pretended to be asleep. His thoughts drifted, entwining themselves with the sounds of the neighborhood. A car door slammed, a dog barked, a child yelled. He heard Nan in the kitchen, clanking dishes and pans. Her whole past was a blank to him, he realized, save for Semenenko's disturbing claim that she was spying on him. There were framed photographs on the dresser top. Nan's husband? Children? He really didn't want to know, he decided. He didn't care about her past, or anybody's past. The tiresome dossiers of dirty little secrets, compromises, and humiliations. Like Rosalie. Poor woman. Looking for a good time. Why the hell didn't the bastard hunting him have better aim?

Warfield opened his eyes and stared across the room. Something he remembered seeing earlier caught his eye. An empty tumbler, resting on the floor by the chaise longue. Slowly he raised himself from the bed. He fought off a wave of dizziness, grasping the headboard to steady himself. After a few seconds, he was able to cross the room and pick up the glass. He sniffed it. Scotch. One of them must have been drinking it before he woke up.

Warfield took the glass and stood by the bedroom doorway and looked out into the living room. He could hear Nan in the kitchen, somewhere past the dining room on the left.

He found what he wanted almost immediately, the instinct of his compulsion guiding him as surely as a hound to game. It was resting on a shelf behind the closed doors of a small breakfront near the sofa. He held the bottle at arm's length, then pulled the stopper out and dumped several inches into the tumbler. The instant it met his tongue he felt transformed. It was indescribably good. He drained the glass, welcoming the warmth that flowed to every corpuscle in his body with a mixture of thankfulness and greed. He poured another two inches into the glass.

Nan appeared from the kitchen, carrying a tray with hot soup and a sandwich on it. She saw him, then saw the glass and the bottle in his hands, and stopped dead. "Oh no!" she cried.

Warfield grinned in guilty triumph. "I feel better already."

Nan deposited the tray on a table and quickly snatched the bottle and the glass away from him. She carried them into the kitchen and poured the rest of the scotch down the sink.

"Nothing to get so damned upset about," Warfield complained, following her to the kitchen.

"You'll be sorry!"

Warfield shrugged, retreated back to the bedroom, and stretched out on the bed. He heard her on the telephone, trying to locate Rosenstock. She found him, finally, at the local drugstore. He listened, amused, as she detailed his transgression to the doctor over the phone.

Then something hit him.

He jumped from the bed, seized by a wave of nausea so powerful he thought that his insides were exploding. Invisible fists pummeled his intestines. He barely made it to the bathroom, collapsing on his knees before the toilet bowl.

For half an hour he writhed on the floor, spewing streams of vomit and mucous into the toilet. When the spasms at last subsided, his throat was raw and his guts ached from the convulsions they had undergone. Too weak to stand, he rolled over on his back and pulled a towel down from a nearby rack to wipe his mouth and dry the sweat from his face and neck.

Rosenstock stood in the bathroom doorway, flicking the ash from a cigarette. "I told you I gave you a shot," he said. "Disulfiram. Two-hundred-fifty milligrams. Produces a violent reaction to alcohol."

Warfield sat back on the tile floor, bracing himself against the toilet bowl. "You son-of-a-bitch!" he rasped.

"I know I have a lousy bedside manner," Rosenstock said, "but nothing is so persuasive as a demonstration."

Warfield hauled himself to his feet.

"I'm sorry I had to do it," Rosenstock continued. "But now you know. With disulfiram in your blood, you can't drink. Period. So put it out of your head. For good. I brought you some from the drugstore in tablet form. Antabuse, it's called. You're going to take it every day."

"You son-of-a-bitch," Warfield repeated. He walked back into the bedroom, feeling some of his strength return. He felt Rosenstock's hand on his elbow, trying to guide him toward the bed. He swung around and hit the doctor in the chest with his forearm. "You murdering son-of-a-bitch."

He picked up a straight-backed chair and hurled it at Rosenstock. It missed and cracked a mirror. Rosenstock ducked quickly out of the room. Warfield picked up the chair again, and smashed it with all his strength against the wall, shattering it into kindling.

Once started, he could not stop. Some fragile last restraint had given way, a seal broken open under the building pressure of his inner fury. He pulled over a chest of drawers, sending a cascade of lamps and vases onto the floor; kicked apart a vanity table; hurled bottles of perfume around the room. He pulled mirrors, paintings, and prints from the wall and broke them over his knees.

Everything that he could smash, he did.

Around dusk he was waking from another long sleep. The tide of rage had ebbed, his anguish subsiding into a kind of torpor. Peace had descended on him like the numb serenity of someone who has been in a thoroughly satisfying drunken brawl.

He surveyed the wreckage of the bedroom. It was past apologizing for. He focused on the old daguerreotype. It hung at a crazy angle; bits of jagged glass stuck out from the edges of the frame.

"I'm sorry," he murmured.

Nan tipped her palm outward in an exaggerated shrug. "It seemed to do you a world of good. And I was about to redecorate, anyway."

"I was out of my head."

Rosenstock nodded in solemn agreement. "Have you decided to live?" he asked.

Warfield shrugged. "I guess you're not going to give me any choice. And I've humiliated myself past the point of worrying about my self-respect. I just feel stupid and ashamed. And depressed."

"Nowhere to go but up," Nan said.

"I think I like it better on the bottom."

"Even at the bottom you're going to have to fight to stay alive," Rosenstock said. "Somebody's trying to kill you."

"I guess so. But how the hell could anybody have known I was at that motel? Maybe it really *was* Rosalie they were after."

"Did you make any phone calls?" Nan asked.

Warfield looked at her. She had washed her hair and changed into a pair of jeans and a light blue sweater.

"Just to Herb's sister. I gave her the motel name and phone number."

"Herb's phone could be bugged," Nan said.

"That would explain it," Rosenstock admitted. "And if my phone is bugged, then that means somebody knows I've been working with you."

"I have a pretty good idea who's after me," Warfield muttered.

The other two looked at him in surprise.

"Did you find that photostat in my shirt? I put it in the same pocket with the pill bottle."

Nan produced it from a drawer in the bedside table, now standing upright again, minus its lamp. "We wondered what it was," she said. "It puzzled us almost as much as the pill bottle."

Warfield explained how he had acquired the photostat and how he'd come to realize that the face behind the wheel of the ambulance was the same as the busboy from the mess hall.

"He's almost certainly the guy Martinez called the Turk. He

poisoned Martinez's food," Warfield said. "I'll bet what's left of my life on it. And I'll bet he poisoned mine as well. That's what's in that bottle—samples from the dinner I didn't eat last night. He delivered it."

"Jesus!" Rosenstock exclaimed. "That's sensational! I'll take it to a lab tonight."

"How did that man get onto the base?" Nan asked.

"Moore is still there," Rosenstock said. "Maybe he can find out for us. I'm counting on him to steal a copy of the autopsy report on Martinez, too. . . ."

"The problem," Nan said, "is that Langley has put us all on indefinite leave of absence. Howard will have a tough time doing anything."

Warfield sipped his tea. It was cold, and he wished it were whiskey. Nan seemed to sense his crisis. She brought him a fresh cupful from the kitchen, thickly laced with honey.

"We've lost the franchise," Warfield said. "Let Friedrich and Semenenko pick up the pieces. Why fight it?"

"But we were just getting somewhere!" Nan protested.

"We don't have much choice. This is the way Langley wants it."

"You might be dead before they find their elbows," Rosenstock insisted.

"Maybe not. I can run. I can hide. I've done it before."

"What about us?" Nan demanded, her voice hard.

"What do you mean?"

Rosenstock interpreted. "Nan thinks we might not be safe, either. Of course, I don't give a damn, but . . ."

"Of course you do!" Nan cut in. "And so does Howard and so do I! We all care! That's why we won't just let you give up, Charles! You got us into this. Now you're going to help get us out!"

She stepped toward Warfield, fire in her eyes. "You've put us all in danger! For trying to help you! And now you have the nerve to tell us you're going to quit?"

A long silence.

Nan stormed out of the room. Rosenstock lit another cigarette. Warfield stared at the TV tray with his cup of tea on it, trying to organize his thoughts.

Nan came back into the bedroom with a glass of scotch in her hand. Her way of telling me to go to hell, Warfield realized.

214 . . .

"Please don't say you're sorry," she muttered, slumping down against the chaise.

Warfield lay back against the pillow and shut his eyes. She was right, of course. Infuriating, but right. They were all in danger. Whoever was masterminding this conspiracy didn't plan to get caught at it. They were getting closer to the truth, and their target obviously knew it and planned to do something about it.

But what the hell could they do to stop anybody? The interrogation was worse than disgraced. Criminal charges would be pending. All access, all credibility, all privilege, was lost.

But he had gotten them into this. He had to help get them out. Sacrifice himself if necessary. That was the singular virtue of his despair. A man shed of his instinct for self-preservation could be truly effective, truly dangerous.

"Okay," he said, his voice rising barely above a whisper. "Okay. As Nan said, nowhere to go but up. Which way is up?"

29

DMITRI SEMENENKO STEPPED from the elevator onto the fourth floor of the elegant mansion on Sixteenth Street that housed the Russian Embassy.

The fourth floor was off limits to all but a handful of embassy personnel. A uniformed guard stationed at the desk by the elevator bank stood immediately at attention and saluted as Semenenko displayed his white KGB card.

The general walked twelve steps down the short corridor toward the rear of the embassy and stopped in front of a steel door. He showed his badge to a second guard, who turned to a small electronic keyboard next to the door and punched in a six-digit number. The code was changed daily, and the guard on duty was required to commit it to memory.

The steel barricade slid aside and Semenenko stepped through to the room beyond. It was windowless, about twenty-five feet long, twenty feet wide, and jammed with electronic monitoring equipment, sophisticated recording devices, and a large computer bank.

Here, four blocks from the White House, thousands of U.S. government radio communications and telephone calls were intercepted every day and recorded, decoded, screened, analyzed, translated, and sent in transcript form back to Moscow Center in the diplomatic pouch. Most of the intercepted conversations were routine. Washington went to great lengths to ensure that nothing sensitive went out over the airwaves within reach of the forest of antennas on the embassy rooftop. Still, the effort yielded occasional nuggets, and the Soviets persisted.

On a normal workshift, six men and women were crowded into the room, reading printouts, tending computers. Tonight the room was empty. Semenenko had ordered all shifts canceled for twenty-four hours.

He walked to a door at the far end and opened it. On the other side was a bare, closet-sized space containing a table and two chairs. Colonel Vladimir Stepanovich, the antenna man, sat in one of the chairs. The table before him held a high-gain receiver, the needles on its glowing green dials flickering. Next to it was located a compact reel-to-reel tape deck, its sound-activated spools of tape standing motionless.

Bolted to the table in front of the receiver and tape deck was a third piece of equipment—a small aluminum box. An umbilical cord of wires snaked out from it across the table and into a large black metal transmitter, resting on the floor under the table. The aluminum box, built, like the other equipment, to special order in a KGB electronics plant outside Sverdlovsk, contained a slot for a key. There were three positions marked around the perimeter of the slot: "lock," "arm," and "fire."

Semenenko sank down in the other chair and donned a headset. Only a thin crackle of static disturbed the silence. He lit one of his brown Egyptian cigarettes and looked over at the antenna man.

"What have you been hearing, Comrade?"

Stepanovich shrugged. "Not much, Comrade General. Some banging around. An argument between a couple of upstairs maids. That was at three this afternoon. Since then, it's been quiet."

Semenenko nodded. "And Mrs. Kamenev?"

"Haven't picked up her voice yet."

Semenenko instructed Stepanovich to arm the mechanism. Reluctantly, the antenna man inserted a small key into the empty slot in the aluminum box, set at the "lock" position. It slipped into place with a precise click. Semenenko consulted his wristwatch. 10:15 P.M. He sat back. He should have to find a book to read, he reflected. It might be a long wait.

At 10:30 the spools of tape began to move. The two men leaned forward tensely. Semenenko turned up the volume on his headset. A door slammed. Then dull thudding noises vibrated in the earphones, as someone walked around the room. Semenenko increased the volume further. The microphone in the hairbrush was remarkably sensitive, he noticed. It even picked up the beep of a car horn somewhere outside the White House.

Suddenly a female voice boomed over his headset: "We shall overco-o-ome, we shall overcome so-ome day-a-a-ay. . . . Oh-oh, deep in my heart, I do believe. . . we shall overcome some day-a-a-ay!"

Semenenko turned the volume down and looked at Stepanovich.

"That's the second time I've heard her today," the colonel said.

Semenenko laughed. "The voice of the oppressed class. She's probably turning down the bed."

"It's frustrating, Comrade General!"

Semenenko scratched his chin, appraising Stepanovich. The antenna man's baptism by fire, he thought, amused at his efforts to conceal his cowardice.

"There's no rush," he replied, his voice silky. "No rush whatsoever."

Warfield awoke from a nightmare, gasping for breath. A cool hand reached out in the dark and touched his forehead.

"You cried out," Nan said.

"I'm all right. What time is it?"

"Around two o'clock."

His situation came back to him. He had fallen asleep after Rosenstock's departure, several hours ago. And Nan, still dressed, had curled up beside him on the other half of her queen-size bed.

"Try to go back to sleep," she said.

"I will."

But he didn't. He lay awake in the strange room, listening to

Nan's even breathing on the pillow next to him, his mind a private projection room of ugly fantasies and bad memories. Disjointed images clicked through the synapses, jarring against each other like jump-cuts in a grim documentary: the assassin, Martinez, dying in his bed, his blind eyes a rictus of terror; the Turk's face in the ambulance photograph, and outside the infirmary, bringing the poisoned food; Rosalie, falling toward him along the motel door; Semenenko's big-toothed grin from across the restaurant table; the reporters on the sidewalk; the derisive laugh of Shanklin, holding that gun on him from the top of the rooming house stairs.

New exhibits to join the old ones in his private house of horrors. He tried to shake the images away, but the moment he relaxed, they slipped back, melded with the more distorted, grotesque forms from the distant past: the men throwing Tanya's body into the back of the Citroën. The unspeakable scene in his rooms on Saad Zaglul Street: the swollen, empty faces. . . .

It was the alcohol that was partly to blame. He had poisoned his brain, and laid it prey to just these sorts of hallucinations.

He felt Nan's head turn on her pillow. "I can't sleep either," she said.

"I'm sorry."

"Stop saying that!" she whispered.

"I'm sorry."

Nan dropped her pillow over his face, then quickly removed it. A tentative attempt at horseplay.

"What's keeping you awake?" she asked.

"Just thinking about the interrogation," he lied. "And where we go from here."

"If the autopsy shows Martinez was poisoned, they should reinstate you," Nan said. "You've made great progress. Far better than anyone else. You got Martinez to talk. You found out about the Turk. There are plenty of leads to follow up."

"It seems that way. But they won't reinstate me. That would mean admitting they were wrong. I'm out of the picture, Nan. All of us are."

"You're not!" she said. "Someone's trying to put you out, though. You've got to find him and stop him!"

"Any suggestions?"

"No."

"Even if I were able to track down this Turk, where would that put us? He's just one more hired killer. He probably doesn't know any more than Martinez did."

"He could lead you to the Instructor."

"What do you mean?"

"He has to meet the Instructor sometime. If you could find him, you could follow him."

Warfield shook his head, amused by the naive optimism of Nan's suggestion. "That's a lot of ifs. And he could be getting his orders indirectly."

"But they *might* still meet," Nan insisted.

"Sure, they might meet—somewhere, sometime. But what does that do for us? We have no leads. Just that imaginary warehouse."

"I *know* they meet!" Nan persisted. "That hairbrush, for example. It had to be delivered. They wouldn't just stick it in the mail or send it UPS!"

"Okay, they meet," Warfield conceded. "Now what?"

"Now you just have to find out where that dark room is located. It must be near Washington."

A picture of a warehouse popped into Warfield's head. It startled him until he remembered what it was: the one in the daguerreotype he had smashed earlier. He sat up. "Where's the light?" he asked.

"You broke all my lamps, remember?"

"Oh yeah . . ."

"*Don't* say you're sorry!" Nan jumped from the bed and flicked the wall switch for the overhead light. "At least you couldn't reach that one," she said.

Warfield retrieved the daguerreotype from the wall, picked some shards of glass from its frame, and examined it. Nan sat beside him.

"Just look at this," he said. He read aloud the legend on the old building's brick facade: "J.C. Fields & Sons, Dry Goods."

Nan peered at him with an expression of concern that made him laugh. "No, I'm not losing my marbles," he assured her. "I was just putting two things together. Warehouses and dry goods. Cotton. Wouldn't bales of cotton be dry goods?"

"Don't ask me. I'm a cryptologist."

"Don't you see," he said. "That would explain Rosenstock's trace evidence—the cotton dust in Martinez's earwax. He met the Instructor in a warehouse!" He paused, suddenly deflated. "But what the hell good does that do us. There must be hundreds of warehouses in the area."

"Not that store cotton, I'll bet."

"How do we check?"

"Easy," she replied. "We'll call my friend Jonathan at the Library of Congress. He's a whiz at research like this. I'll call him right now!"

Warfield laughed. "It's past two in the morning!"

"He won't mind. He'll love it, in fact."

Nan picked up the phone and dialed a number from memory. As she talked, Warfield thought about the odds. Even if it was a warehouse and even if they found the right one, he might have to stake it out for days. He didn't have days. It all seemed so hopeless.

"He'll do it," she exulted, hanging up the phone. "He'll call back as soon as he has something."

"He's going to do it now? In the middle of the night?"

"Sure. He's a VIP at the library. He has access to the building any time."

Nan snapped off the overhead, and in the dark, Warfield could hear her slipping off her sweater and jeans.

"How the hell did you talk him into it?" he asked.

"Some people," she said, pulling down the covers on her side of the queen-size bed, "are susceptible to my charms."

"Is he your lover?"

"I haven't decided yet."

Warfield smiled in the dark. "Speaking of that, I saw your husband the other day."

"Really? Where?"

"In Sans Souci. He was with a delicious-looking blonde."

"Who told you it was my husband?"

"Semenenko."

"Extraordinary."

"He's an extraordinary man."

"I'll say. My husband is in Brazil."

"What?"

"He works for an American bank in São Paulo. We're separated."

Warfield sighed in disgust. "Well, everyone else is making a sucker out of me, why not Semenenko?"

"What else did the extraordinary Russian tell you?"

"He told me you were spying on me."

Warfield waited through a heavy silence. He heard Nan push herself up on the pillow. She seemed to be holding her breath.

"So it's true?"

"Yes."

"Who were you doing it for? Friedrich?"

"Yes."

"That's what I figured."

"My turn to be sorry," Nan said. "How the hell did Semenenko find out?"

"It's possible Friedrich told him when he briefed him—just to reassure him that the CIA is on the ball. I should have expected it."

"Is that why you broke up my furniture?"

"Is that why you didn't complain about it?"

Nan laughed. "Yes. Guilty conscience. I hated spying on you, but I'll have to admit I was pretty good. I once even took a blood sample from your finger. Friedrich wanted to know if you were drinking. But still, I hated it. I was terrified that you would catch me at it. I was really afraid of you."

"Why?"

"I don't know. Your past reputation, I suppose. Rumors about you, things you did . . ."

"What rumors?"

"You know, when you were in covert operations."

"Egypt?"

"I guess that was one place."

"The company rumor mill has probably made me a scapegoat for every botched operation it ever ran."

"Maybe. But it was your manner, too. So grim. It was pretty easy to believe anything about you. And Friedrich said you were unstable. He told me that I was supposed to keep you out of trouble. He made you sound like someone just out of prison—or a mental institution."

Warfield laughed.

"And I *didn't* keep you out of trouble."

"Hardly your fault."

"When you disappeared from the farm, all hell broke loose. Friedrich screamed at me on the telephone for five minutes. I called Herb Rosenstock and learned about your message to his sister. I should have told Friedrich, of course, but I couldn't bring myself to do it. I made Herb drive all the way down here from Alexandria and go out to that motel with me. That's why we got there so late."

"Thanks for not turning me in."

Nan sat up and found a cigarette in the nightstand. He saw the swell of her breasts in the brief glow of the match as she applied it to the end of the cigarette.

"I didn't know you smoked?"

"I don't, normally."

A silent minute ticked by.

"It's a funny way to end up in bed together, isn't it?"

Warfield agreed.

"How do you feel?"

"A little tired. The headache's better."

"I didn't mean that, really. I meant, well, I thought that if you wanted to make love . . . I wouldn't mind. I mean I'd like it."

"I guess not."

"Okay."

Warfield knew he couldn't leave the matter there. "It's not you, Nan. I just don't think I can. Not now. . . ."

"I can understand that. My God, after all you've been through today. I just wanted you to know I would. . . ."

Warfield felt his pulse in his throat. He swallowed hard and reached across the mattress for her hand. He found it and squeezed it hard. She put out her cigarette and lay down beside him.

"It sounds dumb, I know," he said, "but something that happened years ago still hangs over me. The last couple of days have brought it back."

"Can you talk about it?"

"I don't know. I never have."

Semenenko looked up from his book, a copy of former CIA Director William Colby's memoirs that he had found in a Washington bookstore the day before. The material was unforgivably dull, and the effort required to read it in English was beginning to fatigue him. It was two A.M. He had propped open the door to the closet-sized room, but the air still seemed heavy. Stepanovich, in the chair beside him, was wide awake. One virtue of anxiety, Semenenko mused.

The reels of tape began to move. He slipped on his headset. The sound of a door opening and closing met his ears. Then footsteps. A drawer squeaked. A long silence. A clicking noise, then a female voice: "Eliot? . . . Yes. . . . Of course I do. . . . Yes. . . . Later? . . . No, it's not too late. . . . Yes. That would be good. . . . I will."

"It's her! She's on the telephone!" Stepanovich said.

"I realize that, Colonel," Semenenko replied.

Silence.

"You'd think," Stepanovich said, exasperated, "that she'd say something to us. Tell us what's going on!"

Semenenko studied the antenna man's nervous face, then decided he was simply trying to show some bravado. The eye contact made Stepanovich blush.

"I warned her, Comrade Colonel, precisely *not* to do that. Do you suppose they haven't bugged her room?"

"Of course. How stupid of me."

Semenenko grinned. He removed his headset and picked up the copy of Colby's book again.

"Patience," he said. "The moment will come."

30

"I FIRST SAW HER IN ABDUL'S shop, off Mustapha Pasha Square," Warfield said. "Abdul was a black-market money changer. And one of my agents."

He rolled over on his back and looked at the dim rectangle of light seeping through Nan's curtains from a distant streetlamp. He had thought he would never talk about Tanya with anybody, but now, in the wake of the past day's agony, he had to share the pain, to exorcise it before the accumulation of defeats sunk him forever.

"Three things about her attracted me," he said. "She was beautiful, she was Russian, and she had come to Abdul to change Russian

rubles for American dollars. This was absolutely forbidden to Soviet citizens in Egypt. I asked Abdul to find out about her. He
discovered she was married to an Egyptian Army officer who
happened to be the liaison between Egyptian intelligence and the
KGB. I was intrigued with the possibilities of recruiting her."

"What made you think she might cooperate?"

"A sixth sense, I guess. It's always a hell of a risk to approach
anybody, of course, because you have to reveal yourself first.
Abdul and I rigged a simple trap for her. I photographed her
changing money with Abdul and then accosted her with the
photo."

"How did she react?"

"Stunned, at first. Then outraged. She threatened to turn me
over to the police. I thought she might, too. She was in a privileged
position—both as a Russian, and as the wife of an Army officer. I
knew I was taking a risk, too, because the Russians were cashing
large amounts of rubles on the black market for the Kremlin. The
KGB actually ran a regular program, to build up Soviet foreign
hard currency reserves. If she had been part of that program, she
would have tipped off the KGB and that would have been the end
of me. But she was exchanging small sums, so I assumed she was
just improving her own position. Lots of Russians were doing it.
In that case, of course, turning me in would have exposed her and
embarrassed her husband politically." He paused, remembering.
"In the beginning, I paid her a lot of money for innocuous information. Once I had her hooked, I asked for more. Her information,
in time, became first rate."

"What went wrong?" Nan asked.

Warfield pressed a hand against his forehead, where the remains
of his headache still smoldered. "We . . . got involved."

"Go on."

"She didn't love her husband. She didn't sleep with him. She
barely knew him, in fact. It turned out their marriage had been
arranged by the local KGB *resident*. Before I hired her, she was
already spying on her husband for the KGB. When she told me
that, I nearly collapsed. Imagine what a risk I had taken! She could
have sabotaged me in an instant."

"Why didn't she?"

"At first I worried that she had. I broke off contact with her for
several weeks. I had her watched. Nothing suspicious emerged.

Finally, I realized two things. She wouldn't have confessed her KGB work to me in the first place if she had been doubling on me. And she wouldn't have given me such good intelligence."

"But you had blackmailed her into working for you. How could you trust her?"

Warfield sighed.

"In other words," Nan said, "you were in love with her."

"Yes. But I decided to break off completely anyway. It was too dangerous to take the chance that I might be wrong about her."

"And? . . ."

"She found me. She told me she was pregnant."

"So you took her back."

"Yes. And then things got complicated. We had to make a decision. I persuaded her to defect to the West. . . ." Warfield fell silent.

"Go on," Nan whispered.

"I need a drink."

"I know. Go on with your story."

"I hoped to get her out and then join her. It sounds crazy now, but I really thought it possible. I just wanted to go away with her. That was all I cared about. If it meant the end of my career as a spy, I was willing to sacrifice it. . . . I had access to a boat at a dock near the Al Montaza Hotel. She was to attend a big reception there with her husband. There would be a lot of drinking. No one would notice her slip out into the park for a breath of air. . . . The boat would get us clear of the harbor. A mile out in the Mediterranean a fishing trawler was waiting to take us to Israel. . . ."

"What happened?"

"When she came out they shot her—from the back of a truck. Then a car pulled up and two men threw her body in the back and drove away."

Nan gasped.

Warfield lay still, barely daring to breathe, as the apparition of those past horrors crept back into his consciousness again. Nan put her hand on his chest. He was aware of the contrast in their skin temperatures. Hers warm, his cold.

"Do you know what went wrong?" she asked.

"No."

"You never found out?"

"No," he replied. "Two days ago, Semenenko told me the Egyptians were behind it."

"Do you believe him?"

"I don't know. It seems likely. It fits what I know."

"What did you do? What happened to you?"

"I had to assume that everything was blown. I hid out in Shanklin's whorehouse for three days. Finally, I went back to my place on Saad Zaglul Street. . . ."

"And? . . ."

"All my spies were there."

"Yes?"

"I think I need a glass of water."

Nan pushed herself quickly from the bed. "Stay here. I'll get it."

She returned with the water and he sipped it slowly, trying to clear the hard lump in his throat.

"For God's sakes, Charles, don't stop now!"

He took a deep breath. "They were all around my room," he said. "All twenty of them. Some at the dining table, some on the sofa, some in the kitchen, some on my bed. . . ."

"What were they doing?"

"Nothing."

"I don't understand."

"They were all dead. Their throats slit. Someone had gone to the trouble of dragging them there and arranging them in grotesque positions around the apartment. They had been there for two days . . . in the summer heat."

The retelling stirred a powerful rage in Warfield. He drained the glass of water. "I had to leave them there," he said, finally. "I left Alexandria the next day."

He put the empty glass on the floor by the bed and sat, rigid. He clenched his fists and swallowed an enormous gulp of air. He had gone this far, he had to finish.

"There was one other thing," he blurted out harshly. "A large waterproof bag on the kitchen table. Tanya was inside. In pieces. Along with . . . the baby."

Nan turned on her side and pulled herself tight against Warfield's arm. He began trembling, then exploded in uncontrolled weeping. Nan held him for a long time, not speaking or moving.

"I'm glad you told me," she whispered, when Warfield had recovered somewhat. "Tell me the rest. What happened after you left Alexandria?"

"I came back to Langley for a debriefing. I was in bad shape. They gave me six months convalescent leave—sent me to a shrink. I can't remember to this day what I did during that half year. I tried to drink myself to death, I guess. When I returned, they put me in counterintelligence. I kept on drinking."

"Did you ever find out how your network was blown so fast? Did Tanya know the names of your spies?"

"No. They were only in my head. No one knew them. And they didn't know each other."

"She could have been responsible for putting a tail on you."

"I considered that. As soon as I reached Shanklin's whorehouse I sent word out for them to go into hiding. But it was already too late."

"You can't blame yourself for Tanya's death—or their deaths," Nan said. "There's always risk."

"Of course I blame myself. My stupidity cost me everything that was important to me."

"But what was done to you was monstrous! You could never have anticipated something so inhumanly cruel."

The telephone rang. Nan fumbled for it in the dark. "It's Jonathan," she said. She switched on the overhead light and searched for a pad and pencil. Warfield looked at his watch. Five in the morning.

"Guess what," she said, cradling the receiver a minute later. "He found five places in the Washington area that warehouse cotton. And one of them's no longer in use."

"That must be the one we want. Where is it?"

"Off Rhode Island Avenue. Here's the address." Nan handed him the sheet from her notepad. "Are you going now?"

"Might as well. I can check the place out before the neighborhood wakes up."

"Do you want me to go with you?"

"No."

"You sure?"

"Yes. I'll be all right. And the trip may just turn out to be a waste of time. Don't get your hopes up."

"Call me when you've had a look."

Warfield studied her, suddenly suspicious. "You're not going to tell Friedrich, are you?"

"Of course not!"

"He could have bugged this phone, you know."

Nan laughed. "I'm Harlan Robertson's daughter, remember?"

"What's that mean?"

"It means I have an electronic sweep installed in the phone. It's bug-proof."

As Warfield dressed to leave, the phone rang again.

"It's Herb," Nan said, handing him the receiver.

"I'm at the lab," Rosenstock told him. "I decided to analyze your food samples myself. I had a hunch."

"And? . . ."

"And I was right. The poison is Ricin. There are only two places in the world that make it. One's in Hungary, the other's in Czechoslovakia. Exclusive KGB contracts."

"Are you absolutely sure?"

"I'm sure."

"Couldn't anyone else have it?"

"The KGB may share it with some allies. The East Germans, maybe, or the Cubans. But I doubt it. The only other supply of it is at the farm itself, of all places. The CIA recovered some from a defector. They keep it for analysis."

"So who poisoned Martinez?"

Rosenstock was silent.

"Herb?"

"Yeah, I'm thinking. The KGB or the CIA. It's a toss-up."

Semenenko was unable to keep his eyes focused on the page. He closed the book and laid it on the table beside his headset. The digital clock over the console read 5:23.

"I'm going to bed," he muttered, pulling his tie back into place under his shirt collar.

Stepanovich nodded. Semenenko was surprised how alert the antenna man still appeared. Living on his nerves, he supposed.

"Man the monitor and the detonator until eight hundred. If you hear anything interesting call my room. I'll come right up. Otherwise, shut down at eight. We'll try again at eighteen hundred hours."

He buttoned his suit jacket and walked out. He would have to put more pressure on Katya to perform, he decided. The prospect of another night in that room with Stepanovich was more than he could bear.

31

warehouse off Rhode Island Avenue at seven. A steady drizzle transformed the pavements to mud and stained the crumbling facades of the ghetto neighborhood a deeper, uglier shade of gray and black in the dawn light. The streets were deserted.

He had driven his rented car with abandon over the 120 miles from Williamsburg to Washington. Even if nothing came of it, he was glad to be moving, to be doing something.

He parked the Buick three blocks from the warehouse, tucking it into an unobtrusive spot near an empty loading dock. He pulled out the pistol Nan had loaned him and examined it. It was a Beretta Minx, a snub-nosed, .22-caliber automatic. Little more than a toy, he realized, with far less stopping power than the Marine's .45 he had lost somewhere in his drunken revels with Rosalie, but it had its modest advantages. It was far lighter and more compact than the .45, and it held eight rounds. He pushed the button on the side of the hand grip to release the magazine, checked that it was loaded to capacity, and slipped it back into place inside the grip. He dropped the weapon in his right coat pocket, shoved Nan's flashlight in the left, locked the car, and headed for the warehouse.

His body ached from the ordeals of the last two days, and the cold drizzle magnified his discomfort. Still, he felt calm and alert.

He shone the flashlight beam on the small door near the corner of the building and saw a lock. New, but not difficult to open. He withdrew two slim metal picks from his wallet and went to work, tucking the flashlight in his armpit to leave both hands free. No one disturbed him except a stray cat, who rocketed past him from the nearby alley. After five minutes of probing, he was able to rotate the cylinder, snap the dead bolt back, and pull open the door.

Inside, Warfield locked the door behind him and trained the light around the interior. Off to his right lay a stretch of empty, echoing space, the width and depth of the entire building and two floors high, broken by a row of brick columns down the middle. Directly ahead, he spotted an open doorway, and a staircase beyond.

He walked through and directed the light on the stair treads.

The thick coat of dust had been recently disturbed by footprints. He held his own size-ten shoe next to one. It was the same size. Another print was about two inches shorter. Two men, he guessed, one probably short. Both prints had been made by the same style sneaker tread.

He looked for more footprints out on the main floor of the warehouse, but found none. Everyone who came in, it appeared, went straight up the stairs.

Back at the bottom of the stairwell he noticed a third print. He had missed it at first, because its tread was smooth, and obscured by the marks of the sneakers. It was a very big print, and its toe was pointed. A dress shoe.

The trail of all three footprints continued unbroken up through the gloom of the stairwell to the top floor and then down a corridor toward the rear of the building. Warfield stopped occasionally to listen for sounds. A rat scurried past him in the dark.

The top floor appeared to have once been used for offices. The ceilings were lower and the walls showed the cracked skin of old paint. The corridor and the footprints both terminated at a single door. Warfield hesitated in front of it, listening again. He heard nothing.

He twisted the corroded brass knob and gently nudged the door inward. The flashlight revealed a large room on the other side—about twenty-five feet square, with a higher ceiling than the corridor. A solitary wooden chair sat exactly in the middle, its back to the doorway. More footprints were discernible in the dust on the floor.

This, Warfield concluded, had to be the place. The place where the mysterious Instructor dispensed his orders.

He played the flashlight beam around the walls. Two windows on one side, both tightly boarded up. Plaster was peeling off in huge chunks from every surface. Fallen patches of it formed islands of grayish-white on the age-blackened wood floor. The chair in the center was nondescript and old, probably left behind when the building was abandoned. Its seat, he noticed, shining the light on it, was dust free. He grasped the back of the chair and tipped it forward so its rear legs came up several inches off the floor. Distinct clean circles showed in the dust beneath them. The chair had not been moved from this spot in quite a while, but someone had been sitting in it. Recently. Exactly at this spot.

Warfield pondered the strange setup. Why only one chair? And why was it facing away from the door? He sat down on it and tried to recreate the scene in his imagination.

Nothing came. He zigzagged the light beam around the floor, looking for more clues. One clue was missing: the Instructor's larger shoe print.

That meant the Instructor came no further than the doorway. Sitting there, imagining the faceless presence of the man behind him in the dark made the hair prickle on Warfield's neck. An effective way for the Instructor to protect his identity, he realized, and a powerful way to intimidate the hard men who came here for their orders.

Warfield felt for the small Beretta in his coat pocket and pulled it out. If he were to throw himself to the floor, then roll over and shoot, he might be able to hit a man by the door. But it was a distance of fifteen feet, and it would take luck to score a fatal hit. The Instructor, on the other hand, could keep a pistol trained accurately on the back of the chair throughout a whole meeting.

A cautious man, Warfield reflected. And thoroughly trained. He had conscientiously preserved all the advantages.

Did he hear something?

It had been so quiet, the slightest sound made him instantly alert. He held his breath and listened. Nothing. Probably a rat.

He decided he could bug this room and set up a stakeout somewhere nearby. He and Moore could manage it. With luck, the Instructor might hold another class here soon. He had reason to, Warfield thought. The two abortive attempts to kill him must be causing some anxiety among the Instructor's friends.

A sound again.

This time he recognized it as the creak of a floorboard. He stood up and switched off his flashlight. The creaking continued, becoming gradually louder.

Someone on the stairs?

He stepped quickly toward the corner of the room, pressing himself against the same wall as the doorway. The sounds were distinct now, and growing closer. Someone had arrived at the top of the stairs and was walking slowly down the corridor.

Warfield felt with his thumb along the side of the Beretta's grip for the unfamiliar safety catch and slid it forward. His other hand clutched the flashlight, thumb on the button in front of the slide switch, ready to press it down and train the beam on a target.

He cursed himself for dawdling. He should have cased the room quickly and gotten out.

The door handle rattled and turned, and the door squeaked inward on its rusty hinges. It opened to form a temporary screen between himself and the intruder.

A small penlight beam shot across the room and zeroed in on the chair. The door closed, and the invisible figure crossed to the chair and sat down. He played the narrow shaft of light briefly around the dark. Warfield crouched in the corner, a statue. The light missed him and finally clicked off.

The chair creaked as its new occupant settled in. Warfield prayed he wouldn't notice that the seat was already warm.

A full minute passed, the silence mushrooming in the blackness.

The intruder sighed impatiently. It was clear that a meeting was about to take place. Who was in the chair? Was it the Turk?

He gauged the distance between them to be about fifteen feet. He assumed the man was armed. He had to act. And he had to act before the Instructor arrived.

Warfield held one advantage: surprise. But each second he let pass was eroding his edge. The intruder might sense his presence.

He must move now! His hands were sweating. It was many years since he had been in this kind of physical danger. He had lost the instinctive trust of his reflexes. He wanted to wipe the sweat from his hands, but that was out of the question.

Feeling the corner with his elbows for direction, he raised his right hand and trained the Beretta toward its invisible target. With his left, he held out the flashlight, pointing it at the same unseen spot. He felt his pulse jumping in his wrists. It had to be now.

"Freeze!" he cried.

His thumb felt for the flashlight button and pressed it hard. The light blinked on for a brief fraction of a second, illuminating the astonished face of the man in the chair. Then the smooth metal cylinder slipped through Warfield's wet palm and bounced noisily on the floor.

He dove for it desperately. His hands, fanning out on the dirty floor like bird's wings, couldn't find it.

He heard the chair in the center of the room topple over. Rapid steps scuffled to the opposite corner.

He stopped his frantic scrabbling around the floor and pushed himself back against the wall. It was inexcusable to have dropped the light. Disuse had more than dulled his reflexes, it had made him clumsy.

A new and deadly silence swelled in the darkness around him. His mind raced furiously, trying to think clearly, to avoid panic. His companion in the dark must now have a pistol drawn. He would be puzzling out what had just happened. He would know that Warfield was crouched in the corner opposite him, and he would realize that he was armed. The advantage had tipped alarmingly in the intruder's favor. He still had his flashlight. He could pin Warfield in the beam and take the first shot.

Soundlessly, Warfield slid down the wall and flattened himself face down on the floor. He fanned his arms in a wide arc from his thighs to his head, hoping to locate his flashlight. Nothing. He debated whether to risk a noisier search. It *must* be within a few feet of where he lay!

No. The Turk, or whoever he was, would hear him. He might try a shot in the dark, homing in on the sound alone.

Warfield gripped his Beretta with both hands at arm's length on the floor in front of him, finger on the trigger. The distance between them was now thirty feet. Shooting at a *visible* target at that range with a Beretta was a tough hit. In the dark it would be futile. The Turk would probably assume the same thing.

And what else would he be thinking?

Would he risk flashing his light on and pumping out a quick spurt of bullets across the room? And give Warfield the target of the penlight to shoot back at?

Think! Warfield told himself. Think! If the Turk did flash the penlight on, he would probably hold it out at arm's length to one side. If he was right-handed—and the odds were ten to one he was —the gun would be in his right and the penlight in his left, which was to Warfield's right.

So Warfield would aim his first answering shot two and a half feet to the right of the penlight beam. The second shot, two and a half feet to the left. On the third shot, if he was still alive, he would go for the light itself. It didn't sound good. Even if he hit the man, an instant kill was not likely.

The minutes stretched out. How long could he stand the tension?

A soft brushing noise near the floor in front of him sent a jab of adrenalin through his heart. Was the Turk moving? He waited, holding his breath, listening for the noise again. Nothing. Had he imagined it? Probably. He clung hard to the grip of the Beretta, ready to answer an attack.

Several more minutes pounded by. The silence and the pitch blackness were becoming enemies themselves.

His arms and neck began to cramp from the strain. He rested his cheek on the floor and let his arms go limp. He counted out an entire minute in this vulnerable state, then resumed his awkward position, pistol out in front, toes touching the walls on each side of the corner behind him, to align himself in an exact diagonal with the room. His eyes focused on the invisible point halfway up the walls of the far corner, where his nemesis waited.

It was a standoff.

A terrible realization dawned on Warfield. The Turk was waiting him out on purpose. Of course! He had time on his side. Reinforcements in the form of the Instructor would arrive at any second.

If he wanted to live, he would have to act. He must outmaneuver him somehow.

He visualized the room from overhead—a large square, like a boxing ring, with a blind opponent in each corner. If he could work his way along the right-hand wall to the next corner, he could gain important advantages. It would take him out of the location the Turk believed him to be in. It would bring him about ten feet closer. And most important, the wall joining that corner to his right also joined the Turk's corner. He could use it as a guide to position his pistol. By aiming the weapon parallel to that wall, he would greatly increase the odds of a hit.

It sounded good. The problem was moving to that corner without alerting the Turk.

He would have to try. He started, sliding on his belly an inch at a time, using his elbows for traction. Some pieces of fallen plaster caught underneath him and scraped softly on the uneven surface of the floor. He rolled on his side and removed them with his fingers.

He managed a foot. Two feet. Three.

Even while moving, he concentrated on keeping the Beretta in his right hand trained toward the invisible far corner, adjusting the angle fractionally as he progressed along the wall. Nerve racking! But it must be getting to the Turk as well.

Again a faint scraping sound. He felt for pieces of plaster beneath his chest and stomach. There were none.

Four feet. Five. Six.

One elbow pressed painfully down on an exposed nail. He bit his lip and pushed forward.

Eight feet. Nine feet. Halfway there, he judged.

Suddenly he noticed the glow from the luminous dial of his wristwatch, as his sleeve slid back along his wrist. Frantically, he pushed the watchband out of sight further up his arm.

Fifteen feet, he judged. He should feel the corner soon.

Across the room to his left, a faint sliver of light leaked under the door from the corridor outside and then was gone.

He froze. The Instructor!

The doorknob rattled, the hinges squealed.

A shaft of light blazed like a bolt of lightning across the dark, illuminating the toppled chair, and then the Turk.

Warfield gasped.

The Turk was not in the far corner at all. Like Warfield, he had crawled along the wall and reached a point barely a yard from Warfield's left hand. In the next few seconds they would have touched each other.

Warfield saw the Turk turn his face toward the light, blinded momentarily by its intensity. He waved a long-barreled pistol.

"Someone in the room!" he screamed. "Get the light off me!"

Warfield, a yard away, was still in the darkness. Then he was counting explosions. One! Two! Three! Four! They echoed in the empty room like thunder. He saw the Turk lurch repeatedly against the wall, as if kicked by an invisible boot.

Warfield aimed his Beretta at the flashlight and fired, pulling the trigger as fast as he could. The stink of cordite stung his nostrils.

He heard a roar of pain by the doorway. The flashlight snaked out of the room and disappeared down the corridor. In the abrupt blackness, Warfield jumped to his feet and groped his way forward. Heavy footsteps pounded down the distant staircase.

Warfield's toe stubbed against the soft obstacle of the Turk's body. Fingers grasped his leg. He kicked, but the Turk only tightened his grip. He kicked again. A grunt of pain issued from the vise that now encircled his knees. He kicked again.

He must get free!

He reached down and grabbed for the Turk's head in the dark. The hair felt thick, like animal fur. He grasped it, and with his other hand struck repeatedly at the base of the assassin's neck. The Turk's grip went slack.

He groped toward the door into the corridor. The total blackness disoriented him. He found the wall, and ran along it until he came to the door. Outside, in the corridor, it was just as dark. He inched along the wall, then down the stairwell to the outside door. The Instructor was gone. The street, gray and empty, glistened in the cold rain.

He fumbled slowly back up through the darkness and into the room again. With his feet he found the Turk's inert form, and felt around it for his penlight. He found it near the Turk's hand, and flashed it on. Gingerly, he rolled the Turk over on his back and shone the light on his face. He felt a moment of grim vindication. It was the face in the ambulance. And the face of the mess hall busboy. One bullet had struck his leg, another had pierced his chest just over the heart. Warfield marveled that he had survived long enough to put up such a struggle.

In the Turk's coat pocket he found a tape cassette. He tucked it into his own pocket and played the light over the dead man's body. He was wearing sneakers, the tread identical to the footprints he had noticed earlier. He pushed the corpse's legs together and studied the feet again.

Incredible.

One sneaker was nearly two inches shorter than the other. That explained the two sizes of sneaker prints he had observed. In the confused dust of overlapping prints on the stairs and the corridor, he had assumed two men. But now he saw that both were made by the same individual.

He had seen a similar set of unmatched footprints once before —in the park of the Al Montaza, the night they killed Tanya.

A bizarre coincidence? How many men in the world had a right foot two inches shorter than the left? And how many of them were assassins?

But that was not the most incredible thing.

The most incredible thing was the identity of the man the Turk was working for. From his cry of pain by the doorway, Warfield now knew who the Instructor was.

The implications were staggering.

32

WILLIAM WILBERT OPENED the door to the Oval Office and peered inside. President Daniels was sifting through a batch of intelligence reports.

"They've been waiting an hour, Eliot," he said. "You better see them."

Daniels looked across the room at his chief of staff. His expression conveyed suppressed anger. "Okay," he muttered. "But why do I have to put up with this?"

"You're the president," Wilbert said. "That's what it's all about —putting up with things. Just listen to them. That's all you have to do. Tell them you appreciate their concern."

"This is personal," Daniels replied. "It's none of their damned business."

Wilbert averted his eyes. "There are rumors of a demonstration tonight outside the White House. You might be able to head that off with a little diplomacy. I'll interrupt in fifteen minutes if it isn't going well."

The door from the outer reception area swung open and three men and one woman filed in. Isabelle Hatch, Republican congresswoman from Maine led the way, followed by Orville Hainesworth, senior senator from South Carolina; the Reverend Billy James Jaffrey, pastor of the Carteret Street Baptist Church of Memphis, Tennessee; and Chester Catlin, the vice-president.

Daniels spread a hand in the direction of the sofas by the fireplace. "Gentlemen," he cried, in a hearty tone, "Come in and sit down!" He realized his greeting excluded Isabelle Hatch, but he had never been able to figure out an acceptable way to address a gathering of several men and one woman. Besides, he didn't like Mrs. Hatch, and she certainly didn't like him, so there was no need to agonize over pleasantries. In his view, the woman was a dangerous prude.

Senator Hainesworth's presence, on the other hand, wounded Daniels deeply. The president had always admired him. At seventy-three, the senator was an honest, astute, and widely respected public figure. He was also a devoutly religious man, and a strong moral voice in Congress.

The presence of Vice-President Catlin infuriated Daniels. Catlin came from Bible-belt country, and his loudly proclaimed fundamentalist views had helped to swing several border states during the election. Daniels believed Catlin's religious piety, like his patriotism, to be largely opportunistic. The man was an insecure hypocrite, quick to sense shifts in the political wind, and quick to trim his sails to ride them. A weak man. And an ungrateful one as well, Daniels thought. Catlin was the one political deal he truly regretted having made.

What these three visitors had in common was the fourth: they were all members of Billy James Jaffrey's American Christian Crusade. Jaffrey, a hard-driving, ambitious man, had made his movement a political force to be reckoned with by anybody in public office. Himself included, Daniels was forced to admit.

Catlin surprised Daniels by speaking first. "Mr. President," he began, clearing his throat noisily. "We're here on a difficult mission. Mrs. Hatch here, and the senator, and Reverend Jaffrey have graciously consented to be spokespersons in bringing a matter to your attention personally that. . . ."

Daniels gestured impatiently. "Come to the point, Chester."

"It's that Russian woman, Mr. President," Isabelle Hatch broke in.

The president glared at her with his most intimidating expression, the stony stare a Washington columnist had dubbed "The Daniels Death Ray." "Are you referring to the widow of the Russian premier?"

"You know that I am," she replied, the sting of reprimand in her voice.

Senator Hainesworth's soothing Southern baritone rumbled:

"Many people feel that you may be taking too personal an interest in her problems, Mr. President," he said.

Catlin nodded. "What we're trying to say is that the public is upset. . . ."

"There's a wave of resentment against her!" Hatch blurted out.

"What resentment?" Daniels challenged, his voice sharp. "I haven't noticed any resentment. Except yours."

"There's a building consensus on the Hill," Hainesworth said, "that Mrs. Kamenev, through no fault of her own, mind you, may be complicating the international situation. That, and the lack of progress on catching the premier's killers, is making us all a bit worried."

Daniels rubbed his chin, warning himself not to indulge his anger. "I'm frankly astonished," he said, in his most persuasive tone. "Mrs. Kamenev is a guest of the United States. She has lost her husband in a tragic incident on American soil and was nearly killed herself. Two days ago her own government tried to kidnap her. Can you honestly come in here and tell me that I am wrong to extend her our help?"

Daniels studied their faces, trying to gauge the effect of his words. He was being evasive, of course. The truth was that he was completely, desperately in love with the woman, and wouldn't let her go if every damned politician and preacher in the country demanded it. If he was forced to be evasive, he consoled himself with the fact that he was also forced to withhold the one piece of information from them that would instantly quell their protest— that Katya had spied on her government for the United States.

"We don't question your motives, Mr. President," Hainesworth said.

"There are rumors that she's sleeping with you!" Mrs. Hatch cut in brutally.

Hainesworth arched his brows in disapproval of the congress-woman's lack of tact. Catlin and Jaffrey memorized the carpet. Their silence told Daniels that they believed what Hatch had accused him of. He understood what really disturbed them: he was committing adultery. And no matter what the extenuating cir-cumstances, a president of the United States could not expect to get away with it.

How could he deal with this?

With Hainesworth, he knew the answer. He would ask Friedrich to brief the senator on Katya's role as a CIA informant. That would quiet him down fast. And without Hainesworth's support, the opposition would lose a lot of its respectability.

With Catlin, he would have to apply the screws. Daniels had learned recently that he had taken bribes while governor of Tennessee. He didn't know how good a case could be made against him, but the mere threat to sic the attorney general on him would shut him up.

With Hatch and Jaffrey, he had no leverage at all. He wished he could just blurt out a confession to them—admit his love for Katya, explain to them his terrible loneliness. That, of course, would be idiotic. Hatch and Jaffrey were out to crucify him. He would simply have to make a more persuasive case to the public than they could. Americans could be misled in the short term, but he believed they could eventually be brought around to understand his needs. It was just one more political storm to ride out. He had ridden out many. These people didn't represent most Americans. They were repressed, narrow-minded, fearful. He would have to neutralize them, somehow.

"What about you, Reverend?" Daniels asked. "You've been silent so far. What's your view?"

Jaffrey beamed. "We think it's an unfortunate situation," he began, his velvety preacher's voice surprisingly resonant in the large office. "As president of the whole nation, you carry a moral obligation to set an example for the rest of us. We feel that Mrs. Kamenev's presence in the White House, under the circumstances, is having a deleterious effect on the American people. There's an impression of immorality, Mr. President, no matter what the true facts may be. . . ."

"People are afraid," Hainesworth cut in. "That's what we're hearing from our constituents. They don't understand what's going on. The Russian premier is killed, right here in the capital. Nobody seems to know who's behind it—and it's been ten days since the event. The premier's wife asks for asylum and moves right into the White House. You and she are alone up there on the second floor. Then the kidnapping attempt, and millions of Americans see you embracing her at the airport. I submit, this is not a picture that inspires confidence, Mr. President. And I don't personally give a damn about the appearance of morality. I sit in judgment of no man. What I'm concerned about, and what your fellow countrymen are concerned about, is what's going on? Is the president in charge? Does he know what he's doing? They want some answers, Mr. President. They're afraid."

There was reason in the senator's words, Daniels realized. "What would you have me do?" he asked.

"I trust you, Mr. President," he replied. "Most Americans trust you. Talk to them. Tell them the facts."

"A press conference?"

"Or a speech. It doesn't matter. Just get out there before the public and air this issue, even if you don't yourself know all the answers yet. There's too much secrecy. Too many rumors. Dispel them."

Daniels turned to the others. "What else?"

"Get that woman out of the White House," Mrs. Hatch replied.

Daniels leveled his gaze at her. He fervently wished to tell her to go to hell. Something in Jaffrey's demeanor drew his attention away from her. The preacher's upper lip was moist with perspiration, and it quivered, struggling to say something.

"Mr. President," he managed, finally. "The American Christian Crusade has called for a big demonstration this evening. Other organizations are joining in. So you can appreciate how widespread the sentiment against you has become. . . ."

The sneaky, demagogic bastard, Daniels thought. He's using this situation for his own aggrandizement.

"Demonstration?" the president echoed, pretending surprise.

"In Lafayette Park. It will be peaceful, of course."

"At the north fence of the White House?"

Jaffrey nodded.

"I suggest you call it off, Mr. Jaffrey. I'll go on television tomorrow, just as Senator Hainesworth suggests." The next words pained him, but he saw now that Wilbert had been right all along. He would have to move Katya out of the White House. "To further show my good faith, I will ask Mrs. Kamenev to move to Blair House immediately."

"I'm afraid it's not up to me to call off the demonstration, Mr. President."

"Why not? I've agreed to your conditions, haven't I?" Daniels felt his temper rising like a hot air balloon.

... 241

"Well, it's an expression of popular sentiment, Mr. President. As I have previously indicated, there will be many organizations out there besides our Christian Crusade. . . ."

Wilbert appeared in the doorway. Daniels ignored him.

"You realize our security problems, don't you, Reverend? You realize we can't allow any demonstrations near the White House?"

Jaffrey shrugged. "I'm sorry, Mr. President. It's a free land, sir, after all."

"I'm making a fair effort to accommodate you. If you still plan to make a public spectacle of our differences, then I recommend you do it in Potomac Park! Any demonstrators near the White House will be arrested. Including you."

Reverend Jaffrey's cherubic face turned as red as a stop light.

Wilbert broke in to announce that the meeting was over. "Thank you all very much for coming," he said, herding them toward the door. "The president will give careful consideration to everything you've suggested. I'm sorry that more time isn't available. . . ."

33

THERE WAS NOWHERE TO HIDE
the automobile. Every inch in the neighborhood was either road surface, sidewalk, or private property. And Warfield knew the local police patrolled this exclusive slice of Virginia suburb as if it were a missile base. He finally hit upon the perfect solution. He parked the car in someone's empty driveway. He'd rented it with phony credentials, so if the residents came home, no one could trace it to him.

Head down, he walked back out to the street, strode several hundred feet along it, then cut quickly into a driveway on his right and ran across the long, tree-studded expanse of lawn that separated the house from the public thoroughfare.

He saw two lights—one in a second-floor window, the other at the peak of the garage roof, illuminating the pair of overhead sliding doors beneath it. Keeping to the shadows, he worked his way to the far side of the garage and stopped to listen for sounds. The whining of a truck engine, blocks away. Nothing else.

Slowly he circled the garage until he was standing in the open breezeway that joined it to the house. He twisted the handle on the garage door and let himself in. Dim light from the outside fixture filtered through the panes of glass on the overhead doors, allowing Warfield a partial view of the interior. Save for a clutter of objects against the back wall, the near bay was empty. The far bay contained a station wagon. He slipped around behind it, felt about in the dark and found a comfortable spot against the wall.

He sat down and waited.

The numbers on his watch glowed at him in the murky light. Six o'clock. Six-thirty. Seven o'clock.

He heard the faint trill of a telephone inside the house. Was he calling home? Saying he'd be late for dinner? Warfield wished he had a drink.

Seven-thirty. Eight. He dozed off.

The whine of an electric motor and the rattle of the overhead door clattering up its metal track brought him instantly awake. He crept quickly between the front end of the station wagon and the back wall of the garage. He paused there, crouching on the balls of his feet.

A black Mercedes glided into the other bay and stopped. By the time the driver had opened the door and stepped out, Warfield was standing beside him. He wrapped a hand over his mouth, and jammed the Beretta into the small of his back.

"It's Warfield," he whispered, his voice fierce. "I'm not going to hurt you. I just want to talk. Nod your head if you understand."

He felt the nod and relaxed his grip. "Get back into the car," he ordered. "And open the rear door."

Friedrich complied. Warfield jumped into the back seat and pressed the automatic against the CIA director's neck.

"Drive out of here. Head back toward the Shirley Highway."

"You're a damned fool!" Friedrich said.

Warfield could feel him shaking. He had been a desk man his entire career, never exposed to anything more dangerous than a letter opener. He would be easy to terrorize.

"Right, I'm a fool," Warfield said. "But that's not what I want to talk about."

"Come inside and act like a normal human being! We can talk in my study!"

"We'll talk in the car. Drive."

Friedrich backed the automobile slowly out the driveway. At the foot of the drive, Warfield told him to turn right. "Drive slowly. No heroics. I'm a rogue agent, don't forget. A trained killer."

"You wouldn't kill me."

Trying to reassure himself, Warfield guessed. "Probably not," he said. "But I'd maim you. A bullet in the kneecap or the ankle. It wouldn't kill you, but it would raise hell with your Sunday walks in the woods. Keep that in mind."

Friedrich said nothing.

Warfield reached down between the front seats and picked up the hand receiver on the car's radiophone and pressed it against Friedrich's chest. "Call your wife," he said. "Tell her you forgot something at the office. You'll be back in an hour."

Friedrich placed the call. To Warfield's surprise, he handled it without difficulty.

They drove to a shopping center several miles away, and parked in the far corner of the lot, away from the floodlights and the customer traffic.

"Hand me the keys."

Friedrich passed them over his shoulder and Warfield dropped them into his pocket.

"Look, Charlie," Friedrich began, "You're in trouble. Don't make it worse. . . ."

Warfield jabbed the barrel of the Beretta hard against the director's neck. "I'm not interested in any bargains," he muttered, his mouth close to Friedrich's ear. "You've set me up, and I want some explanations."

Friedrich shook his head. "All I did was tell the commandant to hold you at the base until the FBI could get a warrant for your arrest. The president directed me to do that!"

"Bullshit. You intended to frame me for the murder of Martinez."

"I thought you *did* kill him!"

"Why would I do that?"

"I don't know! I didn't trust you. And your whole interrogation was risky. You were using dangerous drugs."

244 . . .

"I wasn't using Ricin."

"What do you mean?"

"I mean Ricin. The KGB's favorite poison. Martinez was killed by a dose of the stuff!"

"How do you know that?"

"I'm guessing it's what your autopsy will show, because he tried the same poison on me. Rosenstock analyzed my sample himself."

"I don't understand. Who tried to poison you?"

"The third assassin. Martinez called him the Turk. He drove the getaway vehicle. He poisoned Martinez's food, then mine."

"He was at the farm?"

"That's right."

"But that's impossible! What was he doing there?"

"I thought you might know."

"I'll call Peary right now! We can still catch him!"

Warfield laughed. "You'll be a little late."

"Why?"

"He's dead."

Friedrich spread his hands in a gesture of defeat. "I don't understand," he repeated.

Warfield described the encounter at the motel, and the shooting at the warehouse earlier that morning.

"The Turk's still there. Top floor rear. I'll give you the address. You can send somebody over to pick him up."

"How did you find out about it?"

"Legwork and luck."

"You see how misled you are," Friedrich said, trying to get back on top of the conversation. "If you hadn't run off, you'd be vindicated by now."

"I'd be dead."

Friedrich turned his head, trying to see Warfield behind him. "Be sensible. Cooperate with us!"

Warfield pressed the pistol harder into Friedrich's neck. "Cooperating with you almost got me murdered. There's a cover-up going on. And you're part of it."

Friedrich twisted his head around and stared at Warfield, speechless. He regained his composure slowly, like a man who thought he'd seen a ghost, only to discover it was a trick of light.

"The CIA is involved!" Warfield insisted.

"That's paranoia."

"Is it? There was someone else in that warehouse this morning. Byron Shanklin!"

Friedrich shook his head in disbelief. "What could he have been doing there?"

"I was hoping you'd tell me!"

"I can't tell you anything!"

Warfield nudged the pistol again. "Are you sure?"

"Of course!"

"Shanklin's the man the Turk was waiting to get his orders from. He's running the hit squad, what's left of it."

It took a long time for Warfield's statement to register with Friedrich. He just kept shaking his head in amazement, as if the idea would go away if he kept at it long enough.

"It's preposterous," he said, finally. "Did you see that it was Shanklin? You said it was dark!"

"I heard him. That was enough."

"You're saying that Shanklin is behind the Suitland Parkway ambush?"

"That's right."

"Nonsense," Friedrich insisted. "Paranoia."

"Is it? I've known him for years, and I know his voice. It's unmistakable. He shot the Turk—either in panic, or because the Turk was compromised. And if you didn't arrange for the Turk to take that job at Camp Peary, then Shanklin must have. Who else knew of the exact location of our interrogation? And who else was in a position to sneak the Turk into the farm with the right credentials? Shanklin, on both counts. And Shanklin must have been responsible for the sloppiness of the first two days' interrogation of Martinez. He was sabotaging it!"

Friedrich shook his head. "This is fantasy! Shanklin's one of our best. It doesn't make any sense!"

"No, it doesn't. That's why I supposed he must be doing this for the company, where senseless activity is so commonplace."

"We're not in the business of assassinating world leaders," Friedrich snapped.

"Some new reform you've instituted?"

"We do not try to kill our own president."

"Well, Shanklin does. Who's he working for?"

"You expect me to know?"

"Make a guess, then! Castro? The Russians? Who?"

"Not the Russians. I'm sure of that."

"Why not?"

"Because the Russians don't assassinate their own leaders, either. And because Shanklin is responsible for the best source we ever developed inside the Kremlin."

"Who is it?"

"You expect me to tell you?"

"Yes. If you hope to convince me you're telling the truth."

"No."

Warfield pointed the Beretta toward Friedrich's leg. "Shanklin's trying to kill me. If you want to save your kneecap, you'll tell me what I need to know. Who's the source?"

"Be reasonable, Charlie!" Friedrich said. "I can't tell you state secrets!"

"You have the perfect excuse. You're being physically coerced. I'll give you three seconds to save that kneecap. One . . ."

"Please!"

"Two . . ."

"Only three people in the government know!"

"Make it four. Who is he?"

"It's a woman."

"How interesting. What's her name?"

Friedrich trembled and shook his head.

"Don't force me to shoot, you silly bastard! What's her name?"

"Katya. Mrs. Kamenev."

Warfield jerked up straight. "She's a spy? For us?"

"Was. Yes. She's defected now."

Warfield slumped back against the rear seat. "How long?"

"Three years."

"And Shanklin was her CO?"

"Yes."

"And he found her? Developed her?"

"Yes."

"He's not capable of anything that sophisticated."

"He did it, nevertheless," Friedrich said, regaining a measure of dignity. "Now perhaps you'll put down that damned pistol and let me go home."

Warfield stared out across the nearly deserted mall. Pieces were falling into place, suddenly. The Turk, Shanklin, Semenenko. First in Egypt, now here. The rage and depression of the past week began to harden into a grim resolve. He faced the same enemies all over again. And he was going to get his chance to revenge himself, after all.

"I have a better idea," he said.

34

THE CROWD STARTED TO BUILD

around dusk.

First to appear were the members of Reverend Billy James Jaffrey's American Christian Crusade. Busloads had been pouring into the capital all day long, coming from points as distant as Detroit, Atlanta, and Portland, Maine. Middle-aged matrons, high school students, small-town businessmen, farmers, laborers, secretaries, clerks, factory workers—they stretched out along the sidewalks of Pennsylvania Avenue and expanded westward, along Constitution, around the Ellipse and the Reflecting Pool, gradually surrounding the White House and its sixteen acres of fenced-in grounds.

Along the north fence, the area closest to the White House, the necklace thickened and bunched into the beginnings of a crowd. The mood, early in the evening, was festive, almost celebratory. Many in the crowd carried home-made signs. The messages were Biblical in tone: THOU SHALT NOT COMMIT ADULTERY; GOD WILL PUNISH YOU, E.W.D; and THE WAGES OF SIN ARE DEATH.

One lone protester, clad in a makeshift monk's habit and sandals, held up an enormous placade with a bold stencil on it that said: GET THE RED WOMAN OUT OF OUR WHITE HOUSE.

As twilight grew, members of left-wing political groups began appearing, protesting deteriorating U.S.-Soviet relations. Competing for attention with the crusaders, they marched in noisy columns back and forth in front of the high iron fence by the north gate, carrying torches and chanting antiwar slogans. The messages on their handmade posters contrasted vividly with those of the fundamentalists: WHO KILLED KAMENEV?; END THE FASCIST STATE; FBI + CIA = MURDER; and COME ON OUT, MR. PRESIDENT! WHAT ARE YOU AFRAID OF?

The icy rain from earlier in the day had vanished, pushed out by a warm front moving into the Potomac basin. The sudden balmy winds seemed to have a stimulating effect on the protestors. The flames of their torches flickered in the dark, and the chanters shouted to be heard above the gusty breezes. The event took on more electricity, more tension—the wind and the dark, the chanting and the torches, transforming it into something tribalistic.

By eight o'clock Captain Eugene Black, of the Metropolitan Police, Traffic Safety Division, received a call from the White House Guard, the uniformed branch of the Secret Service that mans the mansion's gates. The guard wanted Black to send extra men to control the crowd around the north gate. Black, sensitive to the tense situation concerning the president's safety and conscious of the criticism that had descended on the Maryland State Police following the Suitland Parkway ambush, was determined not to be complacent. He called the chief of police, Joseph Franklin, catching him home at dinner, and asked for permission to dispatch the additional men the White House had requested. The Chief, aware of the same factors as Black, gave his consent.

At eight o'clock the crowd around the White House probably numbered fewer than five thousand. The demonstrators were peaceful, but noisy. A fever was in the air. The arrival of van loads of riot police, augmenting the already conspicuous FBI SWAT teams standing guard on the White House roof, raised the temperature of the event. The White House press corps, monitoring the activities from the press rooms in the west wing, called in live reports of the buildup to their stations and newspapers.

The rival protest groups reacted to the growing attention by stepping up the pitch of their demonstrations. As their numbers intermingled on the sidewalks, several minor scuffles broke out. When word of the growing protest reached the airwaves, more onlookers gravitated to the scene. Traffic started to back up around the nearby streets, and Black was forced to call in more police to control it.

At nine o'clock, Captain Black estimated, from his temporary command post alongside the Hay-Adams Hotel on the north side of Lafayette Park, that nearly ten thousand people were massed around the White House fence, most heavily along the north side—the side that faced the windows of the Queen's Bedroom. Thanks to a widely circulated Associated Press report, it was known to be the bedroom occupied by the Russian woman.

The protestors, playing to the cameras, were becoming louder and more aggressive. Captain Black held another telephone consultation with the White House Guard and agreed to call up an additional fifty policemen. He considered requesting a standby alert call to the National Guard, just in case things got out of hand. No, he thought, that would be too alarmist. The Metropolitan Police could handle it.

Semenenko had developed a tic in his left eye. A sign of fatigue, he supposed. And nerves.

Something was worrying him. Had Warfield been able to identify Shanklin in the warehouse? Shanklin had sworn that he had not, but Semenenko was not reassured. He must act on the possibility that Warfield had uncovered Shanklin's role.

Semenenko had risen as far as he had for many reasons, chief among them his ability to see a plan through to its conclusion without flinching in the face of difficulties. One saw the obstacles, he liked to tell his younger colleagues, only when one took one's eye from the goal.

His eye was still on the goal. He must not give Warfield the chance to find Shanklin. Warfield was driven by a compulsion that would make him careless of his own safety. Thus he was extremely dangerous.

He glanced up at the nineteenth-century clock that stood on the mantel of the embassy's second-floor reception room. Past eight o'clock. The bomb must go off tonight. A further delay of even twenty-four hours was not acceptable.

That meant risk. He had been thinking about that problem all day, and had as yet to arrive at a satisfactory solution. Now time was forcing him to act, risk or not.

He sighed deeply, and blinked his eyes to stop the twitch. The best solutions were almost always the simplest. He laughed gently to himself. It *was* risky, what he had decided to do, but only a little.

He picked up the telephone from the table behind the sofa and dialed the White House switchboard, 456-1414.

Five minutes later Katya came on the line. Semenenko spoke to her in Russian. "It's your friend, Yuri, the emigré poet," he said. "You remember we met at that party in Georgetown?"

Her voice sounded frightened. "Oh yes. What do you want?"

"You were supposed to see our mutual friend last night. What went wrong?"

"I'm sorry. Last night I couldn't."

"Tonight, then."

"I'll try."

"Please, Mrs. Kamenev. My friend is leaving tomorrow. You must see him tonight. This is very important to him!"

"Very well."

"Will I hear about the meeting, then? Tonight?"

"Yes."

"Good! That's wonderful! We emigrés really must try to stick together. Help each other. Don't you agree?"

"Yes."

"Good-bye, then. I'll be listening for you."

She hung up without another word. Semenenko replaced the receiver. She'll do it, he decided.

He felt a tinge of sadness. She's ready to betray me, he thought, so he really should feel no regret for what he was doing. But he did. She had been a big part of his life, after all. So much of his genius was invested in her.

He thought of the day in the camp at Dzhezkazgan, where he had first seen her. She was such a beautiful child. He had seen that even through her rags. It was too bad that such beautiful children had to grow up.

But now there would be her daughter to look after. Equally beautiful. Perhaps equally gifted. He would bring the girl up the same way he had trained her mother. He would see to it that she enjoyed the same privileges, developed the same career. That would be his gift to Katya, born Zoya Voloshin. The responsibility of a second Zoya. And a gift to himself as well.

The general stretched, straightened his suit, and walked to the elevator that would take him up to the fourth floor.

A powerful thrill gripped him. Some time in the next few hours, he would change the course of history.

35

WARFIELD RANG THE BELL
and waited. The street, in the newly fashionable neighborhood of
northeast Washington, was empty. He could hear the streetlamps
buzzing. An occasional gust of wind rattled a loose garbage can
cover somewhere.

He pressed the doorbell again. The music of chimes echoed
faintly inside the elegant brick townhouse. He glanced up and
spied the silhouette of a TV camera, hiding like a watchful cat in
the shadows of an overhanging stone lintel.

A small voice spoke from the intercom: "Who is it, please?"

"Charles Warfield."

"Do you have an appointment?"

"I called an hour ago."

"Just a minute."

At least five minutes went by. Warfield pulled his collar up
around his ears. It was warming noticeably, but the wind cut
through his clothes. He felt the Beretta in his jacket pocket.

Finally the door opened. A smiling Oriental girl with long glossy
black hair that cascaded over a brocaded gown ushered him inside.

"Please wait in here," she said, pointing toward a sitting room
to the left of the hallway. "Mrs. Russell will be down shortly."

The sitting room, with its indirect lighting, gilt-framed mirrors,
suede sofas, and deep-pile carpeting, reminded Warfield of the
lobby of an overpriced resort hotel.

Mrs. Russell materialized in the doorway, clad in a dramatic
tight-fitting floor-length white evening dress. A handsome, fleshy
woman in her early fifties with an out-of-season tan, meticulously
coiffed blond hair, and too much jewelry, she carried herself with
the air of a grande dame.

"Mr. Warfield?"

"Yes."

"You've never been here before." It was a statement of fact, not
a question.

Warfield answered it anyway: "No."

"Your friend suggested us?"

"That's right." He felt suddenly embarrassed.

252 . . .

"There's nothing to be afraid of," she said, her tone suggesting otherwise.

"No. Of course not."

"We pride ourselves in being able to accommodate even the most . . . demanding clients."

"I'm pleased to hear it."

A glint of suspicion flickered in the woman's shrewd eyes. "I'll have to ask for some identification. And also a credit card."

The Oriental girl reappeared in the doorway. Warfield fumbled in his pocket and produced a driver's license and an American Express card. Mrs. Russell examined them and handed them to the Oriental girl.

"We've arranged everything for you upstairs. Melody, here, will take you. I hope your visit is a memorable one." She underlined the word memorable with a flutter of her eyelashes and walked away, leaving Warfield feeling more foolish than ever.

Melody took his hand and led him back to the entranceway, with its winding grand staircase that spiraled up to the fifth floor, some sixty feet above them. In elegance and grandeur, it rivaled the staircase of a great estate house.

As they climbed, Warfield asked Melody what the cost of the session would be.

"Three hundred dollars," she replied, matter-of-factly.

From the fourth floor landing Warfield gazed down. It was a long drop to the sea of royal blue carpet below.

"For three bills you should have an elevator," he said.

"Yes," Melody said, and led the way down a corridor toward the back.

They passed several closed doors. From somewhere, a girl giggled. Warfield noticed that the doors contained fish-eye–lens peepholes, mounted backward, so that the room on the other side could be viewed from the hallway.

"We must be able to see that no one is abusing the girls," Melody explained, in her feathery voice. "There can be no locks on the doors, either." She stopped at the door to a room at the end of the corridor. "Please go in," she said. "And enjoy your stay." With that, she smiled shyly and melted away down the hall, leaving Warfield alone by the door.

He put an eye to the peephole. A small room with a large bed.

A very pretty and very young girl with perfectly shaped white legs occupied the center of the room. She was wearing a scanty cheer-leader's outfit and was rehearsing a series of acrobatic moves that looked vaguely like a can-can dance.

Warfield smiled wistfully and turned down the hall to stop at the next peephole. The scene inside was less innocent. A small man with a bald head and rimless glasses was bent over a bench, his wrists and ankles tied to its legs. A tall woman with spiked heels, leather eye mask, black stockings, and tightly laced leather corset was beating him viciously on his bare backside with a sizable whip.

As rapidly as possible, he stepped from door to door down both sides of the corridor, absorbing as he did a kaleidoscope of porno-graphic tableaux in the rooms beyond—living displays torn from the pages of Kraft-Ebbing and the Marquis de Sade; combinations of hands, bodies, breasts, buttocks, tongues, and genitals engaged in a bizarre variety of activities.

Exhausting the peepholes on that floor, Warfield dashed up the stairs to the top floor, and started on the peepholes there. He knew he must hurry before someone noticed him.

He arrived at the last door on the right side of the corridor and slid back the peephole cover. He saw a tall, plump, redheaded woman with very large breasts standing, legs spread apart. In front of her a naked man crouched on all fours, licking the flesh of her thighs in long, slow strokes. The man's neck was enclosed in a studded leather collar with a chain leash attached to it. The red-head held the leash in one hand, while with the other she switched a riding crop alternately against the man's shoulders and buttocks.

Warfield slid the Beretta out of his jacket pocket and pushed open the door. The woman shrieked and dropped the leash and riding crop.

"Go over to the bed," he directed, waving toward it with the pistol. "Sit down and don't move or speak unless I tell you to."

The girl complied. She was nude save for a pair of flimsy black panties with a red-lace trimmed slot cut out around the crotch. She held a hand over the opening in a futile display of modesty. The room was suffused with a sickly sweet smell Warfield couldn't immediately identify. On a table near the bed he saw a silver platter with lines of white powder laid out, like ripples of beach sand, across its surface. A pair of short straws nearby revealed the identity of the substance: cocaine.

The man was still on his hands and knees, staring at Warfield with a stupid, open-mouthed expression. His blotchy skin dripped with sweat, and his massive frame quivered as if from a chill. In addition to the collar around his neck, he was strapped into a peculiar leather harness that fit over his shoulders, back, and chest like suspenders, its sides joined at a steel ring that encompassed his scrotum and penis, which hung, like a donkey's, halfway to the floor. An additional strap circled his waist. The strange rig reminded Warfield of the harnesses strapped onto dogs to take them for a walk.

The man managed a wheezy laugh. "Your idea of a joke, ol' buddy?"

"Sorry to break up your training session, but we need to have a talk."

"Sure, Charlie, sure! Get yourself one of these whores! We'll have a goddamn party!" Shanklin's eyes, dilated from the cocaine, strayed from Warfield's face to the pistol in his hand. "I hope your cock's bigger than that shooter!"

"I've figured it out," Warfield said. "Most of it."

Shanklin sat back on his haunches and draped his arms over his knees. "What did you figure out?"

Warfield stepped over to Shanklin's clothes, folded on a chair. He picked up the suit jacket and found a shoulder holster underneath it. He extracted the pistol and held it up. It was a Mauser Parabellum, an eight-round Swiss pattern nine-millimeter Luger, made in limited production.

"Got that from Interarms," Shanklin said. "Not bad, eh? They run near seven hundred bucks now."

Warfield smelled the muzzle end, then ejected the clip and looked inside. He counted only four rounds. Half empty. Shanklin watched him, tensed like a cornered cat, the muscles bunching across his chest and upper arms. A large flesh-colored bandage covered the top of his left shoulder. Warfield guessed it hid the bullet wound from his Beretta. He glanced down at Shanklin's shoes, parked under the chair; about the size and shape of the dress shoe prints on the warehouse floor.

"How'd you know I was here?" Shanklin asked him.

"You mentioned the place to me on the plane, remember? You always went to a whorehouse after a tough assignment. This morning in the warehouse qualified."

"You gonna let me in on what this is all about?"

"The Turk's dead," Warfield said. He held up the Mauser by its barrel and dropped it on Shanklin's clothes. "You hit him in the chest."

Shanklin laughed. "The Turk? Who the hell are you talking about?"

"You know who the Turk is, you son-of-a-bitch! You've known him since Alexandria!"

Shanklin blinked in surprise. He started to rise. Warfield waved the Beretta at him and he sank back to the floor.

"He threw Tanya's body into that Citroën. I know it was him because I checked his footprints in the Al Montaza's garden. His right was two inches shorter than his left."

Shanklin grinned; the muscles tightened around his eyes.

"I just found out about *Saraband* from Friedrich. It didn't make any sense, at first, that you could have developed a source like that. It was too big. The truth, of course, is that Semenenko *gave* you *Saraband*. He knew that your having a connection like the wife of the Russian premier would make you an instant hero at Langley. Get you promoted to where you could do even more damage. At the same time, he could use *Saraband* to feed the CIA disinformation. Another of his elegant tricks. The man's a genius. How did he turn you, Shanklin? What did he offer you that you couldn't refuse?"

Shanklin's mood shifted perceptibly. "Paranoia, Charlie," he whispered. "Occupational hazard. That's what you catch, out there in the cold, if you survive long enough. Paranoia. You got it bad."

Warfield's mouth felt dry. He licked his lips. "You murdered twenty of my agents," he said.

Shanklin waved a limp hand in front of him. "Now hold on a minute, ol' buddy. . . ."

"You're the only one who could have gotten their names. After they killed Tanya, I asked your help, remember? You said you'd send two of your runners to warn them. I gave you their addresses."

"There's another explanation, Charlie."

"No. Saad Zaglul was your kind of atrocity. Only you would have arranged it."

Shanklin stared at him, expressionless.

"And you knew Tanya was going to defect with me. You sold that information to the Egyptians."

Shanklin's eyebrows went up in surprise. "The Egyptians?"

"According to Semenenko."

"You believe him?"

"Put it this way. If the Egyptians didn't kill her, you did. You and Semenenko."

Shanklin gazed around the room, as if the conversation bored him. "What are you gonna do about it, ol' buddy? Kill me?"

Warfield pointed the Beretta at his groin. "Tell me what happened!"

Shanklin stared at the pistol, his drugged eyes focusing with difficulty.

"Who killed her?"

Shanklin grinned maliciously. "She's not even dead! What do you think of that?"

Warfield's stomach tightened. "Who killed her?" he repeated.

Shanklin's eyes shifted past Warfield to his Mauser, lying on the chair. "The bitch double-crossed you!"

"No!"

"Yes, she did, ol' buddy. She surely did! That shooting was staged. She was on the plane to Moscow that night. Semenenko wanted her to bow out without raising your suspicions about her. She'd fed you a lot of intelligence garbage, after all. And Semenenko wanted it to stay swallowed."

"Impossible!"

"And *she* blew your network, not me! She put the KGB onto you. They tailed you to your agents weeks before the Al Montaza stunt."

"You're a fucking liar!"

Shanklin laughed.

Warfield felt the warm metal of the trigger against his finger. He ached to pull it. "Liar!" he repeated.

"Afraid it's the truth, ol' buddy. Those pieces in that bag. That wasn't Tanya. It was one of my whores! A real pain-in-the-ass broad from Albania." Shanklin burst out laughing. "Albania! Imagine that! Whoever heard of an Albanian whore, right? She was a mean bitch and she had it coming to her. Funny, without her head, she looked a lot like Tanya. She was knocked up, too! How's that for convenience, huh?"

Warfield stared at Shanklin's crouching nude body, momentarily shaken. Could it be the truth? Warfield had never examined the contents of the bag closely. How could he have brought himself to do it? No, no, the man was lying, trying to derail him. He forced Shanklin's words from his mind and concentrated on his plan.

"You're in shit over your head, Charlie," Shanklin warned. "Just like Egypt."

"Am I? What about you? You're exposed. In no-man's land. After what happened in the warehouse, Semenenko will have to get rid of you. And if he doesn't, the CIA will."

Shanklin nodded lazily.

"Your only hope is a triple cross. You can buy your way out with Friedrich. You have something to sell him that's worth the price of your skin."

Shanklin grinned. "And you save your skin by bringing me in. Is that it, ol' buddy?"

"Yes. I'll make the deal with you right now. Right here. Friedrich's waiting to hear from me."

Shanklin appeared to consider it. "What do I have to do?" he asked.

"Tell us what Semenenko is up to. That's crucial. We need that immediately. After that, we want the story of the Suitland Parkway ambush. Everything—all the names, dates, and places. The whole story on the hit team, on Semenenko, the ambush, the kidnapping attempt, the Korean bomb-builder, the hairbrush. . . ."

Warfield stopped. "Jesus Christ," he whispered. "The hairbrush!" The realization was like a kick in the head. "That's how you're going to do it. With the hairbrush! In the White House!"

He felt stunned and distracted. He stood motionless, trying to decide what to do next. The president had to be warned!

Sensing his hesitation, the whore in the ventilated underwear jumped up and ran from the room, banging the door open against the wall as she fled.

It gave Shanklin the split second he needed.

His right hand flew forward and a woman's high-heeled shoe shot out of nowhere and caught Warfield on the bridge of the nose. He fired the Beretta reflexively, but Shanklin was no longer in front of it. He had jumped to his right and grabbed a chair. Warfield fired again, just as Shanklin released the chair. The end of one leg smashed into Warfield's throat, knocking him off balance.

From the floor, Warfield raised the pistol again, trying to find Shanklin in the dim light. Shanklin kicked Warfield's hand with his bare foot and knocked the pistol free. Warfield swept the air with his other arm, searching for a hold. Instead he absorbed a brutal blow to the side of the head. He rolled over, instinct screaming at him to keep moving. The edge of the bed appeared over him and he rolled under it. Shanklin grabbed his ankle and dragged him back into the room.

Shanklin stomped on him with the heel of his foot, delivering punishing blows to his head and stomach. The man's strength was terrifying. Warfield kicked blindly with the toe of his shoe and caught Shanklin a blow in the groin. The big man lurched back, bellowing, clutching his testicles with both hands. Warfield staggered to his feet, swaying. He managed two steps, then slumped to his knees. He saw Shanklin's pistol on the chair, reached for it, then remembered he had removed its clip.

Toe down like a soccer kicker, Shanklin's foot met him under the stomach with a kick that lifted him from the floor. He felt the wind rush out of him. He contracted himself into a ball, guts spasming, lungs sucking for oxygen. The naked man loomed over him. He felt the kicks thudding into his ribs with bone-breaking power. Shanklin could kill him, of course, with his hands or his feet. Defenseless, he waited for the blow that would break his neck or snap his spine.

Instead, Shanklin was lifting him up. He felt a pressure around his throat and waist, and then a fleeting, whoozy sensation as the floor moved away and the ceiling came closer. He lay slung across Shanklin's shoulder and saw the room behind him, upside down. They passed through the doorway into the hall.

He tried to cry out, but had no air in his lungs. He let his head fall against the small of Shanklin's back. Upside down, he saw the balustrade railing around the stairwell rotate toward him. He screamed—or thought he screamed—as Shanklin heaved his limp form off his shoulder and pitched it over the top of the railing.

"I owe you this one, ol' buddy!"

Warfield flung his arms out, the ancient part of his brain crying to his hands to grasp something, catch something, anywhere.

His fingers found the end of the leash, dangling from Shanklin's collar. He squeezed to hold on to it with all his ebbing strength as the walls, railing, and staircase swirled around him and the ceiling fell away.

He clung to the leash with both hands as his trajectory swung him in an arc out over the stairwell and down. The leash pulled taut, and his arms, absorbing the weight of his body, stretched from their sockets. Suspended from the leash, his 180 pounds snapped Shanklin's neck downward and against the top rail of the balustrade. The railing bent and snapped.

Unable to keep his grip, Warfield slipped from the end of the swinging leash and plummeted out and down at an angle that pitched him across the fourth-floor railing and onto the landing. He hit the carpeting and bounced to the wall, ten feet from the stairwell.

His collar wedged between two balusters, Shanklin's nude body plunged out over the well, ripping the balustrade out along the length of the landing until it flopped over the open stairwell, like a section of torn-up railroad track.

For a long moment Shanklin hung suspended at the end of the section of balustrade, poised in the void over four stories of space. He uttered a hoarse cry, and flapped his arms, a fly caught in a spider's web. The section of railing, bending further under his weight, finally cracked, then popped apart with the noise of a rifle volley.

Shanklin plummeted to the main floor, carrying a part of the balustrade down with him.

Warfield, dizzy from the pain of the beating and the fall, worked his way slowly down the remaining flights of stairs. His nose was bleeding and his ears rang. His entire body felt bruised and weak. But there was no time to rest.

In the entrance hall at the bottom of the stairway, a crowd of whores and customers stood in a semicircle, their faces white with shock.

Shanklin had landed on his back, impaled on a broken length of baluster. It had penetrated up through his lower stomach, and its broken end, slippery dark with blood, jutted obscenely into the air, a mock effigy of an erection.

36

edge of the canopied bed in the Queen's Bedroom and listened to the crowd outside, a terrible anxiety in her heart.

Semenenko's telephone call had unnerved her completely. The incredible boldness of it! Even in the White House she was not beyond his reach! She should have told him the truth, that she had left the hairbrush on the dressing table in the suite's sitting room. She had feared it would draw the president's attention if left out on the nightstand by the bed. And in any case, Semenenko would have heard nothing but the intimacies of their lovemaking.

She still sought a way to evade the general's orders, without inviting his retaliation. It was nearly ten-thirty. In an hour and a half she would see the president in his bedroom. She decided the best strategy was to take the hairbrush with her and place it on the large chest of drawers that sat against the south wall. It was some distance from the bed, and perhaps would not pick up their voices very well. That would suit her. Semenenko would no doubt chastise her, but she could claim to be trying.

Katya pulled aside the window drapes to look out. It was a mistake. Her action provoked a roar from the crowd along the north fence. The sound echoed against the building like a perverse kind of cheer—cannibalistic, malicious. An ugly howl that made her shiver in fright. She dropped the curtain and glanced about the bedroom, feeling menace now in even the innocent luxury of the warm rose-pastel walls, the soft Turkish rug, the striped taffeta of the drapes. She didn't belong here.

But where did she belong? Was there anywhere on earth? Or was there only the wistful fantasy of a town on a postcard—a place, like Heaven, that one would not reach in this life?

She caught her reflection in the mirror over the fireplace. Even her face no longer seemed hers. Who was she? Had she ever lived? Ever been herself?

The noise of the crowd unsettled her, provoking irrational fears and imaginings. She must compose herself, she realized. There was really nothing to fear.

She lay down on the bed and tried to shut out the sound of the crowd beyond the windows by simple force of will, a trick she had once learned in the noisy barracks of the labor camps, years ago.

It no longer seemed to work. She turned on her side and folded a pillow over her ears.

The noise still seeped through in a troubled murmur, like the rumble of an approaching storm.

In the president's upstairs study William Wilbert snapped the telephone to his ear before the hammer mechanism inside had time to strike the bell more than once. He listened for several minutes, his eyes resting on the photograph of Estelle Daniels in her wedding dress that sat propped near him on the small table.

Wilbert and the president had retreated from the west wing to this small, comfortable den between the Yellow Oval Room and the president's bedroom as the night had lengthened and the atmosphere around the Oval Office grew more grim.

"I'll get back to you," Wilbert said, hanging up.

Daniels, lounging in a chair in the corner, his slippered feet propped up on a footstool and his hand around a tumbler of Glenfiddich, looked up. The president's face was pallid, his normally piercing green eyes glazed with fatigue. "Trouble?"

Wilbert shrugged. "It's security again. The guards are having a problem keeping the north gate clear. The problem is the press. They've been parading in and out of the west wing like there was an all-night orgy in progress. Every time they let a reporter through, some demonstrators try to sneak past the gate. And the crowd is still growing, apparently. It cheers every time they let someone through, and boos every time they stop someone. The guards are nervous. They're afraid it might get ugly."

Daniels snorted in disgust. "What are we supposed to do? Hold their hands?"

Wilbert was surprised by the sarcasm. Daniels' nerves were more frayed than he realized.

"They want to lock the gate for the night," he said. "Tell the reporters they'll either have to stay in or out until morning."

Daniels scratched his chin. "That sounds like overreacting to me. We've had demonstrations around here for decades. Martin Luther King packed two hundred thousand in Potomac Park once. Some of the Vietnam rallies were enormous. Let's sit tight. They'll get tired and go home."

"We're inviting an incident, Eliot. The crowd and the press feed on each other. One incites the other. Let them lock the gates. The press can bitch all it wants, but if we cut off the traffic in and out of the gate, we'll remove a source of excitement for the crowd. They'll get bored and go home earlier."

Daniels sighed. "Okay. Go ahead. But the press will scream bloody murder. Jerry Stein will be on the phone in minutes."

Wilbert called the chief of security and gave him permission to lock the gates.

Daniels tipped the glass to his mouth and took a long drink. Wilbert studied his boss with concern. The president had deteriorated noticeably in the past several days. In normal times he was an extremely efficient executive, but lately he'd been working far into the evenings, and accomplishing little. Even now, as Wilbert watched the president open up his special copy of the overnight news digest, he could tell that he wasn't really reading it. His mind was elsewhere. On the Russian woman, Wilbert suspected.

Since the kidnapping, Daniels had forbidden Wilbert to bring up her name. It was time, Wilbert decided, to defy that injunction. "The thing about what's going on out there, Eliot, the thing that sets it apart from other demonstrations, is that it's so damned personal."

Daniels glanced up from the page. "What's that mean?"

"They're not out there demonstrating over some issue—war, unemployment, inflation—they're demonstrating against you personally."

Daniels threw down the news digest. "I realize that. And we can blame it on one man—Jaffrey! The sanctimonious Bible-thumper thinks he's found another target to enhance his bogus image as a moral crusader. So we'll just let him indulge himself. It'll backfire on him eventually."

"Maybe," Wilbert said. "But it isn't only Jaffrey motivating that crowd. Some of them showed up because of your press conference."

"Why?"

"Because you stonewalled the reporters this afternoon. You were vague about the progress of the Suitland Parkway investigation; you were misleading about . . . Mrs. Kamenev."

"You want me to admit publicly that I'm sleeping with her?"

"Of course not. But you could have announced what you promised to Jaffrey—that you'll move her out of the White House."

Wilbert expected the president to explode, but he didn't. His face tensed in anger, then softened into a kind of sadness. He rested his glass on the table beside him and threw out his hands in a plea for understanding.

"I have to tell her first," he said. "And I will. Tonight. But I still intend to go on seeing her. She'll stay at Blair House, where we can protect her. When things cool down, we'll work out something else. I don't know what. And I don't pretend that the solution will be easy. But she's my responsibility. And so is Estelle, of course. You understand the situation. Estelle is the past. Katya is the future. I'm in love with her, Willy."

Wilbert was touched by Daniels' confession. "Okay," he said, his voice tired. "But the crowd doesn't know that. You've stirred strong emotions. And crowds and strong emotions are a bad mixture."

Daniels managed a weak smile. "What can they do to me? Storm the White House and drag us out? Tar and feather us?"

Wilbert grinned. "I give up. I'm a worrier, I admit it. Just doing my job, that's all."

Daniels laughed. "I'm beginning to think I'm getting more than my money's worth."

"It's tough, being the political conscience of such a stubborn bastard."

" 'Forceful' is the word," Daniels said. "We'll ride this out, you'll see." He looked at the clock on his desk. "They're broadcasting a rerun of the press conference tonight at midnight. Let's watch it. I'll bet I don't come across half as bad as you think I did."

Wilbert was about to reply that he had to go home sometime, but remembered that he was locked in. That meant another night on the top floor. He'd better call his wife. As he touched the phone, it rang.

He picked it up. "Wilbert," he said. He listened for half a minute. "Put him on."

He pressed his palm over the mouthpiece and looked across at Daniels, his features creased in amazement.

"It's Charles Warfield," he said.

General Semenenko folded the jacket flap over the page he was reading and snapped the book shut. It was past eleven o'clock. The strain was beginning to hurt.

He slipped on the earphones again and listened. The same peculiar rumble and buzz greeted his ears. He turned to Stepanovich. "Have you figured it out yet, Colonel?"

"Yes, Comrade General, I think I have. It's the demonstration going on outside the White House. The brush is probably near a window on the north wall, so it's picking up some of the crowd noise."

Semenenko listened again. "You're sure nothing's wrong with the bug itself?"

"I'll stake my reputation on it, Comrade General."

"You just did," Semenenko answered, a saturnine grin on his lips. "Do you think it could obscure conversation?"

Stepanovich shrugged. "Not completely. No."

"Will we recognize the president's voice against the background?"

The antenna man swallowed nervously before answering. "Yes," he replied. "I'm sure we will."

Semenenko opened his copy of Colby's memoirs again. "Well," he said. "That's all that really matters, isn't it?"

He looked at the page but didn't see the words. It was maddening that the entire painstakingly planned project now depended on the reliability of this one woman. A woman operating under coercion, at that. She did not appreciate the urgency of getting that hairbrush next to the president. She thought she could afford to procrastinate.

Perhaps his orchestration was faulty, he thought. Perhaps he should have told her what the hairbrush really was, let her plant it near Daniels and get clear. No, that would never have worked. She would have refused to do it. He had been over the possibilities a dozen times. Only by deceiving her could he have enlisted her cooperation. And it was better that she die along with Daniels. Her usefulness was over.

Now if she would only collaborate in her martyrdom!

President Daniels placed his hand over the mouthpiece of his extension phone and listened to Wilbert's conversation.

"What can I do for you, Mr. Warfield?" Wilbert asked.

"I want to see the president."

Wilbert reacted physically to the request, jerking his head back sharply. "What for?"

"I have important information for him."

"You can tell me."

"No."

"I might be able to get him on the phone, Mr. Warfield, but it's late. And this isn't a secure line, I'm afraid."

"I know all that. I want to see him in person. Tonight."

Wilbert cupped the mouthpiece and looked over at Daniels. Daniels shook his head.

"That's just not possible," he told Warfield. "Can you give me some idea of what you want?"

There was a lengthy pause at the other end. Wilbert heard a horn beep. The man was calling from an outside pay phone.

"He's in danger," Warfield said. "I understand the plot against him. I want to tell him what's going on."

Wilbert bit his lip. "You could be arrested, you know. If you came here."

"I'll risk it. I want help and protection in exchange for the information."

"You want a lot."

"My information is worth a lot."

"There's a big demonstration going on outside. The White House gates are locked for the night. Why don't you see me tomorrow?"

"Tomorrow's too late."

Wilbert cupped the phone again and looked at Daniels. "What do you think?"

Daniels stood up, agitated. "He must know something pretty important. Can we afford *not* to see him?"

"I'm not sure that I'd trust him in the same room with you."

Daniels shrugged. "What's the Secret Service for? And last week you told me he was an honest man. I'll trust him if you do."

Wilbert agonized. "The Secret Service will veto it," he said.

"Then don't ask them."

Wilbert relented. "How can we get him in?"

Daniels sipped his scotch. "Use the emergency exit," he said.

Wilbert's eyes lit up. "Yes. Perfect." He uncovered the mouthpiece. "Where are you, Mr. Warfield?"

"Ten minutes away."

"You know the Treasury Building? At Fifteenth and G?"

"Yes."

"I'll meet you on the north steps in fifteen minutes."

Estelle Daniels awoke suddenly.

Her sleep, at best, was a brittle thing, a thin membrane that cloaked her senses precariously, and she awakened often during the night, propelled from unconsciousness by turbulent nightmares.

She pushed herself up on an elbow and listened. A dim murmur, sometimes fading, sometimes intensifying, caught her ears. She sat, barely moving, lest the murmuring disappear. Voices were speaking to her, trying to tell her things—important things, bad things. She had heard such voices before, but tonight they seemed more distinct, more urgent.

Contradictory emotions shook her. Dread. Anticipation. Terror. Elation. So many messages, so many voices telling her so many things.

She slipped from the bed and tiptoed to the window. Cautiously she separated the drapes and looked out. It was the same view she always saw: the top of the parapet that enclosed the penthouse roof, and the red glow of the night sky beyond. Tiny winking lights of an airplane climbed through the dark from National Airport.

She pressed her ears to the glass. The voices seemed a little louder. Suddenly the black shape of a figure—a big man carrying a rifle—walked between her window and the parapet. She gasped and let go of the drape as if burned by it. These men. Spying on her. She had seen them all this week. Big men with helmets and guns. They scared her.

Barefoot, Estelle scurried into the nurse's room next door. A small nightlight illuminated the contours of the bed and the bulge of the nurse, asleep beneath the blankets. She slept soundly, Estelle knew. Many times at night she had come into this room and watched the woman's slumber, sometimes touching her softly to test its depth.

Should she wake her now, tell her about the voices? No. The nurse might try to stop them. No. She would do something else. Because there was terrible danger in the air. She could smell it, feel it. The walls, the air, were thick with it.

Estelle reached down and removed the key that dangled from a bracelet on the nurse's arm. Quietly, barely breathing, she crept to the door that separated the suite from the small back hallway and slipped the key into the keyhole. It fit, as she knew it would. She had watched the nurse use it many times.

In the corridor, Estelle locked the door behind her, and, clutching the key in her hand, hurried down the back hall, past the playroom, to the far end, where a stairwell on the left led down to the second floor. She glanced around like an exploring cat, then descended the stairs.

At the second floor Estelle paused at the threshold of the east sitting hall, and listened. The rumble of voices seemed louder here. The white inner drapes were pulled across the huge arched window. She didn't dare approach it to look out, because behind her would be the long, wide hallways that ran the length of the floor. And open spaces meant people. Eyes. Danger.

Instead, she crept along the wall to the last door on the left and ducked into the sitting room that adjoined the Queen's Bedroom.

Lamps on a vanity table were lit. She froze, expecting to be accosted, but no one appeared. The voices were much louder here. She stepped across the room to the window, hesitated before it, then cautiously pulled open the drapes and looked out.

A ragged, trembling cheer welled up from below. She uttered a cry and let the drapes fall back. The sound wavered and gradually died. She opened the drapes again. Again the thunderous cheer. A sea of people was massed against the fence along its entire length, and spilled back across the street, deep into Lafayette Park. Voices yelled and chanted. Frightened again, she closed the drapes.

For a long time Estelle stood by the window, wondering at the meaning of it. Once more she drew the drapes aside; once more an echoing cheer went up from the crowd.

There was no doubt. They were calling after her! They wanted her! A deep thrill suffused her, an elation so intense it caused her to tremble. Some apocalypse was at hand. And somehow, it centered on her!

She stepped back from the window, still dazed by the excitement, and wandered about the room, nervously touching things, picking up things, dropping them again. She must get dressed, she decided. She must look her best!

She gravitated toward the vanity table. It was a fancy one, draped in white cloth and festooned with tasseled cord. In the center of it sat a Chinese lacquered chest with an oval mirror mounted on it. She would make herself up, she decided. She would dazzle the crowd. She would requite their vast outpouring of adoration!

She sat down and gazed at her reflection. She studied herself greedily. There were no mirrors in her room, and her face was a rare and prized sight for her. She gazed for a long time, experimenting with expressions, from simple smiles and frowns to more subtle faces—sad and happy, comic and coquettish. Entranced by this new game, she quickly forgot about the urgent voices outside, begging her to come to them.

The glass-topped surface of the dressing table was littered with an array of bottles, jars, combs, and brushes. Estelle examined each item carefully, holding it up to the light and turning it around. She wondered whose treasures these were.

Tenderly, she picked up the hairbrush that sat at the table's edge. She admired the fat contours of its wooden handle. It looked very clean and new. Not a strand lay caught in the bristles.

Estelle gazed into the mirror again, and with a deep thrill of pleasure, she ran the brush through her hair.

37

WARFIELD WAITED IN THE shadows on the north side of McPherson Square. Traffic around the White House was backed up for blocks by the demonstration, and horn-blowing competed with the chants of the crowd to create a cacophony unlike anything he had ever heard outside the streets of Cairo.

He saw a figure materialize on the steps of the Treasury Building across the square. He watched him carefully, to see if he was alone. He appeared to be. To a degree Warfield knew he would just have to trust his instincts about Wilbert. He crossed the square quickly, and met Wilbert at the bottom of the steps. Wilbert offered a curt nod in recognition.

"Let's go," he said, and started back up the Treasury Building steps.

"I thought you were taking me to meet the president," Warfield said.

Wilbert stopped and turned around. "I am," he said. He waved his hand, urging Warfield to follow.

The president's chief of staff led the way through a door at the top of the steps, then along an echoing, dimly lit, and deserted stone corridor to an elevator bank at the rear of the building.

"If it's a question of trust," Wilbert said, as they stepped into the elevator, "consider that I'm about to reveal a little state secret to you."

Mystified, Warfield watched as a series of small buttons on the elevator control panel lit up in a rapid downward sequence: G, B, B1, B2. The elevator car hushed to a stop and they stepped out into a low-ceilinged corridor lit by overhead florescents. Warfield followed Wilbert along a rabbit warren of narrow passages that took them past storerooms, boiler rooms, equipment rooms, and finally, to their destination—a small closet at the dead end of a dingy corridor.

Wilbert produced a key, opened the closet and stepped inside; Warfield joined him. The room, painted an institutional gray over cement block, was barely ten feet square. It was empty and featureless, save for a single light recessed in the ceiling and a massive steel door built into the back wall.

"You realize," Wilbert said, "that we have to frisk you."

Warfield nodded, expecting the Secret Service to jump from behind the steel door.

"I'm going to do it myself," Wilbert said, "The fewer people we involve in this the better."

Warfield removed the clip from Shanklin's Mauser from his inside jacket pocket and handed it to Wilbert. "Believe it or not, that's it. But go ahead and do·your job."

Wilbert dropped the clip into his pocket and ran his hands awkwardly over Warfield's clothing. Satisfied, Wilbert moved in front of a small console, blocking its view from Warfield, and punched in a code.

The door swung inward to reveal a long, brightly lit underground passage. The floor was tiled and tilted upward slightly as it receded into the distance.

Warfield understood immediately.

"It goes right into the White House subbasement," Wilbert explained. "It really isn't good for much. As far as I know this is the first time it's ever been used."

Police Chief Joseph Franklin's limousine, its detachable pod light flashing from the driver's side of the roof, pulled up next to the Hay-Adams at Sixteenth Street, on the north side of Lafayette Park. Captain Eugene Black, hunched over a two-way radio, saw the chief's car and immediately rushed over.

The chief, a dapper, precise man in his early fifties with a thin mustache and a formidable temper, appeared irritated, as if somehow this whole mess was Black's personal doing. "What's the picture, Gene?" he asked, tapping the edge of the limousine door impatiently with his fingernails.

"We've closed off the major approaches," Black answered. "Pennsylvania, New York, Vermont, Connecticut, and Fifteenth and Seventeenth between Constitution and H. We're leaving Sixteenth open for emergency vehicles. It's causing a hell of a traffic backup, but it's stopped the crowd buildup on this side."

Franklin narrowed his eyes. "What do you mean, this side?"

Black ran a nervous hand through his hair. "They've started showing up along the south side of the fence, and backing up onto the Ellipse. In fact, except for the west front of the EOB, it's wall-to-wall crowd all the way around the fence."

The chief frowned, looking at the crowd surging back and forth through Lafayette Park. "Any incidents?"

"Several people tried to sneak through the north gate when they opened it to let some journalists through. But they've closed the gates for the night now. One man tried to climb the fence. A few fistfights. Nothing ugly . . . yet."

"What's the size estimate now?"

"McCullouch says eighty thousand."

Franklin cocked his head, impressed. Everyone on the District force knew McCullouch's estimates were always conservative. "So we're talking a hundred thousand plus."

"And growing," Black added.

"They handle bigger crowds every weekend at the Rose Bowl."

"We can handle this one," Black asserted.

Franklin studied his captain's broad face. "You'd better be right, Gene," he said. "For all our sakes."

Stepanovich snapped his fingers and gestured urgently to Semenenko. The general slipped on his headset.

A peculiar crackling sound—a long, drawn-out scratching, like someone running fingernails across a coarse surface—met his ears. The sound repeated itself at regular intervals. A two-second crackle followed by a split-second pause, then another crackle.

Semenenko looked at Stepanovich questioningly. The antenna man threw up his hands. The two Russians hunched intently over the console. The rhythmic scratching continued.

Suddenly a loud female voice sent the needle on the VU meter jumping. Semenenko recoiled from the unexpected blast against his eardrums.

"Will you, won't you . . . will you, won't you . . . will you, won't you. . . ."

The accent was American, and the words a tuneless singsong, like a child reciting a nursery rhyme: "Will you, won't you . . . will you, won't you . . . join the dance?"

Stepanovich had a sudden intuition. He yanked off the earphones and faced the general. "Some damned woman is combing her hair with the brush!"

Semenenko's face went pale.

"Will you, won't you . . ." scratch, "will you, won't you . . ." scratch. . . .

Beads of sweat rose on Semenenko's forehead.

Wilbert ushered Warfield through the White House subbasement, then up the elevator to the second floor, and into the west sitting hall. President Daniels was sprawled on the sofa, waiting for the telecast of his press conference to begin.

Daniels raised his lanky form slowly from the sofa and shook Warfield's hand. Wilbert noticed an immediate tension between the two, almost a hostility. The president, he supposed, blamed Warfield for some of his recent problems. The death of the captured assassin Martinez was a terrible blow. And Warfield's disheveled appearance would offend anyone. As for Warfield, he probably saw in Daniels the cause of his current fugitive state. The man was a maverick, anyway, the type who always held authority in low esteem.

"Have a drink, Warfield?" the president offered.

"No thanks."

Wilbert winced. He should have remembered to brief Daniels on Warfield's drinking history.

Daniels sat back down on the sofa, leaving Warfield standing. The TV set was just beginning the rerun of the press conference, and Wilbert could see that Daniels would be distracted by it.

"Mr. President. This would be better done in your study. Mr. Warfield should have our undivided attention."

Daniels shot Wilbert a killing look, but he shrugged and got up clumsily from the sofa. Wilbert realized that the president was half drunk.

In the study, Wilbert seated Warfield by the fireplace and took up his own spot by the telephone again. Daniels wandered behind his desk and sat down heavily.

Wilbert nodded at Warfield. "You're on," he said. And you'd better make it good, he thought to himself as he watched the president's eyes examine with disdain the disreputable-looking figure by the fireplace.

"Sorry about my appearance," Warfield began. "But what I have to tell you couldn't wait for a change of clothes. The Suitland Parkway ambush was the work of Bulgakov's faction in the Kremlin. The original purpose was to kill both you and Kamenev. I don't pretend to understand their motives. Obviously Kamenev's death has put them in control at the Kremlin. But why they want to kill you too is not clear—at least not to me."

Wilbert's jaw dropped almost to his chest. Daniels glanced from Warfield to Wilbert and then back to Warfield again, as if not sure that he was hearing correctly.

"Go on," he said.

"I believe the actual planning and execution of the ambush was the work of six people. The three members of the hit squad itself —who are now all dead—received their instructions from Byron Shanklin, a CIA agent stationed at Camp Peary."

"Shanklin's working for the KGB?" Wilbert asked, incredulous. "He's a double agent?"

"Was. He's dead."

"Dead!"

"Yes. He died about an hour ago. In a whorehouse a few blocks from here."

"You were there?" the president asked, his voice rising in astonishment.

"Yes."

"You killed him?"

"You could say that."

"That's four you've named," Wilbert said. "And they're all dead. Who are the other two?"

"The operation is directed by Dmitri Semenenko, the man you invited in to monitor our interrogation."

"You have proof of all this, I assume," Daniels said.

"I have proof of none of it."

Daniels caught Wilbert's eye. Clearly he thought Warfield deranged.

"This Semenenko," Daniels said, measuring Warfield carefully over the rim of his scotch glass. "You think he's still trying to kill me?"

"Yes."

"And that's what you've come here to warn me about?"

"Yes. I believe his plan is to sneak an explosive device into the White House."

Daniels laughed. "That's pretty wild, don't you think?"

"Maybe. But the device is already here."

Wilbert was seized by a terrible premonition. He saw the direction Warfield's remarks were taking them. "You said there were six people involved in the plot," he interjected. "You've only named five."

Warfield's hands trembled as he clasped them together in his lap. "I have no proof. It's possible I'm wrong. But it fits the way he operates."

"Come to the point, Warfield," Daniels demanded. "Who is it?"

Warfield met the president's gaze head on. "It's the premier's widow. Katya Kamenev."

Unable to sleep, Katya opened her eyes and stared up into the big canopy suspended over the bed. In the dim light of the chandelier, it appeared like a hovering shadow. A tall antique clock on the mantel began to strike the hour. Katya counted the chimes: twelve. Midnight.

She rose from the bed, smoothing the spread absently. The chanting outside the windows sounded louder than ever. She walked into the adjoining sitting room to ready herself for the president.

She was several steps into the room before she saw a woman in a blue bathrobe sitting at the dressing table.

The woman caught her reflection in the small vanity table mirror and jerked her head around.

Katya gasped. The president's wife! The woman's eyes narrowed. Katya stood, momentarily paralyzed by indecision. The woman twisted around to confront her, crooking an arm menacingly over her shoulder. The muscles in her neck tensed, and her mouth contorted in a snarl.

Katya started to back out of the room when she noticed what the woman was clutching so fiercely in her hand.

The hairbrush!

She must get it away from her immediately! She thought to say something, to coax her to put the brush down, then she realized that Semenenko was undoubtedly listening in at that very moment. To mouth a single word would reveal that she had stupidly let the brush out of her possession.

She calculated the distance to Estelle's chair: ten feet. Between them stood a heavy pedestal table. Katya edged swiftly around the table and lunged at Estelle, reaching out with both hands to wrest the hairbrush away.

Semenenko and Stepanovich sat in rigid silence, headsets in place, trying to decipher, through the cacophony of sounds, what was happening. Stepanovich bit the end of his thumb; Semenenko sat straight up, teeth clenched, fists bunched tightly on the table in front of him. *Damn her!* he repeated to himself. *Damn her to hell!*

The silence that greeted Warfield's declaration hung in the room like a sorcerer's malediction, casting a spell of immobility. Wilbert became aware of the barely audible murmur of the crowd on the north side, and of the sharp ticking of Daniels' old-fashioned desk clock. It said four minutes past midnight.

"It's Semenenko's method," Warfield said at last. "He likes to use beautiful women to get what he wants. He did it to me in Egypt in 1972."

"You don't understand," Wilbert interrupted. "Mrs. Kamenev worked for *us.*"

"That's what Friedrich told me. But she's a double agent. She has to be. Shanklin was her control."

Daniels found his voice. "My God, man, do you realize how idiotic your accusations are?" The words exploded out of him. "Katya was in the limousine with me on the Suitland Parkway! If Semenenko is behind this, and she was working for him, why would he have tried to kill her?"

"I don't know."

"And why did he try to kidnap her?"

"I don't know."

Wilbert watched anxiously as Daniels' face flushed a deep red. "And now," he cried, "you claim she's going to blow me up!"

"Something like that. The bomb's hidden in a hairbrush."

Daniels rested his scotch glass on the table. "Warfield," he said, "it looks as if you're here to try to save your own neck, not mine."

Again Warfield met his gaze. "Let's ask Mrs. Kamenev."

Daniels didn't answer. He turned to Wilbert. "It was a mistake, bringing him here. He should be arrested. Call McCormick."

"I gave him my word," Wilbert said. "And what the hell—why not bring her in?"

Estelle screamed as the bad woman came toward her. She was terribly afraid. She wanted to run, but she was cornered. The bad woman would hurt her!

Clutching its fat handle in white-knuckled panic, she swung the hairbrush at the woman's face. But the bad woman caught her wrist and twisted it, forcing the hairbrush out of her hand. It fell to the floor.

Estelle struck the woman across the ear. The woman did not hit her back. She was bending down, trying to pick up the hairbrush.

Estelle brought her knee up, propelled by the panic surging through her, and caught the bad woman in the face before she could straighten up. The woman's head cracked against the edge of the pedestal table. She slid to the rug, rolled on her back, and closed her eyes.

Estelle grabbed the brush from the floor and ran from the room.

"Let's give him the benefit of the doubt," Wilbert argued. "If he's wrong, what harm is done? But if he's right. . . ."

The president was standing now, facing Warfield from behind his desk. "Damn it, Willy, you've hated Katya from the beginning! I think you're jealous of her!"

"You're in love with her," Wilbert said, unruffled. "She may be deceiving you. Let's bring her in here. Let Warfield confront her. If you're right, I'll be the first to apologize. And if you're wrong, you might thank us for saving your life."

"Shit!"

Warfield stepped back from the verbal crossfire. He was sure Katya was a Semenenko plant. But he was not sure that he could prove it. Finding the hairbrush would be the key, of course. He watched the president. Daniels seemed twisted in agony. Warfield felt sympathy for him; he knew what he was suffering.

Finally Daniels ran a hand through his hair. "Go get her, then, damn it!" he said.

Estelle scurried down the center hall, her heart pounding. In the double doorway that separated the center hall from the west sitting hall, she stopped and pulled her bathrobe around her.

She had heard a voice nearby. Cautiously she peered into the west hall and discovered that the voice emanated from a screen in the wall. She ducked around the corner of the wide doorway and stood inside the room, her attention transfixed by the image on the screen. The voice and the face were familiar. Yes. Of course. It was Eliot!

Clutching the brush in her hand, she moved up close to the screen. She wanted to tell him about the bad woman!

Wilbert came running back into the study, his eyes wide with shock. "Something's happened!" he shouted. "Katya's on the floor, unconscious! I've called Sam to get the doctor!"

Daniels' mouth fell open. He jumped from his chair and dashed out into the central hall behind Wilbert. After a moment's hesitation, Warfield followed.

Colonel Stepanovich snapped upright in his chair, his hands cupping his headset. "I think that's him," he whispered. "The president!"

Semenenko forced his mind to remain calm. He had heard the voice, too. Stepanovich was right. It was President Daniels. He turned up the volume and tried to make out the words: ". . . The answer to that lies, I think, in the work that the FBI, Secret Service, and the CIA is still heavily involved in pursuing. . . ."

"It's him!" the antenna man repeated. "I'm sure of it!"

"Yes. Be quiet! Listen. . . ."

"We might lose him!" Stepanovich said, agitated. "We don't know what's happening!"

"All the more reason to wait, Colonel."

But having said it, Semenenko could not, finally, bear to wait. He pointed a finger toward the detonator, inviting Stepanovich to man it. "Very well," he said. "Let's get it done."

The antenna man removed his headset and placed a shaking thumb and forefinger on the igniter key. He looked over at Semenenko. "Remove your headset, Comrade General," he warned.

Semenenko complied.

Stepanovich took a deep breath. His hand trembled violently. He removed it from the key, flexed his fingers, and placed them back on the key. But they did not turn it.

Semenenko stared, disbelieving. "Go on! Turn it!"

The antenna man closed his eyes, opened them again, and gazed blankly at his fingers, as if he no longer had control over them. He withdrew them and placed the other hand on the key. It too trembled, and refused to turn the key.

"Hurry up, for God's sakes, man! Turn it!"

Stepanovich gritted his teeth. A whimper escaped his lips. His whole upper body shook. "I can't!" he moaned. "Dear God, I can't!"

Semenenko pulled his small, Czech-made automatic from his breast pocket and pointed it at Stepanovich's head. "Turn it, you idiot! I'll count to three!"

Stepanovich buried his head in both hands and collapsed against the chair.

Semenenko slapped the pistol against his cheek and pushed him out of the way. The KGB general's other hand fell quickly onto the igniter key and twisted it, in one emphatic motion, from "armed" to "detonate."

38

THE SUDDEN CLANGING OF AN
alarm bell in the White House subbasement caused Secret Service
agent Ken Stout to drop the copy of *Playboy* he was reading,
remove his feet from the edge of the desk, and knock over half a
cup of cold coffee.

A red light was flashing on the computer console in front of him,
the first time he had ever seen that happen except during a practice simulation.

Words popped up on the green console screen: FIRE . . . WEST
HALL SECOND FLOOR

Stout jumped to his feet and was halfway out the door before he
remembered the drill. He returned to the console, shut off the
alarm bell and the red light, flicked on the emergency communication channel, and waited, his eyes scanning the screen. He wondered how many agents were available at this hour.

As he waited, a second line appeared on the screen under the
first: FIRE . . . CENTER HALL SECOND FLOOR

Frantically he dialed the agent's lounge in the first level basement. Thank God, someone answered.

"We've got a fire!" Stout shouted at him. "Family quarters—
west hall and center hall!"

Stout disconnected and called the guard station. No answer. He
dialed the chief usher's office, using the regular White House intercom system. No answer. He guessed the usher on night duty might
have already gone upstairs to check.

He hoped it was just another false alarm. A wastebasket fire
could create enough smoke to trip the sensitive detectors in the
ceilings—even in adjacent rooms.

He glanced at the console again. New information was coming
up on the screen:

FIRE . . . WEST HALL SECOND FLOOR
FIRE . . . CENTER HALL SECOND FLOOR
FIRE . . . DINING ROOM SECOND FLOOR
FIRE . . . PRESIDENT'S BEDROOM SECOND FLOOR
FIRE . . . PRESIDENT'S STUDY SECOND FLOOR

"Jesus Christ!" Stout exclaimed aloud. "How is that possible?"

He tripped the switch that would automatically feed the computer information to the district fire department headquarters

and the stations nearest the White House. Then he began dialing every station around the White House itself—the west wing, the east wing, the ground floor, first floor, second floor, third floor, the EOB—watching the screen with growing panic. The fire—or whatever it was—seemed to be marching right across the second floor:

FIRE . . . YELLOW OVAL ROOM SECOND FLOOR
FIRE . . . KITCHEN SECOND FLOOR
FIRE . . . ELEVATOR LOBBY ONE SECOND FLOOR
FIRE . . . ELEVATOR LOBBY TWO SECOND FLOOR
FIRE . . . WEST STAIR HALL SECOND FLOOR
FIRE . . . NORTH SIDE BEDROOM ONE SECOND FLOOR

Only a few saw the actual explosion.

A network cameraman, situated near Blair House on the southwest corner of Lafayette Park saw it best, through his zoom lens. For no reason that he could later recall, he had swiveled the camera up from the boisterous group by the gate at West Executive Avenue, and trained it on the large, fan-shaped window that looked out from the second floor of the White House west wall. He saw the entire window burst outward, followed by long tongues of gold drapery, which slapped against the sides of the mansion.

Thousands saw what happened next. Behind the concussion, a billowing orange and black fireball rolled through the sudden hole and blazed toward the roof.

Captain Black dropped his two-way radio and gaped in disbelief. Chief Franklin, sitting in the limousine, bit his cigar in two.

For a few seconds the din of the crowd died, as it absorbed the shock of the event. Then an odd, wavering moan went up—an eerie, inhuman wail of fear and thrill. It grew in volume for nearly a minute, metamorphosing into a barbaric cheer. The noise reverberated against the nearby buildings, seizing the throng of a hundred thousand with the frenzied ecstasy of a football stadium. Those who were there and heard it would never forget it.

The fire, conceived in the hairbrush in Estelle Daniels' hand, burst into being in a sonic cataclysm, rending the air with the scream of its birth.

Estelle, only inches from the concussion and the intense heat of the combusting chemicals, was incinerated instantly.

Near her, a sofa and chair burst spontaneously into flame. Snakes of white magnesium, thrown outward by the blast, sizzled in molten fury against the walls, ceiling, and floor, igniting the layers of paint, the carpeting, and the wood beneath it.

In milliseconds, the west sitting hall became a furnace. Five oil paintings, a mahogany drum table, a satinwood commode, a pair of eighteenth-century Adam armchairs, a Hepplewhite bookcase, and half a dozen other pieces of combustible furniture blazed like kindling in a stove.

Fanned by the strong wind blowing through the shattered Palladian window, the fire burst quickly from its west hall cradle out through the broad archway to the center hall, igniting everything before it.

Flames licked through the open doors into the president's bedroom, into the upstairs dining room, into the back halls by the number one and two elevators, and into the upstairs kitchen, finding fuel in the paint and the wood of the doors, frames, and moldings.

In less than a minute from the time of the explosion, the fire had taken hold throughout the family quarters. Heavy clouds of smoke rolled through the entire floor and seeped to the floor above.

Warfield was in the passage between the president's study and the center hall when the bomb exploded. The president was just ahead of him, stepping through the doorway. Wilbert had already moved down the hall.

He heard a wall-rattling concussion, followed by a blast of hot wind. Daniels swept past the doorway like a leaf. Warfield shut his eyes and threw his arms up over his face. He stumbled backward into the study, ears ringing, throat gagging from the acrid gases.

When he could steady himself and look up again, he saw smoke obliterating the passageway. He ducked down, groped for the door, and slammed it shut. To his right, a doorway off the passage led to a small bathroom. He snatched a towel from a rack, soaked it under the tap, and wrapped it around his face, covering his mouth and nose.

Back in the study, he saw only one other way out—a door on the left that opened into the Yellow Oval Room. He ran through. On the other side smoke was boiling into the spacious salon through a wide doorway that opened onto the center hall.

Clasping the towel to his face he ran to the doorway and started to close the double doors. As he swung them shut, he saw Wilbert, crumpled in a heap ten feet in front of him.

He dropped to his knees and crawled out into the center hall. To his left, through the wide archway into the west hall, nothing was visible but a pall of gray brown smoke and crackling red flame, whipped by heavy turbulence. He grabbed Wilbert by the wrists and dragged him back inside the Yellow Oval Room.

He took a couple of deep breaths, stretched the towel back over his face, and started back out, to look for the president. Crawling on his stomach, Warfield could just make out the shape of a man through the smoke. He was lying motionless against the legs of a round table, his limbs tangled around them.

Warfield crawled forward, blinking against the sting of the smoke. The heat burned his forehead as if he were facing the open mouth of a blast furnace. A line of incandescent white flame hissed along the carpet near the president's feet.

Warfield reached him, grabbed a wrist, and pulled him away from the table, losing his towel in the process. Lungs bursting for air and unable to see, he dropped the wrist and scrambled, on all fours, back to the safety of the Yellow Oval Room.

He found another bathroom, wet another towel, soaked his head in cold water, and forced himself to clamber out on his knees to the president again.

Over the roar of the inferno around him, he heard shouts. Dimly, he perceived figures trying to enter the center hall from a stairwell near the archway into the west hall, now completely enveloped in flame. The heat and smoke drove them back.

The president was much heavier than Wilbert, but with extreme effort, Warfield managed to drag him fifteen feet before he was forced to crawl back, with ragged breath and burning eyes, to the Yellow Oval Room.

When he tried the hall a third time, he saw a geyser of foam arching in from the stairwell, hissing against the walls and furniture. It had no effect on the flames. He heard more shouting, but the voices seemed to be well down the stairs.

He pulled the president into the Yellow Oval Room, dragging him alongside Wilbert, and banged the doors shut.

He slumped to the carpet. His eyes, throat, and nostrils felt scorched, his lungs choked with smoke. He coughed, mopped his head and face with the towel, and looked around for a way out. He had done all he could for them. He hoped they would live to appreciate it.

Secret Service agent Dan McCormick stood at the bottom of the west stairs, three other agents from the bodyguard detail beside him. He watched the two guards come scrambling back down the steps, casting their fire extinguishers to the floor.

"It's bad!" one of them yelled. "The whole west end of the floor is burning!"

"Never mind that!" McCormick yelled back. "Can you see the president?"

"No! You can't see anything up there!"

McCormick turned to his three agents. "The Grand Staircase! On the east side! Come on!"

At the top of the staircase, the four men were forced to halt. McCormick was appalled at the amount of smoke. He dropped to the carpet and tried to see ahead. It looked as if they might be able to make it as far as the middle of the center hall. No farther. The Yellow Oval Room door was there. Through it they could penetrate to the president's study and bedroom along the south side.

"Head for the Oval Room!" he cried. "We'll work our way back!"

Warfield heard the voices and the footsteps in the hall. Help on the way. He should stay, but that would invite trouble. His presence in the mansion was known only by Wilbert and the president. They might not live to vouch for him. He'd better find his own way out.

The door to the right led back to the president's study. That was toward the fire. No good. The three windows in the room opened onto the balcony over the south portico. No good, either.

Near the fireplace on the left wall he noticed another door, cut flush into the wall and partly hidden behind a side chest. He ran to it, pushed the chest out of the way, and groped for a handle. He found it—a small flush-pull, hidden in the strip of wainscoting that ran across the wall and door at waist level. The lower corner of a painting intruded over the edge of the hidden door and came crashing down when he pulled it open.

On the other side was a shallow vestibule and another door. He pushed against it and propelled himself into the Treaty Room, a dark green salon with Victorian furnishings and a massive table that dominated the center. He glanced around. Two windows on the south wall, a fireplace on the east wall, and only one door, which he realized must open back out into the center hall. He knelt by that door, took a deep lungful of the still smoke-free air, and cracked it open. Directly across the hallway a wide staircase descended to the lower floors. He was about to make a dash for it when an extraordinary sight stopped him.

Four men emerged through the haze of smoke, like soldiers in the midst of a battle, gagging and coughing. One pair clutched the legs and arms of Wilbert, the other pair carried Daniels. Flames had caught on the pants-leg of the last man. He must have felt it, Warfield thought, but he refused to drop his burden to slap them out.

Swaying and lurching with their loads, the men banged down the staircase. The moment they had cleared the top step two guards rushed to swing out massive steel fire doors from the walls on either side and clang them shut.

Warfield cursed to himself at his missed opportunity. But there must be other ways down. He opened the door from the Treaty Room and dashed past the blocked grand staircase into the east hall and immediately found another, smaller stairwell to his left. But it led only upward, to the top floor.

He moved to the next door. It opened into a rose-colored bedroom. He slammed it shut and tried the next door. It revealed a narrow vestibule with several more doors off it. One must be a stairway going down, he prayed. To the right, he found only a bathroom. To the left, a doorway back into the rose-colored bedroom. He dashed straight ahead to the one remaining door, and found himself in a small blue room at the corner of the mansion. A dressing room. He turned to leave, then caught sight of a form crumpled on the rug behind a pedestal table.

Of course! In the trauma of the explosion, he had forgotten. She was the one they were all headed for when it happened.

The Russian woman.

McCormick and his men lay Wilbert and the president down on the tiles of the main entrance hall at the foot of the Grand Staircase.

A chaotic mob was now swarming through the first floor—guards, agents, staff, the SWAT team, which had been evacuated down the same stairs minutes earlier, the third-floor staff and others, including Estelle's nurse, Irene, who had to be rescued from her locked room.

McCormick, stifling a coughing fit, looked himself over. He had suffered burns on the back of his hands and neck. Painful as hell, but not serious, he decided. He forced himself to his feet to take charge of the evacuation of the president.

Wilbert was sitting up, coughing and dazed. A crowd had gathered around him. Of greater concern was the condition of President Daniels. He was alive, but unconscious. The nurse, Irene, was examining him, and administering first aid.

McCormick pulled over two of his men on the bodyguard detail. "We've got to get the president to a hospital," he told them. "Get the limousine to the north entrance. Alert Bethesda and Reed and every hospital nearby to clear the decks! All emergency wards, burn units, CPRs, the works! And get the goddamned fire department here before the whole house burns down!"

Franklin was screaming. Captain Black had never seen him behave like this. His face was purple, apoplectic, and his voice was raised so high that it kept collapsing into a gravelly screech as he tried to pump more power into it.

"Clear a path!" he shouted, over and over, standing by the door of his limousine, shaking his fist at the crowd. "Clear a fucking path!"

The situation was getting worse. Fire trucks were stalled in traffic on Sixteenth Street, Vermont, and Connecticut. Black was trying to radio for another station house to try to get trucks to the White House via the Elipse, but he couldn't even get his call through.

Five minutes earlier, Black had dispatched a hundred men and twenty horse-mounted troops to push a path through the mess on Sixteenth. It was taking a long time; Black knew they were making progress only because he could see, from his vantage point on the north side of the park, a hook and ladder inching along past Eye Street. It would still have to maneuver around the park to get to the north gate.

As his eyes scanned the north face of the White House, the lights suddenly blinked out. First the outside spots, trained on the walls, then the lights of the mansion itself. Every window went abruptly dark. A rumbling growl, like a dragon's roar, issued from the crowd.

He guessed someone inside had shut the power off on purpose, for safety or security reasons, but in a peculiar way the sudden blackout was as frightening as the explosion had been. It was as if the great house had suddenly died. He could see the flames more clearly against the darkened interior. They licked out from the shattered window on the west side, and glowed a dirty orange inside the two windows on the north face closest to the fire.

Captain Black had grown up in the slums not far from the White House. He had passed the place thousands of times in his life, and he had come to consider it the most important building in the world. It was an old, faithful friend, an anchor of enduring strength in a turbulent world. Now, as he watched the flames and smoke eat away at the magnificent residence, he thought he might cry.

Warfield knelt beside the woman and felt for her pulse. It was beating steadily. He drew a glass of cold water from the bathroom tap and trickled it over her forehead, noticing, as one notices irrelevant things in a crisis, that the roots of her hair were dark. She was not a natural blonde.

No less beautiful for that, though, he thought.

He poured the remainder of the water on her wrists and massaged them briskly. Her features were almost *too* perfect. She must be near forty, and yet she looked much younger—her face, her neck, smooth and unblemished.

She was responsible for this, he realized; apparently she had miscalculated. The bomb must have gone off in that sitting room. Daniels had been there earlier, when Wilbert first brought Warfield in. But what had happened to her? Had someone seen her with the bomb and knocked her out? He knew he should leave her and get out before he was arrested or trapped in the fire, but he remained, looking at her, unable to pull himself away.

She stirred. Her eyelids fluttered faintly.

Then the lights went out.

Warfield yanked open the curtains on the window, gaining a

glow from the streets that dimly penetrated the room. The crowd outside seemed bigger than ever, and more restless. He could see a wedge of uniforms trying to clear a path to the north gate, but as soon as the phalanx advanced twenty feet, the crowd closed in behind it. Sirens wailed, seemingly from everywhere—from the street directly below, and from the wide web of avenues that radiated out from the White House. A helicopter rumbled overhead.

He knelt beside the Russian woman again. She had propped herself up on one elbow. In the faint light he saw her big eyes, wide with fright.

"What happened?" she whispered.

"I don't know," he said. "You were out cold. There's been an explosion down the hall. The place is on fire."

"She knocked me out."

"Who did?"

"His wife. She was here."

Warfield helped her to a sitting position. "I don't know what you're talking about, but we both better get out of here."

The Russian woman made no move to rise. Warfield, still kneeling beside her, put a hand under her arm and lifted gently.

"The hall outside is full of smoke," he told her. "And they've closed a fire door across the main stairs. We have to find another way out."

"Who are you?" she asked. "Why are you here?"

Warfield looked at her. The light from the windows was at her back, hiding her face in shadow. He could feel her eyes on him.

"Come on," he said. "Let's get going."

She struggled to her feet. Warfield was surprised she was so tall. He felt her arms circle his neck.

"Can you walk?" he asked.

She didn't answer him. Her head leaned against his shoulder, then pressed into it. He tried to pull her arms away, but they tightened around him. Is she in shock? he wondered.

He slipped his arm around her waist and tried to help her toward the door, but she refused to move. She squeezed herself against him harder than ever. Sobs racked her chest, and her whole body seemed to quiver and shake as if from the cold.

"What's the matter?"

"Charles!" she whispered.

At first he didn't realize that she was speaking his name. She repeated it, her voice broken by sobs.

"How do you know my name?"

The Russian woman pressed her mouth against the curve of his neck, then close to his ear. He felt warm tears wetting his skin.

"It's Tanya," she whispered. "It's me. Tanya."

39

WHEN WORD CAME DOWN that the gates would be locked for the night, CBS White House correspondent Derek Johnson and his cameraman elected to remain inside. They set up to broadcast on Johnson's customary spot on the north lawn, about halfway between the mansion's north portico and the north gate. From this unique no-man's land, Johnson had a good view of everything—the milling crowd along the fence on one side of him, and the progress of the fire in the White House on the other.

CBS put him on the air live at eleven-thirty, and he had been covering the situation continuously for nearly an hour:

"The fire on the second floor still appears to be spreading. From here you can see the flames through the windows all the way across to the portico roof. Smoke is leaking from several spots now on the main roof, and the fire may have spread up to the third floor, which is not visible from down here. . . . We're told the third floor has been completely evacuated. . . . Meanwhile, nothing is yet known about the cause of the explosion, or if there have been any casualties. Concern is growing, however, with every passing minute. There have been several reports, still unconfirmed, that the president was in his study on the second floor at the time, with his chief of staff William Wilbert. He was thought to have been some distance from the blast, but we cannot confirm any of this. White House press secretary Jerry Stein has no word yet on the president's condition. He has assured us only that Secret Service agents were

able to reach him on the second floor. . . . We have no word at all on the Russian woman, Mrs. Kamenev. Several people in the crowd we talked to earlier said they saw her looking out the window over on the east end of the mansion. That would be the Queen's Bedroom, where she is believed to be staying. . . . The lights have been out inside the mansion for nearly ten minutes now, and there is no sign of any activity on the second floor. . . . What's amazing is that there seems to be no organized effort to bring the fire under control. We've seen several dozen people— Secret Service agents, guards, domestic staff—running around the ground floor and first floor, but the scene is one of terrible confusion. . . . Meanwhile nearly two dozen fire trucks are still stalled in the streets outside. . . . A few minutes ago my colleague Anne Davis talked to Police Chief Joseph Franklin at the north side of Lafayette Park. He informed her that a path was being cleared to the north gate to allow the trucks through. . . . You can see the north gate right over here to my left. There are a lot of policemen among the spectators and demonstrators, but so far they have failed to open up that path Chief Franklin promised. . . . You can see the fire trucks. The nearest is about a hundred feet from the gate. The others are further back. You can hear the sirens. And the blinking emergency lights form a necklace through the crowd, snaking all the way around Lafayette Park and up Sixteenth Street, toward the Russian Embassy. . . ."

Johnson broke off his monologue and pressed his earplug to his ear. Information was being relayed from the White House press room.

"We have this latest word," he said. "The president has been brought down from the second floor. . . . Let me repeat that. President Daniels has been rescued from the fire, still raging on the second floor. . . . We have no information on his condition, but we assume this means he must be alive. . . ."

"They changed my face," Tanya said, still clinging to Warfield in the dark room. "Surgeons operated on me when I was in a coma."

Warfield's heart was pounding furiously. He felt that he might choke from the shock.

"Please, you must forgive me, Charles, for everything that happened! If you knew everything, you'd understand!"

"Explain it to me, then, damn you!" he whispered, his voice fierce with the tumult of his emotions. "Explain it to me!"

Tanya pressed her hands to his cheeks. "I meant to come with you that night," she said, her voice breaking. "Oh how much I wanted to! More than anything in my life!"

"But you didn't!"

"There's so much to explain. I loved you, Charles. I truly did! You must have felt that!"

Warfield said nothing.

Tanya broke out in sobs again, and was unable to continue. The noises outside were growing. Sirens. Helicopters. He knew they must get out immediately, but he felt nailed to the spot.

"I was supposed to pretend to be killed," Tanya said, finally. "Just as you saw. So that the operation could be ended. So that I could be withdrawn."

"So you could betray me! So Semenenko could roll up my network!"

"I didn't give him the names of your network! I lied to him! I told him I had learned them, but I hadn't! I promised to give them to him after my staged murder! But I was going to run out, to defect with you! Just as we said!"

"Then why didn't you?"

"Because they really shot me! It wasn't faked. I was in a coma for three days. Somehow the general discovered our plan. I was flown to a special hospital outside Moscow. They repaired the damage from the gunshots. And . . . did this to me."

"Why?"

"So everyone would believe me dead. You. My husband. Everyone. So Tanya could die."

"Your name isn't Tanya?"

"No."

"What is it?"

"Zoya Voloshin. I wish I had told you, Charles. I wish I had told you many things!"

"You let him use you again."

"Yes."

"Why?"

Tanya buried her face in her hands.

"Why!?" he repeated.

"I had no choice," she murmured.

"You're a liar," he said.

"No!"

"Why didn't you get word to me? All these years, I thought you dead! Butchered!"

"I know. It broke my heart! But it was better that way. I couldn't let you think I'd betrayed you. That would have been truly unbearable!"

"But you did betray me!"

"Because it would be so hard for you to understand the truth!"

"How in the world did you come to marry Kamenev? Did Semenenko arrange that too?"

"Yes. He saw that Kamenev would be the next premier. Kamenev's wife had died the year before. Some say she was poisoned. The general may even have done that, too, I don't know. Such things are possible in this terrible world. He arranged for us to meet. Kamenev didn't need encouragement. He asked me to marry him the third time he saw me. I did it. I didn't want to, but I knew my life would be better as his wife. And I had no choice."

"That's no explanation! You wrecked my whole goddamned life!"

Tanya pulled herself away from Warfield and slumped in a nearby chair.

"You're Semenenko's secret weapon. He uses you to seduce and destroy. The president falls in love with you, and you move in, like a praying mantis, to kill him."

"No! no! no!" Tanya wailed. "It's not true! I agreed to spy on him. That was all!"

"What about the bomb?"

"It must have been in the device he gave me. The hairbrush. I didn't know it!"

"Hard to believe."

"Yes! But it's the truth!"

Warfield felt utter desolation. He wished more than anything on earth to believe her. Otherwise, finding her alive again was a worse punishment than thinking her still dead. But to believe her protestations of innocence required an act of faith that defied common sense.

"What you're telling me is absurd. How could Semenenko force you to do all these things? What hold could he have on you that could be so irresistible? What does it matter any longer? Tell me the truth!"

She slammed both fists against her knees. "Yes, yes, I am telling you the truth! He does have a hold on me! He always has! Oh Charles, I should have told you all this in Egypt, I know. Then you'd have understood. But don't you see? I thought I was going away with you! I thought I was escaping! I wanted, I prayed I could keep my past from destroying our new life together!"

"What hold does he have on you?"

Tanya was crying steadily now, but her voice was strong. "The general took me from a labor camp when I was eleven! I had nowhere else to go! No family, no way to make a living. I would have been sent back to an orphanage."

"You weren't his slave!"

"He adopted me. He changed my life totally. Gave me the best —clothes, schools, privileges, everything! Can you imagine what that meant to me, after my wretched childhood? Of course I did what he wanted. I studied politics, joined the KGB. Because that was what he wanted. What right did I have to do otherwise?"

Tanya stood and reached her arms out to embrace him, but he shrugged her off. She dropped to her knees and hugged his legs. "Then you came along," she whispered. "I dared to have new dreams. Now I know I was wrong to have them."

Tanya moved away and lay on the floor, curling up self-protectively on the soft Aubusson rug. "After Alexandria," she said, "I stopped having dreams. It was hard, but my life had been hard before. I hate what I've had to become, and I've tried to escape from it. First in Egypt. Then here. Now I know that I can't!"

A sudden jealousy seized Warfield. "Was Daniels your lover?" he demanded.

"Yes."

"What about Semenenko?"

Tanya was silent, her face hidden.

"Was he? Was Semenenko your lover too?"

"Yes."

"When?"

"When I was eleven."

Warfield felt split open—turned inside out. He listened to Tanya crying softly in the shadows, and tried to suppress his pain.

White House correspondent Derek Johnson was still talking to the camera:

"Speculation is that the explosion was another assassination attempt on President Daniels by the same unknown group responsible for the Suitland Parkway ambush ten days ago. How an explosive device could find its way into the White House under the very heavy security precautions of the past week is just one more incredible mystery to add to the sizable number surrounding events of recent days.... They've cleared an area around the north gate. There, you can see what looks like a troop of about a hundred District policemen forming a solid double phalanx out from the gate toward the fire truck.... Apparently the police have given up attempts to arrest demonstrators because they simply cannot get them from the crowd to the police vans. We saw several fights here a while ago. Since the fire, attention has been riveted on the White House itself. The mood of the crowd seems part festive, part awestruck.... They're opening the gates, now. I'll have to shout to hear myself over the noise of the sirens and the crowd. Guards are swinging the two sections of the gate open. This gate is used to let vehicles in and out of the enclosed portion of West Executive Avenue and the driveway to the north portico entrance of the White House.... The police you can see are special riot police. Some of them are pushing against the crowd with nightsticks, and I can see several skirmishes between the cops and some of the demonstrators. One just got hit over the head with a placard. ... The gate is open now but the fire truck still hasn't come through. I'd guess it's only thirty feet away, but as you can see the path in front of it is collapsing against the weight of the crowd. There's a good deal of pushing and shoving.... We'd heard earlier they intended to use tear gas, but we've seen none so far.... Wait a minute! Wait a minute! There's a big scuffle by the gate! Police cordons have collapsed. Now they seem to be trying to form a line across the front of the open gate. No wonder! Look at that! The crowd is pouring right through! The crowd is pouring right through! They're coming right through the gate! Police are trying to push them back, but the sheer numbers are overwhelming them! I see the guards trying to close the gate, but it's useless! The crowd is packed solid right through the opening! They're coming through in a flood! I've never seen, never imagined anything like this! A helicopter just dipped down close over our heads! We could

feel the breeze from the rotor blades. I can see the lights of other helicopters in the sky over by. . . . The crowd's really streaming through now! Fanning out all over the north lawn! It's an unbelievable sight! The fire truck is getting nowhere! I haven't been able to check the. . . . Wait a minute! That was tear gas over . . . where is it? Over on the edge of Lafayette Park! I can see a cloud of gas rising up over there! . . . The fire inside the White House, meanwhile. . . . It looks like our position here is going to be overrun. I'm . . . we're going to have to . . . pull back. If we can. Wait a minute! Excuse me! . . . Hey! Goddammit! . . ."

Correspondent Johnson disappeared from view.

"Is the president dead?" Tanya asked.

"I don't know. They got him downstairs, anyway. How was that bomb detonated?"

"I don't know. I didn't know it was a bomb."

"By remote control, then. If Semenenko was listening from the embassy, then he must have detonated it from there. That makes the third time he's almost killed you. In Alexandria. On the Suitland Parkway. And here."

"It's because I've been trying to escape from him that he's willing to sacrifice me. But you won't believe me still."

Warfield didn't answer.

"You saved my life," she said. "If you hadn't come, I would have been with the president . . . and the bomb."

"Don't think about it. Let's get out of here."

"Everything is over for me," she said. "Leave me here."

"No. I need answers from you."

He walked to the bathroom, soaked two towels under the tap, and returned to Tanya's side. "Let's go to the bedroom next door," he said. "It's closer to the stairs."

In the Queen's Bedroom it was totally dark. They felt their way along the wall to the door that opened into the east hall. Warfield handed her one of the towels.

"Wrap it around your neck and cover your mouth and nose. Keep your eyes closed as much as you can. The smoke will be thick. Don't breathe it. You'll choke. We'll go on hands and knees. The closer to the floor, the less smoke. Don't stand up, and don't panic."

"All right."

"We'll go for the main staircase first. They closed firedoors across it, but I might be able to open them. If we get through, run down and keep on going all the way to the ground floor. Don't let anybody stop you. Follow me closely. The best way out is through a tunnel under the east wing to the Treasury Building. I came in that way tonight. If we can't get down the main stairway, we'll have to go up those nearer stairs, just outside this door. I don't know what we'll do on the top floor, but it'll be safer than staying here."

Warfield helped her tuck the towel around her face. Touching her in the dark stirred the aches of old memories. As they knelt on their knees before the door, Tanya's fingers found his hand and squeezed it.

From the west sitting hall the fire had grown in the course of half an hour to engulf the entire length of the center hall, feeding on its rich clutter of furniture and books. It ate into the wall moldings, the carpets and their underpadding, and into the ancient, tinder-dry herringbone parquetry and the wooden subfloor beneath it.

The fire burned as well in the president's bedroom and study, the dining room and kitchen, the two small bedrooms under the north portico, in the Treaty Room, and the Yellow Oval Room.

It burned throughout the second floor of the mansion, save for the east sitting hall and its two guest suites, the Lincoln Bedroom and the Queen's Bedroom.

No one remained on the floor, except Charles Warfield and the Russian woman.

They crept into the dark east hall and scrambled toward the Grand Staircase. The heat was intense. Twenty feet along Warfield opened his eyes briefly and saw, in the crackling of the flames, the staircase entrance to their right, with the firedoors closed across it. He reached out, grabbed the handle on one door and tugged at it, burning his palms against the hot metal. It refused to budge. He kicked the doors with both feet. Nothing. They were firmly locked from the other side.

He dropped onto his stomach, pressed the towel over his eyes to wash out the smoke, then glanced at Tanya, just behind him. He shook his head. She understood.

To try to slow the fire's progress, Warfield slid shut the pair of heavy wooden doors in the archway between the center and east halls. Then they retreated back to the other stairs in the east stairhall. Dim light from an emergency battery lamp in the stairwell ceiling illuminated the steps up to the third floor through the shrouds of gray smoke.

Warfield sucked in a deep breath through his towel, and plunged up the stairs, Tanya behind him. At the top he encountered another fire door. In the swirling heat he beat against it, pulled on it, rattling the steel handle with desperate strength. It didn't budge.

He felt Tanya tugging at his jacket. He gave up.

They ran down the stairs and retreated back to the Queen's Bedroom, eyes burning, lungs rasping. Warfield stumbled over the furniture in the dark, groping for a window. He found one, pulled aside the drapes, yanked up the sash, and leaned out to gulp in draughts of fresh air.

"We can stay here," Tanya said, pushing her face out beside him. "Just keep the door closed and wait until it's over."

"The fire's too damned close. And there's no sign of the fire department."

"The phones might work," she said. "We can ask for a ladder to the window."

"They'll arrest us," he said.

"Maybe not."

"They won't be getting any ladders to these windows. Look."

Tanya bent out the window. The crowd swarmed in a near-solid mass over the entire lawn below them.

"My God!"

One of the fire trucks, stalled near the gate, steadied its searchlight on their window. The crowd below saw them and began yelling and pointing. They ducked back out of sight and sat on the floor just under the windowsill. Warfield studied her in the bluish white light streaming over their heads. He looked for the face of the Tanya he thought he had remembered so well, but saw only a blurred likeness. The eyes alone remained familiar, their translucent seductiveness stirring him again, the way they had so many nights in the parks and sidestreets of Alexandria.

She smiled at his puzzled stare. "It's not just the plastic surgery," she said. "I'm ten years older, too. You don't look the same either."

"Of course," Warfield said, smiling back. He felt a powerful wave of nostalgia overtake him, and the emotions triggered a concern long buried by the years he thought her dead.

"You were pregnant," he said.

He saw her nod in the shadows, and he waited for her to elaborate. She didn't.

"What happened?" he asked, suddenly fearful.

"I had the child. Her name is Zoya. She's ten now."

Warfield felt an electric, exhilarating thrill surge through him. "Imagine!" he stammered. "My God! Imagine! And I thought. . . ." He stopped. "What's she like? I mean is she okay? Where is she now?"

Katya found his hand and squeezed it. "She's smart and beautiful. And she's fine. There's no time to explain it all now. . . ."

Warfield pushed himself to his feet and pulled Katya up after him. "I have a million questions! My God. A million! Let's get the hell out of here!"

Dan McCormick thought he was in a nightmare from which he soon must waken. The White House in flames, the president dying on the stretcher beside him on the south lawn helipad.

And now this. The crowd.

He saw them coming around the corners of the east and west wings, trickling through the trees like jackals in the woods. The first ones had skulked cautiously in the shadows, aware they trespassed on forbidden ground. The ones that followed became more careless, emboldened by their numbers.

McCormick searched the sky overhead and turned to one of the other agents, Sam Warner, standing by the helipad with a radio in one hand, an Uzi submachine gun in the other. "Where in Christ's name is the president's helicopter?" he shouted at him.

"On the way, Dan! It's on the way!"

He pointed to the scurrying figures silhouetted in the orange and yellow shafts of light cast from the second-story windows of the White House. "We're going to be overrun, Dan!" he said. "We should carry the president farther down the lawn! Take him out the southwest gate!"

"No, goddammit!" McCormick roared back. "The gate's surrounded. He has to go by helicopter. And this is the only spot where the chopper can land. We stay here!"

The agent glanced around the acres of lawn. "We're all armed," he replied. "We can protect the president by forming a ring around him. But there aren't enough of us to do both that and keep the helipad clear."

"Then get the goddamn chopper down here!"

The dozen agents formed a circle around the unconscious form of President Daniels and cocked their guns, prepared to fend off any threats. McCormick stood by the president, his fingers anxiously testing the pulse in Daniels's wrist, his eyes scanning the night sky for signs of the helicopter that would deliver them from this hell.

"They're dropping tear gas," Warfield said.

Tanya looked down. Widening smudges of white smoke, like giant puffballs, drifted on the brisk wind. The crowd, jammed together and unable to flee, began coughing and choking and falling to the ground.

By the north gate, police in gas masks were clubbing demonstrators to force them back from the fence. Meanwhile, another fire truck—a pumper—had crept up alongside the stalled hook and ladder, fifty feet from the gate. Two firemen stood on top of it behind the wheel of a deluge gun and directed its nozzle toward the crowd around the gate, exploding into it with a powerful stream of water.

Warfield ran to the door to look into the east hall. The sliding doors he had closed across the archway were almost burned through. Smoke seeped around the edges, and flames licked up underneath, burning the floor under the doors. He returned to Tanya.

"I've got one last idea," he said. He pulled the mattress from the big double bed and dragged it into the east hall in front of the Palladian window that looked out over the east wing.

He pointed down. About twenty feet directly below them ran the wide, flat roof of the pavilion connecting the main part of the mansion to the east wing. "This is our only way out," he said. "It's less of a drop from here than anywhere, and the roof will keep us away from the crowd. We'll throw the mattress down on the roof and try to land on it."

The Palladian window didn't open. Warfield picked up an armchair and rammed its legs through the panes at waist level. The glass and sash bars shattered. He punched out the jagged edges of glass left along the bottom and threw the chair aside. Tanya helped him force the mattress out the hole. The smoke, sucked in their direction by the sudden new draft, threatened to engulf them.

He looked down to the roof of the pavilion and at the dim outline of the mattress, lying at a diagonal beneath him.

"You go first," he told her. "Try to land on your feet. Collapse when you hit and fall on your side. It's not very far. Even if you miss the mattress you probably won't be hurt."

Tanya pulled off her shoes. Warfield tore the silk damask drape from its rod and laid it over the bottom sash, to cover the small edges of jagged glass that still remained. Bracing herself on his shoulder, Tanya stuck her legs out the window and sat, balanced on the ledge.

"Go ahead!" he urged. "I'm right behind you!"

Tanya twisted around, pulled his face to hers, and kissed him hard on the lips. "I still love you," she said. "No matter what happens!"

She pushed off the ledge.

Warfield looked down. Tanya hit the mattress on its corner, and fell sideways onto the roof. She jumped quickly to her feet and waved up at him. Relieved, he tossed her shoes down to her.

Clouds of tear gas drifted through the air. He realized they might need the wet towels again. He hesitated, then dashed back into the bedroom to get them.

In that handful of seconds, his luck changed.

On his way back, the sliding doors that formed the last barrier between the east hall and the fire, burst open. The blaze, sucked through by powerful wind currents, swallowed the east hall in one cataclysmic roar. Warfield fled back into the Queen's room and slammed the door against the sheet of flame.

He knew he was cut off; he had not the slightest hope of getting back to that window. The thought of Tanya stranded out on the roof, watching the fire flash against the window where he had been standing seconds before, brought him to the edge of panic for the first time. She would think him dead, and that was unbearable. It was not even whether he lived or died. It was the separation again, another gulf to divide them before they had bridged the old one.

One option remained.

He climbed out the open bedroom window facing the north lawn and surveyed the situation below. He would have to stand on the ledge and push off hard to clear the wide cement casements around the ground-floor walls. He guessed it was a twenty-five-foot jump. And he would almost certainly land on top of someone.

He didn't. He crashed through the branches of an evergreen bush, twisted over, and hit the earth on his back. The air went out of him, and for several seconds he blacked out. His rib cage contorted with muscle spasms. He sucked desperately for air and inhaled tear gas. He pressed the towel still in his hand over his face and forced himself to his knees. Intense pain speared his left shoulder.

The tear gas had failed to disperse the demonstrators, packed in too tight to go anywhere. Many lay on the ground, choking from the gas.

It was several minutes before he could stand. Finally, pushing aside bodies with frantic determination, he fought his way around to the east wing. On its south side the crowd was less dense. He ran across the south lawn, back toward the mansion. Near the edge of the garden that bordered the east wing pavilion he could see the arched window on the White House second floor, belching flames. Below, on the pavilion roof, he saw no one.

She must have jumped down, he thought. It was an easy jump from the edge of the roof into the garden. He looked for her among the shadows of hedges and paths, but didn't find her.

What would she have done? Where would she go? He gazed forlornly across the vast spread of the south lawn, milling with thousands of people. How would he find her?

A large helicopter hovered overhead, splashing brilliant shafts of light toward the ground, and pinning, in their beams, an eerie tableau of a circle of men around a stretcher.

The helicopter settled to the lawn in a whirl of wind, and the men quickly loaded the stretcher on board and disappeared inside after it. The president, Warfield guessed.

The craft lifted instantly from the lawn and swooped off southward, its red lights blinking in the night.

Several fire trucks had managed to work their way to the gate on the south lawn's eastern perimeter. The iron grilles had swung open and the first truck was roaring through, sirens screaming.

Warfield ran down a short path and onto the wide gravel drive that formed a circle between the south portico and the fountain, halfway down the lawn. Hundreds of people were running across the grounds—yelling, whooping, laughing. The tear gas had not reached this side. Warfield threw away his towel.

Near the gate, helmeted police were laying into the demonstrators with clubs, beating them to the ground as they tried to slip through to the lawn. Some threw rocks in retaliation.

Warfield scanned the running figures, looking for a head of blond hair. He saw one, and ran toward it. A cop clubbed her as he approached, and she crumpled to the ground, screaming, hands on her head.

Warfield leaped at the cop from behind, jammed his forearm under his Adam's apple, jerked upward, and squeezed. The cop dropped his club and clawed at his neck. Warfield slammed a fist upward into the man's chin with a swift motion that snapped his jaw against his temple and knocked him out.

Warfield moved to the woman on the ground. It was not Tanya.

A club struck him from behind—a glancing blow near the base of his skull. He staggered forward, his head exploding with pain. Steadying himself, he swung around in time to see a second cop advancing at him. He dove into the man headfirst, butting him in the stomach and knocking him to the grass.

Uniforms swarmed around him. He whirled and kicked, ran, stumbled and fell, regained his footing, and was knocked to the ground again. He curled up in a fetal position, threw his arms around his head, and let the blows rain down on him. They thudded on his feet and legs, his sides and back, his arms and hands. He grunted, and prayed for a kick that would knock him unconscious.

A tear gas grenade burst nearby, and saved him. The crowd of uniforms surrounding him melted suddenly into the clouds of white gas. He lay there, trying to catch his breath, but the gas forced him to his feet. He tried to see through the smoke, but his eyes burned and streamed tears. Demonstrators, coughing, hands over their faces, staggered around him like drunks.

Through his tears he caught the distorted image of another blond head and ran toward it. Another stranger.

Running against the flow of the crowd, he made his way out through the gate to East Executive Avenue. He sucked in lungfuls of poison-free air, and cried out Tanya's name. The sound was swallowed up by the cacophony around him.

His lungs felt seared, and his eyes watered so badly he couldn't keep them open. He leaned his head against the fence, clutching the irons rails with both hands for support and tried to clear his head.

Where had she gone?

He forced his eyes open, straining to penetrate the shadowy chaos, the battleground of running figures, yelling voices, flashing lights and sirens, bullhorns and helicopters.

Where had she gone?

He trotted a few steps north up the avenue, refusing to face the possibility that he had lost her. Then one figure, running north up Executive Avenue, caught his attention. She was moving against the grain of the mob, and ran with more purpose, like someone with a destination. He followed.

At the southeast corner of Lafayette Park the figure paused, then ran north, toward Vermont Avenue. Lights from the park illuminated her hair briefly. Blond. Tanya!

Warfield, his heart pounding with hope, tried to move faster, to close the gap between them. Fatigue weighed him down.

At the northeast corner of the park, she stopped again and looked each way down H Street, as if uncertain of which direction to take.

Warfield ran, closing the gap. He yelled her name. The syllables, ragged and hoarse, seemed to float off in the dense night and die in the wind. He yelled again. She looked his way briefly. He was closing the gap. Only a hundred feet.

"Wait! Tanya! Wait!"

The figure hesitated. He was close enough now to make out the clothes and the woman's shape. Far enough away not to see the changes wrought by plastic surgery, he saw instead all the remembered, familiar things—her stance, her silhouette, her manner of movement. The images of a loved one as recognizable as one's own face.

She started to run again, heading west along the north edge of the park.

He cried her name again. Surely she had heard him! Why did she still run?

Halfway along the top of the park she turned north into Sixteenth Street.

Warfield stopped, gasping for air. Abruptly a dark panic closed over him. He knew where she was going! With pain constricting his throat, he began running again, putting every last ounce of his fading energy into the effort.

She disappeared for a moment in the crowd, then reemerged. He ran, forcing his legs, which seemed caught in the slow motion of a nightmare, to close the distance between them.

"Your postcard village!" he cried. "I found it! . . . I found it. . . . I live there! . . ."

She reached the intersection of K Street and crossed it, taking long, almost masculine strides, her hair bobbing and trailing like ribbons in the gusty breeze.

"Tanya!" he called. "We can live there!"

At the intersection of Sixteenth and L, she lost her balance and almost fell. He gained several strides on her.

"Our daughter," he gasped. "I want to see her! I have a right, Tanya. . . ."

Between L and M Streets she disappeared from view. He wanted to shout again, but could not. He needed to conserve everything for a last effort to overtake her.

She was no longer on the street.

Warfield arrived at the middle of the block and staggered to a halt. He heard a gate snap shut.

The streetlights cast a ghostly white light on the four-story graystone mansion. The windows were shuttered, and the small yard with the high wrought-iron fence around it was shrouded in darkness. A security camera hidden in the heavy shrubbery near the walls gleamed in the reflected light from the street.

A shutter on the top floor cracked open. Against the faint interior glow Warfield could distinguish the silhouette of a woman. He called after it repeatedly, but it offered not the slightest gesture of a response. The shutter closed.

Warfield grabbed the railings with both fists and began to shake them hard. "I want to see her!" he cried.

A guard stepped out of the shadows on the other side and warned him to go away.

Warfield collapsed against the gate and slid down along it until he lay in a heap on the pavement, his arms still clutching the cold iron bars.

"Tanya," he whispered. "I want to see her. . . ."

A half hour later, a police cruiser arrived and three policemen pried his fingers from the embassy gate and carried him into their car.

40

carrying the mail and the morning newspaper. "My God, you're up," she said, surprised. "Only sixteen hours of sleep last night!"

Nan tossed the newspaper on the bed and flopped onto the chaise across the room. Warfield glanced at the paper, then threw it on the floor. "I've had enough news to last me well into the next century."

Nan laughed. "I know what you mean. Anyway, there's some *good* news for a change. The Senate and House passed the White House restoration bill. Work will begin at once. And the president's condition is improving. He's out of his coma. The doctors say he'll recover."

Warfield shrugged. "Sure. In a year or two. After the skin grafts take and he can remember his full name. They'll have to remove him from office. The Twenty-fifth Amendment."

"Maybe. But there's tremendous sympathy for him. And support in Congress, too. Something might be worked out. He might be able to hang in there."

"Well, nobody wants to see Catlin take over, that's for sure."

Nan sifted through the mail. "They want you to testify as soon as possible. Senator Rollins wants to talk to you. I told him absolutely no. But I can't stall him much longer. The subcommittee hearings start in a week."

"He'll have to get in line. He can have what's left of me after the attorney general, the FBI, the CIA, and the Secret Service take their cuts. Not to mention the prosecutors for the state of Virginia and the District of Columbia. And, of course, my lawyer."

"You left out the press," Nan said. "Some of them are still camped on the lawn. Who's your lawyer, by the way?"

"Wilbert's promised to help."

"Well, you'd better call him, then. And Herb Rosenstock and Howard Moore. They're very hurt you haven't seen them yet."

"I'll call them tonight."

"The swelling seems to be going down," Nan said, looking over at him with an appraising squint of the eye. "You're returning to your original shape."

"But not my original color. Look at this." Warfield pulled open the robe. Large areas of purple, black, and yellow bruises ran from his chest across his stomach to his thighs.

"Hmmm," Nan said. "You don't match the new bedroom decor at all, now. I liked the red and blue stage better. . . . Oh . . ." She held up an envelope. "Here's a letter for you. Sent care of this address." She tossed it over to the bed. Warfield picked it up and turned it over.

"Funny," he said. "Who would know to send it here?"

"Read it later," Nan replied. "I have something more important to show you."

Without elaborating, she jumped up, disappeared into the other room, and returned with a tape recorder.

"You remember that cassette tape you removed from that man in the warehouse?" she said, sitting beside him on the bed.

"The Turk? Sure. I'd forgotten about it."

"Well, *I* didn't," Nan said, her voice suddenly full of mystery. "Listen to this."

She pressed the playback button and placed the recorder on the bedside table. It hissed for a few seconds and then, through a lot of background noise, he heard a disjointed conversation:

> *"Hello, Chester. . . . I thought those fellas might mug me. . . . What's this?"*
> *"I'll explain. Just go down, please!"*
> *"Don't you have an elevator?"*
> *"It doesn't work. Just go on down!"*
> *"Ten thousand. . . . A campaign contribution from the*

Spengler Construction Company. . . . Aren't you gonna count it? You always count it."

Nan turned the cassette player off and looked at Warfield. "Recognize a voice?" she asked.

"No."

"It'll get clearer. Listen." She turned the recorder back on.

"I'm not going to open it. You can take my word for its contents."

"Well?"

"Two hundred and fifty thousand dollars, Otis. In hundreds. Everything you've given me. I want you to take it all back."

"What the hell are you talking about?"

"I want you to take it all back. I want to get it all out of here. Right now! This morning! I never want to see any of it again, ever! Do you understand?"

"Understand? You're talking crazy!"

"I'm scared, and I'm not afraid to admit it. Do you realize how close I came to becoming president last week?"

"Chester, I'm disappointed in you. You can't give the money back. You've already taken it. It's all clean, untraceable. It's yours."

"You saw them when you came in. Secret Service. Police. They're swarming all over the place, following me every step I take. And there's a hit squad somewhere still gunning for the president. Do you realize that if Daniels is killed they'll be in here, within hours, moving our belongings over to the White House. It's just not safe! I can't keep large amounts of cash on the premises. I want it out of here! Right now! And you're taking it with you, dammit!"

"Chester, I want you to think this over carefully. . . ."

"I have thought it over! If I become president, I'll be in a fishbowl! Somebody—some reporter somewhere—will dig this business up! I'll be ruined! . . . It's all there. Two hundred and fifty thousand. Take it, and let's never discuss this business again. No more envelopes. Ever."

Nan turned off the recorder. "There's more," she said. "But you get the gist."

Warfield whistled. "Catlin! On the take!"

"It's worse than that," Nan said. "Think it through."

"My brain's still convalescing," he replied.

"You found the tape on one of the assassins, right?"

"Right."

"He was working for Shanklin, right?"

"Right."

"Who was working for Semenenko, right?"

Warfield sat up straight. "Right. Jesus! . . ."

"Jesus is right. Semenenko was positioning himself to blackmail Catlin."

"Who may soon become president," Warfield whispered, completing the thought.

"That's why Semenenko wanted Daniels dead," Nan said. "So he could control the new president! Catlin!"

They looked at each other. "What do we do now?" he asked.

"We expose Catlin, obviously. This tape is just what we need to bail you out of your mess!"

Warfield shrugged. "It'll take more than a tape recording, Nan."

Nan looked at him, a hurt expression compressing her lips.

He avoided her eyes. A week he had been in her apartment, he thought. A week since she had sprung him, with Wilbert's help, from a D.C. jail. She had been remarkable: a nurse, a confessor, an adviser, a protector. A shepherd guiding him through the Slough of Despond. Against long odds, she had held him together. It was too soon for him to feel any gratitude. Later, he thought. Everything would have to come later.

But now he could see that she was beginning to show signs of strain. "I've been an ordeal for you, I know," he said.

She nodded, her eyes sad. "I'm not doing it out of pure altruism," she said.

"What do you mean?"

"I helped you because you needed it, of course. But I was helping myself, too."

"How?"

"You were worth saving. For me."

Warfield looked down at the blanket.

"But I guess I miscalculated," she said.

Warfield didn't reply.

"You still love the Russian woman, don't you?"

Warfield nodded.

"It'll have no end, then."

"Everything has an end."

"No. You're obsessed. I can't compete with that. I don't even want to try."

"I just need to find out what happened to her. It's not a good time to talk about it."

Nan turned and walked out of the room. "I'll fix us some lunch," she said, tears in her voice.

Warfield stared out the window. March was a kind month to Washington. It was a beautiful spring day outside. Renewal was in the air.

He glanced down on the bed and saw the unopened letter. He picked it up and absently ripped open the edge of the envelope with a forefinger and withdrew a folded piece of stationery.

A color photograph fell out from between the folds. He retrieved it from the blanket and held it up before him. It showed a young girl, about nine or ten years of age, with dark hair and large, remarkable eyes. She was dressed in a ruffled blouse with a petticoat vest, and smiled shyly at the camera, like someone not used to having her photograph taken.

Warfield's heart thumped wildly as he unfolded the letter.

My Dear Charles,

I thought perhaps you would enjoy having a photograph of your daughter, Zoya, who of course you have never seen. She has her mother's eyes, don't you think?

As her legal guardian, I now oversee her affairs entirely, and I am happy to tell you that she is doing very well. She is popular with her schoolmates, gets excellent grades, and hopes one day to become a dancer.

Zoya's well-being, and the fulfillment of her bright promise, depends at the moment, however, on her natural father.

There is a certain matter outstanding between us concerning a tape recording that I understand you are in a position to resolve. You are aware, of course, that any indiscreet disclosures on your part could be harmful in the extreme, not only to future U.S.-Soviet relations, but to your daughter's future as well.

I know you will want to cooperate fully and return to me the property that I have paid dearly to acquire.

I am sure you see the tremendous importance I place on this matter. Forgive me for pressing my case so strongly, but this is an issue that transcends the welfare of any single individual.

The responsibility is yours.

Most sincerely,

S.

Warfield rested the letter gently on his lap and picked up the photograph again. That explained it, of course. The hold he had on Tanya. Her daughter.

His daughter!

Was Semenenko your lover, too?

Yes.

When?

When I was eleven.

Warfield dug the heels of his hands into his eye sockets. Outrage upon outrage. If he thought about it, he would go mad. But how could he ever think about anything else?

41

WHEN DMITRI SEMENENKO'S black Zil limousine reached the southeastern outskirts of Moscow, it turned right off the broad Kutuzovsky Prospekt and onto the Rublevo Road. It was a Friday evening in late April, and the sun, still over the horizon at seven in the lengthening spring days, flashed through the tall stands of pine and birch as the car sped toward the small village of Uspenskoye, twenty kilometers away.

Semenenko turned to his companion in the rear of the limousine. "I don't think you should be wearing lipstick," he said. "Please take it off before dinner."

"But Uncle Mitya," Zoya complained. "All the girls in the school wear it now!"

The KGB general shook his head firmly. "You're only ten years old. There will be plenty of time for lipstick later on."

"Kolya and Valya let me," the girl protested.

"I'm not Kolya and Valya. Now that you're living with me, there will be no makeup. Is that clear?"

Zoya slumped in the seat and began to pout.

Semenenko regretted his stern tone. With Zoya to himself at last, he was determined to relax and be cheerful, to get their relationship off to a good start. The strain of the last few weeks, solidifying his new position in the Politburo, had fatigued him. This weekend he must put his work behind him and enjoy the budding of spring and the presence of Zoya. He would have to cheer her up.

"Did you shop today?" he asked her, looking down at the parcels piled by her feet.

She nodded, still sulking.

"Where did you go?"

"Granovskovo Street."

"Is that all?"

"Detsky Mir."

"Ah! My favorite! The world's greatest toy store! It was right across from my old office on Dzerzhinsky Square. Did you buy anything?"

"A Matrushka doll."

"Really? You have three already. Are you starting a collection?"

"It's for my mother."

Semenenko frowned. "I see."

"You promised I could see her next weekend."

"And so you shall, little darling."

"Why can't she come and stay with us?"

"She's sick, Zoya."

"What's the matter with her?"

Semenenko sighed. He would have to curb the girl's inquisitiveness. It was apparent that Valya and Kolya had spoiled her rotten.

"She has a mental illness," he said. "The psychiatrists call it 'sluggish schizophrenia.' "

"What does that mean?"

"It's difficult for you to understand. The psychiatrists are convinced that the trouble she endured while in America caused a kind of nervous collapse. She has come to think that Soviet society is the cause of her problems. Such an antisocial attitude is considered a serious mental aberration."

"But she'll get better, won't she?"

"We hope so. We'll have to wait and see."

Semenenko studied the girl out of the corner of his eye. She seemed nervous. He would have to treat her carefully, be patient with her. And get her some attractive clothes.

"I got something for you, too, Uncle Mitya," she said, suddenly, a curious teasing quality in her voice.

Semenenko made a point of showing her a broad grin. "How nice! A present! Something from Detsky Mir, I hope. You know I like beautiful toys."

"No," she replied.

He waited for her to elucidate. Instead, she reached down among the packages by her feet and found a small one, wrapped in heavy brown paper. She placed it on his lap.

"Am I supposed to guess?" he asked, trying to play to her mood.

The girl shook her head.

He shrugged and began to remove the heavy brown paper wrapping. It bore no markings, but the special store for the elite on Granovskovo Street made it a point to use nondescript wrappings to avoid arousing the envy of those not among the privileged *nachalstvo*. He removed a small rectangular plastic box, about the size of a cigarette case. The legend "BASF 90," emblazoned in white against a black and red background, jumped out at him from the face of the box. Beneath that, in smaller lettering, appeared the words "performance series," in English. It took several seconds for him to recognize what it was. When he did, he sucked in his breath.

"Where did you get this?" he asked, keeping his voice as casual as possible.

"A man gave it to me."

"Where?"

"In Granovskovo Street."

"Who was this man?"

"I don't know."

"What did he say to you?"

Zoya straightened up in the seat. "He said to give this to you. You were waiting for it."

Semenenko swallowed, feeling a pleasurable swell of excitement. "Those were his exact words?"

The girl shrugged elaborately. "Well, I think so. He said you needed it very much."

"That was all?"

"I think so. What is it?"

"A tape cassette," he replied. "Was this man a foreigner?"

"He spoke Russian."

"Did he look foreign?"

"I don't know. Maybe. He was well dressed."

"Is that all you remember?"

Zoya wrinkled her brow. "He was just a man, Uncle Mitya."

Semenenko dropped the subject. He had never thought much about how the tape might find its way to him; he knew only that it would come. The chauffeur turned up the long private drive past the big NO ENTRY signs, and in another minute they were slowing to a stop in front of his two-story *dacha*. More than a country home, it was an estate, secluded on a heavily guarded expanse of forest and meadowland.

He sat at dinner with Zoya at the big Finnish teakwood table in the dining alcove. His Latvian cook served them delicious veal cutlets with fresh vegetables from his greenhouse. The girl, still shy in his presence, said little. His eyes kept returning to the tape, sitting in its box on the breakfront nearby.

After dinner a man arrived from the KGB lab in Moscow. He X-rayed the cassette for Semenenko, and subjected it to other tests to make certain it wasn't booby-trapped. Finally, he pronounced it safe and left.

Semenenko sent Zoya to bed at eleven, showing her to her own little room in back on the second floor, decorated in bright wallpaper and piled with stuffed animals. Tomorrow night he would bring her to his room.

He poured himself a snifter of Napoleon brandy and sat at his desk in the small den on the ground floor, staring thoughtfully at the cassette. Shanklin had said only that it was a recording of Vice-President Catlin talking openly about his payoffs. The KGB had gathered other evidence on Catlin, but this was crucial—an explicit admission, straight from the man's own lips.

Semenenko closed the door and loaded the cassette in his Sony portable, which he kept by the telephone. He pressed the playback button and watched the cartridge spin forward, winding the small tape slowly from one spool to the other with a gentle hiss.

Semenenko listened, but heard nothing. He raised the volume on the Sony. Still no sound emerged, beyond the background static. He let the tape run for five minutes, then, tired of waiting, he pressed the fast forward button.

Nothing.

He snapped off the machine and looked at his watch. Near midnight. He felt incredibly tired. Every muscle ached. He turned the recorder back on and let it run at normal playback speed, determined to miss nothing.

The machine continued to emit the same low, empty hiss. He was surprised. Perhaps he was playing the wrong side of the tape.

A terrible headache began pounding in his temples. The suddenness and the severity of it startled him. He had been pushing himself too hard these last few weeks. Now it was catching up with him. And he was overdue for his physical at the polyclinic.

The gentle hiss seemed to mock him.

The headache intensified. He felt inexplicably weak. His breathing became labored and his eyesight blurred. The headache seemed to shoot through his entire body. The pain made him want to cry out. He reached for the snifter of brandy and knocked it off the desk. He heard it tinkle faintly on the floor. It sounded far away.

He made a desperate effort to rise from the chair, but was too weak to move his arms. He could barely draw a breath.

True panic seized him now. Something was dreadfully wrong.

The pain was squeezing his eyes, pressing against his chest like the weight of the waters at the bottom of the sea. He was drowning.

His heart pounded like a blacksmith's hammer on an anvil, louder and louder, harder and harder, slower and slower, until the beats filled his brain with thunder. All his emotions, all his thoughts and memories, constricted into a tight ball deep inside him, then exploded and drifted away from him, as if caught on a gust of wind.

His senses faded, consciousness bled away.

A voice out of the void spoke to him: "Can you hear me, Semenenko? That's GS gas you feel. Courtesy of my government. It's state of the art. It's coated electromagnetically onto the surface of the tape. As the tape crossed the playback head on your recorder, it released it into the air. It's odorless, colorless, and breaks down fast. But in the meantime, it's the devil itself. It seeps through the skin and attacks the nervous sytem. Only takes about a minute to act. I understand it's a terrible way to die. . . . What was it you said to me in the restaurant? 'Ruthlessness is the cardinal virtue, vulnerability the cardinal sin.'? Something like that. . . . I like to think you're paying this price for your virtue, not your sins. . . ."

Semenenko grasped blindly for the recorder, caught it by the tips of his fingers, and pulled it toward him. He found the stop button, pushed it, then let the recorder fall from his hands.

In a last spasm of energy he managed to stand. He balanced on his feet for a second, then took a step toward the door and collapsed onto the rug, his heart stopped by the enveloping crush of death.